NIGHT SHIFT

Also by Charlaine Harris from Gollancz:

MIDNIGHT, TEXAS
Midnight Crossroad
Day Shift

SOOKIE STACKHOUSE
Dead Until Dark
Living Dead in Dallas
Club Dead
Dead to the World
Dead as a Doornail
Definitely Dead
All Together Dead
From Dead to Worse
Dead and Gone
Dead in the Family
Dead Reckoning
Deadlocked
Dead Ever After
A Touch of Dead
After Dead
The Sookie Stackhouse Companion

HARPER CONNELLY
Grave Sight
Grave Surprise
An Ice Cold Grave
Grave Secret
The Harper Connelly Omnibus

The First Aurora Teagarden Omnibus
The Second Aurora Teagarden Omnibus

The Lily Bard Mysteries Omnibus

Wolfsbane and Mistletoe (co-edited with Toni L.P. Kelner)
Many Bloody Returns (co-edited with Toni L.P. Kelner)
Crimes by Moonlight
Death's Excellent Vacation (co-edited with Toni L.P. Kelner)
Dead But Not Forgotten (co-edited with Toni L.P. Kelner)

NIGHT SHIFT

CHARLAINE HARRIS

GOLLANCZ
LONDON

First published in Great Britain in 2016 by Gollancz
an imprint of The Orion Publishing Group Ltd
Carmelite House, 50 Victoria Embankment
London EC4Y 0DZ

An Hachette UK Company

1 3 5 7 9 10 8 6 4 2

All the characters in this book are fictitious, and any resemblance to actual persons, living or dead, is purely coincidental.

A CIP catalogue record for this book is available from the British Library.

ISBN (Hardback) 978 0 575 09292 1
ISBN (Export Trade Paperback) 978 0 575 09293 8

Printed in Great Britain by
Clays Ltd, St Ives plc

www.charlaineharris.com
www.orionbooks.co.uk
www.gollancz.co.uk

For the people who've kept me floating all these years:
Paula Woldan; my literary agent, Joshua Bilmes (go, JABberwocky!);
my left coast agents, Steve Fisher and Debbie Deuble Hill at APA;
my website mods (you know who you are, VK, LB, MS, ME);
the great staff at Penguin (past and present);
and most of all my husband, Hal.

ACKNOWLEDGMENTS

I appreciate all the great advice I've gotten from my writer buddies Dana Cameron and Toni Kelner, aka Leigh Perry. Joshua Bilmes really helped me out on this one, too. Witch and writer Ellen Dugan was especially generous with her time and expertise. All mistakes I may have made are due to my own frivilous nature.

The first suicide arrives one early October night.

He is a middle-aged man with a scruffy beard. He parks his battered pickup in front of the Midnight Hotel. The six-to-midnight clerk, a junior college freshman named Marina Desoto, later tells Deputy Anna Gomez that when she saw the pickup pull to the curb, she assumed the driver would come in to rent a room. Marina does not add that she had been a little excited at the prospect, since in the months she has worked at the hotel only six people have asked for a room during her shift.

Marina's hope is dashed pretty quickly.

Peering out the glass door, she watches the man fall out of the pickup "like he was drunk," she tells Deputy Gomez and Sheriff Arthur Smith.

Since Gomez knows Marina's family, she also knows Marina is fully conversant with the behavior of drunk people.

"What did he do then?" the deputy asks.

"He walked funny, kind of leaning, like a big magnet was pulling him into the middle of the crossroad. And then he . . ." Marina's voice trails off, and tears roll down her face. She lifts her hand to her head, forefinger pointed and thumb cocked, and mimes pulling a trigger.

"You saw this from the front desk?" Smith asks. He's checked the line of sight, and he's skeptical.

"No, you can't see the whole intersection from the desk," Marina says immediately, but not as if she's really thinking about the question. "I had gotten up and walked to the door to lock it, after I saw him get out of the truck. Because he was acting so weird."

"Smart," Gomez says. "So he was just carrying a gun in his hand?"

"He pulled a gun out of his waistband. And he shot himself."

Gomez makes herself keep her eyes on Marina, though she's tempted to turn to look at the dark heap still crumpled by the road. An ambulance is waiting to take the corpse to the nearest medical examiner's office.

"He didn't say anything? You didn't see him make a phone call?" Sheriff Smith says instead, going over ground already covered. He's seen a cheap cell phone in the man's shirt pocket.

"No, sir," Marina tells him. "He didn't do nothing but get out and shoot himself." And she starts crying again. Deputy Gomez sighs and pats Marina on the shoulder.

Anna Gomez has never liked Midnight, and its people are all guilty until proven innocent to her, no matter what her boss says. But even Gomez can't hold the Midnighters responsible for this suicide, though she'd love to find a way.

Gomez gives in to the prickling on her skin and turns to look around her, feeling the eyes on her. The locals are awake and watching. Though this is surely a normal human reaction to a lot of lights and sirens late at night, it doesn't make her feel any more comfortable.

Midnight and its people give Gomez the creeps. But she has to admit, none of them approach her to ask questions, and none of them try to get close to catch a glimpse of the body.

It never occurs to Anna Gomez that this is because they are all well aware of what a body looks like.

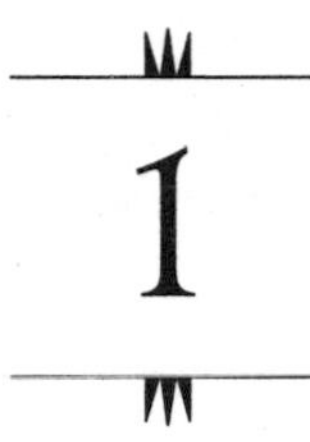

The next night, almost all the people in Midnight went up the steps to gather in the pawnshop owned by Bobo Winthrop, owner and proprietor, who worked the day shift there.

Midnight Pawn was a very old store with wooden floors that creaked in a friendly way. It was crowded with many curious items. The big open area at the front of the shop was hospitably full with chairs of all descriptions and ages, which made it a natural meeting place. The counter, with its high stool, was to the left, parallel to the wall. Normally, that was where Bobo sat when there were customers.

But when there weren't, like tonight, Bobo sat in his favorite velvet chair. It was very old, and the velvet was worn, but Bobo found it comfortable and stylish. He'd positioned it to give him a good view of his domain, from the loaded shelves that held the strange discards of the human race, to the display cases in which objects gleamed and glittered. There was a whole shelf of sanders, for example. And one of bubblegum machines. And jewelry, both real and fabulously fake.

And there was one secluded corner full of magical items. Fiji Cavanaugh, the witch who lived across Witch Light Road, had suggested that Bobo let her inspect those before they were placed on display.

Tonight, Fiji came in first. She smiled at Bobo and found a place to sit where she could see everyone. The witch, a brown-haired woman in her late twenties, was literally well rounded and had lovely skin, at least in part because she kept it protected from the Texas sun.

The Rev and his ward, Diederik, took up chairs beside Fiji. The Rev was a sparse man; short in stature, short of words, thin and bony and dry. His thinning dark hair was combed straight back. The Rev always wore the same ensemble: a white shirt, black pants, a black coat, and a black cowboy hat and boots. He sported a string tie with a turquoise stone fixing it around his neck. Wearing the same ensemble every day simplified his life.

The Rev's companion, Diederik, provided a sharp contrast. Diederik radiated health and vitality. The boy looked as though he were nineteen, perhaps entering college like Marina Desoto, but that wasn't so. Diederik had a broad olive face, wide violet eyes that slanted a bit, and thick dark hair. He was built like a wrestler, and he moved with grace.

Before he settled into his chair, Diederik gave Fiji a kiss on the cheek. She smiled at the boy, hoping the smile held nothing but motherly interest. When she'd met him a few months ago, he'd been a little boy. Now he was a full-grown male with a lively interest in females.

Fiji looked over at Olivia Charity, the only other woman present. Did Olivia, too, have a few slightly conflicted feelings about Diederik? But she sensed Olivia didn't; that, in fact, he was barely a blip on Olivia's radar.

But Olivia let Fiji know who she was thinking about. "Lemuel's still working on those books," she said to Fiji, who hadn't asked. "In fact, he eats, drinks, and sleeps those damn books."

"Golly," said Fiji, who couldn't think of anything more helpful to say. Lemuel could focus like a laser beam, but she'd never seen him concentrate like that on anything. The volumes in question had been hidden in the pawnshop for decades, and for decades Lemuel had looked for them. Then Lemuel had sold the pawnshop to Bobo, staying on as night manager. Bobo had found the cache, not realized its importance, and moved it up to his apartment, planning to examine the books someday. Now Lemuel had discovered he couldn't read the script in one, and naturally, that was the one that was most important, though Fiji didn't know why.

Chuy Villegas and Joe Strong, the couple who ran the Antique Gallery and Nail Salon, nodded easily to Bobo as they entered. Chuy patted Fiji's shoulder. Diederik rose and hugged them, and scratched their dog's head. The two took odd chairs, side by side, and set their little Peke, Rasta, down. He snuffled around the room, visiting everyone in turn, and then settled by Chuy's feet.

Manfred Bernardo, the psychic who rented the house next door to Bobo, hurried in and threw himself into a chair by his landlord. He gave everyone a wave or a word. Manfred, almost as small and spare as the Rev, was pierced liberally and with great effect, and lately he had begun getting tattoos. He pulled up his T-shirt sleeve to show the new one on his left shoulder, an ouroboros, to Fiji, and she shook her head, smiling.

"Why volunteer for pain?" she said.

"It's for my art," Manfred said dramatically, and they all laughed. Manfred regarded the tattoo with admiration. "Actually, I think it makes me look badass."

No one raised the topic of the evening.

They were all waiting on Lemuel, who would be there when the sun set.

In the early part of October, the sun went down a little before seven thirty p.m. One of the clocks in the pawnshop chimed the half hour, and a minute or two later, Lemuel Bridger came up from his basement apartment. There was a sense of completion when he took his place in the circle to Bobo's left.

The two were as much of a contrast as the Rev and Diederik. Bobo always seemed relaxed, and now that he was in his thirties his blond hair was a little faded, and his blue eyes were a little sad. But he still could have been featured in an advertising campaign for something casual but expensive, like sunglasses. Lemuel could never pass for human. He was too white, white as bleach, and his eyes were a strange gray. He didn't even move like a human being.

"Did anyone know the man who killed himself last night?" Fiji asked the little crowd. "Joshua Allen, right, Manfred?"

"That's what they said on the news."

"I didn't know him," Lemuel said. His hoarse voice was at odds with his white, gleaming appearance. "But I knew the first one."

There was a moment of absolute silence.

"The first one. The first what?" Olivia said.

"The first suicide." Lemuel's pale eyes went from one of them to another. If he was looking for someone to nod in agreement, he was disappointed.

Fiji was stumped. "Are you looking back a decade or something?" Vampires could lose track of time.

"I'm looking back a week," Lemuel said, in a bored way. "The first one was at three in the morning last Tuesday. A homeless woman stabbed herself to death right under the traffic light. I knew her, a little. Her name was Tabby Ann Masterson."

Even Olivia had not expected this bombshell. "You didn't tell me," she said.

"I could not imagine that it had anything to do with Midnight," he said. "No one was awake but me."

Lemuel was up all night, of course. Though the pawnshop was up a few steps from the ground level, and though he was often behind the counter, the pawnshop sat at the northeast corner of the only intersection in Midnight: the crossroads of Witch Light Road and the Davy highway. And from behind the counter, Lemuel could get a somewhat abbreviated view of what was happening there. If he happened to be closer to the window, his view would be unobstructed.

Fiji smiled to herself at the long silence. Even if Lemuel had said he'd been facing the wall when it happened, none of them would have dared to question his word. Lemuel, the oldest of the town's inhabitants by a century, was not a joker, a kidder, or a fantasist.

"I've met Tabby Ann," she said. "She used to come by my place, looking for my aunt. Evidently, Great-Aunt Mildred used to give her leftovers. I gave her some food once, but the next time I wasn't there, and she peed on my back porch. I cast a spell to find out who had done it, because Mr. Snuggly didn't see."

"Where is her body, then?" Manfred asked. "Tabby Ann. What did you do with her?" There was another profound silence. "Wait, sorry, don't need to know." He waved his hands, palms forward, warding off unneeded information.

Lemuel smiled at Manfred, briefly. "Tabby Ann Masterson was a homeless woman," Lemuel said, "as you call it now. I knew her during her better days, when she had a man and children and a home. She had no one left any longer."

"Two suicides," Joe Strong, who looked exactly like his name, said. "In the same spot, in the same town. Joshua Allen can't be a copycat, since he couldn't have known about Tabby Ann."

Manfred said, "The article I read about him online said he was an itinerant laborer."

"Which is another way of saying he didn't belong anywhere." Olivia's voice was harsh. "But why choose Midnight for his death? Could it be a coincidence?"

Fiji felt doubtful, and she saw that same expression on the faces of everyone around her.

Bobo said, "This seems like a magic thing." These were the first words he'd spoken all evening. Bobo had seemed a little broody for days, though no one was sure why. Fiji, who was always aware of Bobo, was a little hyped up by the fact that she was almost certain that he was staring at her even when she wasn't speaking. She didn't know why; she sadly suspected it was not for the same reason she liked to look at him. In fact, looking at Bobo was one of her favorite things to do.

Fiji made herself concentrate on the moment as she brushed her wild hair away from her face. "It would have to be because this is a crossroads," she said slowly. "It might be a coincidence that two people committed suicide here in a week, but they killed themselves in the same spot. That just can't be a coincidence."

Reluctantly, Chuy Villegas raised a hand. When they all looked at him, he said, "The ghosts have been agitated."

Manfred sat up straight and stared at Chuy. Short and swarthy and in his forties, Chuy did not look like the kind of man who would talk about ghosts in a very prosaic way. (Manfred himself, with his piercings and tattoos and dyed platinum hair, *did* look like such a person.) "You see ghosts?" Manfred said, keeping his voice matter-of-fact with an effort.

"We do," said Joe. Joe was just as muscular as his partner, but taller and fairer.

"Do you see Aunt Mildred?" Fiji asked, startled. Her great-aunt had left her the cottage she lived in, and Fiji had adapted to life in Midnight as if she'd been born to it.

"All the time," Chuy said.

"She's okay?" Fiji looked anxious.

"Right as rain," Joe reassured her. "But lately, along with all the other ghosts, she's been breaking routine."

Manfred *so* wanted to ask what "routine" was for a spirit, but that would be veering off the subject. "Maybe I can ask some questions later," he said. Chuy nodded and looked resigned.

"So they are feeling the pull of the crossroad, too," Lemuel said, though not as if he were completely sure. "Or maybe something is coming to Midnight, something bad, something we should be afeared of."

Fiji cleared her throat. "I think it must be already here. Otherwise, why two deaths on the same spot?"

Diederik said, "Can we kill it?" The boy was definitely excited.

"Not until we know what it is and what the consequences would be." Joe turned to Lemuel. "Is this what you've been looking for in the books? Facts about something magical here in town?"

"I'm working on a translation," Lemuel said rather coldly. "The books are all books written by vampires. For a few of them, the volume I have is the only volume remaining in the world. As I examined them, I found one that I thought would lead me to information about Midnight. It seems to be a history of magical sites in this country, from the map included. I had to find someone who could tell me what language the book was written in."

"When was it written?" the Rev said.

"It was written a couple of hundred years ago, so it is the most recent of the books. But it was written in a language that has not been spoken for two thousand years, or longer."

The Rev nodded. Fiji could not tell if the ancient minister was glad, surprised, or irritated at this information.

"Who would be the intended reader of such a book? And how come you have to translate it?" Fiji was curious. "If it's about America, shouldn't it be in English?"

Lemuel said, "It was written by a vampire who was touring the U.S. before I was born."

"But the book's only a couple hundred years old?" Fiji didn't get it.

"Yes. I believe from the binding and the printing that this book has only been around for two centuries, give or take. But it may have been written long before it was printed."

"But . . ." She stopped, deciding to think rather than talk, which was always a good idea around Lemuel.

"The vampire was from a long-dead culture," Joe said.

Lemuel nodded. "Before the Romans. I believe the vampire was Etruscan. I found a rough dictionary, written by a child of the only Etruscan vampire I've ever heard of. That's a help, but it's still very slow going."

Rasta whined at Joe's feet, and he picked up the little dog and settled it on his lap. Chuy reached over to scratch Rasta's head.

"Is there any way you can skip around a little in the book to find out if our crossroad is in there?" Manfred said tentatively. Offering Lemuel advice was a risky proposition.

"I dare not skip around because I may miss the very thing I am reading the book to discover," Lemuel said. "This place wasn't named Midnight until the late eighteen hundreds, so it's simply described in this book, if it's in there at all. In the meantime, I'm real sure we need to be on the watch for more suicides."

"More?" Bobo said. He gave Fiji a dismayed look.

Lemuel said, "Why stop at two?"

"At least they're dying at night," Fiji said, trying to find something to be glad about. "And at least no one else knows about the first one."

"And that's better because?" Manfred looked at her with his eyebrows raised.

"Because we have a chance of covering it up," Diederik said promptly. "As Lemuel did the first one."

"Can you imagine the news coverage?" Bobo spoke quietly, but everyone listened. "The headlines? 'What Draws Suicides to This Remote Texas Town?'"

"Honey, I think they're urging you to read quick as lightning," Olivia said to Lemuel.

The vampire smiled. "I can get a lot done on night duty here," he said. Lemuel worked the night shift at the pawnshop, which was closed from late afternoon until dark, and from dawn until nine o'clock, or whenever Bobo got down to open it up. The doors were shut only between dawn and eight (or nine) a.m. and five or six p.m. to dark.

"Should we set some kind of watch?" Fiji asked. "To stop people?"

Manfred's mouth turned down with distaste. Joe and Chuy looked grim. Olivia hunched her shoulders. Even for the Midnighters, who were used to weird and even bloody events, this seemed like an unpleasant prospect.

"I'm not sure how we could stop them," Bobo said. They all looked at him. "If someone's determined, he just walks out there and shoots himself, like the guy last night." He shrugged. "No way to stop that guy, right?"

"But we had no warning, and now we know," Fiji said.

"I don't think we can stay awake all night for the remote chance that someone else will stop to off himself," Manfred said. "We'd have had to have been *right by* Joshua Allen last night. He got out of his truck, took a step or two, pulled out the gun, and *blam!* What if one of us had tried to stop him? Would he have shot us, too?"

There was a scattering of nods.

"So we won't keep a night watch," Lemuel concluded. "But I'll do my best to spot any others who appear at the crossroad."

"Did you see that there's a new guy at Gas N Go?" Olivia said.

Chuy and Joe, who lived one vacant building away from the corner convenience store, smiled simultaneously. "You should see him," Chuy said. "He's . . . remarkable."

Fiji, who was removing the spell that had kept interlopers out of the store during their meeting, finished her task and rejoined the conversation. "Not going to give us any hint?" Fiji said.

"Nope. Go see." Chuy laughed. "Teacher was in to fix our showerhead and faucet yesterday, and he was delighted to be free of the Gas N Go."

"He didn't have to take charge," Joe said.

"He said the money was good and steady." Olivia shrugged. "Hard to turn down when you have a baby. Madonna said she enjoyed knowing where he was all the time. But even she'd gotten pretty aggravated at him always being busy."

"I'm surprised she talked to you enough to tell you that," Joe said.

It was true that Madonna was not much of a talker. None of the Midnighters felt they knew her. And no matter how friendly her husband, Teacher, was, he never seemed to tell them anything of importance about his life or his past. These reasons were good enough to keep the Reeds out of town meetings.

"I'll go down to Gas N Go soon. It's always nice to have a new community member," Fiji said brightly, as they all stood up to leave.

Joe and Chuy laughed.

Before Fiji could ask them to explain what was so amusing about the newcomer, a customer came in.

They all turned at the ringing of the bell over the door.

The customer was haggard, and very young, and he was towing a girl by the hand. She was in her teens, but she hadn't gotten there easily. From the way her eyes ping-ponged around, she'd enhanced her world chemically.

"Here!" the boy said to Lemuel, shoving the girl toward him. "I want to pawn her!"

They all froze, waiting to hear what Lemuel would say.

"I don't take live people or live animals," the vampire said mildly. "And lest you should think that means I want her dead, you best think again."

"Then I'll pawn my soul!" The boy laughed again, defiant and dramatic, obviously feeling he was making a grand gesture.

"Never say that." Chuy made his way through the chairs to where the boy stood. "You only have one. You can't imagine the price of it, or the cost of losing it. What is it you need money for?"

Under Chuy's serious eyes, the boy wilted a little. "I owe someone a lot of money, and I was going to sell some Ecstasy, but she *took it all*," he said, giving the girl a petulant slap on the butt.

"You mean she ingested it all?" Manfred said, alarmed. "Doesn't she need to go to a hospital?"

This had obviously not occurred to the boy, who gave a violent sort of shrug, as if to throw off this petty concern when his own problems were so much vaster. "So anybody want her for anything?" he demanded. "She won't mind. She won't even remember."

Manfred's fists clenched and he took a step forward. Fiji had the same reaction. Somewhat to Fiji's surprise, Chuy was faster than either of them. He'd been pulling out his keys, but now his hand went instead to the boy's face. He put his thumb in the middle of the boy's forehead and spoke a word, though Fiji could not remember afterward what the word was. Immediately, the tension drained out of the boy's body, and he let go of the hand of the addled girl, who sagged into a chair the minute she was free.

Chuy removed his thumb.

The boy said, "I'm sorry." His gaze was almost as blank as the girl's, but his stance was relaxed and receptive. "I'm sorry," he said again. "I should be getting home. To figure out my problems. I shouldn't involve anyone else. Selling other people is bad."

"Yes," said Chuy sadly. "It is, boy. You are a bad one, but a young bad one. You may be able to change."

"I'm going to try," the boy said. Without another word, he left the pawnshop, and they heard his car start up and drive away.

Fiji said, "What do we do with her?"

Joe crouched by the girl's chair and took her limp hand. "Her parents are Margaret and Louis Hatter. They live in Davy," he said with assurance, and no one asked how he knew.

Manfred looked the address up on his phone, which he then laid down on the counter and forgot. "I'll run her home," he said. "Feej, you want to come with me, in case they think I took advantage of the little idiot?"

"Okay," she said, casting a glance at Bobo, who was looking at her (again!) with an expression she couldn't read. He appeared to be lost in some unpleasant place, and as she watched, he went out the side door leading to a landing. He was mounting the stairs to his apartment in the last glimpse Fiji had before the door swung shut.

Fiji sighed heavily, not even aware she did so, and she turned back to help Manfred. Between them, they supported the Hatter girl across the pawnshop driveway to Manfred's. With some difficulty, Fiji taking her head and Manfred her feet, they maneuvered her into the backseat of Manfred's car. During the short drive to Davy, the girl's eyes were open. She seemed to be admiring the texture of the roof.

The search for the Hatters' house took longer than Fiji had anticipated, since street signs were not abundant in Davy and Manfred had run out without his phone. Finally, Manfred parked in front of a small ranch-style home on a modest street.

Manfred tugged the girl's hands until he got her out of the backseat. Then Fiji looped one of the girl's arms around her neck, and Manfred did the same with the other one. With the girl propped between them like a barely ambulatory sack of laundry, they lurched across the small lawn to the front door and rang the bell. A fortyish woman opened it. When she saw the girl, her shoulders sagged with relief. Or maybe it was resignation.

"Oh, Marilyn," she said sadly. "Again."

"You're Margaret Hatter?" Fiji asked. "Her mom?"

"Yes." Margaret Hatter didn't sound happy about it. "Here, I'll take her." She didn't ask Fiji any questions or level any accusations during the awkward process of transferring the limp young woman from two people to one.

Fiji said, "We found her like this." She wanted to make it absolutely clear she and Manfred had had nothing to do with Marilyn's condition.

"All right," said the woman, as if Fiji had asked her to believe something quite impossible. "Sure, honey."

Stung, Fiji opened her mouth to protest this implied judgment.

"I hope she gets better," Manfred said rather loudly, and yanked Fiji away from the door.

It was closing, anyway.

On the drive back to Midnight they were mostly silent. When he dropped her off at her house, Fiji said, "I just didn't want her to think . . ." The conversation had been gnawing at her.

"Give it up, Feej," Manfred said. "Mrs. Hatter didn't ask a single question. She was going to think the worst if we'd had wings and white robes and a heavenly choir."

"I can't really blame her," Fiji said.

Manfred sighed. "Neither can I," he said.

"I hope this is the end of the trouble," Fiji said after a short silence.

"We all do. But you know it's not."

From her front porch, Fiji watched Manfred's car begin moving. Since there was no one coming, he backed across Witch Light Road. She stayed outside for a few more minutes, looking at the crossroads. She half expected to see another hapless soul staggering toward the center, some weapon of self-destruction in hand. But the only thing to see was Midnight's one traffic light, resolutely following its pattern. The intersection of Witch Light Road and the Davy road was the reason Midnight was alive. The little community had been founded because of those roads, when they were just trails.

Catty-cornered from where she stood, Fiji could see that the lights inside Gas N Go were still on, and someone was moving around inside. As she watched, the lights went out and a man emerged, locking the doors behind him. He walked north, to the house where the previous Gas N Go manager had lived. He moved quickly and lightly, though

Fiji couldn't tell anything more about him. Now she was curious about the new resident. She would have to bake something for him.

After a moment, Fiji went inside and opened a locked drawer under the counter in the shop. There was a curious selection of items in the drawer: a crumpled tissue, a lipstick, a napkin, a knife, an ink pen, a squeeze bottle of hand sanitizer, and other mundane items. All of them were used. To this odd group, she added a folded dollar bill that had fallen from Chuy's pocket in the pawnshop. She put it on top of an index card already prepared with Chuy's name. She slid the drawer closed very gently and relocked it.

Instead of going to read in her bedroom, her original thought, Fiji returned to the window to look out at the traffic light and the pavement below it.

Fiji tried to detect something different about the intersection, but there was nothing visible, even to a witch.

But Fiji was sure this particular crossroad was exerting some malignant pull. She hoped it would not spread a pall over all the people who lived around it, but she could not believe they'd all escape it.

No coincidence in the world would allow for two people, who presumably did not know each other, to commit suicide in the same place within a few days. This crossroad was not a famous site like the Golden Gate Bridge or Niagara Falls. This was a place where two small roads crossed in a very small town not particularly close to anywhere notable.

Or was it? Wasn't that the kind of cosmic joke that made regular people decide places were haunted, or cursed?

"Well," she told her marmalade cat, Mr. Snuggly, who'd come to stand beside her, "I guess we'll know soon."

2

The next morning, Fiji was working in her yard, one of her favorite pastimes. Getting her fingers in the dirt, watering, planting good things and removing weeds, checking for bugs and harvesting herbs and tomatoes in season . . . these were all good things for a witch to do to keep in touch with the elements of earth, air, and water, and for a Fiji to do to keep herself grounded and content. The shop was fun for connecting with humans, but it wasn't organic.

The Inquiring Mind stocked everything pertaining to "witchcraft lite," as Fiji called it. She carried very little of what she thought of as the heavy-duty stuff, because there was very little local market for such things. She'd never met another real witch besides her great-aunt Mildred Loeffler, who had owned the cottage before her. Aunt Mildred had been a widow, obliged to support herself, and she'd done okay with selling herbal medicines out her back door and occasionally casting a spell or two for a few people. She had also been an excellent cook and had had a sporadic business as a caterer.

Fiji was thinking about Aunt Mildred that morning while she

worked. She'd been a little rattled when Joe and Chuy admitted they saw Aunt Mildred around Midnight, all these years after her death. Fiji had to wonder what that meant in terms of Aunt Mildred's soul. Did she dare to ask Joe or Chuy if Aunt Mildred was roaming the earth because she wasn't fit for paradise? Did she herself even believe there was a heaven, or Hell?

On the whole, Fiji thought she did.

As she turned over the soil in the vegetable bed, Fiji wondered about the soul destination of Tabby Ann Masterson, the first suicide. Catholicism had always given suicide a really bad rap. For all Fiji knew, it was accounted a terrible sin in any religion. But how could you find out for sure? You couldn't. What if you were in terrible pain and there was no hope for recovery? Would she ask someone to help her depart this earth? She chewed around the edges of that dilemma for a few minutes before abandoning the train of thought. *No point wondering about something you can't know,* Fiji figured. *At least Tabby Ann won't pee on my porch again.*

Though it might be fall in most of America, in Texas it was still summer, though the nights and mornings were cooler. Fiji was grateful for the early-morning temperature. Mr. Snuggly came to sit with her. He liked to watch her work, especially when she was working in the sun. Mr. Snuggly had caught a mouse the day before, and he couldn't stop preening himself.

"Don't tell me about that mouse again," Fiji said.

The cat shot her an injured look.

"And don't give me the look, either," she said. "You'd think it was a lion, the way you go on about it."

Mr. Snuggly said, "Fine. Next time I'll let it chew on your bread." He stalked off, tail upright and stiff, and located a sunny spot on the other side of her garden.

"What's up with the cat?" Bobo Winthrop said. She'd heard his footsteps, so she wasn't startled, but she kept her face down. She knew she had a habit of smiling too much when Bobo was around.

"Oh, he's pissed off because I'm tired of listening to his story about killing the mouse," Fiji said, pulling another weed and tossing it into her bucket. "I might be willing to hear about it again, if he hadn't put the corpse in my shoe."

Bobo laughed. He did it well, because it was natural for him. In the past few months she hadn't seen him laugh enough. He'd been running; he was wearing an ancient sleeveless sweatshirt and even more ancient gym shorts. And he was sweating, though the air was pleasantly cool.

"Pull up a chair and tell me what you know," Fiji suggested. She sat back on her haunches. Instead of getting a stadium chair from the porch, Bobo folded down onto the ground to sit with her. She sighed inwardly. Bobo was flexible and fit, the right weight for his height, though he was years older than her. "How old are you?" she asked abruptly, giving in to gravity and settling on the ground, too.

"Thirty-five," he said. "How come?"

Fiji felt heavy and depressed. "Oh, nothing!" she said, doing her best to sound upbeat. "What brings you over here today?" He was due to open the pawnshop soon. And she would have to shower and unlock her own business.

"You know what we need, Feej?" He was looking very serious, and her heart began thudding, just a bit.

Fiji could think of several things they needed, or at least she needed.

"What?" she said, trying not to sound as though she were strangling.

"We need a vacation."

She wanted to be absolutely certain what Bobo meant before she made a fool of herself. Cautiously, she said, "Do you mean we need to go to a desert island? Or the Grand Canyon? That kind of vacation?"

"I don't know of any other kind," he said, smiling. "Yes, that's what we need. How long has it been since you've been out of Midnight for more than a couple of hours?"

"Two years," she said promptly.

"I've been gone overnight maybe three times, but I can't remember being gone longer than that. Even Lemuel went traveling when he was trying to find someone to translate the books. Chuy visits his kin, and Joe goes to antique shows. Manfred goes to Dallas or Los Angeles or Miami for a couple of days every few months. Olivia is gone half the time!"

"Not the Rev," Fiji said.

"No, not the Rev, I'll give you that one. And not the Reeds. And Diederik's only lived here for a few months, so he doesn't count."

Fiji was thinking that it surely *sounded* as though Bobo was proposing they go somewhere together. Like a couple. But she could hardly believe it. She tested the idea. "You think you and I should go to see Hawaii, or Death Valley?"

"That's what I'm saying." He looked serious enough to mean it. The morning wind blew his light hair around.

Fiji had waited for this moment for so long. It was like a clear, perfect, shimmering crystal of happiness. Then Bobo shifted slightly and looked anxiously into her face.

"Of course, we can get two rooms," he said.

For the life of her, she could not interpret his tone. The crystal shattered.

Fiji mustered every smidgen of self-control she could summon to keep her face from showing her painful disillusion. Something inside her snapped, and she lost hope. "I just can't do this," Fiji said into her hands. "You have to leave now."

Her dearest friend and longed-for lover looked shocked, but maybe not so shocked that he could claim ignorance of his offense. "Let me backtrack," Bobo said urgently.

"*No.*" She stood up, pushing off the ground to rise to her feet, for once not caring how heavy and clumsy she might look in the process. "No. I'm going in. Do what you like." She flicked her hand to show how little she cared. She walked away, into the back door, and closed and locked it behind her. Somehow Mr. Snuggly had beat her inside.

"I'm done with him," she told Mr. Snuggly. "I can't live like this anymore."

Wisely, Mr. Snuggly said nothing.

In the shower, you could not tell the water beating down from the tears.

"Fiji," Fiji told herself out loud, "you are a fucking idiot."

It was a harder, tougher witch who turned off the water and toweled herself dry just in time to unlock the front door. A car stopped in front of the shop. *Good, I need something else to think about,* Fiji told herself. But then she took a second look. To her puzzlement, the car was a familiar one. Fiji was even more amazed when she recognized the woman who got out.

Her first customer of the day was her sister.

"Kiki?" she said, incredulously.

"One and the same," her sister called gaily.

Waikiki Cavanaugh Ransom was four years older than Fiji. Though all the Cavanaugh women were inclined to be well-rounded, Kiki had starved herself and exercised herself so she would never reach that pleasant state. Kiki was a little taller than her sister, and she wore bright green contact lenses that made her eyes extraordinary. That was new. So was the color of Kiki's hair, a sort of golden wheat. In the time it took to register all this, Kiki had reached the front porch.

The sisters hugged. For about six seconds, Fiji was simply excited her sister had driven up from Houston to see her. Then her knowledge of Kiki's nature reasserted itself.

"Not that I'm not glad to see you . . . but I'm surprised," Fiji said, trying to soften her actual impulse to say, "What the hell are you doing here?"

It wasn't like *any* member of her family had come to see her since she'd claimed her inheritance. And her one trip home for Christmas two years before had been a terrible mistake.

"Well, it was just time, Fiji! You're the only sister I've got! You know I've regretted that big scene. Mom thought she should have gotten the house, and it may have seemed like I sided with her, but I thought the better of it. I know there were a lot of hard words spoken."

"You've waited two years to tell me this? After maybe three phone calls in the intervening time?"

"Give me a break! I'm trying to make nice!" Kiki held her sister away and gave her an admonishing smile.

But Fiji was not having any of it, not today. She folded her arms across her chest. "I'm not in the 'giving a break' business. Out with it. There must be some reason you left Houston and drove all the way up here. Let's have a seat. You tell me about it."

Fiji gestured to the two armchairs on opposite sides of the little table in the middle of the shop, and Kiki sank into one.

Since she sat down when I asked her to, now she's going to ask me for something, Fiji thought.

"All right," Kiki said. "By the way, I could use a cup of coffee."

Right on the money. "I'll do the polite hostess thing after you tell me what your trouble is," Fiji said. She didn't know where this new tougher Fiji was going, but so far it felt good.

"I left Marty," Kiki said, almost tearfully. "I just wanted to get out of town for a while, but I don't have any money, so Mom said I should come stay with you, since you had a house all your own."

"Fake house envy," Fiji said. "You didn't like Great-Aunt Mildred, you never spent any time with her, and you thought this place was a dump. You didn't keep that any secret. And yet you and Mom have the gall to be surprised that Aunt Mildred left it to me."

"I never told *her* I felt that way," Kiki said childishly. "Aunt Mildred, I mean."

"You think she was dumb? You think she didn't know?"

That was exactly what Kiki had thought. As if a few smiles and hugs and flattering comments would pull the wool over Aunt Mildred's eyes.

"So you really *like* this place?" Kiki was truly amazed.

"I love it," Fiji said fiercely. "I love the house, I love my business, I love the town." *Despite everything,* she added to herself, without spelling out what "everything" was.

"I just figured you'd fix it up and sell it." Kiki laughed.

"To whom? You noticed a booming housing market around Midnight?"

"Well, no," Kiki said, still smiling. "You really do like living here?"

"I really do." Fiji smiled back, just a little, showing her teeth. "So you left Marty, huh? What did he do to break the camel's back?"

"He stole some of my jewelry and pawned it. Then he tried to tell me I'd lost it."

"Why'd he need the money so bad?"

"He's developed a gambling addiction," Kiki said stiffly. "He isn't getting any help, and he's lost almost all his money, so to save myself and my own things, I had to get out. I put some stuff in Mom's attic, and then I lit out."

"So you came here." Fiji smelled a large rat, much bigger than the little creature Mr. Snuggly had stowed in her shoe.

"Yeah, I came here."

"Mom wouldn't let you stay?"

"She made it clear that if Marty came by her house, I couldn't expect any help from her."

"What about Dad? He used to be pretty much ready to defend his darling." Fiji had always been sure she wasn't included in that defense.

"I don't know how much you talk to Mom . . ."

"Hardly at all. What?" Fiji was suddenly alert. There was a serious note in Kiki's voice, a note that said, "Sit up and listen close."

"Dad has the onset of Alzheimer's," Kiki said.

Fiji could only stare at her sister. "Mom didn't think she needed to tell me? And you didn't call to tell me?" she said, without any inflection.

Kiki pursed her lips. "I'm telling you now. This is pretty new. I stop by their house maybe twice a week, and I didn't notice anything wrong for a long time. He was absentminded about things—but he didn't do any one thing that scared me. It was just like, 'Where'd I put my car keys? Where'd I leave my phone?' Stuff like that." She looked around the shop as if she were appreciating Fiji's arrangements, but Fiji knew better. "Then one day he called me from the hardware store. He couldn't remember how to get home."

"But he could remember how to call you?" Fiji groped to understand.

"He liked my picture by my phone number, so he hit that one." Kiki shook her head. "Could have been much worse."

"That must have been really scary. For him. For you."

Kiki nodded. "No shit."

"So you decided to come here upon the breakup of your marriage, instead of Mom's?"

"Yes," Kiki said firmly. "You know she's always hated Marty, and I couldn't stand to listen to her gloat. Plus, helping her with Dad is really stressful. I need to unwind, not get more tense."

Since Fiji had no intention of going home to help her mother take care of her dad, she hardly had the moral high ground, she realized. "I can understand that," Fiji said. And she did. But Fiji also knew there was more that Waikiki Cavanaugh Ransom had to tell her, and she supposed sooner or later she would have to hear it. She could hardly tell Kiki to turn around and drive back to Houston, though for a moment that seemed like a delightful possibility. But the bond of family prevailed, somewhat to the new Fiji's disappointment.

"Well, then, the guest bedroom is just back here," Fiji said. "I'm sure you recall." When the family had visited her mother's aunt, of course Kiki had come, too. "There's not that much house to remember."

Fiji walked down the little hall. The bathroom was on her left, her own bedroom was on her right, and the guest room was after the bathroom on the left, across from the kitchen. It was a small room, but now it was a real guest bedroom since she'd bought a shed for the backyard.

Bobo had helped her put it up. Well, Bobo had put it up, with assistance from her and Diederik and a few hours of skilled labor provided by Teacher Reed. The happy memory turned sour in a second, now that she knew she would always be a buddy, never a lover. Fiji pushed back the wave of misery. She would not show weakness in front of her sister.

The bed was a single and covered with a bright patchwork quilt. There was a red bedside table holding a lamp and a box of tissues. Otherwise, the room now contained only a narrow chest of drawers (purchased from the pawnshop) and a narrow wardrobe (likewise).

Kiki looked around her, her lips pressed tight together. It didn't take a mind reader to tell that Kiki had a low opinion of these accommodations.

Fiji let that roll off her back.

"Okay, I'll go get my suitcase," Kiki said. She jerked her thumb down the hall. "That's the only bathroom?"

"Yes. I know it's not what you're used to, but we're lucky Aunt Mildred put one in. She used to have an outhouse."

"Ew." Kiki's disgusted face was enough reply. She pivoted to go to her car out front.

"You can move your car back behind the house with mine," Fiji called after her sister. When Kiki was out the door, she sat in the chair behind the counter and put her head in her hands. Ordinarily, she'd be calling Bobo to tell him the big news—a family member had actually come to see her. But of course she could not do that. She thought of telling Manfred, but somehow that didn't suit her mood, either.

My sister is here and there's more to that story for sure, my dad's mind is disintegrating, and I just broke off emotionally from the guy I've loved for three years. So what else can happen today? Fiji asked herself.

The bell on the door tinkled as it opened, and Fiji stood up to see an actual customer coming in. "Hi," she said, hoping she sounded passably sane. "What can I do for you?"

"Do you have any ceremonial daggers? I'm not sure how to pronounce them. Athames?" The middle-aged woman peered around the shop as if one would materialize in front of her. She looked faintly familiar.

Fiji looked at the woman more closely, wondering where she could have encountered her new customer. Fiji would never have pegged this woman for a serious practitioner. On the short and stubby side, she had a graying perm with a severe, almost militant, curl to it. Bright pink lipstick was her only makeup. Her clothes were strictly Chico's, and her sandals were something good but practical, like SAS.

"Don't I know you?" Fiji said.

The customer looked up reluctantly. "Maybe," she answered vaguely, and looked around the shop again. Fiji began to get the feeling something was distinctly off about this woman. This had been a day for encounters that weren't what she'd expected, and it wasn't even ten o'clock.

"I have a few athames," Fiji said. "I keep them here inside this counter, if you'd care to come look."

The woman approached, and Fiji pointed through the glass of the countertop. There were seven or eight athames on display, of different types, sizes, and styles. The newcomer peered down, apparently fascinated by the blades. Fiji was ready to tell her the different materials used in carving the handles, but the woman didn't ask a single question. The bone one was plain and simple, a steel one had designs chased all the way down the blade, another had a wicked and practical look, another was modeled on a Scottish *sgian dhu*.

While the customer looked at the display, Fiji looked at the customer. She was convinced she'd seen her before.

"Athames have very specific usages," Fiji offered, to break the silence. "Would you like me to explain?"

But the woman shook her head. "I want that one," the customer said after another moment of contemplation. She pointed to the sharpest one, made of stainless steel—the most utilitarian-looking of the bunch, and the only blade that looked as though it could do real damage. Athames didn't have to be sharp; they were meant to direct energy. Some witches did use their athames as daily tools, on the theory that usage gave the blades power—but most were strictly ceremonial, like Fiji's, which she kept locked away.

"So when are you going to use it?" Fiji asked directly, though she took care to smile as she did so.

The woman looked blank. "Oh, you know . . . I'll take it when my coven meets," she said finally.

Wrong answer. Usually, only the priestess used an athame during a coven ritual. And if this woman was a priestess, Fiji was a hole in the ground.

Fiji had never faced a problem like this before. *Wouldn't you know it would be today*, she thought bitterly.

"You have a coven?" she asked, trying to sound as nonconfrontational as she possibly could. "I've never heard of one around here. That's so interesting."

"Oh, yes," the woman said vaguely. "You'd be surprised."

I certainly would, Fiji thought. *But what's the harm?* After all, it wasn't like this woman couldn't go into any Walmart or hunting store and purchase a knife even longer and sharper, right?

So Fiji extracted the athame, let the woman examine it more

closely—which she did, but not as if she really understood what she was seeing—and then took the woman's proffered cash.

While the woman's billfold was open, Fiji caught a glimpse of her driver's license. She was hoping for enlightenment, but the name Francine Owens was unfamiliar. Fiji was still cudgeling her memory for where she'd seen the woman before as she dropped the receipt and the knife into a bag. Fiji felt an overwhelming wrongness emanating from this customer. But she had no evidence, no proof, no information.

"Have you ever come to the class I hold on Thursday nights?" Fiji asked.

"What?" The woman stared at her, bewildered. "Maybe the first one you ever had," she said, after a significant pause.

"Then I'm glad you returned to visit the store. Enjoy your purchase," Fiji said automatically, and as Francine Owens walked out of the store, Fiji heard Kiki coming out to stand by her.

"Customer, huh?" Kiki sounded unmistakably surprised.

"Yep," Fiji said, barely aware of speaking. She went to the front door without knowing what she was going to do, and she opened it just as, across Witch Light Road, Manfred Bernardo whipped open the front door of his house and began to run . . . toward Francine Owens, who was walking toward the intersection with her shoulders braced back and a ground-eating walk that seemed close to marching. She'd discarded the bag, which was bouncing east with the wind. The bare knife was in Francine Owens's hand.

Fiji began running, too. Manfred had had a good head start, and before Fiji could reach the woman, he launched himself from the pavement to tackle Francine Owens just as she would have sunk the knife into her own abdomen. The north/south light had turned green, but thank the goddess, there were no cars coming from either direction.

Fiji reached the struggling couple within seconds. Francine Owens was fighting Manfred. She was a hefty woman and Manfred was a slight man. Fiji landed on her knees beside them. She performed the spell at which she excelled. She froze Francine Owens.

"God almighty," said Manfred, rolling off the woman. "Thanks, Feej." He sat back, panting.

"Don't thank me, it's my fault," she said, her voice coming in jerks as she caught her breath. Fiji looked down at what she'd done. Owens was still and her eyes were open, and she was fixed in the position she'd been in when Fiji had cast the spell. Her right hand was up to slap the side of Manfred's head, and her left hand had been gripping the athame, perhaps to bring it up to use on him.

Or herself.

"Thank you," Fiji said. "Thank you, Manfred. So much. For stopping her."

"She came out of your shop?" He was paler than ever, and his silver piercings glinted in the sun. She could see the black roots on his platinum hair.

"Yes, she bought the athame," Fiji said. "The knife. But . . ." Fiji had to gasp in a huge lungful of air before she could continue. "But it seemed so strange that she was buying one, and she didn't seem to know what she was doing. So." Another heave of her chest. "I watched her, but you got it first."

"I had a twitch on the thread," he said, and after a second, she understood. Manfred had a strong psychic ability, which was unreliable but undeniable. He'd felt that he had to prevent a disaster, and he'd obeyed his instinct. "This woman coming up behind you must be your sister?" he said. "There's a resemblance."

"Damn, forgot about her," Fiji said. "Brace yourself."

"What the *hell?*" said Kiki, from behind Fiji's back.

"Manfred Bernardo, this is my sister Waikiki Ransom," Fiji said. "Mostly known as Kiki."

"Your parents had a thing about islands and beaches," he said.

"I'm lucky I wasn't named Capri," Kiki said. "So, what happened to the crazy woman? Didn't look like she got hit, thanks to Speedy Gonzales here, so what's up with her?"

"Your sister put a spell on her," Manfred said, pushing slowly to his feet. "If this lasts as long as the last time she used this one, the woman will be out for maybe five more minutes. So what do we do with her?"

Fiji stood, too, with considerably more effort. She glanced up at the window of the pawnshop to see Bobo staring out at them. He opened his hands, wordlessly asking if he should come help.

The last thing Fiji wanted was another encounter with him. She shook her head vehemently.

"Oooooh, who's that?" asked Kiki. "He's cute!"

Fiji stood and turned to face her sister. "Don't go there," she said, in a deadly voice. "Just. Don't. Go there."

Kiki nodded, her eyes wide. She took a step back.

"Manfred," Fiji said, wheeling back to the psychic. She wanted to make it clear the subject had changed. "We need to get this lady in her car and get her out of town. Lest she wake up and try to kill herself all over again."

"So you think this was a deliberate . . . ?"

"Sure," Fiji said. "In the next few seconds she would've stabbed herself, right at the intersection. With the knife she bought from me. Dammit."

Kiki said, "I guess you're going to explain this to me later?"

Grimly, Fiji said, "I guess I will."

"Seems like all we do is haul unconscious women around," Manfred said, getting to his feet. "This is beginning to seem weird."

"I agree," Fiji said. "But I don't know what else we can do. Wait . . . let's get her into the shop!"

Diederik made a timely appearance just then. If Kiki had been smitten with lust at the sight of Bobo, Diederik made her mouth fall open. But even Kiki had to be mindful of how young Diederik was, though she could never have guessed quite how young. Diederik said, "Miss Fiji, can I be of help?"

"Yes, you certainly can," she said. "We're going to pull this lady upright and see if we can get her into my place. I'm hoping she can wake up there naturally."

It took the three of them (Kiki stood a distance away and offered verbal supervision) to get poor Francine Owens in an upright position. They managed to sort of lift her and move her a few feet, then a few more, until they got her up the porch steps and into the Inquiring Mind.

"Shall we just lay her on the floor?" Diederik said brightly.

"Yeah, I think so." Fiji got a cushion from one of the chairs and put it under Ms. Owens's head and put a light throw over her legs. "Now she looks cared for," she said, checking the effect. "Kiki, would you get a glass of water?" Fiji had chased down the store bag with the receipt still in it, and now she placed it and the athame behind the counter where they could not be seen. She put the purchase price of the athame back in Francine Owens's purse.

Fiji was actually a little surprised when Kiki returned with the water. But she accepted the glass without comment, and when Francine opened her eyes, Fiji was squatting beside her looking solicitous.

"Oh my goodness," Francine Owens said. "What happened?"

"Do you know where you are?" Manfred said, his voice gentle.

"Why, no, I don't believe I do." She looked terrified, even more so after she gave a second glance at Manfred's glinting silver piercings and spiky platinum hair.

"You're in Midnight, in a store called the Inquiring Mind," Fiji said. "You came in to look around, and I think you fainted."

"But I've never done that before," Ms. Owens protested weakly. "My gosh, I must have scared you to death! You . . . haven't called the ambulance or anything, have you?"

"We were just going to," Fiji said. "You've only been out for a few seconds. Maybe you'd feel better if you got checked out?"

"Oh, please don't call," Ms. Owens said. "The fuss . . . and all over nothing, I'm sure."

Fiji felt like the lowest form of life possible.

"Really? Because we'd be glad to."

"I'm absolutely sure. Here, help me sit up. If you wouldn't mind."

"Of course not." Fiji took one arm and Manfred the other, and in a jiffy Ms. Owens was sitting up and smiling with relief.

"That's better. I feel just fine. I'm sure I can get myself home."

"No, ma'am," Manfred said firmly. "One of us will drive you in your car, and one of us will follow to take the driver home."

"Thanks for taking such good care of me," Ms. Owens said, genuinely surprised. "Though . . ." She looked hard at Fiji. "I feel like we've met before. I mean, recently."

"I felt just the same way when you came in," Fiji said. "But for the life of me, I can't recall where. Have a drink." She handed the glass of water to Ms. Owens, who took a long gulp and handed it back.

"Thanks. If you wouldn't mind, I know I'd feel even better at home," she said.

"All right, we'll get you up then," said Manfred, and he signaled for Diederik to take Fiji's place at Ms. Owens's side. She was up on her feet before she had time to worry about the procedure.

Fiji asked Diederik to help customers if any came in while she was gone, and then she grabbed her keys and purse so she could follow Manfred to Ms. Owens's house in Davy.

"What am I supposed to do while you're gone?" Kiki demanded.

For a few pleasant moments, Fiji had forgotten all about her sister's presence. "I won't be gone long," she said. "Unpack. Or fix lunch. That would be nice. And helpful." And then she started out back to her car, only to spin on her heel.

"And leave the kid alone," she said.

"Oh, for God's sake. How old is he?" Kiki was partly angry, partly curious.

"Younger than you think."

"Too young to drive the woman back to her house?"

"No driver's license," Fiji hedged.

"Why?"

"He's foreign."

"He sure doesn't look Mexican."

"He's Dutch," Fiji said. "Now, I've got to go." And she made good her very temporary escape.

3

Manfred gave the sister—Kiki?—a nod and a wave as he got into Francine Owens's car. The sister nodded back, but without enthusiasm. That was okay with Manfred. She wasn't impressed with him; he surely wasn't impressed with her, either. And he'd seen the way she looked at Fiji when Fiji's back was turned.

Manfred couldn't drum up much conversation with Francine on their short drive to her house. She asked if he'd lived in the area long, seemed relieved that he hadn't (so presumably he wouldn't gossip about her fainting in the store), and thanked him several times for helping her, though his appearance clearly made her very uneasy. She had no idea how much he had helped her, but that was okay with Manfred.

Her house was a small ranch in a neighborhood of similar homes. Gardens and basketball goals and barbecue grills and the smell of cut grass, though it was the tail end of mowing season in Texas.

After Francine Owens had thanked them both several more times, and they had reassured her that they'd been glad to help and they hoped she recovered completely, they were all able to part ways with ill-concealed relief.

Manfred climbed into Fiji's car and leaned back, heaving a sigh. He didn't feel like talking about Francine Owens again. It was simple to think of another topic of conversation.

"So how come your sister showed up after all this time?" he asked. "Didn't you tell me none of your family had come to visit you in Midnight since you inherited?"

"Truth. Kiki says she's here now because she's broken up with her second husband. And also, my dad has Alzheimer's. So she doesn't want to stay with Mom and Dad."

"Two reasons, huh? One wouldn't do? You don't have a telephone; she couldn't call ahead?"

"Yeah, it seems pretty weak to me, too," Fiji told him. "I can sort of see her not wanting to go to my mom and dad's if Dad is getting hard to handle. She never has liked to take responsibility for someone else. But the split with her husband—that seems pretty hinky to me."

"I don't know what 'hinky' means, but the situation does seem kind of suspicious. More explanation called for."

"Right."

"Doesn't she have a job?"

"Good point, Manfred. Yes, last I heard, she was working at a Banana Republic or something. A mall clothing store. And even if she and her husband split up, it seems like she'd need to work. Maybe especially."

Manfred didn't know a lot about conventional families, since he'd never known the name of his father and he'd spent a bit of his childhood and almost all his adolescence with his psychic grandmother, Xylda Bernardo, who'd never met a camera she didn't like. "So are you thinking she's come here for some other reason entirely? Or that she's got bad news about your mother, too? Or what?" He glanced over at Fiji, who was clearly mulling over possibilities.

"I'll find out, I'm sure," Fiji said. "Even if I'd rather not."

"And your parents picked a theme to name their children?" It was time to lighten the atmosphere.

"Beach people," Fiji said, with a shrug.

"They actually went to Fiji?"

"On their seventh anniversary. Saved for five years. Mom got pregnant with me while they were there."

"And Waikiki?"

"Third anniversary."

He choked back a laugh. "Really?"

She tried not to smile. "Really."

"I never had a sibling—one I knew of, anyway." Maybe he had six brothers by his unknown father. Just with other women. "But it's got to be weird to be obliged to stick by someone you didn't pick as a friend. Or am I crazy?"

He glanced over to see that Fiji looked taken aback.

"I never thought of it that way," she said slowly. "You have to stick by family, unless they've done something truly terrible to you. I know there are families who are sadistic or neglectful. I suspect Olivia's was."

Manfred was careful just to nod, because he didn't want to interrupt the flow of Fiji's thoughts.

"There's a bond when you've been brought up in the same household together," she said finally. "Whether you want there to be or not. There are times, growing up, when you get into trouble together. When it's kids versus parents. I love Kiki, but that love is tempered with . . . a lot of wariness."

"Interesting," was all he could think of to say. After they drove a few more miles, he said, "We have to tell everyone about Francine Owens."

"Yeah," she said, without enthusiasm. "Maybe you could take care of that?"

Again, Manfred was surprised, and not in a good way. Keeping everyone in town on the same page was a Fiji thing. Something was going on with his friend, something beyond the unexpected arrival of her sister. Cautiously, he said, "There anything you want to talk about?" He half hoped she'd say there wasn't.

"I think having my sister turn up, on top of suicides and a suicide attempt, is enough," she said, after a pause that was just a little too long.

"Okay," he said, hoping his relief didn't show. "But you know where I am if you need me."

The adrenaline that had fueled his great tackle of the about-to-be suicide had long faded, leaving him dragging and dull. Now that they'd gotten rid of this last body (fortunately, still breathing), Manfred found himself longing for his computer and his telephone and his privacy.

"If your sister stays for any length of time, I'll take you two out to dinner one night," Manfred offered as Fiji dropped him at his house. "And not at Home Cookin. All the way to Davy, or even Marthasville. I spare no expense!"

"Thanks, Manfred," she said, sounding surprised. Fiji threw the surprise back over to his side of the fence by giving him a hug.

Manfred knew his return of the hug was a bit awkward, but it was sincere. He was pleased. Unfortunately, as soon as he touched her, he knew what Fiji's secret was. She had had a falling-out with Bobo—or rather, with her dream of the possibility of a relationship with Bobo. That made him sad, but he was not about to comment on it.

Fiji let go and leaned back in her seat. "Oh, I just remembered!" she said.

"Remembered what?"

"Where I'd seen Francine Owens before."

"Where was it?"

"The last time I went to the grocery store in Davy. She was ahead of me in line."

"How can you possibly remember who was ahead of you in line at the grocery store?" Manfred shook his head disbelievingly.

"You'd remember her, too," Fiji said, though she wasn't completely sure about that. In her limited experience, men remembered different things than women did, at least sometimes. "She was one of those shoppers who had a coupon for every item. And she asked the cashier about a dozen questions. Like if the second package of napkins had to be the same style as the first one for the coupon to be good." She'd also waited until the items had been tallied to begin writing a check, which was one of Fiji's pet peeves. *If you're gonna use a debit card, fine. If you're gonna write a check, by golly, start filling it out.*

If Fiji hadn't been in a hurry (she couldn't remember why), she would never have recalled the little incident, which had irritated her quite a bit.

She explained all this to Manfred, who said, "So you disliked her, based on that incident."

"Well, yeah. Of course, today I just felt sorry for her. But she was definitely on my shit list for about five whole minutes." Fiji smiled to make sure Manfred understood that being on her "shit list" was not a permanent thing.

"That's interesting."

"I don't see why! At least now I can lose that nagging feeling you get when you can't quite remember something."

"Fiji," Manfred said, and stopped dead. He'd been about to explain his tentative theory, but he thought better of it. "Nah, don't worry about it." He smiled at her. "I'm glad you remembered, and I'm glad the lady's okay, and I hope your sister leaves soon."

"Those all sound like good wishes to me."

"And whatever else is wrong, I think it's gonna be okay, too," Manfred said, and turned to go in his house before she could ask him any questions.

4

That night, Lemuel was back at his task of puzzling out the translation of the book—the most important one, the one about the origin of magical sites in the United States. The only one in Texas he'd seen mention of so far was the Devil's Sinkhole, south of Midnight. It would have been more accurate to call it "*a* Devil's Sinkhole," according to the author of *The New World and Its Places of Interest.*

Lemuel had seen older books than the one to which he was paying so much attention, but he was sure this was the right book. He'd come across the first pawnshop owner's notes in his second year of working for Bobo; it was ironic that it had taken him all these years to find the really interesting piece of history that had become his obsession. But the builder of Midnight Pawn, which had originally been a general store, had bought and sold a good many things, both ancient and modern, new and used.

"A consignment of ancient books," the original owner had written. "Which I now believe to be of the Devil, so I have hidden them. If the owner returns to redeem them, I will kill him." Lemuel had been intrigued, of course. He'd had trouble discovering what had happened to the original owner, but he'd run across one mention of a terrible accident in an old county newspaper, which had made him even more curious.

Lemuel had not been able to claim ownership of the pawnshop continuously for all those years, because someone would have noticed his odd longevity and his aversion to daylight. Though he was very strong and fast, humans in a group could defeat him. By various subterfuges, he'd remained in the area. But he'd never been able to find the trove of books.

Bobo had discovered them by accident, which was galling. And funny, too.

The cover of the book Lemuel was studying, which had been created from the skin of a werewolf, was still in excellent shape, and the pages, though spotted and yellowed, were quite legible . . . if you could speak the language they'd been written in.

That was what had taken so long—finding someone who could still speak the ancient tongue.

"You taking a break?" Olivia asked. She'd set up a card table behind the counter and was working a jigsaw puzzle. "A thousand pieces," she'd told him, looking determined.

"Just for a few minutes," Lemuel said, getting off the stool and stretching.

"I have to go to New Orleans in a couple of weeks. You want me to look up that Quigley, thump him good?"

"I felt lucky to find him at the time," Lemuel said. "A descendant of the vampire who wrote this book? Hadn't expected that."

"It would have been a better discovery if he'd been smart," Olivia said.

"Yes, indeed. Maybe I should have taken some wooden slivers with me, asked a few more questions. I know Quigley has a child, and he wasn't the first vampire Arria Auclina created. There's an older child somewhere, a female."

"What about Arria Auclina herself?" Olivia was all for going directly to the source.

"She would squash me like a bug," Lemuel said gently. "Ones that old, they don't care a thing about a comparatively new one like me, especially since I'm the rare breed."

"I think being able to take blood from humans *or* sap their energy makes you a lot more diverse," she said. "I bet they all wish they were like you."

"Not the purists," he said, with a slight smile. "Though it was much easier for me when I was only a hundred or so, to go amongst people. It was hard for them to tell what I was. Now, there's no question."

"Shall I ask Quigley nicely to give us another source?" She perked up at the prospect of action.

Lemuel looked at Olivia steadily. She was brave and strong and lethal, but she'd never understand that a vampire could snap her spine in a second. Any vampire. "Olivia, please don't approach him unless I ask you to," he said, making sure she saw how serious he was.

Lemuel squatted by the card table to pick up little puzzle pieces that had landed on the floor. As he began returning them to the table, he glanced up at Olivia. Her brow was furrowed as she tried to match piece after piece. Though he had never told her—and she had never asked—Lemuel planned to make Olivia a vampire someday. She was bright and wounded and lethal and loyal. Only her mortality kept her from being nearly perfect in his eyes. She was about to speak again; she turned away from the puzzle.

"Listen, I guess there's no shortcut you could take, or you would have taken it already, right?"

"What shortcut did you have in mind?" Lemuel lay the book down and simply looked at her.

"Like scanning the text for the word that means 'Midnight,' or 'Crossroad.' Something like that." Olivia shrugged, to let him know she thought her idea feeble.

Lemuel reached up to put his cold hand on her cheek. "Remember, I told you that whatever happened to make this place so odd and queer must have happened before this crossroad was even called Midnight?"

She nodded.

"I think the town is here because of whatever event took place."

"You think people have come to this spot because they were drawn to it because of the event," Olivia said slowly.

"Yes."

"I knew this wouldn't be easy," Olivia said, and her voice was just shaky enough to remind Lemuel to remove his hand before he took too much energy from her.

"If you have any other ideas, I will be glad to hear them," he said. "Never keep one to yourself."

"I won't." Olivia flashed him a smile, and Lemuel said, "That's my bold woman." He spied one more bit of puzzle and leaned beneath the table to retrieve it.

The bell over the door tinkled as a man came in, a rough and hairy man with a coarse brown beard. A gust of cool air came in the door with him.

"Evening," Olivia called, standing up and moving behind the counter. Lemuel, out of her sight, stiffened.

"I came to redeem my knife," the man said, his voice deep.

"Got your ticket?" Olivia asked. Lemuel glanced up and nodded to himself. Olivia knew what he was. She had remembered to smile with her teeth covered, as you should around a werewolf.

"I do." The customer fished around in his jeans pockets and came up with a bit of cardboard, which he put on the counter. He paused and sniffed. "Do I smell a dead . . . *kinsman*?" His own teeth became very apparent, and they seemed longer and sharper than they should have been.

"I have no idea what you smell," Olivia said. "But I bet you're getting a whiff of metal, buddy." She was holding a gun in her hand.

Lemuel thought, *I did not tell her about the bookbinding.* He stood. At the sight of him, the werewolf stepped back a little. "So overcome by the cover of an old book that you couldn't smell me?" Lemuel asked, his voice rusty and slow. "This shop is under my protection. That includes everyone who works here."

"I can take him," Olivia said. She sounded remote, calm.

"I know you can, Olivia. But in this case, I just about owe this man an explanation."

The werewolf looked surprised. "My name is Theo Barclay," he said more civilly. "I wait to hear it."

"See this book, Theo Barclay?" Lemuel held it up. "You can see it is ancient. I had nothing to do with the construction of it. As you smelled, some person used the skin of a were to construct it."

"It should be buried with respect."

Lemuel paused before he spoke. "I have to read this book, because magic is brewing here, magic that will do none of us any good. If I can find out what is going to happen, maybe I can prevent it. The answer lies here." He tapped the book to emphasize his point. "When that danger is passed, I will give the book covering to your packmaster. Until then, I have to keep the book intact, lest something I can't foresee might happen to it if I simply remove the cover."

It was Barclay's turn to think out his response. "That's a deal," the werewolf rumbled, finally. "I'll tell my packmaster. Now, I want to redeem my knife."

Within minutes, Barclay was out the pawnshop door, his very fine knife in its custom sheath on his belt.

Lemuel could feel Olivia simmer during this whole exchange.

"I could have handled him," Olivia said, the minute the rumble of Barclay's motorcycle faded in the distance.

"Woman, I know you can kill," Lemuel said. "This is not an issue we need to debate. And you are proud. You should be. But this incident had nothing to do with pride. It had only to do with the werewolves' right to bury their dead, if that is how they want to honor her."

"It's a female?" Olivia looked at the book, impressed but also a little disgusted.

"I think it is," Lemuel said. "I can't know how she died, or when, but I know it was many, many years ago."

"So she's not likely to be Barclay's literal kin?"

"No."

"Well, all right."

Lemuel wasn't sure what Olivia had resolved within herself as a result of this discussion, but he could tell she was at peace with him now, and that was what he cared about.

That, and reading this damned book.

John Quinn came into the Inquiring Mind the next morning with Fiji's newspaper tucked under his arm. She realized she'd forgotten to go out to get it that morning. It had been an atypical and incredibly irritating day, and it was only nine a.m. Until Quinn entered, Fiji had been sitting behind the counter, gripping the edge with both hands, staring straight ahead with her teeth in a line, listening to her sister sing in the shower. Every word was perfectly audible, and it was all in the wrong key.

Fiji had never realized before how simple her life was merely because she was the only person living in the house. She had to make an effort to smile at Quinn, which was a first. Like most women, she'd always found it easy to be happy when she saw him. Quinn was tall, bald, and muscular, with pansy-purple eyes. Pleasant to look at, pleasant to talk to.

"Here you go," he said, handing her the folded paper.

"Thanks," she said, and dropped it on the counter. Ordinarily, she took time during the morning to read it. Ordinarily, she was cheerful. Ordinarily, she was content in her own shop. Now, her routine was all shot to hell.

Quinn stood listening to Kiki's dreadful warbling. He blinked a couple of times. "You have a musical visitor," he said politely.

"Well, I have a visitor who likes to sing. Sorry for the serenade," Fiji said. "Muzak would be better, and I never thought I'd say that." She shook her head dolefully.

Quinn's smile returned.

Fiji had to restrain an involuntary sigh. Despite the fact that she'd considered her affections taken until the day before, other parts of her felt free to rejoice in sexual attraction. Quinn was hot, no two ways about it.

"When did you get in to town?" Fiji asked.

"Last night. I just finished a big ascension ritual, and I missed my son. Diederik's growing so fast!"

That was God's truth. "The tiger growth rate," Fiji said. "It's just incredible. By the way, my sister doesn't know much about supernatural stuff."

Quinn nodded. "Like weretigers? Point taken. Before she joins us, then, Diederik tells me there are troubles here."

"Very serious troubles. When are you going to be able to take him with you?" It would break the heart of everyone in Midnight if anything happened to Diederik. They'd all had a hand in raising him, however short a time that had taken.

"He's almost mature," Quinn said. "When I'm sure he can protect himself, he'll start traveling with me."

Weretigers were popular as fighters in the pits, a supernatural gladiatorial contest held in secret. The contest was along the order of "Two creatures enter, one creature leaves." No one went into the pits voluntarily. Fighters were either coerced or kidnapped. More than anything else, Quinn did not want this to happen to Diederik—because it had happened to Quinn, and he still bore the mental and physical scars. And pit fighting had reduced the weretiger population down to a scary level.

"I'm pretty sure Diederik is all grown up. Marina at the hotel sure thinks so." Fiji tried not to grin.

"I had noticed that. We've had the 'safety first' lecture."

"Glad to hear it."

"Who's out there?" Kiki called from the bathroom. "You got a customer, Feej?"

"Yes, Kiki," Fiji called back. "I'm shutting the hall door." She stepped to the door that shut the living quarters away from the shop area, but before she could close it, Kiki stepped out of the bathroom with a towel wrapped around her and nothing else. Her hair was piled in a haphazard bun on top of her head, and a gust of steamy air enveloped her. She gave Quinn a look that Fiji could only term "come hither" before she sashayed down the hall to the guest bedroom, giving Quinn a great view of her rear end.

Fiji, casting her eyes up, shut the door and returned to her company. "Ew, sorry," Fiji said.

"I've seen women's butts before," Quinn said.

"It's just . . . she's separated from her husband and I think she's . . ."

"Trying to test the waters?" He smiled down at her.

"Yeah, something like that." Fiji felt relieved. "She's not really . . ."

"That easy?" Quinn said.

"Yeah." Though Fiji thought maybe Kiki *was* pretty easy; she just didn't want her friends to know that. Fiji struggled with the idea that Kiki's sexual activity wasn't her problem for all of thirty seconds. Then she admitted to herself that if Kiki were a slut, it would make her feel embarrassed for them both.

"Feej," he said. "Everyone here knows you. We don't know her. We don't expect her to be like you. You're one of a kind. My son has told me many times how great you've been to him, how much care you take of your neighbors, how much concern you have for this community, how much genuine talent you have."

"You talking about Feej's baking? Because she is a mighty fine cook," Kiki said, opening the door from the hall. She managed to sound both sassy and provocative. Fiji couldn't believe how quickly her sister had shoehorned herself into tight jeans, an aqua T-shirt, and no bra, a lack that was quite obvious.

"Fiji is a fine witch," Quinn said. "I am surprised you don't know that."

Kiki tossed her head. "Riiiight," she said. "You and the guy across the street have *both* told me that my sister's a witch. And I'm from Area Fifty-Four. You all take yourselves pretty seriously here in Midnight. By the way, I'm Kiki Ransom. Fiji's sister."

"My older sister," Fiji murmured, and winked at Quinn with the eye that Kiki couldn't see.

"Slightly older," Kiki amended, though with good humor. "And you are?"

"This is Quinn," Fiji said. "Diederik's father. You know Diederik, the young man with the beautiful eyes?"

"I see where he gets 'em from," Kiki said. "Well, it's a pleasure to meet you. Do you live here year round, Quinn?"

"No," he said pleasantly. "I travel a lot. That's why Diederik stays here."

"So he can go to school," Kiki said, nodding. "I get it."

Diederik "went to school" by learning from each of them. He took religion and hard work from the Rev, he learned magic and shopkeeping and reading from Fiji, he learned basic math and form-filling from Bobo, computer skills and thinking quickly from Manfred, and he learned the evaluation of old things and the way to deal with customers from Joe and Chuy. He'd even had cooking lessons from Madonna and gotten paid for his janitorial work at the Midnight Hotel.

"Yes, school," said Quinn. "Will you excuse us a moment, Kiki? I need to talk to Fiji before I get back to the hotel for a conference call." He turned to walk out to the front porch, and Fiji followed, a bit baffled and apprehensive. Quinn spent time in Midnight as often as he could, but she didn't feel as though she truly knew him.

The front porch was stone, like the rest of the house, and there was a broad knee-high wall on the outer side running between the squat stone pillars. Fiji and Quinn sat on the wall. She was full of curiosity.

"As we've been saying, Diederik is almost the right age for me to start taking him with me," Quinn said.

"We'll all miss him," she said, because that was safe and sincere, and she didn't yet see where this conversation was going.

"Thanks," he said. "He's very good-natured, like his mother was. Maybe stubborn like her, too."

Fiji nodded. She'd never met the late Tijgerin, but from what little Quinn had said, she'd been determined to raise Diederik old-school, away from his dad, and it was at least probable that her death had been a result of that decision.

"I have always planned on him learning my job, and I hope he takes to it," Quinn said. "It would be great to have a helper, and eventually he could take on his own clients." Quinn was an event planner for supernatural occasions, like vampire weddings, Were coming-of-age parties, packmaster contests, and other rituals too secret to be discussed.

"That sounds ideal, if he enjoys the work," she said, still puzzled. "I know it takes a lot to get a business like yours going."

"But he loves it here," Quinn said. "He's still a kid in a lot of ways. This little town is familiar to him, and he's surrounded by friends."

"Aw, I'm so glad he feels that way." She beamed. It made her feel warm inside to hear that their affection for the boy was returned.

Even though Diederik's childhood had lasted only a year.

"What I was considering," Quinn said, after an awkward pause, "is that maybe Diederik and I might buy one of the empty cottages here, so we could spend our downtime in Midnight."

It was a pleasant change to hear good news. "What a great idea," she said. "He'd feel like he had a home here, and you'd have a place to spend a week or two now and then. I guess you've had an apartment somewhere all this time?" She hadn't thought about it before.

"Yes, but it's just an apartment, and I really want something more rooted. So I'd thought about checking out that one," Quinn said, pointing at the house to the east of Fiji's.

The house was very similar to Fiji's, but in bad repair. It had sat empty for a long time. She had a thread of memory that the woman who'd lived in it, a widow named Gertrude something, had looked down her nose at Aunt Mildred.

"I was just wondering if that was one that interested you," Fiji said. "No, of course I wouldn't mind. It would be great to have someone in it." She'd have to pay attention to whether her curtains were drawn . . . but they traveled a lot . . . she was lost in these details until Quinn said, "Earth to Fiji."

"Oh, sorry! Just thinking about how different it would be to have neighbors," she said. "The Rev's not in the chapel or pet cemetery at night, ordinarily, and that house has been empty since before I moved in. It belonged to Gertrude . . . Flannigan, that was her name! She died about five years before Aunt Mildred."

"You remember the next of kin, by any chance?"

Fiji closed her eyes to concentrate. She could almost feel Quinn looking at her through her eyelids, a strange sensation. Surely Aunt Mildred had talked about the house? Yes.

"He was named Tommy Flannigan. Thomas R. Flannigan," she said. "He lives in Waco."

"That's a huge help. You've saved me hours in the courthouse or on the computer," he said. "Can Diederik and I take you out tonight to say thanks?"

"Umm, well, I appreciate the thought, but there's Kiki," Fiji said awkwardly. She didn't think she could stand Kiki making eyes at

Quinn for a whole evening. And she didn't even want to think about what she'd do if Kiki made a pass at Diederik.

"Then you have a rain check," Quinn said. He gave her an unexpected kiss on the cheek before he loped off toward the hotel.

Fiji sat for a moment, smiling to herself as she thought over the conversation. After a minute, she went into the shop, where she had to answer Kiki's million questions about Quinn. With some exasperation, Fiji said, "You haven't even gotten rid of your current husband yet. Why start thinking about another one?"

This might have been a little too brutal: but then, most of Kiki's questions hadn't had to do with Quinn's character, but with his income.

"Anyway," said Kiki cruelly, "I don't think he's smitten with *you*."

Fiji said, "I never thought he was." But she kept her eyes lowered, because after this morning, she did think that might be a possibility.

This is the darker side of my big sister, Fiji thought. When Kiki was unhappy, she struck out against the people around her, especially the women. Kiki thought of herself as a sexual goddess.

Could she really be such a siren? Fiji wondered. Sure, Kiki had been married twice. But did that really prove anything? Reviewing the men Kiki had married and the men Kiki had dated, Fiji thought, *I don't think so.* Surely that couldn't be the basis for Kiki's self-regard. So what was her sister really good at? She certainly couldn't sing. "Are you good at art?" she asked abruptly, and Kiki gaped at her.

"Nope, I can't draw a lick," Kiki said. "What a weird question."

They were sitting at the table in the kitchen, eating lunch. Fiji poured some more tea into their glasses.

"Why'd you ask?" Kiki said, as if simply being quiet bugged her.

"I just wondered."

"That guy Quinn said you were a witch," Kiki said, looking off in another direction, as if merely bringing this up made her uneasy.

"You know Aunt Mildred was," Fiji said bluntly. "That was how she made her living."

"So you make herbal teas for women with headaches? And read their futures in a crystal ball?"

"Future? No, that's for psychics," Fiji said, smiling. "You might try Manfred, across the road, if you're interested in learning about your future."

"That's a bunch of crap." Making a face to show how disgusted she was, Kiki got up to scrape her scraps into the garbage can and wash her plate. They'd shared a salad; not much of anything to put away or clean up except the cutting board. "I don't believe in reading palms or casting spells, stuff like that."

Apparently, Kiki believed Francine Owens had genuinely fainted.

"Okay," Fiji said, still smiling, but with an effort. "That's fine." *Just deny my whole life and my beliefs. That's okay!*

"Maybe I'll go down and get my nails done this afternoon." Kiki had spotted the Antique Gallery and Nail Salon sign that morning, and she'd been peering at her hands ever since. "Do I need to call and make an appointment?"

"I don't think so," Fiji said, maintaining her smile. "Go do that. Tell Joe and Chuy I said hi."

And very soon after, that was what Kiki did. The relief of having her gone was ridiculously keen. As soon as Kiki's feet touched the sidewalk, Mr. Snuggly appeared by his food bowl. He fixed Fiji with a baleful glare, and she hurried to pour in his kibble and spoon a little Fancy Feast on top.

He had earned the treat.

Kiki had called Mr. Snuggly "Blubberbutt" three times, within the cat's hearing. Though Kiki had no idea that the cat could understand her, Fiji had winced every time, sure that eventually she'd pay for her sister's tactlessness..

"She'll leave sooner or later," Fiji said, scratching Mr. Snuggly's head. She tried to sound confident. *Maybe I can stand it for a week,* she thought doubtfully, and her fingers slowed. The cat butted her hand to get her attention, and she resumed scratching. "Sorry, buddy."

When Mr. Snuggly felt he'd been adored enough, he ate his food, every bit, and exited through the cat door into the backyard in what Fiji considered a very pointed way. This time of day, he normally took a nap in the basket under Fiji's counter.

Fiji felt she'd apologized enough for Kiki—in fact, she'd thought of calling Joe to apologize for whatever her sister was saying right now—but she knew that was ridiculous. *My sister's character is hardly my fault. Kiki's a grown woman,* Fiji reminded herself. As Quinn had said, people would form their own opinions of Kiki, which would not necessarily influence or affect their opinions of Fiji.

She told herself that several times.

Just when Fiji was beginning to feel more calm, if not exactly cheerful, Francine Owens came into the Inquiring Mind. The near-suicide was not in the trancelike state of yesterday, but she didn't seem to be the self-assured woman who'd held up the grocery store line, either. Fiji stood up.

"Good afternoon," she said. "Welcome back. How are you feeling?"

"Maybe you can help me," Francine said. She hesitated, looking around her as if she were seeing the store for the first time. "I know I fainted in here yesterday, and I appreciate how kind you were in getting me home safely. But I don't seem to remember coming in here. Do you think it's because I passed out, that I can't remember? It just seems so odd. I'm not really sure why I'd come in this store. I mean, it seems charming, but not my kind of thing, normally?"

Fiji thought hard as she came out from behind the counter. It had never occurred to her she'd see Francine Owens again. She had no story prepared to cope with this situation. What could she say?

Fiji hated the idea that Francine Owens might put herself through expensive medical or psychological testing to find some physical issue that had caused her to pass out. "When you came in yesterday, we had a little conversation," Fiji said slowly. "You were wanting to buy a gift for someone."

If you could say the sun was coming out on someone's face, that face was Francine Owens's. "What a relief," she said. "I wonder who the present was for?"

"I don't believe you told me. But you know what? After you fainted and I left my friend minding the store, when I was taking you home? My friend smelled gas, and he called the gas company. They came out and fixed a gas leak. So I guess you must be extra sensitive to it, cause I sure never smelled it. But you must have."

"Oh my goodness." The woman sat down heavily in one of the wicker chairs. "I'm so glad to know why I fainted like that! I can cancel my doctor's appointment. Now I just wish I could remember about buying a gift. Maybe it was for someone in my book club? We have a little harvest party coming up."

"Know someone who likes wind chimes, or sun catchers, or scented candles, something like that?"

"I think Pearl might like wind chimes; she loves her garden," Francine said, though she still sounded doubtful. "I drew her name."

"Really, don't let it worry you," Fiji said. "You know we're just a short drive away, if you decide your friend might like something from the Inquiring Mind."

"That's true. I just felt so foolish, not remembering why I was here." She looked at Fiji apologetically.

To Fiji's relief, another customer came in just then, a woman who regularly came to her Thursday night group. Most of the women who attended were simply seeking some excitement, or some way to stretch their emotional and mental muscles in search of something that fulfilled them or interested them. Denise Little, who was living at the Midnight Hotel while waiting for an assisted-living center vacancy, was a great reader and very curious. Denise, who was in her seventies, made her slow way east at least twice a week to visit with Fiji. She almost always bought some small thing to show she understood the Inquiring Mind was a business.

"Hi, Denise," Fiji said, with maybe overdone enthusiasm. "This is Francine Owens. Francine, Denise lives here in Midnight, at least temporarily."

Francine seemed reassured by Denise's white-haired respectability. "I'll take these wind chimes," she said, clearly glad to conclude her time in the shop.

Fiji rang up the purchase and wrapped the wind chimes in tissue paper, feeling she would be just as glad to see Francine leave. While she was doing this, Francine politely started a conversation with Denise about living at the Midnight Hotel. "I hear it's real nice," Francine said.

"I'm just there until a place opens up at Big Sky in Marthasville," Denise explained. "My house sold much more quickly than I ever expected, so I had to go somewhere. It's been a real boon for me, and really comfortable."

"How long do you think you'll have to wait for Big Sky?" Francine asked. "I guess you're on a list?"

Denise shrugged as she sank into one of the padded wicker chairs. "Just waiting for someone else to die," she said baldly. "I'm third in line. I've got my furniture in storage, and I can have my own things in my room there. But it's nice not to make my own bed or clean my own bathroom at the hotel. I'm pretty damn tired of housework."

Francine was visibly shocked to hear a woman older than herself curse. But she hurried to agree with Denise. "You do get tired of doing the housework after so many years. I never thought I'd say that." She smiled, which looked odd on Francine.

"That's why I come down here," Denise said, and Fiji silently said, *Thanks, Denise.* "Gets me to thinking about new things."

Francine looked blank.

"Spiritual-type things," Fiji explained. "Reading material for people seeking to expand their consciousness. Meditation techniques."

"Well. I can't imagine being interested in those things." Francine's face went from bewildered to embarrassed. "Not to be rude, I've been a Baptist all my life."

Since the ill-assorted trio seemed to have reached a conversational standstill, Fiji said, "I know you must have other things to do, so I'm grateful you stopped by today to let me know you're all right."

"I can't thank you enough," Francine said. She was on firmer ground here, since she was on her way out the door.

"You take your time getting back to full speed," Fiji advised. "But we'd be glad to see you again any time." She gave a considerable shove of her will when she said this, and Francine stiffened.

"Well, you have a nice day," Francine said by way of bidding them farewell. When she'd gotten safely in her car and driven away—back toward Davy, Fiji watched to be sure—Fiji made a cup of coffee for Denise, and they sat and had a long chatter. Fiji didn't have anything pressing to do, and she liked Denise. So she listened to Denise's stories about her courtship and widowhood, and she confirmed that the new woman in Midnight was her sister, and she agreed that Lenore Whitefield, who managed the hotel, was a stick in the mud.

It was clear that whatever was brewing in their little community, it had not yet affected Denise.

Fiji was relieved and wondered how long that would last.

She felt a lingering guilt about Francine Owens. Fiji didn't believe Francine had ever done anything awful in her life. (Being persnickety in a grocery store hardly counted.) Yet Francine, for an unknown reason, had been drawn in by the Evil Thing and very nearly committed suicide—a lifetime of propriety thrown away because she'd been targeted by something wicked.

During her conversation with Denise, Fiji turned the corner from being frightened to being angry. She had to force herself to pay attention and make appropriate responses to Denise's remarks. By the time the older woman had left, Fiji was calmer. That was a good thing, since Kiki came back from her excursion to the Antique Gallery and Nail Salon with so much news that they might as well have been in a city.

First, Fiji had to admire Kiki's fingernails, which were truly beautiful. Chuy always did a great job. Kiki planned to return for a pedicure the next day. "No point getting everything done at one time," she snorted. "Since fun here is not a big commodity."

"Feel free to go back to Houston any time," Fiji said.

That stopped Kiki dead in her conversational tracks. "Oh, you know what I mean," she said, with assumed gaiety. "Anyway, I stopped in the Gas N Go on my way back, because I was looking for something to munch on."

Didn't want to hurry back to talk to her sister, Fiji translated.

"And you won't believe who's running the Gas N Go! Just started a couple of days ago!"

"Who?" Fiji was actually curious about the guy, because she hadn't heard any report on him yet.

"Well, he's a full-blooded Native American. . . ."

"What tribe?"

"I don't know, and it seemed a little rude to ask him," Kiki said, which was inexplicable to Fiji. "But the thing is, he's gorgeous! In kind of an inscrutable way. And maybe he's a little rough around the edges. But he's got the long black hair and the copper skin and the manly man thing going for him. Yum!"

"Huh. What's his name?"

"Here's the kicker. Sylvester!" Kiki widened her eyes. "Have you ever met a real person named Sylvester?"

"No," Fiji said truthfully. "Sylvester what?"

"Something Indian," Kiki said. "Like Bearclaw, or something."

"That really is interesting," Fiji agreed. "Well, I hope he stays a while. I assume he's living in the house that comes with the store?"

Kiki nodded vigorously. "I think so. And he said he was going to look for someone to work part time so he wouldn't be spending sixteen hours a day there."

"That would be pretty awful." Gas N Go had been open limited hours while Teacher Reed had been in charge, because Teacher simply refused to work that many hours. And he hadn't found anyone to split the shift with—at least, anyone who lasted more than a week.

"Maybe he'll bring in someone just as hunky," Kiki said.

"Or maybe his wife." Fiji was willing to concede this was a little mean of her, but Kiki seemed determined to rub her the wrong way. Ordinarily, Fiji would be quite interested in a hunky new guy at the convenience store. She had to admit that Kiki made her feel contrary. This was not a huge revelation.

"He didn't mention a wife, and he didn't have on a wedding ring," Kiki said triumphantly.

"Well, that's good news," Fiji said, scolding herself severely.

"What did you do while I was gone?" her sister asked. She looked at Fiji in the bright-eyed expectation that Fiji would have done absolutely nothing.

"Had a couple of customers, talked to them," Fiji said. "Sold some stuff." Denise had bought a book about star signs.

"Oh. Well, good!" Kiki fidgeted around some more, going through the stack of magazines on the table between the two wicker chairs, picking up this item or that item and examining it, only to return it to not-exactly-the-right place.

"So," Kiki said, when she'd exhausted the possibilities of the store, "what do you think Quinn's doing now?"

"Probably visiting with Diederik, because that's what he came here to do," Fiji said. "Or if Diederik's busy, Quinn's working up in his hotel room on his laptop."

"Why would Diederik be busy?"

"He has a couple of . . . jobs," Fiji said. "He helps the Rev out. And he works over at the hotel doing janitor work in the evenings."

Kiki decided to rearrange the wicker chairs and the table. "Who's the Rev?"

"The Rev is the older man who wears the black suit and hat," Fiji said between clenched teeth.

"Why is he helping to raise Diederik?"

Fiji had to think quick to come up with an answer for that one. She wasn't going to tell her sister that the three men were weretigers. "The Rev is a distant relation. Quinn travels all the time, so the Rev's glad to keep Diederik here until he can go along with his dad. We're all helping."

"So he's been here for years?"

In tiger terms, yes. In human terms, not so much. "We've all watched him grow up," Fiji said truthfully.

"Quinn had quite a chat with you today out on the porch. All by your lonesomes."

"We're friends."

"You never thought about making a play for him?"

No, because I was blinded by my love for Bobo. "I never did," Fiji said calmly.

"Because, seriously, he looks like he would be a tiger in the sack."

Fiji snorted with laughter. "I'll bet he would," she said. She had a strong conviction it was not the first time that observation had been made about John Quinn. She thought for a moment about how it would feel, going to bed with Quinn, all that olive skin at her pleasure. She felt a twinge, and knew it would be a memorable experience, but somehow Fiji didn't think she'd follow that up.

She glanced at her watch. "Kiki, you want to cook supper tonight?"

"Oh. You don't feel like it? What were you going to have?"

"I have some chicken in the refrigerator in the meat drawer. How about chicken baked in spaghetti sauce over pasta, with a salad?"

"Got any garlic bread?"

"There should be some in the freezer."

"Then you got a deal," Kiki said.

It was really nice not to have to cook this evening, but not quite nice enough to make up for the aggravation and tension that Kiki's presence caused her. At least Fiji kept busy that afternoon. Three women from Marthasville stopped by to exclaim over the philosophy books, the witchcraft books, and the astrology charts. They even bought two or three things apiece. And as the afternoon came to an end, Fiji could smell cooking from the back of the house, a novel assurance that she could sit back and relax, maybe work on the store's books for a while.

Though the chicken was a little overdone and the salad a little overdressed, Fiji enjoyed eating a meal that she hadn't had to prepare. Dinner was even more pleasant when Kiki ran out of small talk. But Fiji could tell there was something else on her sister's mind. She wasn't sure she wanted to know what that might be, but automatically she began reviewing the possibilities.

After a moment, Fiji realized that Kiki hadn't said one word about hearing from her husband or their parents since her arrival. Kiki specialized in adversarial phone conversations. This dearth of controversy seemed very odd. *I haven't even seen her pick up her cell phone*, Fiji realized. Significant, but in what way?

There was a knock at the front door just as they'd finished eating. Fiji peered out to see through the glass pane that her caller was Teacher Reed. Though she was surprised, Fiji hurried through to unlock it.

Teacher said, "Sorry to bother you, Fiji, I know you're closed. But my truck has just died, right here." Fiji peered past him. Teacher's old pickup had pulled in just off the road. "Can I leave it there until the morning? The tow truck will come get it then, early, I promise."

"Sure, that's fine," Fiji said, feeling Kiki coming up behind her. The woman was as curious as a ferret. "I hope it's not too broken."

"Bad enough that I can't fix it myself," Teacher said. In Fiji's observation, Teacher was a man who liked to listen more than he liked to talk, who would rather do than be done for, and he seemed to have a personal goal of self-sufficiency. Fiji found all that admirable, but not endearing. "I had big plans for tomorrow, now that I'm free of working at Gas N Go," Teacher said.

"I'm glad for you. And I know everyone in town will be relieved now that you're available as a handyman again!"

"Good to hear. But I'm giving myself a few days off. I was going to Killeen in the morning, but I guess now I'm staying home. I'll let you know when I can get it moved. Sorry." And with a wave, he walked off.

At least after Teacher had gone Kiki didn't ask questions. It wasn't that Kiki disliked men of color, or looked down on women who dated men of color—at least, Fiji didn't think so. Kiki simply didn't see them as suitable play partners for her, so they didn't register with her as male.

About an hour later, Manfred called her. "What's broken at your place?" he asked.

"Not a thing, unless you know something I don't know."

"Teacher just stopped in for a visit?"

They both knew how unlikely that was. "Right," Fiji said, laughing. She was holding the phone to her ear with one hand while she put a bookmark into an Anne Rice novel with the other. "No, his truck broke down, and it's beyond his power to fix so he's in a state about it. Plus, he had an appointment in Killeen tomorrow and now he can't go."

"Killeen? Huh. I have to go to Killeen tomorrow. I should give him a call."

Manfred didn't sound too excited about it.

Fiji said, "He won't know, if you don't spread it around. I guess you two aren't soul mates?"

"It just seems so random," Manfred said. "That he should need to go where I'm going. And that it should *also* be somewhere I've never gone."

"Got your spidey-sense tingling?"

"Yes," Manfred said.

"Don't call him, then," she advised. "It won't kill him to wait a few days until his truck is fixed. Killeen will still be there."

"I'll think about it," Manfred said. "I feel like I owe him for fixing my sink. He came over at ten at night after he'd closed the convenience store. That was kind of above and beyond the call of duty. Okay, well, glad nothing's wrong with your water heater, or your plumbing."

"Me, too."

"Hey, I got a couple of bottles of that pinot grigio you like so much. It was on sale. Want me to bring one over? We can talk about the state of the world."

"Sure, come on over. We just cleaned up after supper, but there are some leftovers if you're hungry."

"Nah, I've eaten. But I'm walking over with the wine."

Fiji put down her phone and said, "Kiki, let's put out those cheese straws in a bowl."

"Company's coming?" Kiki said, trying not to sound too eager. Kiki's face lit up at the prospect of having someone else to talk to besides her sister. Truth be told, Fiji felt the same way.

"Manfred, and he's bringing wine. So if you could get out some glasses? They're on the second shelf of that cabinet." Fiji pointed.

Thirty minutes later, the three of them were sitting around the wicker table in the shop portion of the house. Fiji had rolled her office chair around the counter for the third seat.

She understood that the conversation was stilted, but she didn't really know how to cut the thread of awkwardness. She and Manfred had a comfortable relationship. Adding Kiki to the mix had put in roadblocks.

Oh, her sister could have a conversation . . . the famous people she'd "happened" to meet, the odd customers who'd come into the mall clothing store where she worked. The punch line of each story was (always) Kiki setting them straight in their opinions and life styles with a pithy phrase or put-down.

Manfred was very polite about the lopsided conversation. He could say "Really?" or "You did not!" as well as the next person.

But Fiji became more and more embarrassed. Finally, she was compelled to stem the tide. At the next pause in the monologue, she jumped in. "Why are you going to Killeen, Manfred? Do you have a private reading there?"

He smiled ruefully. "Yes, but a nonpaying one. I won't tell you the whole long story, but I owe my lawyer one. You remember Magdalena, I'm sure."

"She's dating Arthur Smith now, isn't she? You're just a cupid, Manfred!"

He made a mock-modest face and bowed.

"The sheriff and his lawyer sort of knew each other, but Manfred brought them together," Fiji said in an aside to her sister.

Kiki had taken the change of subject with good grace and was doing her best to look interested. Possibly she'd remembered conversation is a two-way street.

"Tomorrow I'm giving Magdalena's mom a private reading. The first time we scheduled it, her mom had to cancel. But tomorrow, I'm driving to Killeen to clear the board." He said this with more relief than Fiji would have expected.

"Has Magdalena been bugging you about it?"

"You have no idea," Manfred said, shaking his head. "She's tenacious, which makes her a great lawyer. But she's a very uncomfortable person to owe a favor to."

"How far is Killeen?" Kiki said.

"It should take about three hours to get there," Manfred said. "Oh, by the way, Feej, I called Teacher and he jumped at the chance to ride with me. I figured as long as I was canceling out a favor I owed, I might as well cancel another one, too."

Fiji smiled. "I like your reasoning. It's a good thing to be square with Teacher."

"The guy who left his truck in front of your shop?" Kiki said, to make it clear she was feeling left out.

"You met him," Fiji said. "He just texted me to tell me a tow truck would be coming early in the morning to get the pickup out of the way."

"Want some more cheese straws?" Kiki asked their guest, determined to insert herself into the conversation.

"Oh, I'm not company," Manfred said easily. "I'll get my own." And he did.

After twenty more minutes, Manfred made leaving sounds. He offered to wash the wineglasses, but Fiji said, "I give you a pass on helping this time, since you brought the wine. You have to get an early start in the morning, anyway."

After he'd departed, Kiki could hardly wait until the door slammed behind him before she began asking questions. The fact that Manfred was a real Internet presence had escaped her until this evening. She wanted to know all about him.

Fiji answered the questions she could and shrugged at the questions she couldn't. She did point out that Manfred was at least eight years younger than Kiki, whose face went sour at the reminder.

"It's like you're telling me I can't flirt with anyone in your precious little town," Kiki said. Her voice was sharp and her face was hard.

Fiji made herself pause before she snapped back. She gave Kiki's accusation a minute's thought. "I'm just pointing out facts," she said. "Flirt with all of them, if you want." She spread her hands to indicate the buffet of men available in Midnight. "I didn't think you'd be interested in someone whose age is so different, that's all."

"Same difference as between you and the Diederik boy," Kiki said meanly.

"What?" Fiji had turned away to dry the last glass. Now she swung to face Kiki again.

"Well, he is really tasty looking," Kiki said with a smirk. "And he doesn't look at you like he's thinking how old you are."

Fiji exhaled heavily, trying to control her impulse to jump on her sister and beat her about the head. But a thread of honesty kept her from it. It was true that when Diederik was helping the Rev dig graves in the pet cemetery, with his shirt off, it was hard not to think about him . . . carnally. If she just happened to be there at the time. But all Fiji had to do to bring herself back to reality was to remember Diederik as he'd been less than a year before, a very little boy who was really scared.

That memory was cold water. Ice water.

"Kiki, I really don't want to hear that again. I've known that boy since he was a toddler, and I don't even want that idea to cross my own mind, much less anyone else's."

"Oh, Fiji, I was just kidding!" (She hadn't been.)

"Don't kid anymore." Fiji let the water out of the sink. "I'll put the dishes away in the morning. I'm going to read for a while, and then I'm going to bed. Do you need anything else?"

"No, I'm just fine." Kiki looked angry because she felt guilty, and Fiji thought there should be a word for that. Guilter? Anguilty?

"See you tomorrow." Fiji escaped to her room, shutting the door behind her with great delicacy.

The only television in the cottage was in the shop portion, and it was no great TV set. Fiji didn't care that much about watching, though she heard all the time there was good programming that she really ought to see. But she always seemed to have something better to do. As Fiji, in her nightgown, padded to the bathroom to brush her teeth, she heard the television come on and saw the glow. Just as gently as she could, she closed the door between the shop and the residence. Mr. Snuggly came through the cat door, stopped by his bowls, and jumped up on Fiji's bed the minute she climbed in. Fiji read some more of the Anne Rice novel, and worked a crossword puzzle, and caught herself yawning. She switched off her lamp and wiggled down in bed, Mr. Snuggly curled up at her feet.

Fiji said prayers every night, though she varied whom she prayed to. Tonight, she prayed for a smooth trip for Manfred and Teacher, and she also prayed that her sister would finally tell her why she'd really come to visit, and then find a reason to go.

6

At seven the next morning, Manfred and Teacher left for Killeen.

Teacher walked into Manfred's yard holding a travel mug of coffee and looking morose just as Manfred was stowing his valise in the backseat. The two men nodded at each other, and Teacher got into the passenger seat. After a brief pause while Manfred put Agnes Orta's address into his GPS, they drove south.

After Manfred had had his favorite morning beverage, Coca-Cola, and Teacher had worked on his coffee, Manfred found himself casting around to think of a topic of conversation. Manfred hadn't met the new manager of Gas N Go yet, and he asked Teacher about the newcomer. Teacher told Manfred that he was okay. Teacher cataloged the repair jobs that had accumulated while he was employed at the convenience store and let Manfred know he was plenty upset about his truck failing him.

"What do you need to do in Killeen?" Manfred asked, after they'd listened to the morning news on the radio and agreed that the world was in sad shape. "I hope something that'll take a couple of hours? I'll be at least that long, I think."

"I've got a friend there who handles this brand of tools I like a lot, so rather than order a few over the Internet and guess which one I'll really use, which one feels the best in my hand, I thought I'd take a look at 'em," Teacher said. "He just e-mailed me to tell me he'd gotten in some new things, and I didn't have a job scheduled for today, so I'd planned on driving down there. Kind of a treat to get away for a day. Thanks for letting me know you were going, man."

"Fiji told me," Manfred said. "It's no big thing. Glad I could help. I guess these are pretty specialized tools?" Manfred only knew the basics about home repairs and tools, and he was trying to imagine how "special" a wrench could be.

"Some of them are special enough that I don't know how often I'll use them. The main thing is they're very well made. So they're pretty damn expensive," Teacher said. "But my daddy always told me, don't do to buy cheap tools."

"Really? Huh."

"Your daddy tell you the same thing?"

"I never met him, so he didn't have the chance." Manfred had had his whole life to get used to this state of affairs, but it was usually a shock to anyone else. Sure enough, Teacher turned and stared.

"That sounds pretty rough," Teacher said, after an appreciable pause.

"I'm used to it. Where did you grow up?" Manfred asked, just to get the conversation across that abyss.

"Alabama," said Teacher.

"Never been there," Manfred said. "You meet Madonna there? Childhood sweethearts?"

Though Manfred was focused on the road before him, he got the impression that Teacher shot him a sharp look. "We've known each other a long time," Teacher said.

A curiously nonspecific answer, Manfred thought, and not what he'd expected. "So you grew up in the same town."

"Nearabouts."

"Can everyone in her family cook as well as Madonna can?"

"She says her granny could, but the talent sure skipped her mom. We'll have to see about Grady."

"Today Home Cookin, tomorrow *Top Chef*," Manfred said, smiling. "Wouldn't that be something?"

"How about you, Manfred? Where'd you grow up?"

"Tennessee," he said. "A town outside of Memphis."

"Had a big houseful?"

Manfred laughed. "No, just me and my mom, or more often me and my grandmother," he said. "You have lots of siblings?"

"I did have a few," Teacher said. "Two sisters and a brother."

"Do you all keep in touch?" This conversation was on life support.

"Yeah, more or less. We talk at Christmas, but we don't visit a lot."

Manfred thought he could let it drop now, and they drove in silence for some time. Manfred was thinking about his business, and the ominous stain he'd noticed on the ceiling after the last rain. He was pretty sure his rented house needed a new roof. He'd have to hit up Bobo, his landlord. Bobo had been in such a bad mood the past few days that Manfred didn't relish the prospect.

"Have you ever put a roof on?" he asked Teacher.

"I can. A roofing crew can do it a hell of a lot faster."

"That's something to think about," Manfred said. "Hey, you need to make a pit stop? I could use some tea." Tea was not available at the convenience store, but Manfred was glad enough to get another Coke. While Teacher bought a tube of powdered sugar doughnuts, Manfred enjoyed a gulp of icy sweetness. This road trip was turning out to be—not a disaster, certainly, but less than pleasant. Manfred felt uncomfortable at the prolonged close proximity to Teacher.

After another hour of listening to the radio and exchanging a few more terse comments on the news, they reached Killeen. Manfred couldn't tell how Teacher felt about it, but Manfred was relieved. Teacher was able to direct Manfred right to his friend's shop in the older part of town, the main street. Manfred pulled into an empty parking space to let Teacher out. He noted that there were some small restaurants on the same block, and he was relieved to know that if his session with Agnes Orta took longer than he expected, Teacher wouldn't be sitting on the sidewalk twiddling his thumbs. "I'll call you when I'm through," he said. "You good?"

"Yeah, I'm fine. If I get through with my business ahead of time, the pie at Mary Lee's Café—over there, see the red awning?—is really, really good. Don't tell my wife I said so."

Manfred said, "I won't. Have a good time with your tool guy."

Teacher nodded. "Okay, man, see you later." And he was out of the car and opening the door of the hardware store.

He walks like a different person, Manfred thought, watching Teacher go inside. Teacher looked freer, somehow; happier. Either his friend in Killeen was someone really special or Teacher found Midnight oppressive. Manfred navigated his way to Agnes Orta's house, thinking only a little about Teacher as he drove. Mostly, Manfred felt pleased to be alone.

Magdalena Orta Powell's mother lived in a neat white house built in the fifties, with a small and well-kept front yard. There was a whimsical statue of a squirrel in one flower bed (the squirrel was smiling), and in another flower bed there stood a painted wooden cutout of a woman with a big butt, bending over. In case Mrs. Orta was looking out the window, Manfred did not make a face. Instead, he knocked on the door, which had recently been repainted dark green. It opened immediately.

"Mrs. Orta?" he said, and she nodded vehemently.

"Well, if this isn't wonderful!" Agnes Orta said. "I'm so excited. I feel like I'm meeting a movie star. Call me Agnes, I'm not so old!"

Agnes Orta really wasn't old, even to Manfred's eyes. She must have been very young when she'd had Magdalena. Agnes was short, and if she had bent over she would have looked very much like the wooden cutout in the yard. He appreciated her sense of humor a bit more when he realized that.

Agnes's hair was still thick and glossy, though there were a few threads of gray running through it. A beautiful silver comb held it away from her face, and the comb contrasted sharply with the orange-patterned top and brown pants that hugged Agnes's generous curves.

"Come in, come in!" she said, and he moved past her into the sunny house. "Can I get you some tea? Some coffee?"

"Thanks," he said. "Some tea would be great."

"And if you need the bathroom, it's right there," his hostess told him, pointing at a door to the right of the little living room.

"Thanks," Manfred said, relieved, and availed himself of the offer.

When he emerged, she called him to the kitchen, which (though small) was bright and clean and full of plants. Mrs. Orta saw him looking around. "I brought in my rosemary and my basil," she said. "The nights are getting too cold for them, even on the patio."

"They make the kitchen look so nice," he said, wishing his vocabulary had a better word for what he meant.

"My Magdalena bought this house for me," she said proudly.

"What a great thing to do." He meant it.

"She said she had met you in her professional capacity," Mrs. Orta said. "I know Magdalena can be a forceful woman, so I hope she didn't bulldoze you into coming to see me. I know it was a birthday present from her, but I also know that was quite a drive."

Now that Manfred had met Agnes, he felt much happier about repaying his debt to Magdalena this way. "I'm glad to be here," he said. "Magdalena told me you're a fan of mine. I'm so flattered to hear it."

"Oh, she don't believe, but I do," Agnes said. She put a mug of tea in front of him, along with a spoon and a tiny jug of milk and one of sugar. "And my priest understands."

Manfred was surprised. He put a spoonful of sugar and a dash of milk in his tea in silence. In his experience, priests and ministers had strong feelings about psychics and fortune-tellers, and he'd been on the receiving end of plenty of lectures. He didn't want to hear another.

"But he won't be showing up here today to watch, I take it," Manfred said gently.

"Oh!" Agnes laughed, a big infectious huff of merriment. "Not Father Antonio. He just said, 'I'll see you on Sunday, and you better be there!'"

Manfred tried a sip of his tea and told her how good it was, trying to hide his relief that a Catholic priest would not be part of the morning's program. He unpacked his valise, bringing out the tarot cards, the crystal ball (which he used as a focusing object), and the Ouija board, which he simply despised but lugged along, anyway.

Agnes looked at his tools with excitement and anticipation. "Can my friend Linda come over?" she asked. "I didn't know if you would charge Magdalena more if I invited someone or not? Linda's just as big a follower of yours as I am, and she lives right next door. It would be such a treat for her; she don't get out much. She's been poorly."

"It would be fine if Linda was here," Manfred said. He did not tell Agnes that he was doing this for free; that was between him and Magdalena. *After all, I might as well add another old lady to the reading,* Manfred thought. He would definitely have gone above and beyond what was required to discharge his debt.

Agnes was on the phone with Linda in a New York minute. While they were waiting for the neighbor to arrive, Manfred looked around, trying to pick up more clues about this nice woman's life. He asked a few gentle questions. Knowledge was always handy when it came to the psychic business. He was beginning to build up a picture of Agnes and her world when there came a gentle knock at the kitchen door.

Linda Ortega was definitely not what Manfred had expected. She was at least twenty years younger than Agnes, and she was in the process of dying. The certainty hit Manfred like a hammer.

Does she know? Manfred asked himself, because everything depended on the answer. When he shook Linda's hand, he had his answer. She did know, but Agnes did not.

Linda's eyes were huge and dark and melancholy, but not tragic. She'd accepted her death sentence. She didn't want to talk about it. Manfred nodded, having gotten his cue. He sat at the kitchen table with the two women.

"Let's talk about how we're going to do this," he said cheerfully, and fell into his professional patter. "There are different ways to lay out the cards, if you want to go with the tarot. What information are you seeking?"

"Can you explain?" Agnes asked.

"If you want to know if there are spirits in your house, we can try the planchette, though they may not cooperate," he said. "If you want a reading on your future, we can lay out the tarot cards. If you want to find out what's looming over you personally, we can use the ball to focus the spirits to give you an answer. If you want to see what spirit has a message for you specifically, I can link with you and we can explore that." He had to go over all the options again before Agnes could make up her mind, but that gave him time to figure out how to handle the Linda-dying situation.

Agnes, as it turned out, wanted a little of everything.

Manfred did a tarot reading for her first, giving the cards to her to shuffle and laying them out in the familiar square. To his pleasure, the cards cooperated in a wonderful way. They hinted at a romance for Agnes, which put the older woman in a gale of giggles. Even Linda smiled.

Agnes was also delighted to hear she would have grandchildren sometime in the not-too-distant future . . . and that her daughter would be the vehicle by which those grandchildren would arrive. Manfred shuddered when he thought of the possible repercussions of that prediction. Magdalena would scalp him. Fortunately, Manfred had determined ahead of time that Magdalena was not Agnes's only daughter.

When Agnes insisted Linda have a tarot reading, too, Linda stopped Manfred from handing her the cards to shuffle.

"No cards. Just hold my hands," the young woman said. She switched places with Agnes, who was all smiles and excitement, and Manfred reached across to take her hands. They were cool and bony. The last time he'd done a private reading, his client had died while he was summoning her deceased husband. He tried not to shudder as he remembered how that had felt.

"Is there someone in particular you want to talk to?" he asked.

"Yes, my mother," Linda said. "Lucy Trujillo."

Manfred opened the other eye inside his head. He didn't always think of it as an eye; sometimes it was a window, and sometimes it was a door. But today, it was a third eye, and its lid flew wide. Someone was close, waiting for Linda to ask. Feeling very encouraged, Manfred said quietly, "Lucy Trujillo, visit your daughter Linda. She's waiting for you, Lucy." He hoped the spirit would show up.

But Lucy Trujillo had nothing to say to her daughter that day; someone else wanted to speak. Manfred had to comply.

"Do you know a Donnie Trujillo?" he asked Linda. Her hands clenched his convulsively.

Agnes gave a thrilled gasp. (She really was the best audience you could possibly hope for.) "Oh my God, Linda, that's your brother!" she whispered. As if Linda would not have recognized the name otherwise.

"Yes," Linda said quietly. "I know that's my brother." She was not nearly as excited—more resigned than anything, if Manfred could judge. The spirit was circling him, waiting to be invited. When Linda didn't speak again, Manfred said, "Donnie, you may approach and talk to your sister."

Donnie did not want to use his own voice, and he wasn't strong enough to use Manfred to speak. Manfred was grateful, because possession wore him out and was not a little frightening. Manfred relayed the message he was given. "Donnie says, 'I've missed you, LindyLou, and I'll be glad to see you.'"

Unexpectedly, Linda smiled. "It is him," she said quietly. "That's what he called me."

"He misses you," Agnes whispered. "Oh my God." Manfred regretted that the older woman hadn't chosen this method of communication, since she was so thrilled by Donnie's appearance.

Donnie said, "Tell her not to worry."

Manfred dutifully repeated the message.

"I'm not worried," said Linda, managing to smile.

Liar, thought Manfred. But he finally felt someone coming for Agnes, and it was lucky he'd done some research because it helped him identify the spirit. "Donnie says he'll see you in the blue hereafter," Manfred said. "Excuse me, but there's someone here to see Agnes." Wide-eyed, Agnes took Linda's place. Linda seemed content to move back to another chair, and she seemed at peace with the message she'd received, too.

"Agnes, it's Anna," Manfred said. "You know an Anna?"

"Anna!" Mrs. Orta was wide-eyed. "Anna, what do you want to tell me? Are you happy? Are you in heaven?"

"It's beautiful," Anna said, through Manfred. "Agnes, Mama's ring . . . it's in the sewing machine." Manfred shook his head, puzzled. But that was what Anna was saying. "In the button box?" he said. "Does that make sense?"

Evidently, it did. Agnes didn't wait to see if Anna had any other words for her. She was on her feet and hurrying into the next room, trailing exclamations like scarves behind her. There were sounds of vigorous rummaging. While Manfred and Linda waited, two tears slid down Linda's cheeks, and she blotted them hastily on a napkin. She said, "Thank you," very quietly.

A second later, Agnes burst back into the kitchen, carrying an ancient dark blue metal tin that had once held King Leo, whatever that was. She spilled the contents out on the table.

"Wow," said Manfred involuntarily. There were buttons of every description imaginable on the table, many of them far older than he was. Some were metal, some covered in velvet, some were carved wood, some modern plastic. Agnes bent over them and began stirring them with an urgent finger.

"There," said Linda, who had gotten interested in the search. "There it is!"

Sure enough, a pearl ring lay jumbled in with the buttons.

Agnes couldn't stop repeating "Oh my God," and Manfred was feeling pretty damn proud of himself. A genuine, tangible, result of his work! This didn't happen often.

Agnes, the ring on her little finger, was turning it this way and that, exulting. Impulsively, she took Manfred's hand and Linda's, and said, "What a wonderful day this is!" But the link between the three of them flung Manfred back into the realm of spirits, and he was abruptly confronted with his grandmother.

He was horrified.

Seeing Xylda again, as a spirit, was almost unbearable. She wasn't in color, which was very strange. He could only imagine the red of her hair, which was being whipped around her head. A wind was battering at her; soon it would rip her away. Xylda was desperate to tell him something. She reached out as if she were trying to physically grab his shoulders so she could hold on long enough to deliver her message. "Watch out," she said. "Watch out. Get away from the crossroad! It's waking up!"

And then she was gone, and the kitchen was silent, and both Linda and Agnes were looking at him with alarm. "I'm sorry," Manfred said. "I hope I didn't scare you?"

Agnes said, "You just looked scared and pretty upset for a minute. We didn't know what was happening with you."

"I saw someone I didn't expect to see," Manfred answered honestly. "It shook me up. I . . . was surprised. I'm fine, now." He forced a smile.

Agnes was ready to be reassured, and Linda too absorbed in her own problems to spend a lot of time worrying about Manfred. They both accepted his explanation and returned to the topic of the ring.

Manfred could tell that Agnes was not only delighted to discover the ring but also proud that her whole belief in spiritualism had been validated by the ring's reappearance. Since anything else he told Agnes would have been anticlimactic, Manfred extricated himself slowly and politely from Agnes's hospitality. He took a moment to give Linda a quick hug. He was sure he would not see her again.

Because Agnes was so thrilled, it took Manfred a bit longer to actually get into his car and leave. With some relief, he returned to the main street, hoping to meet Teacher and get back to Midnight without further incident. Manfred had had a text from Teacher: *I'm at Mary Lee's Café. Pie still good.*

Manfred entered to find Teacher sitting at the counter, a big metal box on the floor beside him. It certainly looked heavy enough to contain real he-man tools. Manfred sat down with Teacher long enough to wolf down a sandwich, and then they were on their way.

Manfred had a lot to think about. Fortunately, Teacher took the hint when Manfred answered a couple of questions in a clipped way. Drawing out his cell phone, Teacher played a game most of the way back, at least in the areas where he had service.

When they reached Midnight, Manfred dropped Teacher off in front of his trailer, glad to have done a nice thing for Teacher but even gladder to have completed that nice thing and gotten rid of him. Manfred was itching to get back inside his own house, sit at his own computer, and catch up on the work he'd missed while he was in Killeen.

He was almost at the point of having to hire another "Manfredo" to help him with the website, because if he slackened, he had to hump to get back to keeping abreast.

Even with Manfred's plunge into work, it seemed to take a very long time for the sky to darken outside. Finally, he felt so tired he stopped working. Though Manfred was preoccupied with his vision of Xylda and her alarming message, he also felt relieved to have discharged his debt to Magdalena. She was not a woman he'd wanted to owe, especially since she was his lawyer. Manfred knew he'd hear from Magdalena. He knew that Agnes would call her daughter today, assuming she hadn't been on the phone the second he'd backed out of her driveway.

It surprised him, though, when Magdalena showed up in person just as he stood up from the computer. She was not alone. Sheriff Arthur Smith was with her, and he wasn't in uniform.

Manfred liked Arthur, who not only seemed more flexible than most lawmen, but also seemed like a decent person. Manfred also knew that Arthur had been married three times already, since Arthur had told him that. In fact, the third divorce was only a month past. Magdalena had been married, too, at least once. Manfred was not optimistic that their couplehood would endure.

However, Manfred told himself sternly, it was none of his business, and Arthur and Magdalena were certainly old enough to chart their own course.

"How you been doing?" Arthur asked, and Magdalena said, "You sure made my mom's week."

For a good five minutes, they talked about the ring discovery. Manfred could have predicted every word of the dialogue, just like a bad movie. Normally he would have been at least moderately glad to see the two, but tonight he had other fish to fry. And urgently. It was almost dark. And lately, dark had meant a higher chance of a suicide at the crossroads.

Manfred glanced at the window, trying to conceal his impatience. He'd been carrying Xylda's warning around with him all day, and it was a heavy burden. He needed to spread the word. If he hadn't been so eager to get back to normal after his road trip . . .

"Okay, how the hell did you know about the ring?" Magdalena demanded, not for the first time. Manfred sighed, but he'd known she'd demand a "rational" explanation for one of the cleanest and clearest readings he'd gotten in his life. "I don't know how you could have done that! Mama's been looking for that ring for years."

"I guess she hasn't sewed on a button in that long," Manfred said. "Your aunt showed up and told her that was where the ring was, in the button box. Believe me, I was just as surprised as your mom. She's a wonderful lady, by the way."

Magdalena's face softened. "Yes, she is," she said. "My dad died young, and she did a good job raising us."

"That neighbor of hers," Manfred said awkwardly. "Linda."

"What about her?"

"She's pretty sick." This was something he didn't want to talk about, but he felt he had to warn Magdalena. Agnes Orta was going to take Linda's death hard.

"She's young," Magdalena said, smiling, but without conviction. She knew there was a reason he'd brought up Linda's health.

Manfred just shook his head. Her smile vanished. After a tense moment, she nodded, just a jerk of her head.

Arthur broke the silence by asking Manfred how things had been going in Midnight. "Any more suicides?" he asked, trying to lighten up the conversation. He couldn't have imagined that just made it worse.

"That would be pretty stunning, wouldn't it?" Manfred said.

Arthur laughed. "Even in Midnight, that seems pretty unlikely," he said.

Manfred offered them a drink, pretty sure Magdalena and Arthur would turn it down and see the offer as a signal to depart. Sure enough, Magdalena thanked Manfred but turned down the drink. Soon after, she and Arthur rose to take their leave. They were going to stop by the Cartoon Saloon for a sandwich and a beer, and then catch a movie in Marthasville.

When their taillights were out of sight, Manfred walked over to the pawnshop. As he'd expected, Lemuel was behind the counter. The old book was open in front of him and a spiral-bound notebook was beside it. Lemuel was busy writing when Manfred came in, but he put down his pen to regard Manfred. "What brings you out this night, neighbor?" Lemuel asked in his rusty voice.

"I got a warning today," Manfred said. "A true warning."

Lemuel's cold gaze intensified, which made Manfred shiver. It felt odd and unpleasant to be the object of Lemuel's interest.

"Tell me about it."

As concisely as possible, Manfred related his grandmother's warning. "She said it was waking up," he said.

Lemuel said, "I think we are very close to catastrophe."

"Do you know what lies underneath the crossroad?" Manfred asked.

"I suspect I do." Lemuel laid his hand on the book.

Manfred wanted to tell Lemuel to hurry up, but a strong sense of self-preservation stopped him.

"Since I have to finish the translation, it's slow work." Lemuel's tone made it clear this was not an apology, but an explanation. "I dare not skip anything. It's too important. A crossroad is a place where hunting trails cross, a place where criminals are executed, or a place where shrines are set up. This crossroad may be all three, but I have to be sure what we're dealing with."

Manfred could only nod. He turned to go, but Lemuel had more to say.

"I understand Teacher went to Killeen with you today," Lemuel observed. "What did you think of him?"

"Interesting you should bring that up," Manfred said. "I wasn't comfortable with him, and I don't know why. He seems like the easiest person in the world to get along with, in general conversation, but one-on-one . . . I just can't figure him out."

"Did he seem to want to know you?"

"Yes, he asked several questions. I kept telling myself it was only natural when you don't know someone, to ask those questions, but you know what? It felt like filling out a form for a job. So I tried to ask him the same questions, see how he liked it. He didn't." He told Lemuel about Teacher's visit to the hardware store.

"Interesting," Lemuel said, and dismissed Manfred by becoming engrossed in the pages of the book.

Manfred shook his head and left. He would have been surprised to know what Lemuel did about three a.m.

7

When everyone else in Midnight was asleep, Lemuel left the pawnshop. He drifted through the night, which was as close to silent as an inhabited place can get. The electronic sounds of the stoplight were small and easy to ignore. The bugs were not too noisy at this time of year. A coyote yipped to the north, a lonely and feral comment. He listened, but the sound was not repeated.

Lemuel paused at the hotel to listen. He heard Lenore Whitefield, the manager, get up and visit the bathroom. He heard her husband snoring. One of the senior citizens on the ground floor stirred restlessly in her sleep. Lemuel moved soundlessly past the hotel, then past Home Cookin, and then drifted behind the restaurant to circle the double-wide trailer where the Reeds lived.

Grady woke up crying, perhaps sensing Lemuel's presence, and Lemuel listened to Madonna plod into Grady's little bedroom. Her voice and words were softer than he'd ever heard them as she gave the toddler a dry diaper and a soft kiss. Grady settled back into sleep almost immediately, but Madonna went into the kitchen to get a drink of water. Moving around the outside of the trailer, parallel to the woman inside, Lemuel followed her, his fingertips brushing the siding.

He had long wanted to search the Reeds' trailer, but they were never gone long enough at night. He could trust Olivia to do a good job while the Reeds were gone during the day, if he could only be sure enough to tell her his suspicions.

If this had been a different day and age, Lemuel would have broken down the trailer door. Lemuel would have gone in and killed the Reeds, perhaps taking Grady to an orphanage if he was feeling merciful.

There were many things Lemuel liked about here and now. He did not have to hide what he was anymore. He had friends, and a lover who accepted him for what he was. Some of his friends would willingly feed him the energy he needed to thrive. If not, he could visit a bar. He could travel, too, with some care and forethought. That delighted Lemuel, who had been tied to the area around Midnight for decades and decades.

The downside of the modern world? His natural tendency to settle things in a permanent and drastic way had to be curbed. Law enforcement was much more consistent and effective, at least in part because communication was instant. Ways of tracking those who broke the rules were scientific and relentless; or at least, they seemed so to Lemuel when he considered the past, where moving from one area to another had rendered him practically invisible. Now, he had to think twice before he acted.

So he circled the trailer, pondering his options, until he had to return to Midnight Pawn because a car pulled up in front. He was in the side door and on the stool at the counter just before the customers entered, hooting and hollering and stumbling: three males, young, all drunk.

Lemuel would have sighed if he'd needed to.

Predictably, the young men had come in to pawn the television that they'd probably stolen from one or another of their kin. Lemuel took a picture of them with his telephone (the novelty never ceased to entertain him) and kept the television for the police to collect, giving the kids each forty dollars, just enough to get them to leave. When their car taillights flashed, he called the highway patrol and gave them the license number.

"Lemuel Bridger, good citizen," he said out loud after he'd hung up. "That's me." And he smiled, all to himself. He'd had a gulp of energy from all three. He wrote a note for Bobo and taped it to the television. The police would pick the set up tomorrow. Possibly, they would stop the boys before they'd had time to spend the money, and he would get it back.

Olivia had been out of town all day and would return sometime this night. He kept watch for her, while he sat and translated. Every now and then he would go out to look at the crossroads, but no one appeared. In between watching and looking, he translated, but it was slow going. He was ever conscious that if what he suspected was true, he was running out of time.

They all were.

8

Fiji got up extra early the next day so she could work in her garden without her sister's constant, irritating presence. It was not a huge surprise when Diederik joined her. The boy enjoyed gardening almost as much she did, though perhaps being free of Rev's presence and being outside had as much to do with that pleasure as the actual work did.

Today, Diederik had pulled his dark hair back into a ponytail and he was wearing a cowboy hat and cutoffs. No shirt. Fiji had to glance away to stifle a giggle. Diederik looked like he was about to go on stage at a male strip club. The boy's olive skin was a beautiful even tone all over. Fiji told herself to not drool, not even for a moment. Though her sister's cruel words had appalled Fiji, she had to admit that this morning she noticed the way Diederik looked at her. Kiki was right. Diederik was aware that he was a man and Fiji was a woman.

To reinforce her maternal role in the boy's life, she offered Diederik some biscuits.

He was *delighted* at biscuits. She'd figured he would be. Diederik loved food, especially home-cooked food. Perhaps the way he looked at Fiji was because he thought of her as the source of deliciousness. She smiled to herself at the thought as they sat on the back porch with tea and a plate of buttered goodness.

"What's your dad up to today?" she asked.

"My father is at the hotel, still, working on the Internet." Diederik licked some butter off his fingers. Fiji looked away. "He is preparing for a packleader challenge in Wyoming."

"Soon you'll be going with him."

"Yes, and I want to see some of the world," Diederik said, slowly and thoughtfully. "I do. I don't really remember the journey here. But I love Midnight, which my father thinks is strange. Apparently, most people my age are not content with their homes."

"It can't be very exciting living with the Rev," Fiji said gently. "He is a great man and I admire him, but no one would think of him as fun."

"In some ways, no," the boy admitted. He pointed at the last biscuit, asking a silent question. Fiji nodded. He ate it slowly. "But he tells wonderful stories about the creation of the world and all the animals in it, including humans, and he prays a lot, and he tells me how to be grateful for work and friends. And now I know how to read, and my father got me an account on the Internet, and I can go over to Mr. Manfred's house and order books directly onto my e-reader. Mr. Bobo is teaching me how to play the piano. And Madonna shows me how to cook. And Marina who works at the hotel at night . . ." He stopped in his conversational tracks and smiled. It was a look both delighted as a child's and satisfied as an adult's.

"Oh, Diederik!" Fiji tried not to be taken aback by this honesty.

"But Marina, she was not a virgin," he said anxiously. "I know that if she had never . . ."

"No, no, it's not that. It's the birth control issue. I know your dad talked to you about that," Fiji said. She could not imagine the consequences if a weretiger got a human girl pregnant, especially since Marina was in her teens and clinging on to her junior college scholarship. Fiji knew Marina needed the money she earned at the Midnight Hotel. She also knew that Marina's huge extended family was a drinking and fighting clan who never missed a weekly Mass.

"She takes a pill," Diederik said. He beamed at Fiji. "So she will not become pregnant."

"I'm very relieved to hear that," Fiji said. "But you know, Diederik, there are diseases people having sex can catch from each other. Some of them are very terrible."

"STDs," Diederik said, very matter-of-fact. "I'm a weretiger, and I can't catch them."

"Good," Fiji said weakly. "That's really good." She took a sip from her cup. "I'm glad you're happy here," she said, knowing it was a weak ending to the conversation. Fiji could hear Kiki moving around in the house, and she was thankful the conversation had been concluded before her sister came out to find out who was visiting. (Kiki did not like anything happening that she didn't know about.)

Diederik's acute hearing had also informed him Kiki was up. He leaned over, gave Fiji a quick kiss on the cheek (just as his father had), and bounded away to find someone else to play with.

From inside the kitchen, she heard her sister say, "I smell biscuits. Where are they?"

Fiji sighed. Something else she'd have to explain.

9

The next morning, Bobo was glad to hear the bell ring as soon as he'd unlocked the door. For days, he'd been brooding over his catastrophic failure with Fiji. He'd called himself the chicken who wouldn't cross the road. (What happened to the chicken who wouldn't cross the road? Nothing. Ever.) He had made up his mind to go over to Fiji's house and straighten things out. If she'd let him in.

But Fiji's sister was there, and Bobo had to admit to himself he was not a fan, from the little he'd seen of Kiki. She'd visited the pawnshop, asked him a lot of questions about his romantic status and income in a not-very-subtle way, flirted with the same blatant obviousness. He couldn't think of way to have a heart-to-heart with Fiji with her sister around.

He'd bungled asking her to go on vacation. He should have led with his strength; he should have told her he found her beautiful and kissed her, and then asked if they could spend time together. But he'd been trying to lead up to that, and in trying not to sound presumptuous, he'd blown his chance. It had taken him too long, anyway, too long to realize that he had a wonderful woman right across the street, too long to understand that she cared about him, too long to appreciate that she was keeping her feelings clamped down so she would not intrude on their friendship. Too long to realize he felt the same way about her as she did about him. His blunder had alienated the person he most cared about.

Maybe over time she'd return to her former warmth? But Fiji seemed really, truly put out with him.

Fiji was so smart, and powerful way down deep, and the way her hair fluffed around her face . . . it turned him on. He found himself dreaming of sex with her, and (even better) after-sex, when he would put his arms around her and hold her to him and nuzzle her neck. Bobo hadn't known guys could dream of cuddling—and it was embarrassing, sort of.

But it was also massively alluring.

It was an understatement to say that Bobo was preoccupied that morning. He scarcely registered the truck pulling up in front of the pawnshop until the bell rang. His first reaction was pleasure. He needed to think about something else.

Then he recognized the newcomer. Instantly, Bobo tensed up and retreated behind the counter. "What are you doing here?" he asked Price Eggleston. He hadn't seen Price in months, and that had suited him just fine. Price was a right-wing fanatic, and he'd tormented Bobo and kidnapped Fiji a few months before.

"Leave," Bobo said.

"I'm here to buy a gun," Price said quite calmly.

Bobo glanced down to be sure he had his own gun handy. "I don't believe you," he said. He was almost certain Olivia had returned during the night: her car was in the parking lot behind the pawnshop. He pressed the buzzer under the counter. It couldn't be heard up here, but it sounded in Olivia's and Lemuel's apartments. Lemuel would not hear the buzzer in the daytime, but Olivia would. The way

Bobo's luck was running lately, she was probably in the shower with the water turned up to full volume.

"Why not?" Price said, and it took Bobo a second or two to realize Price was responding to his statement. Finally, Bobo noticed how odd Price was acting. The man seemed almost mechanical.

"Because you can't stand me," Bobo said, watching Price closely. "Because we thwarted you when you wanted to beat me up and rob me last time. Because you sent a woman to pretend she loved me, in order to get information."

"That's ridiculous," Price said, still very matter-of-fact. "I just want to buy a gun."

"But you *have* guns," Bobo said, even more confused and aware something was seriously off. "Why do you need to buy one from me?"

Olivia flew out of the trapdoor, her bow and arrow in hand. She'd been experimenting with holding her arrows in her bow hand and firing that way after she'd watched a video on YouTube. After hours of practice the results had become impressive, judging by the target in the open ground north of the pawnshop. She was ready to try her new technique out in live action, and she was smiling.

Bobo felt relieved now that she'd appeared, and he expected Price to back down, even leave. But Price was looking at Olivia as if he'd never seen her.

She stood, clearly ready to shoot him.

He didn't react at all.

This situation was getting stranger and stranger.

"Olivia, this is Price Eggleston, in case you two haven't ever met formally," Bobo said quietly. "I figure you remember him from Aubrey's funeral."

"I know who he is," Olivia said, lowering her bow perhaps an inch. "What does he say he wants?"

"To buy a gun," Price said promptly.

"Sketchy," Olivia said.

"But true," Price said. "That's what I want."

"What do you want a gun for?" Olivia said, a question Bobo had never thought to ask.

"I'll kill myself with it," Price said, in an absolutely calm voice.

Olivia lowered the bow and arrow she'd held nocked and ready. She exchanged a shocked glance with Bobo.

"Why will you do that?" she asked.

"Because that's what he wants me to do." There was still no emotion in Price's voice.

"Sell the man a gun," Olivia said to Bobo, smiling again. "You heard him."

"That's just wrong." Bobo glared at her.

"Even him?" She jerked her head in Price's direction. "Him that planted Aubrey here to betray you? Him that ruined her funeral? Him that terrorized us all and had you beat up?" Olivia might have lost sight of her grammar, but she'd held on to her point. She laid down the bow and her arrows on the counter.

"Even him," Bobo said, grinding his teeth together. "He doesn't know what he's doing."

"You wouldn't have said that a few months ago." Olivia's voice was almost taunting.

"I'm saying it now."

Price had been looking from one speaker to another—not as if he understood the result of their argument meant his life or death, but more as if he were mildly curious. He shifted from foot to foot, his only sign of impatience. He'd gradually moved a little closer to them.

With a suddenness that made Bobo and Olivia both jump, Price grabbed an arrow from the counter and pounded out the front door. As they launched themselves in pursuit, Price, standing on the dirt margin at the curb outside, gripped the arrow and drove the point into his own neck.

Even Olivia shrieked.

It was a horrible death. As soon as the arrow was lodged in his flesh, Price appeared to come to his right mind, choking on his own blood and terrified. His eyes were wide with horror. He looked directly into Bobo's face.

At least his death was quick, though it might not have seemed so to Price Eggleston.

And once again, the ambulance and the police came.

10

Now that Midnight was again the center of a lot of attention, everyone was angry except Kiki. She had been bored already, but for the rest of the day she entertained herself with the media people, especially the fringe bloggers and those people who reported for websites like Paranormal America and Eerie Homeland USA.

Fiji had always known that her sister was a smooth liar, but she had never appreciated the scope of that talent until now. She would hear snatches of conversation in which Kiki, representing herself as a longtime resident, hinted at wild orgies and secret sacrifices. At first Fiji was entertained, but then she was embarrassed, and after a short and stern visit from the Rev, she was alert to the real harm Kiki was doing to Midnight.

With some reluctance, Fiji began to marshal her arguments, and after an afternoon in which she'd had no customers at all because they didn't want to be somehow urged to kill themselves, she sat down with Kiki over a supper of salad greens tossed with chicken and bacon and blueberries, and sourdough bread.

"What is it? You look like you're going to spit nails," Kiki said, after a moment. But she wasn't really taken by surprise. The consciousness of her outrageous behavior was there in the way she avoided Fiji's eyes.

"You have to stay away from the news people," Fiji said. "Or leave."

Kiki's upper lip lifted in what was almost a snarl. "Are you gonna make me? You're going to throw out your own sister, after I came to you for help?"

A deep voice said, *I'll kill her for you.*

Fiji froze. She did not waste time disbelieving what she'd heard. And she did not imagine she was going crazy. She had heard the voice of the thing under the crossroad.

"Why?" she asked.

Kiki looked at her oddly. "That's what I'm asking you. I came to you to ask for some sisterly protection. Now you're telling me I have to leave?"

I've been calling the ones who've done you wrong. The voice was deep, and gloating, and seductive.

But I'd never met the man who shot himself, she said, hoping he could hear her internally.

I had to get enough strength to start the summoning, he said pettishly.

She said, *Don't talk to me now.*

Fiji took a deep breath, pushing away the outrage that such a creature would speak directly to her. She had to continue this conversation with her sister. Fiji pictured several ways she could make Kiki leave, and that helped her calm down. She felt collected enough to continue the conversation, taking care to make her tone reasonable. "Kiki, you haven't done anything since you got here but bitch about how small and dull Midnight is. You've told me you don't want to be with your husband anymore, and you don't want to help Mom with Dad. But you haven't told me why you left your job. Were you fired? Again?"

Kiki glared at her. "Maybe I wouldn't have had to work outside the home if my husband earned enough for us to live on. Or if I'd gotten a fair break from my own relatives," she snapped.

"Riiiiiight. In addition to bitching a lot, you throw in a hint every now and then that you think you should have gotten a share of this house." Fiji shook her head. "But you didn't, because you never paid any attention to Aunt Mildred. I did, because I loved her. I was interested in her life and I admired her self-sufficiency. You haven't offered significant help. You also haven't offered to pay toward the household expenses. Since I'm making my own living, I don't take that too well. So, yes, I'm telling you, you have to leave tomorrow morning."

Fiji's kitchen was so quiet you could almost have heard a pin drop. Instead, Fiji heard the sound of Mr. Snuggly coming in the pet door. The cat came up to the table and sat with his tail wrapped neatly around his paws. Mr. Snuggly stared up at Fiji, and then fixed his gaze on her sister.

"Effing cat," Kiki said.

"Effing woman," the cat said.

Kiki froze. Fiji put her hand over her mouth to cover her smile.

"What did you say?" Kiki asked Fiji. She had the suspicious look of someone who thinks she is being hoaxed.

"Not a thing."

"You're a ventriloquist now?"

Fiji shook her head again.

Mr. Snuggly was highly offended. "Are you implying that she speaks for me? That I don't have a mind of my own?"

Kiki's eyes got even wider, and she looked from the cat to her sister and back again a dozen times, as if she thought that she would discover some means of voice transfer if she could catch them at the right moment.

"So why'd you really come?" Fiji asked her, to catch Kiki off-balance.

"I really did want to get away from Marty," Kiki said. "It's a sour marriage, and I can't take it anymore. And he's not . . . he hasn't been faithful." It mortified Kiki to admit that, and Fiji's heart softened for a moment. "But I can't move back in with Mom and Dad, either, not with Dad going nuts," Kiki continued. "All Mom does is fuss about him. He can't be left alone in the house. Sometimes he doesn't make it to the bathroom. I'm not a nurse. I'm not cut out for that."

Whine, whine, whine, boomed the voice. *You're not like that at all.*

"What happened to your job?" Fiji was maintaining her focus with difficulty.

"I got fired because that bitch of a manager thought I was taking things home with me."

"Without paying for them?" inquired Mr. Snuggly. He licked a paw while he waited for Kiki's answer.

"Hell, for what they paid me, they ought to be giving me clothes," Kiki said, not even looking at the cat. She was pretending she didn't know words were coming from Mr. Snuggly. This was turning into the most confusing conversation Fiji had ever had.

"So you were stealing." Fiji put down her fork. "You're lucky she didn't have you arrested."

"Lucky!" Kiki said bitterly. "She's the one Marty was seeing on the side."

"Humans!" Mr. Snuggly said, disgusted. "Ugly." He began cleaning his other front paw.

Delightful, said the voice.

"Some days I agree with you," Fiji told the cat.

"Your effing cat *talks*? And you're standing in judgment on *me*? Who's the crazy one around here?"

"Weird doesn't equal morally bankrupt. You need to go in the morning," Fiji said. "It's not only that you're not offering help, you're actually embarrassing me by making things worse with the media people."

"So I have to go back to help Mom wipe Dad's butt? I have to find a lawyer to get divorced, and I have to look for a damn job, while you just loll around here on your fat ass," Kiki said.

Fiji looked at her sister for a long moment. “Yep, that’s about the size of it,” she said.

There was a tap at the back door that startled both of them—though not Mr. Snuggly, who looked positively pleased.

“Yes?” Fiji said, and Diederik came in. He was obviously holding himself in check with an effort, and his face was flushed. He spoke to Kiki in a choked voice. “You may not say such things to your sister,” he said. “You may not insult someone who has been kind and loving to me since I came here. We all think Fiji is beautiful. It is you who are ugly.” The boy was so menacing that Kiki, who’d risen from her chair, took a step back.

“So that’s how it is,” Kiki said, her face red and her lips pressed tight. “Robbing the cradle, Feej? You’re smarter than you look.”

Fiji stared at her sister, for the first time seeing her as a stranger, and one she didn’t particularly like. She said, “Pack up your stuff tonight.”

Kiki’s face grew even uglier, and she planted her feet to loose a volley of anger. But then she faltered.

Diederik looked like a very big boy, or a very young man, but either way you counted him, he looked formidable, Fiji thought. And Fiji hoped that she herself was projecting the confidence she felt.

Kiki deflated.

To Fiji’s relief, Kiki went into the guest bedroom without further words, slamming the door behind her. She packed as noisily as possible, slamming and banging and kneeing things until it seemed as though a poltergeist were at liberty. Fiji hoped nothing of hers was going into Kiki’s suitcase.

In the kitchen, Diederik reached out to take Fiji’s hand. She let him and felt comfort in the contact, but Kiki had succeeded in awakening active shame in the fertile ground of Fiji’s conscience. After a minute, she withdrew her hand. “I guess you’d better leave, Diederik,” she said. “It’s going to be pretty uncomfortable here until she goes.”

“You will maybe need protection,” he said.

"I can handle her. You're a good friend to have," she said. "I can't thank you enough."

He grinned, to her surprise. "I feel strong and tough, now!"

She would not have thought so a moment before, but she could smile, too. "You are plenty strong and tough," she agreed.

Around suppertime, Kiki came out of the guest room and marched down to Home Cookin, without saying a word to Fiji, who was making supper for both of them.

Love the atmosphere of your home, gloated the deep voice.

The minute the sky was dark, Fiji called Lemuel. "It's talking to me," she said.

For a long moment, he said nothing. "I'm coming," he said. Fiji heard him saying, "Olivia, please mind the shop for a few minutes," and four seconds later he knocked on her back door.

"Where is the sister?" Lemuel glanced through the hall at the shop.

"She's still at the restaurant. I've asked her to leave in the morning. The voice told me that he's trying to kill my enemies to placate me. I'd asked her to leave, anyway. She's unhealthy for the community. But in view of the voice's agenda . . . Lemuel, what is it?" Fiji didn't mind showing Lemuel how frightened she was.

Lemuel's cold hand brushed her cheek. "Fiji, don't feel singled out. Do you know why it's speaking to you?"

"No, but I hope you do."

"You are its target because you alone can stop it."

"How?" She was excited and terrified by the prospect.

"I don't know yet."

Fiji deflated in a hurry. "Lemuel, how can you know one thing and not another?"

"Because I'm still reading the damn book, woman."

"You need help. We need to speed this process up."

"What is coming up on the witch calendar, Fiji?"

"That's easy! Samhain."

"What does this mean to you as a witch?"

"Not too different from what it should mean to the nonpagan community. It's the day when the souls of the dead can come through. People used to dress in disguises so the dead couldn't recognize them, and they used to leave food out for the spirits. Now we call that 'trick or treat,' and it's fun for kids." She shrugged. "Also, it's a thin day, a day when the spirit world is close to ours, and fairies and other supernatural creatures can enter our world. There's lots more, but those are some of the aspects of Samhain . . . which I celebrate on the night of October thirty-first. Some celebrate it on November first." She looked askance at Lemuel. Lemuel knew that she had a big Halloween party and decorated her house starting days ahead of time.

"I think you should not have your party this year," Lemuel said. "Fiji, I'll do anything I can to unearth the information we need as soon as possible."

Kiki came in the back door as Fiji was digesting this. Kiki's expression had been angry, haughty, her jaw set hard and ready for a fight. But when she saw Lemuel, she became wary.

"Hello," Kiki said, and realized she had to pass Lemuel to get to her room. She stopped dead.

"You'll be leaving tomorrow?" Lemuel said directly to Kiki, his icy eyes locking on hers.

"Yes, first thing in the morning," she said, as if the words were being wrenched from her throat.

"You are not a good woman," Lemuel said. "I hope you will not return."

"God, no!" Kiki exclaimed. "Not for love or money."

"I doubt either will be offered you," he said, and stood aside so that she could walk through the kitchen.

When the guest bedroom door was shut, Fiji said, "I'm afraid he'll try to get her out there to kill herself tonight."

"Olivia and I will take turns watching," Lemuel said.

Despite that reassurance, Fiji was awake for most of the night, listening for sounds of movement in her house. She got up very early and quietly made breakfast, thinking it was the least she could do. Now, she felt vaguely guilty, though leaving might save Kiki's life. She put on a pot of coffee and left biscuits and jelly on the table. When she glimpsed Kiki going into the bathroom, Fiji went into her own room to make her bed and pull on some clothes. Then she sat and waited, identifying each noise Kiki made until she heard the good-bye sound of suitcase wheels. After the back door slammed, Fiji emerged and watched out the back window as Kiki slung her suitcase into her backseat and got into the car herself.

It was a profound relief, in many ways, to see the car pull onto Witch Light Road. Kiki turned south at the light, and Fiji hoped she was on her way back to Houston.

11

Rasta ran away that afternoon. The little Peke had been acting oddly the past few days, growling at nothing and barking at shadows. Despite all the extra petting and reassurances Joe and Chuy lavished on the dog, his atypical behavior accelerated. Rasta refused to go for his walk on the Midnight streets; he tugged and tugged until Joe or Chuy took him out behind the shop.

The two men were baffled. Rasta had always enjoyed visiting the other people of Midnight, who often had dog treats to offer him. (Though the hospitable Fiji was not on Rasta's visiting list, because Mr. Snuggly would seldom permit Rasta to come into the yard.) The hotel residents had quickly become favorites, but now Joe could not even drag Rasta over to see them.

The morning Kiki drove away, Chuy had to carry the dog down the steps from the apartment and then turn left instantly to take Rasta into the backyard, which they'd never succeeded in turning green. As soon as Rasta was empty, he'd demanded to be picked up again. After a windy and chilly morning had passed, Joe opened the door of the Antique Gallery and Nail Salon, intending to sweep off the sidewalk.

To Joe's shock and astonishment, Rasta suddenly darted out past him. Hampered by the broom, Joe could not lunge fast enough to stop the Peke. No one else witnessed Rasta's mad dash, even Chuy, who was upstairs in their apartment doing ten minutes' prep work for their evening meal.

The little brown streak dashed east, sprinting without pause across the Davy highway—thankfully, he wasn't hit by the pickup truck slowing to a stop at the light—continuing past the pawn shop (unseen by Bobo, whose attention was on the computer), and passing Manfred's house at only a slightly reduced speed. Manfred happened to be collecting his previous days' mail. He dropped the bundle of envelopes and started his pursuit.

"Rasta!" he bellowed. "*Stop!*" Rasta, perhaps not in his right mind, did not stop. But the Peke's little legs were tiring, and he was gradually slowing down. Rasta didn't seem to be aware that Manfred was closing in behind him. Manfred staked everything on a flying forward tackle. He landed on the hard ground with a bone-jarring, tooth-rattling thud, but he had his hands around Rasta.

The dog bit him.

Manfred said, "Shit!" And then he said it several more times. But he didn't let go, which he thought was quite noble, especially since he'd never had a pet as a child. He was content to lie in the dirt for a second, listening to Rasta pant and whine and yip and snap.

Or maybe, he thought, *that's me.*

Manfred was relieved to hear Joe pounding up.

"Rasta," Joe said, "BAD BOY!" Joe was a regular runner, so he wasn't as winded as the dog and Manfred, but since Joe'd gone from zero to warp speed, he was doing a little gasping of his own.

"Can you take him, so I can get up?" Manfred said, still feeling noble.

"You're bleeding," Joe said. He squatted and took the Peke, holding him to his chest while all three of them recovered.

"Yeah, well." Manfred rolled onto his stomach and then pushed up, trying not to be obvious as he inspected his hand.

"What's the blood from?" Joe asked anxiously. He was inspecting the dog for any sign of harm, and Rasta was trembling.

"He bit me," Manfred said bluntly.

"No!" Joe was clearly shocked to the core. "Not Rasta!"

Manfred looked down at himself. He was literally covered in dust. (It hadn't rained in three weeks.) "Yeah, *Rasta*," he said. "I hardly bit myself!" Then he was ashamed of being so put out. "Sorry, man, but it was him," he said in a more civil tone. "He just seemed terrified. Something scare him?"

"No," Joe said, bewildered. "He's been jumpy lately, but he hasn't been scared by anything or anybody. In fact, we were happy that he'd finally gotten used to Diederik. They're big buddies now."

Chuy arrived at as fast a pace as Joe had. "I saw out the upstairs window. What happened?" he said, and the whole event had to be gone over again. "Manfred, I'm so sorry you're hurt. But thanks, thanks so much."

"De nada."

"It's the crossroad," Chuy said, turning to his partner. "Joe, we're going to have to board him with Dr. Tappet until this is over."

Manfred's hand was throbbing. He didn't want to be pouty or whiny, but he was not really concerned with the dog's neurosis just at this moment. At least he could be confident that Rasta's shots were all completely up-to-date, since Rasta was a regular visitor to his vet, Dr. Tappet, in Davy.

"Well," Manfred said stiffly, "I'm just going to go home and clean this up. And just for the record, I'm tired of tackling suicidal creatures."

"We're so sorry," Chuy said again, looking a little confused. "Thanks for taking off after him like that. We appreciate it, Manfred."

"You're welcome," Manfred said, waving his good hand weakly. He began making his way back to his own house. To his surprise and chagrin, the combination of the spurt of adrenaline, hitting the ground hard, and the bite was making him feel the tiniest bit shaky. He looked forward to shutting the door on the world and acting like a great big wuss.

He was not best pleased to see Olivia waiting.

"I saw you take off after the dog," she said. "Figured you could use some help. It's kind of a shock, isn't it? Being bitten? You expect it from a wild animal, but when it's a critter you trust . . ."

Manfred was even more ashamed when he became almost soppy with gratitude that someone understood and was worried about him, just as Joe and Chuy were worried about Rasta.

He stifled the gratitude in its birth and said, "Great," far too gruffly. Fortunately, Olivia didn't take offense. If he'd had the energy to be surprised, he would have been astonished at her outfit. Olivia was still in sleep pants and a T-shirt. "All you need is a teddy bear," he said.

She laughed, a sound he seldom heard from the fearsome Olivia Charity. "I was up late last night, making sure that Kiki Cavanaugh didn't commit suicide," she said.

"I don't even want to know about that. At least I didn't have to run after her and tackle her." At the last minute, he suppressed a natural tendency to express surprise that Olivia had been involved in saving a life, rather than taking it. It didn't seem likely to him that Olivia had actually liked Kiki. She didn't care for outsiders, as a rule, and Kiki was not a Midnight sort of person.

Other than the fact that Olivia killed people, she was just an ordinary Midnighter.

Other than that. He began laughing.

When Manfred was sitting in his kitchen and Olivia was looking over his scant first-aid stock, he asked the question that everyone in town was chewing over. "When do you think Lemuel will find out what's happening?" he said.

"We all want to know," she said. "He's working on it almost every waking moment. I wish I could help more." She began to clean the bite with peroxide, a process that felt every bit as unpleasant as Manfred had expected. "I hope that little rat of a dog isn't carrying any diseases," she said absently, bending closer to peer at Manfred's hand.

"You know he can't be," Manfred said. "They take better care of Rasta than most people take of their kids."

"Want to know what I found out?" she asked, after she'd dabbed at the torn skin on Manfred's hand. The antiseptic didn't sting as much as he remembered from when he was a child. Either he had improved, or the antiseptic had.

"I guess so."

"I found out that there's no such person as Teacher Reed."

Manfred's eyes opened wide, and he forgot all about his hand. "What about Madonna?"

"Not her, either. The Reeds are not real."

"That's interesting, but not totally unexpected," Manfred said. When she asked him why, he told her about the uncomfortable drive to and from Killeen.

"Where did you drop him off?"

"Handyman Hardware on San Jacinto Street," Manfred said.

"That's a very prompt and specific memory." Olivia had paused in her doctoring to stare at him.

"That's because I had to remember, to tell Lemuel yesterday."

Olivia's eyes widened. "I haven't talked to Lemuel enough lately," she said. "There hasn't been time with everything else he's trying to accomplish. I've wondered about the Reeds for a while, and he asked me to avoid them."

Manfred grinned.

"That does sound snobbish, doesn't it?" she said. She got some sterile gauze and wound it around Manfred's hand, tying it off neatly with a bright purple self-adhesive strip.

Manfred snorted. "It might sound snobbish if being a real Midnight person were something anyone else in the world aspired to," he said. "That's like saying someone doesn't really fit in with the Weirdo Club."

Olivia laughed for the second time. Manfred looked up at her, smiling faintly. "So you avoided them physically but tracked them online? Do you think that's what Lemuel really meant?"

"Nope, but I gotta be me," she said cheerfully.

"Thanks for the first-aid job," he said. "If you ever need a career to fall back on, you might want to think about being an EMT."

"I'll write that in my diary," she said.

"To revert to the previous topic. It would be too good to be true that a great cook like Madonna really chose to live in the back end of nowhere," Manfred said. "And I've said at least ten times that I didn't know how they kept Home Cookin open, with only a small circle of steady customers."

"And we didn't listen," she said. "Because we were so glad the restaurant was open at all."

Manfred started to say something, stopped. Started again.

"Out with it," Olivia said.

"I hope the same thing doesn't happen with them . . . that happened with the Lovells." He was aiming for "firm but not threatening" and he hoped to hell he'd gotten it right.

"No need for it to," Olivia said, not even pretending to sound surprised. "Did that upset you?"

He stared at her incredulously. "Of *course* it upset me," he said.

"Do you blame Lemuel for the outcome?"

Lemuel had taken decisive action when the rest of them had been paralyzed.

"Do I blame him?" Manfred thought about it. "No. I don't. Because no matter what we did, there was no fixing that situation."

"It didn't make me *happy*," Olivia said.

"I never believed it did. But I also believe you can't rearrange the world to suit yourself, like we did, and not pay for it some."

"Not pay for it a lot," Olivia said quietly. After looking his bandage over and nodding in a satisfied way, she added, "I think that's what we're doing now."

Manfred sat at the table for a few minutes after the door closed behind his neighbor, thinking about that awful night and the anguish on Shawn Lovell's face. When the reckoning had come, Manfred hadn't been living in Midnight long. While he'd fallen into the Midnight way of thinking pretty quickly, Lemuel's justice had been brutal. But they'd all tacitly agreed with his verdict.

Manfred wondered how Creek Lovell was faring. He'd had a crush on her the size of a boulder, and he'd never figured out if it was returned. She'd called him once without saying her name, to tell him that she was okay, with her dad, and working as a waitress. By now, he hoped she'd gotten to go to college somewhere. Now Creek was free of the millstone she'd carried around her neck for years. She should have the chance to make a life for herself.

Manfred also hoped she'd moved away from her father. If anyone was to blame for the situation they'd all found themselves in, it was Shawn Lovell.

12

Olivia returned to her apartment to think. She could not think of a single thing that would make her feel happier with life right at the moment, except helping Lemuel with his all-important task.

When Price Eggleston had taken his own life at the crossroad the day before, Olivia had been in for a hard time with the police, especially Officer Gomez, who did not like Midnight or its citizens. After all, the arrow that Price had stabbed through his own neck had belonged to Olivia, a fact she freely admitted.

Though the police didn't know the half of Price Eggleston's history with the people of Midnight, much less what Lemuel and Olivia had done in retaliation, it was still hard for the police to take Olivia's word that she hadn't had anything at all to do with his bizarre suicide.

Fortunately for Olivia, Price had killed himself in front of witnesses—not only herself and Bobo but also an insurance agent from Davy, who would regret to the end of his days that he'd been stopped at the red light when Price had stabbed himself in the neck.

And one of the guests at the hotel had been looking out a window, too, which Olivia thought was a little strange. But as a result, Olivia wasn't seriously worried about her legal position. She could not have had anything to do with his death besides inadvertently providing the weapon that had killed him.

But Olivia loathed police attention.

Even Arthur Smith's tactful interrogation had felt invasive. Between answering his questions, she had been looking around her to make sure her friends were close. Her eyes had met Chuy's, and he had nodded. Bobo, who'd answered almost as many questions as Olivia had, had been sitting on the front steps of the pawnshop, still looking stunned. Olivia had wondered why Fiji wasn't there with him. The Rev had stood framed in the doorway of his chapel across the street. Manfred had not issued forth from his house.

Then Olivia had spotted a face she didn't recognize. An unfamiliar woman had been standing at the edge of the furor. Olivia had homed in on her, because the woman was inexplicable. She was not the press, she was not law enforcement, and she wasn't one of the Midnighters.

Olivia had thought, *I'd swear she's a lawyer.* But she herself had certainly not called a lawyer. The woman, who appeared to be in her forties, had met Olivia's eyes, and Olivia had decided the stranger looked simply curious.

But Olivia had been distracted by the arrival of Price's parents. Mr. and Mrs. Eggleston had arrived on the scene to find someone to blame for their son's death. The older Egglestons knew of an enemy of Price's who lived in Midnight, and Olivia couldn't fault their logic when they assumed that Fiji Cavanaugh was the cause of their son's death. Since Mr. and Mrs. Eggleston were reluctant to explain to the police that Price had kidnapped Fiji months before, their choice of the witch as murderer was incomprehensible to Sheriff Arthur Smith, who had ascertained the whereabouts of every Midnight resident (including the hotel residents) before and during Eggleston's suicide, as quick as quick could be.

Fiji had had some good luck, too. She'd had a customer at the time; a very credible customer, too—Bonnie Vasquez, wife of a local rancher, who'd wanted to get a pretty rainbow sun catcher for her granddaughter. Kiki had been at Gas N Go buying some Coca-Cola, which Fiji didn't keep in the house, and chatting up the new manager. The Rev and Diederik had been weeding in the pet cemetery behind the church. Chuy had been doing a pedicure for Lenore Whitefield, the manager of the Midnight Hotel, who had never in her life had one, and Joe had been a tactfully busy spectator. Manfred had been working alone, of course, but he'd been on the phone with a frequent caller who would *love* to testify that she'd been talking to him. All the transient guests of the hotel had been gone, and the residential guests had been napping or watching television in the lobby . . . except for the one who'd been watching out his window.

It was amazing how all the townspeople were in the clear.

Olivia had described the whole event to Lemuel at length. He was usually entertained by her accounts of things that happened while he was in his day-sleep, and she had figured he'd be glad that Price Eggleston was off the board. But Lemuel hadn't reacted the way she'd anticipated.

"Olivia," he'd said, in that voice with its antique cadence, "do not go over to talk to Fiji or the Reeds by yourself."

It was very seldom that Lemuel told her what to do. She had glared at him. "Like I'm scared of the Reeds," she'd said. "They don't even exist, right? And no one's scared of Fiji."

"You do like her," he'd said, as if he were confirming something. "She's very powerful."

"Of course I like her. When I'm not completely irritated with her. She's practically the town puppy. I don't know where you get the power?" Olivia had kept the glare up. "And what's with the Reeds? You think they're outlaws on the run? You think Grady's gonna bite me?"

"No, that's for me to do," Lemuel had said, smiling, and a rush of heat from her groin to her cheeks made Olivia kiss him. They hadn't talked about the Reeds anymore after that. But in the light of day, Olivia realized that Lemuel knew what sparked her lust better than anyone ever had, and he might have deliberately diverted her.

Not that they both hadn't enjoyed the encounter. A lot. Olivia had gotten so accustomed to Lemuel's physical coldness that she didn't think of it anymore, except to be grateful in the summer. And she didn't mind the energy being siphoned off; in fact, it was a relief. She was a calmer and more thoughtful person as a result. But back to the cause of the diversion.

Olivia considered the Reeds, surprised that she hadn't spent more time puzzling them out. Manfred was right; several times, he'd brought up the anomaly of the Reeds, to the point where she'd wanted him to shut up and accept the fact that the Reeds were part of the town. Now, she could see his point. And Lemuel needed her help, which was rare. *Surely,* Olivia thought, *there's something I can to do to help him.*

She decided she needed to go for a run.

Olivia was not a reader, and very little on television interested her. She liked to shoot: arrows, bullets, whatever. She liked to walk and run. So today she went to run in the bare stretch of land between the pawnshop and the Roca Fría River. Unlike track or road running, this involved lots of watching: for rocks, snakes, and cacti. After dodging the various hazards, she ran back to Midnight, still too restless to return to her small apartment.

Virtuously, Olivia did not walk over to Fiji's, though she noted that the obnoxious sister's car was gone. And she did not go to Home Cookin for lunch, either. Another gold star! Instead, she went to Gas N Go to meet the new manager. She did not mind at all that she was sweaty and had some hair plastered to her forehead.

When she pushed open the glass door, Olivia thought for a second that the new guy had brought a wife. She saw black hair that was long and shining. But when he turned around, she realized she'd made a very false assumption.

The new manager was very male and a Native American. Olivia estimated he was in his thirties—short, slim, and clad prosaically in a Gas N Go T-shirt and jeans. He was someone who sent off a strong vibe. And that vibe said, "Don't fuck with me, or you'll be sorry." She approved.

"So, hi, new neighbor," Olivia said.

"Hi."

"Welcome to town."

A nod in return. Okay, this was going to be uphill. "I'm Olivia Charity. I live in an apartment below the pawnshop."

"Sylvester Ravenwing," he said.

She blinked. "So . . . Sylvester. You moved into the house the Lovells had?"

"The Lovells were the people that ran this place before me?"

She nodded.

"Yeah, the company offered me the use of the house, so I'm in it, for now. It's a strange place. Locks on all the doors, some of them on the outside of a bedroom."

"They had an unusual family situation," Olivia said.

Sylvester didn't ask any questions, which was odd. He seemed sorry to have said that much. And he wasn't giving her any encouragement to continue the conversation. He'd returned to loading cigarette packages into the slotted box over the counter.

Olivia wandered down an aisle, and from among the little powdered doughnuts, the Slim Jims, the chocolate-covered peanuts, and the Red Hots, she spied something she actually wanted: Cheez-Its. She bought a large box and a bottle of water, at exorbitant convenience store prices. Sylvester Ravenwing had to look at her while she paid for them, so it was worth the money.

"Thank you so much," she said sweetly, in as good an imitation of Brenda on the *The Closer* as she could manage.

"Welcome," he said dryly. "Good-bye . . . Olivia."

Olivia shook her head at his having to make an effort to remember her name. Carrying her purchases, she went to the door, thinking, *Well, at least he is interesting.* As she pushed the door open with her shoulder, she had a thought that made her turn back. "Have you been reading the papers?" she said. "Do you know what's been happening here?"

Now he looked surprised. "What?" he said, and then looked as though he regretted showing curiosity.

"You really ought to get a paper out of the vending machine by the door and give it a read." She smiled and left, pleased at having had the last word.

13

Manfred was glad for absences. Kiki was gone, and Rasta was at his vet's kennel being coddled by the staff, or so Chuy and Joe were assured when they called. Kiki had added nothing to Midnight, and she had taken away some of its harmony. He only hoped Fiji was not too upset. Diederik had told him that Kiki had been mean to Fiji in some way that Diederik didn't specify. Manfred didn't ask. He had enough on his plate. His hand looked better today, but it was still sore, and constant typing hadn't helped that situation.

Manfred quit work a little early to give his hand a rest. He was propped on his elbows at the desk, looking out the front window. With a sigh, he stood and stretched and walked over to peer at Fiji's. She had a customer. Behind him, phone lights blinked as callers were given a message that said, "We're closed for the day. We'll reopen tomorrow at eight a.m. Central Daylight Time. Please call back then." Overnight, the e-mails would accumulate on his websites. Tomorrow morning, he'd start another day of prophesying and giving advice . . . and making money.

Sometimes Manfred thought there was no human problem under the sun he hadn't encountered. Quite a few of them he heard every damn day. Cheating spouses and unfaithful boyfriends, mostly. Bosses who "had it in" for you. (Manfred often suspected those bosses had good reason. A lot of those contacts happened during business hours.)

It was dusk, and no one else had committed suicide in Midnight today.

Manfred would have been a good interview for more marginal reporters who'd swarmed the town, and he'd considered it. Being featured in the blog of "PNGirl, roaming Paranormal America, looking for news of the weird and uncanny" would probably have generated some business. But he'd thought twice. A connection with suicide would hardly do him any good.

So Manfred had remained shut in his house on Eggleston's suicide day, curtains drawn. And the next day he'd only ventured out to get his mail and rescue the stupid dog. Today, he'd worked straight through with only a short break for lunch. He found he was tired of slaving over the telephone and the Internet, giving people advice for their unpleasant—or sometimes sad and pathetic—problems.

I think I have a curse on me. No one seems to like me.

I just got fired again. I need to know the name of the person who goes to my bosses and complains about me. I gotta stop them.

I lost my money and my house in the bad economy. Tell me what lottery number to buy.

Tomorrow, Manfred was taking part of the morning off to visit some of his favorite people: Tommy, Mamie, and Suzie, who now lived in an assisted-living center in Davy. They were all rascals; Mamie and Suzie would never have baked cookies and shown their grandchildren how to make chicken and dumplings. Tommy would have been better at teaching his kids how to bust kneecaps than how to bait a fishhook. But they were lively and entertaining company. If they all felt well enough, Manfred would take them out to lunch. He'd been doing that at least once a month since they'd been shifted from the Midnight Hotel to Safe Harbor Assisted Living and Nursing Home in Davy, which had several degrees of nursing care and was closer to a hospital, doctors' offices, and shopping.

Manfred, who checked on them once a week either over the phone or in person, had gotten Tommy to list him as a relative. He was now Tommy's great-nephew, in the eyes of Safe Harbor management. When that had been done, Manfred had gained the right to ask questions about Tommy's bills.

"Paid by a corporate office," the assistant manager of Safe Harbor had told him.

"Why?" he'd asked.

"Past service," had been the reply.

"To whom?" he'd asked.

"To the corporation, I guess," the accounts receivable clerk had said, shrugging. "Tommy should know. Ask him."

And Manfred had. Not entirely to Manfred's astonishment, Tommy refused to worry over who was taking care of his bills. Having been in a dive in Las Vegas where they'd been terrified of being robbed every day, the three old people were just grateful to be housed in a clean place, fed, and safe. Suzie, the smartest of the three, was more suspicious than Tommy or Mamie. But ultimately, Suzie was just as relieved to have found a literal safe harbor. She didn't pursue the source of that safety as doggedly as she would have in her heyday.

On his way to Davy the next morning, three days after Price Eggleston's death, Manfred was looking forward to seeing Tommy, Suzie, and the frail Mamie. He was in a lighthearted frame of mind.

No reporters in sight, a morning away from work, and a conversation with three former Las Vegas reprobates to anticipate: fun things. Tommy, who tended to be on the peppery side, amused Manfred; Manfred felt he'd learned a few things, too, from Tommy's attitude about life.

Besides seeing his friends, Manfred found he was also more than a little buzzed at the possibility of encountering Estella Hardin, a nurse's aide working at Safe Harbor while she attended junior college. He hadn't known he had a type until he was smitten with Estella. Like Creek Lovell, Estella was short and of medium build, olive-skinned and dark-haired. Also like Creek, Estella was intelligent and had been through some hard times. When she completed junior college in May, she'd have four or five semesters at a four-year college to face before she could become a registered nurse. Manfred, who'd only taken some college-level computer courses, admired Estella's determination and ambition.

The day became even brighter when Estella was the first person Manfred spied in the Safe Harbor lobby. Still dressed in her scrubs, she was dawdling around the check-in desk. He hoped that meant she'd been waiting for him, since he'd called Tommy the day before to tell him he was coming. Manfred signed the guest register, nodding at the pink-coated volunteer in charge of the information desk, and turned to Estella.

"Hey, how are you?" he asked, wishing he could think of something more original to open with.

"I'm good. You?" The maroon scrubs worn by the nursing staff didn't do anything to prevent Estella's looks from shining through. Her glossy black hair was pulled back in a ponytail (regulations) and her nails were unpolished (also regulations), but she wore a little makeup and her pants fit nicely on a figure that was not voluptuous or bony, but just right.

"I'm fine," he said. "How are my people?"

"Well, they'll tell you," she said, smiling. But he could sense that under the smile lurked a worry.

"What's wrong?" he asked.

"It's Mamie," she said. "I don't want to give you bad news. But she's not flourishing."

They'd been strolling toward the left wing where Manfred's friends were housed. Now they stopped to face each other. "Tell me," he said.

"I'm not a nurse yet," Estella said. "But I've worked here a while now. Mamie's getting weaker. She's not walking much anymore, even with a cane or a walker. She's not eating enough. I know she's eighty-five, but this seemed to come on pretty suddenly." She paused. "She's losing her grasp, Manfred."

Her grasp on life. Manfred understood. "What can I do?" he asked.

"I don't know if there's anything specific worrying her," Estella said. "If there is, of course taking that load off her would help. Otherwise, I think it's going to be time for her, soon. Again, I'm not a nurse, and I may be speaking out of turn. But that's my take, and I'd feel really bad if I didn't tell you."

"You think losing Mamie would be really hard on Tommy and Suzie?" he asked.

To his astonishment, Estella looked dubious. "It might," she said. "But sometimes the very old can seem . . . surprisingly offhand about death. In fact, about any disaster happening to someone else. I think it's because they're so close to the end themselves, and they've lost so much by the time they get there."

"My grandmother, Xylda, wasn't that way. But she wasn't nearly as old as Mamie," Manfred said. He found himself smiling, despite the bad news. "Xylda was flamboyant to the end," he said.

"What did she do?"

"She was a psychic, like me. In fact, she taught me the business."

He was pretty sure Estella had already known what he did for a living. He could see the staff talking about him sometimes; he was a fairly unusual-looking visitor.

"How long ago did you lose her?"

Manfred had to think. "It's been at least two years. Maybe longer."

"I'd like to see a picture of her sometime," Estella said.

"Totally doable. I'll go through my photo box, Estella." He held his breath, trying to look like he was perfectly at ease.

"My friends call me Stell."

"Stell, are you ever free to have time off?"

"What's that?" She laughed.

"You work. You go to school. You study."

"I might be able to arrange a little free time," she said, smiling back at him.

"Can we spend some of that time together? So I can show you my grandmother's picture?"

"I think I can spare a few minutes," she said, to his vast relief and excitement.

He put her on his contacts list, and she wrote his number on her arm with an ink pen.

"I'll put it in my cell phone when I'm off work," she said. "By the way, I'm traditional—in some ways. I'll wait for you to call me."

"Good to know the rules." Manfred was feeling positively buoyant. He was having to struggle to keep his smile under control.

"Okay, I'm going home to get some sleep," Stell said. With a final wave, she peeled off to vanish through a door marked EMPLOYEES ONLY.

Manfred was still smiling when he knocked on Tommy's door. "Come in, Bernardo!" Tommy called.

Tommy's room looked like a studio apartment. It had a little kitchen area, a double bed, and a sitting area. Though the room was small, it was attractive and comfortable—if not very personal, since Tommy had arrived with only the clothes in his suitcase. In his heyday, Tommy Quick had been a leg-breaker in Las Vegas. He had had a long, varied, and colorful life. This room in this town seemed like a bland end for such a man, but Manfred had come to understand that when you reached your eighties, safety was more important than lots of other considerations.

Tommy was dressed and shaved and sitting in the strawberry-red armchair. He looked ten years older than the last time Manfred had seen him, which was saying something.

"Hey, Tommy," Manfred said, shaking the man's hand. Tommy still had a good grip. "How are you?"

Tommy waved his hand to show that they were going to bypass the preliminaries. "Listen," Tommy said. "And listen good."

Manfred sat in the other chair and listened good.

"Mamie is trying to get out at night," the old man said.

Manfred thought, *Oh, no. Please tell me she's not . . .*

"She wants to walk down the highway, get me? *Walk* to Midnight!" Tommy was scared and furious.

"Why does she want to go back to Midnight so bad? Has she told you?" Manfred tried to sound casual, but he didn't fool Tommy.

"I can tell this isn't a total surprise to you," Tommy snarled. "We read the papers here, you know! We're not total ignoramuses!"

"Did she say why?" Manfred was equally persistent.

"She's gonna kill herself there, she told us." Tommy regarded Manfred with a cold eye. "Now, you got something to tell me?"

"You know about the suicides," Manfred said, because that much was public knowledge. "We don't know why they're happening, but we think there's some weird influence going on."

"Woo-woo stuff," Tommy said.

Manfred nodded.

"Can you get Mamie to quit this?" Tommy asked. "Suzie and me are going nuts, getting no sleep trying to make sure she don't get out of here. They were already talking about moving her to the nursing home wing."

Manfred knew that for the residents, moving to the nursing home wing was the last step before the graveyard. Sometimes residents recovered from a fall and got to go back to the assisted-living wing, but that was rare. "Could she really get out? Aren't the doors locked at night?"

"Yeah, except when one of the staff goes outside to smoke and forgets to lock up. That's happened twice. And a few times, one of us walks out as visitors walk in, and no one notices. One of the Alzheimer's ladies was out in the parking lot trying to break into a car! Chet Allen was halfway to his ranch before they caught him."

"Do the nurses know what Mamie is trying to do?"

Tommy shook his head. "They just know Mamie's getting worse. They're talking about tying her to the bed."

Manfred recoiled, imagining ropes or handcuffs.

Tommy noticed. "Naw, you idiot, they use these soft restraints. But we hate to see that happen to Mamie. When she gets back to being okay, it'll embarrass her something awful."

"So what do you want me to do?" Manfred felt totally at a loss.

"Do some mojo on her. Make her quit thinking about this."

"I need to send for Fiji. She's better at that kind of stuff. I'm just a two-bit psychic."

"Well, Mr. Two-Bit, you get in there and try." Tommy got up slowly, stiffly. He and Manfred made their way to the room next door, Mamie and Suzie's room.

The two women were dressed and sitting in matching armchairs identical to those in Tommy's room, and the television was turned to a game show. Mamie's curly white hair was flattened on one side, which would have mortified her if she'd been aware of it. Suzie, whose parents had immigrated to the States from Hong Kong, was carefully combed and made up, as usual. But she looked as exhausted as Tommy.

"I like the hair, Suzie," Manfred said, when she turned to the door. In the weeks since he'd seen her, Suzie had dyed her steel-gray hair its original black.

"Thank you," she said. "And how are you and that pretty Estella?"

"Hey, we traded phone numbers," he said, not at all surprised that Suzie had picked up on his admiration for the nurse's aide.

"That's good," she said. "Now, let's see if you can help Mamie, here."

At the sound of her name, Mamie opened her pale blue eyes. She turned slowly and painfully to look at Manfred.

"Hey, honey," she said, her voice wispy. "I didn't hear you come in. Hey, Manfred, give me a ride back to Midnight? I need to . . . do something there." She looked sly.

"No, Mamie," he said. He sat on the bed closest to her and reached over to hold her thin hand. "I can't do that. It's not healthy for you there right now."

"I don't have anything to live for," she said, tears running down the fine pale skin of her cheeks. "I'll just go there, to the roads, where they cross, and I can put an end to this."

"Miss Mamie, what would Tommy and Suzie do without you?"

She smiled faintly. "Oh, they'd manage, same as always. Come on, Manfred, put me in that car of yours and let me go home with you."

He had seldom felt more at a loss.

"I can't. There's stuff going on in Midnight that's bad. We have to clear it up before you come back for a visit."

Mamie said, "All right." She'd suddenly lost the thread of the conversation. She glanced over at Tommy. "Tommy? Is it time for lunch yet?"

"Not yet," he said. "In an hour, honey." But Mamie had already focused her attention on the television screen, though from her blank expression she wasn't really engaged with what she was seeing.

Manfred tried again to think of a way he could help his friends. And he came up with nothing.

He said as much to Suzie and Tommy. "All I can do," he said, "is ask Fiji if she's got any ideas. And try to solve this problem in Midnight as soon as possible."

"People just show up and . . . *blam!?*" Suzie shook her head.

"That's how it's happened," Manfred said. "No motive, no warning."

"Mamie never was too big on Fiji, but I don't think she'd care anymore, long as she gets better," Suzie said wearily.

"All right, buddy-boy," Tommy said. "You run back to Midnight and you fix things up with Fiji. Mamie shouldn't be suffering like this."

Manfred signed out in the lobby, only vaguely conscious of the curious look the volunteer was giving him at his quick departure without his friends, whom he often took on an outing.

Manfred walked slowly to his car. The temperature was only in the low eighties, but he was too preoccupied to enjoy the relief from the summer's heat. He'd never had such a jarring visit at Safe Harbor. He found himself dismayed and worried to a degree that surprised him. Until this moment, Manfred hadn't realized how much he'd come to rely on his visits with Tommy, Mamie, and Suzie. He missed his grandmother; their conversation had somehow eased the loss for him, but he hadn't even understood that. *Some psychic I am,* he thought.

As he started his car, planning to drive right back to Midnight and talk to Fiji, Manfred found himself—nonetheless!—excited at the prospect of calling Stell. He wondered how long he had to wait until he could punch in her number. "I must be really shallow," he muttered, and he drove back to Midnight thinking of a jumble of things, both happy and sad.

Fiji had customers, so Manfred waited until they'd left before walking over to the Inquiring Mind. He found his friend sitting in one of the wicker armchairs, and she was definitely in a serious mood.

"What?" she said, as he sank into the chair opposite her. She turned her face to his abruptly, as if she'd been interrupted in a conversation with someone else.

"Maybe I should come back tomorrow?"

"No," she said wearily. "That's okay. Let me guess. There's some problem I have to help solve."

"Ahhhh—yeah."

"Gee, I'm surprised."

Manfred had never heard Fiji fall back on sarcasm. "You don't seem to be in the mood to put yourself out," he said. "Is there something I can do to help you?"

For a terrible moment, he thought she was going to cry. To his profound relief, the moment passed. Fiji kind of shook herself and then forced a smile onto her face. "So, what is it?" she said.

He explained about Mamie, leaving any mention of Stell out of the story, though he was in the mood to drag her into every conversation.

"So you want me to drive up to Davy and cast some kind of spell on poor old Mamie so she doesn't want to walk to Midnight to commit suicide," Fiji said. "And you want me to do this without anyone at the assisted-living place being any the wiser." She rubbed her face with her hands.

Manfred hadn't really thought about the difficulty of his request. "Yes," he said. "That's about the size of it. I'm sorry, Fiji, I probably wouldn't even have brought it up if Tommy hadn't been so positive one of us could do something about it. He thought I could, but I can't think of any way a psychic could change Mamie's mind when this awful thing, this impulse, is hijacking her."

"So that's what you think is happening?" Fiji seemed to be considering the idea. "Maybe you're right, Manfred. Did you ever watch *Buffy the Vampire Slayer*?"

The change of subject left him teetering. "Ah . . . sure. My grandmother loved it."

"Do you ever wonder if Midnight's on the Hellmouth? Like Sunnydale?"

Manfred laughed. "That's exactly what it feels like," he said. "You must be Willow, and Olivia must be Buffy. And Lemuel is Angel."

That brought a smile to Fiji's face, too. "I would classify Olivia more as Faith," she said. "Bobo can be Xander."

"So Diederik would be Oz."

For a reason Manfred couldn't fathom, Fiji flushed.

"As long as we're having a neighborly chat," Manfred continued when she didn't speak, "I'm thinking something's wrong with the Reeds."

She looked at him doubtfully. "You mean, they're sick or worried or something?"

"Nope. I mean, there's something really hinky about them. Lemuel and Olivia think so, too."

"Oh, I agree. Even with the economic slump, them settling here is strange. But I'm just so glad they're here. He can fix everything, just about, and getting a repairman to drive out to Midnight is not easy. And she's such a great cook. Besides, it's nice to have a real kid around."

Though Manfred didn't think much about Grady one way or another, he nodded. He didn't want to seem anti-baby. "This is the equivalent of Tommy not wanting to question the good luck that put him in Safe Harbor," Manfred said. "Lemuel wonders about the Reeds, too."

"Lemuel? Then I'm glad I'm not Madonna or Teacher," Fiji said. She stood up. "You want me to go to the nursing home this afternoon?"

"Assisted-living center," he corrected. "They're in the assisted wing, not the nursing home wing. And the sooner, the better. I'm sorry. I'm imposing." Though she hadn't said a word, he could tell from the way her mouth turned that she was reluctant.

She shrugged. "I'll go tomorrow. Business is slow anyway." Fiji looked tired and dispirited.

"Listen, I'll keep your shop open." Suddenly, Manfred realized this was the least he could do. He tried to suppress the thought that he would miss a lot of business that way, and it was probable that Fiji would not have a single customer.

She brightened. "That would be great. I don't think Diederik's quite up to that yet, and he's the closest we've got to a free person. Teacher is measuring down at the Antique Gallery and Nail Salon to see if he can build some internal stairs. Chuy and Joe are tired of going outside every time they go to and from the shop. And you could bring your laptop, right? Maybe you could kind of keep up with your work that way."

Manfred brightened. "We'll do a favor exchange, right?"

"Okay," she said.

Manfred thought they both felt better, and he hoped Fiji could do Mamie some good.

14

Lemuel loved the fall and winter, especially after the time change. Through the years, people—including, most recently, Olivia—had tried to explain to Lemuel how a government could decide what time it was.

"I still think it's arrogant," he'd told Olivia. "But since I'm up while people are still awake, I like it."

"I thought you didn't like company," she'd said, smiling.

"I like to talk to people. I like to be with you. I like more customers during the night."

This was all true. Unfortunately, night customers were sometimes human, and often drunk and therefore tedious, but at least he could take some energy from them.

He was talking to a monk at the moment.

"You haven't been hearing the giant voice?" the man in the robe asked.

"I haven't," Lemuel said. He did not know if the man was mad, or if there really was a giant voice. "What does it tell you to do?" Lemuel said.

"It told me to come here to kill myself, that as a man of God my death would be especially sweet, but I know that is a mortal sin," said the self-proclaimed monk. "So I have told it to get behind me, and I decided instead I'd pawn this silver fork."

It was a meat-serving fork, not a dinner fork, and it was very old. Since it was silver, Lemuel handled it wearing a glove. "Yes," he said, turning it over to look at the maker's mark, "why would a monk need a meat fork?" The front door opened, and Lemuel glanced up to see Fiji come in.

Lemuel made short work of the transaction with the monk so the man would go on his way. Fiji looked troubled, but not only that—she was exhausted.

"A real monk?" she asked, as the door shut behind the visitor.

"I don't know. He wears a robe and lives by himself somewhere south of here, and he walked in. I am not sure how to designate him. A real monk or a false one?"

"A Catholic one?"

"He wore a crucifix. Beyond that, I couldn't say."

"Lemuel, it's talking to me more and more."

Lemuel stayed silent, because he had several different reactions. He felt sorry for Fiji, but startled at the quick approach of the oncoming crisis. He was glad that Fiji had the will to resist. He was dismayed, because it couldn't be coincidence that the monk had said the same thing. And he was mighty apprehensive, because this was a very ominous sign.

"You must tell me about this," he told the witch.

And she did.

Lemuel kept his silence when she was finished. "Fiji, he's trying to seduce you," he said at last.

"He's the only one," she muttered, but Lemuel chose to ignore that.

"Who do you think it is?" Lemuel asked. He suspected he knew, but he wanted to hear what Fiji believed.

"I think it's something bad and old, and I think it's picking on me because, in some way, I threaten it."

"I think you are absolutely right," he said. "Sister, you need to leave town for a while."

"I can't do that," Fiji said. "I have to keep the shop open. And I promised Manfred I would go see Mamie tomorrow afternoon. She's being pulled to the crossroad, Lemuel."

Lemuel looked into Fiji's scared brown eyes. "I understand," he said. "And I'm thinking on this as hard as I can. Don't despair, friend."

After she went back to her house, Lemuel left the pawnshop. With his very sharp hearing and sight, he could tell when anyone pulled up in front of the shop, and he could be back in the store almost before they'd gotten out of their vehicles. (The night he'd circled the diner and the trailer had been a case in point.) Now, he went to "visit" the Reeds almost every night, and they were beginning to have bad dreams, even Grady. Madonna and Teacher were getting jumpy and irritable without knowing why.

Lemuel didn't care.

Lemuel had nothing against Grady, but he was not sentimental about babies. He had been born in a time when early mortality was the norm, and there were no hospitals, no medicine, no doctors for many miles in any direction. Babies routinely did not live to reach adulthood. His own mother had lost three, he knew, though he did not have clear memories of those babies.

When he returned to the pawnshop after his run, after his nightly visitation to the Reeds, Olivia was waiting for him.

"I was thinking about my childhood," he said by way of greeting.

"Did you have siblings?"

"If you mean sisters and brothers, I was the only surviving son. I had two sisters who lived. Susan Mary died when she was pregnant with her first child at seventeen, and the baby died, too. Hester May died at twenty-seven when she had some infection in her stomach."

"Appendicitis, maybe?" Olivia asked.

He shrugged. "Maybe. She left two children alive, their names were . . . Luke and Phillip—Webster?" Lemuel dimly recalled Hester's husband, David, but Lemuel himself had died a year later, so he didn't know what had happened to David and his sons.

"So it's possible you have kin through your sister's children."

"I suppose," he said. "Every now and then, I think of tracking them down."

"Maybe your sister's descendants are computer programmers or astronauts," Olivia said. She obviously thought that was funny. "Shouldn't there be written records somewhere?"

"Back then there weren't so many," Lemuel told her, and for a moment the past came alive to him. He remembered how it had been, and he'd told Olivia about how he'd gone to work as soon as he could ride. Lemuel had been a cowhand, working for this rancher and that, whoever could afford to pay him. He had learned to read when he was fourteen, while he was tending cattle for a man named Marvin Middleton, sometime after 1850.

Middleton had been a strange bird, as Lemuel put it when he was telling Olivia about him.

"He was a schoolteacher back east," Lemuel said. "Then he inherited this spread when Horace Middleton got bit by a rattlesnake. Mr. Middleton was swung to come west by what he called 'the romance of it all.' He brought along his wife, Belle, and their daughters, Mabel and Daisy, and they became a ranch family."

"How did they like it?" Olivia asked him.

"Not much, on the part of Mrs. Middleton and Daisy. Mabel took to it right smart," Lemuel said. "One night when we were out with the cattle, Mr. Middleton found I couldn't read, and he decided to set that right."

"I would have thought you'd have been too tired to think by night-time."

"Dropping in my boots," Lemuel said. "But he was relentless. Learned a lot of words, too."

"What happened to them all?"

Lemuel looked back through the decades. "Well, Mr. Middleton got throwed off his horse about the fifth year I worked for him, and he broke his neck. Mrs. Middleton took it pretty hard and headed back east as fast as she could pack and go. Daisy went with her."

"What about Mabel?"

"She and I were hitched," Lemuel said. "So we worked the ranch, and I hired someone to help me as I'd helped Mr. Middleton, a man named . . . well, I cannot remember his name. Then a gunslinger named Donald Lee Coe came to town. That name I remember."

"You had a gunfight," Olivia said, her eyes wide. "Like the OK Corral!"

"Those damn Earps," Lemuel said, shaking his head. "One as bad as another. No, ma'am. I was a good shot, but no gunslinger. I got wounded in the crossfire between Donald Lee Coe and the marshal, Harvey Burns. The town was quite a bit south of here. It was the closest town to our ranch, and it was called Baileyville."

"Wounded where?" Olivia had a professional interest in wounds.

He pointed to his left side. "Took out a hunk of meat," he said. "But it was the infection that got me. After a day, I was nigh unto death."

"Your first death. Who caused your second?"

"My wife, Mabel."

"You're kidding!"

"I would never make this up, Olivia."

"How did she—? How had she changed, herself?"

"While I was lying in town in the back room of the saloon, bleeding all over a table, Mabel had a visitor at the ranch. He'd come from town to tell her about my mishap, you see, and as soon as he told her he had news of me, why of course she invited him in."

"And he was the same kind of vampire as you are?"

"Yes. Blood or energy. Like a hybrid car," Lemuel said. It was his favorite joke since he'd learned that such cars existed. "So he bit my wife and bid her bring me the favor of life, as he put it. She was knocked sideways by the whole experience, since she had never heard a story about such a thing, and it was outside her Christian thinking and her education."

"I understand," Olivia said.

"But she felt that God had planned this rescue for me and she must be the one to deliver it, as the Indian had bade her. So into town she comes at night, though she had to wait for the three days to rise again, and then she had to kill the ranch hand to get her some strength. By which time I was as good as dead."

"And then?"

"And then she told the 'doctor,' who was really a quack who pulled teeth and suchlike and had this awful patent medicine that was nothing but alcohol and worse things, to get out of the room, that she wanted to tell me farewell in privacy. Since there was nothing more he could do for me—and he'd already done plenty in the way of drugging me—he left. Mabel had had the foresight to pay for a round of drinks, so we were left alone for quite a time. She related to me what the Indian had done to her. I could scarcely understand it, what with the drugs and the illness and the pain, but I agreed to her proposition. Though it was mighty painful, it wasn't that much more painful than the gunshot and the infection, and it was over quicker."

"And then?" Olivia was so wide-eyed she looked like an owl.

"And then, she went out into the saloon and told them all that I had died, which was no surprise to anyone. And she told them she would take me back to the ranch to be buried, which was also no surprise, since many people did that. They helped her out by tying me over her horse. The horse, though mighty skittish, got us back to the ranch that night."

"People didn't think it was strange she wanted to ride at night?"

"She told them that in the daytime, with the sun, I would be bloated by the time we reached our place."

Olivia nodded. "So, when you got back to the ranch . . . ?"

"She buried me, as she had to. There was no ranch hand to help her! And when I came out of the ground she was waiting. One of the men in the bar had ridden out to see how she was faring, and perhaps to see if he could console a grieving widow. She had kept him alive for me."

"But what happened to Mabel after that? What did you do during the Civil War?" Olivia asked.

"Enough history for tonight," Lemuel replied.

She wondered if she'd been insensitive, asking questions about events so long past. "Does it hurt to remember?"

He thought about that. "Not exactly. But it's not comfortable, either. And I don't always remember clearly." He shrugged. "It's been a long time."

Now, as Lemuel pored over books, he was grateful to Mr. Middleton for teaching him to read. Even Mr. Middleton could not have imagined that the man he'd known as Bart Polson would be able to read an ancient language. In truth, Lemuel's progress was tedious and slow. He was always aware that time was ticking away at the crossroads. He felt it, like a heavy hand on his shoulder, resting heavier and heavier as the nights passed.

Slowly, he translated a sentence out loud. "And when he rises, he will have help by powerful creatures, because he can talk to them while he is still confined. To others, he is silent." Lemuel thought that over. It seemed ominous, and he began to worry even more whether Midnight could survive the crisis that was surely coming. He bent back over the book, hoping to find another passage that would explain this cryptic sentence, which was in the middle of a paragraph he couldn't crack.

After an hour of hard work on the text, with no further results, Lemuel was so tired that he left the pawnshop for three hours straight. He hunted. He ran through the scrubby bushes and cacti; he leaped over rocks, unseen and ecstatically himself. He found four passed-out teens camping out to the north by the Río Roca Fría. He took blood from them but left them alive.

Lemuel felt much better after that. Energy was good, reviving; but sometimes, he just needed the blood. He would have enjoyed killing the teenagers, because the energy of the passing was an incredible rush. However, these kids were so well nourished and glossy that he knew they would be missed.

On his way back to the pawnshop, Lemuel thought about the conversation he'd had with Olivia. It had been a long, long time since he'd thought about his past. It was a great thing, to be able to read. He thought of the computer, and how Olivia used hers all the time, while he let Bobo do the computer work for the pawnshop. He felt uneasy using the machine, though he knew the basics. It seemed likely that Olivia could look up his sister's descendants somehow on the damn thing.

Descendants, Lemuel thought. *Descendants.* And suddenly, he had an idea. Olivia had gone to bed, but he went down the stairs to wake her up.

15

Fiji was holding Mamie's hand. Mamie was restless in her dozing state, her legs moving feebly as if she were walking. Her hands were still, though, and Fiji felt how soft Mamie's skin was, how thin over the bones. Sometimes old people got worn down from the inside out, and that was the case with Mamie. The former Las Vegas showgirl was a shadow of herself.

"She's only eighty-five," Tommy Quick said hoarsely.

"She's always been so tough," Suzie said. The rhinestones on her glasses frames glittered in the overhead light. "Real tough. Till she had that fall in Vegas on the stairs. And now this obsession with Midnight. Can't you stop it, Fiji?"

Fiji considered. None of Aunt Mildred's spells would cover this. Mildred Loeffler had had spells of cooling and heating, spells to freeze people in their places, spells to hold things just as they were until the spell was rescinded (useful in keeping food from spoiling), spells to make the subject more attractive, spells to make the subject more hateful, spells to help your garden grow, spells to protect you or others from harm . . . and a lot of herb work to combine with the spells for better effect. One or two of these had been lethal. But Fiji could not recall any spell that would take away a dangerous and painful call from some supernatural source. If she had known such words, she would have used them on herself.

Fiji didn't think Mamie was hearing the voice she heard, but clearly, Mamie was experiencing a summoning. *Probably the same one all the suicides heard,* she thought. *Luring them to Midnight and to their doom. But why Mamie, of all people?*

Fiji knew two Mamies. If the one being summoned had been the other Mamie, Price Eggleston's mother, Fiji would have understood. You didn't raise a son that hateful unless you had an overabundance of hate yourself, in Fiji's opinion. But this Mamie seemed so helpless and frail! It was hard to remember that she hadn't always been that way.

Now Fiji had to comprehend that, because Suzie was thrusting a picture in front of her, a picture of a young woman with a pert round face, heavily made up, and clad in a plumed headdress, high heels, and very little in between.

"Wasn't she gorgeous?" Suzie demanded.

"She was," Fiji said, keeping her voice quiet. She didn't want Mamie to rouse completely, because she was going to try a spell of her own.

"Aren't you going to say some words?" Suzie asked.

"Magic is will, my great-aunt always told me. You may have a set of words to say, but you may not." At first this had been incomprehensible to Fiji, but now she got it. If you had the magic, the will and intent would form the words, or the sounds, to bend the magic to do what you wanted. She wanted Mamie to forget about Midnight. She began to hum, moving back and forth a little, as she forced her will into a magical channel and put Mamie at the end of that channel.

The magic formed up nicely and began flowing toward the old woman. Fiji held Mamie's hand and rocked and hummed, and after a time she became aware that Mamie's legs were quiet under the white bedspread, and that Tommy and Suzie were slumped in their chairs, asleep.

Her magic had slopped over. Not very professional.

At least Fiji herself was awake. She extricated her hand from Mamie's and sat back. Getting to her feet, she retrieved her purse and tiptoed out of the room. Once in the bright hall with its gleaming linoleum and constant bustle, Fiji breathed a long sigh of relief.

She had done as Manfred had asked, and she'd given Mamie some relief. It wouldn't hurt Suzie and Tommy to catch up on their sleep, either. Fiji deserved a reward, she felt. Maybe she'd stop by Sonic after she'd been to the grocery store. She glanced at her watch and called the Inquiring Mind.

Manfred answered.

"Hey, I did it," she said. "She's asleep and not dreaming about walking to Midnight."

"Fiji, I owe you."

"No, you don't," she said wearily. "And you might as well close up. It's close to time, anyway, and no one's going to come in this weather."

"Okay. Thanks again."

Fiji got out her grocery list, realized she couldn't put off shopping any longer, and drove to the store. When she emerged from Piggly Wiggly, the temperature had dropped dramatically and it had begun to rain. Fiji wished she'd brought a jacket to add to her long-sleeved shirt, and it would have been even nicer if the fictional jacket had been rainproof. She turned on the heat in the car.

The rain increased in intensity as she drove toward Midnight. It was pounding down as Fiji parked behind her house and prepared to dash to the back door.

She gathered her cloth grocery bags and purse, braced herself as much as she could, and dashed the short distance to the back porch . . . only to shriek and jump back at colliding with another person.

Fiji and Teacher Reed were face to face, and he had his hand on the doorknob. He'd just come out of her house.

"Teacher, what are you doing?" she said, in what she thought was a remarkably calm voice for someone who'd been taken by complete surprise.

"Shit!" He sounded just as rattled as she had.

"Were you in my house?" It didn't occur to Fiji to be afraid. She was growing very angry as the outrage sunk in.

"I confess," he said, making a show of hanging his head. "I was on my way down the street, and the rain started. I got under your back porch, and I knocked. Just kind of absently, I turned the knob, and your back door was unlocked. So I went in the kitchen."

This was a little more credible since the rain was pounding into the back porch, with about twelve inches of dry left. But she didn't believe him. He could have sheltered on her front porch, where there was a broad covered area with chairs. He would have been welcome. But this was an invasion.

"I'm going in now," she said evenly. "But only after I watch you leave my yard. I'm seriously upset." That was what her mouth said, while her brain was thinking of spells to use.

"I'm really sorry I scared you, Fiji," Teacher said, waving his hands in the air as if to pat it softer, soften the offense.

"You mistake me. I'm *angry*."

Another tiny corner of her brain was wondering what it was about thunderstorms and men making her mad, since her abduction by the now-deceased Price Eggleston had occurred during just such a storm.

Teacher seemed to expect her to say something else, but Fiji stood mute. No matter how wet she was getting and how scared she was becoming, she would not enter the house until he was gone. She would not be trapped inside with him.

After a second more of waiting, Teacher dashed off into the rain. She watched him, her will pushing him away faster.

As soon as she was sure he was gone, Fiji went inside, slammed the door and locked it, and wedged a kitchen chair under the knob. And then she did something she had promised herself she would never do again, and she did it without any conscious deliberation. She called Bobo.

"Fiji!" he said, and his voice was full of surprise and happiness. Ordinarily, she would have basked in that for a moment. Instead, she said hurriedly, "Listen, the weirdest thing just happened." She explained.

"Did he really stay in the kitchen while he was in your place?" Bobo asked.

"Maybe. I only see wet footmarks in the kitchen. But that might just mean he heard me pull up and realized he had to get out of here."

"Or maybe he was smart enough to take off his shoes and leave them in the kitchen while he was roaming around your house."

"That's a horrible thought." As the anger drained away, Fiji felt her eyes brimming with tears.

"What could he have been looking for? I'm not doubting your instincts; I'm just wondering." Bobo sounded like he was suppressing a strong emotion himself.

"I have no idea," Fiji said. Her hands were trembling.

"You need me there?" he asked, as though he could see her hands, too.

"No, you've got a customer," she said. She'd just walked into her shop area and looked out the front window, as if being a few feet closer to Bobo would make her a bit safer. A car was parked in front, and its driver door was opening.

"Shit. Okay, I'll come over in a while," he said. "If anything else happens, just run over here, okay?" And he hung up, as Fiji saw a huddled figure dash up the steps to the door and enter Midnight Pawn.

The cat, she thought, as she turned away from the window. She looked under the counter to see that Mr. Snuggly was curled up in his cat bed. He blinked at her to prove he was alive, and she nodded and went into the kitchen.

Fiji gradually became calmer as she put her groceries away. "Mr. Snuggly!" she called. "Let's talk."

In a moment, the cat flowed in from the shop. "Is it dinnertime?" Mr. Snuggly inquired, in his bitter little voice. "The rain makes me hungry."

"Everything makes you hungry," Fiji said. "Where did the man go when he was in the house?"

"He left his shoes in the kitchen," the cat replied. "And he went through our house with his socks on. But he didn't find me! I hid very carefully."

Fiji sat down at the table abruptly. She had hoped to hear that Teacher had done exactly what he'd told her. After a moment, she roused herself to say, "You think he was going to steal you?"

"Why else would he come?" the cat asked, bored. "What else is there here worth having?"

Fiji thought seriously about this question. She discounted the possibility that Teacher was actually looking for Mr. Snuggly, since Teacher did not know the cat could talk; also, he'd said in Fiji's hearing that he didn't care for cats. She remembered such things.

What could Teacher have wanted? Fiji didn't have much cash in the house, and after she'd opened the till, she knew he hadn't touched it. Mildred Loeffler's diaries were important to Fiji, but she couldn't imagine them being interesting to anyone else, especially since Aunt Mildred's writing was extremely challenging to decipher.

What else?

Fiji looked around her as she went from room to room. There were only five, so it didn't take long. She had very little jewelry of value, and her good earrings were still in her jewelry box. She had no correspondence that would be interesting, but it did seem to her that her files of business papers had been slightly disarranged. If she hadn't known someone had been in the house, though, she doubted she would have noticed. Since Fiji considered business papers boring, she couldn't imagine what anyone might want with them. Insurance, utility bills, bank statements, supply orders, receipts. Things she saved for the tax season, when she carted them all to a CPA in Davy.

None of the goods she sold in the shop were very valuable, either, and they were all present and accounted for. Athames (she checked those first), books, statuettes, wind chimes, incense, Ouija boards, oils, tarot decks, Wiccan calendars, candles, mortars and pestles, tote bags . . . even one little cauldron, which she'd had on the shelves for two years. Her shop was definitely Witch Lite. Nothing really powerful to take, in and of itself.

So why would Teacher Reed search it?

After an hour of checking, Fiji was almost certain Teacher had not taken a thing.

But she felt his presence in her house now, like a horsefly buzzing around her head. This impression was almost impossible to dispel. It disturbed her greatly.

Can I kill someone for you, witch? asked the deep voice.

She didn't answer. She knew it wasn't wise to turn this weird conversation into a dialogue. She forced herself to get back in the thinking groove.

Fiji was fond of little Grady, and she'd always respected Madonna, if she didn't exactly like her. Her feelings were even more wounded by Teacher's invasion because she'd thought of Teacher himself as one of the most useful people she knew, and warm and affable, to boot.

Horns of a dilemma, Fiji thought. As she checked to make sure the front door sign was turned to CLOSED and gave Mr. Snuggly a treat for his accurate reporting, she wondered what the hell she was supposed to do about this.

Fiji couldn't let Teacher get away with it. *Not that I'm vindictive,* she told herself, hoping that was true. *But I have to have respect.* And respect could only be maintained if she protected her territory and her property.

Fiji asked herself the question that had gotten her through a lot of crises. *What would Aunt Mildred do?* Though Fiji was not the same person as her great-aunt had been—she was essentially more social and her heart was more tender—she was determined to stand her ground and defend her home.

It was time to assume her aunt's mantle.

16

Fiji unlocked the drawer below her work area, a broad shelf below the high counter where she took payments. The shelf was the right height for her rolling chair, and on it she did the gift wrapping, worked on the books, and studied Aunt Mildred's journals. These were not Mildred's anecdotes about her own life, but an accounting of what spell she'd performed for what person, what service she'd provided, what favor she'd granted. Some of these were dubious, some outright gruesome.

But most of these transactions were pretty straightforward. "Amulet to help Hetty W find her mother's wedding cake recipe. Successful. Spell to help Julio R's favorite cow calve. Calf lived, cow died."

The dubious ones tended to be things like, "Provided Linda H with herbs. Early enough." In other words, Aunt Mildred had provided "Linda H" with a mixture of herbs to cause an abortion.

The gruesome ones? It had taken a while for Fiji to puzzle them out. What "Ult" meant next to someone's name was that Aunt Mildred killed that person.

If Aunt Mildred had kept accurate and honest records—and Fiji was assuming she had—it had been rare for Mildred to resort to such a drastic measure. She did so when she had reason to worry about her own survival.

You had to do some really careful reading to figure out those entries. "Israel T, threat. Iced tea. Ult." The unwise Israel T had threatened Mildred with (perhaps) jail or exposure, and she had poisoned his tea.

Maybe even at a church picnic.

Aunt Mildred had been no Christian, but she had gone to church regularly; there had been an ordained Baptist minister in Midnight then, and a larger population. The church had been full on Sundays.

Fiji tried hard not to judge Mildred for her actions, since she didn't know precisely what Israel had done to her great-aunt. Mildred had had a hearty sense of self-protection.

Fiji hoped she never had to kill anyone. But she knew for sure that if she didn't stand up for herself, she would be walked upon. Kiki's visit had been a timely reminder.

As Fiji considered all these things, she'd been staring down into the open drawer. She'd been looking at all the little items she'd collected to keep inside it, but not really seeing them. Now that she'd reached a decision, Fiji carefully lifted the index card marked "Teacher Reed" and placed it on the counter. On top of the index card were a quarter and a nickel.

That had been her aunt's first lesson; keep something of everyone's, no matter if you love him or hate him.

Fiji had never loved Teacher.

Fiji lifted each coin with tweezers and dropped them in a special bowl. It had never held anything else.

Bobo came over five minutes later. Fiji gently slid the bowl behind a display on the counter before she let him in. "Are you all right?" he asked anxiously. "Did you find out if he'd searched the house?"

"Yes," Fiji said. And then she stopped speaking.

"Talk to me," Bobo said.

"Bobo," she said, and then couldn't figure out how to continue. Every time she looked at him, she could feel her heart hurting. "Listen, I'm so glad you came over and I thank you for it. But I'm going to handle this myself. I should not have called you. It's an old habit. It won't happen again."

"What does that mean?" he asked, and to Fiji's chagrin, he looked suspicious and wounded.

She stood and came around the counter, and to her own astonishment, she put her arms around him. After a second, he hugged her back, and it was a moment both of great contentment and great regret.

"I haven't been living up to my potential," Fiji said against his chest. "It's time to become what I was supposed to be."

There was a long moment of silence.

Finally Bobo said, "I hope whatever you become, you will remember . . ." And then he couldn't seem to finish the sentence, and Fiji was left to wonder how it would have ended.

"I'll see you later," Bobo said quietly. "You know I'm there."

And with that, he was gone.

17

In the kitchen of the diner, Teacher said to Madonna, "She almost caught me going through her drawers. If I hadn't taken off my shoes . . ."

Madonna was staring at him, and her expression wasn't happy. "You took a foolish chance," she said. "What did you hope to find, searching her house? Fiji is as sweet as candy and harmless as a mouse."

"You're wrong," he said. He didn't often say that to his wife, but when he did, she listened. "I know you don't believe in half the stuff that goes on in this town, but that Fiji can do some serious shit. You didn't see that private eye after Fiji got mad at her."

"You're right," Madonna said, glaring at him. "I don't believe half you tell me. This is a crazy place, and the sooner we get out of here, the better. I can't believe we haven't gotten a million questions. These people aren't dumb."

"You like the café. You told me so. You like the work."

"Yeah, I do. But we're not moving *forward*." Forward momentum was key to Madonna, whose father had been a garbage truck driver in

Dallas. "We can't stay here. As soon as the job is over, we have to get out of here. Sooner or later, they're going to cotton to who and what we are."

"You really believe they don't already suspect?" Teacher looked incredulous.

"They don't," she said, as if it were chiseled in stone.

"But honey . . . These aren't normal people with normal resources."

His wife gave a scornful snort. "Yeah, like I believe that some magic person casting some spell is gonna make us look normal to the natives."

Madonna went back to work serving dinner. Grady was occupied with smearing his mashed potatoes all over the counter and occasionally putting a piece of carrot in his mouth.

Teacher said, "I'm going to file a report."

"Fix that drawer in the kitchen that keeps sticking," Madonna said.

"Okay."

"There's plenty of leftover roast beef for a sandwich," she reminded him.

"Thanks, babe," he said, and went out the back door.

When Madonna closed the restaurant that night a little after eight o'clock, she scooped up Grady and stepped out the same door. She locked it, having to fumble because she couldn't see. "Huh," she muttered. Madonna turned to find that the trailer was dark. This was so unusual that she froze in place for a moment. Grady said, "Mama?" and gripped her a little more tightly.

The door to the trailer was unlocked, so Teacher had made it across the few intervening yards. Cautiously, Madonna reached a hand in to flip the light switch by the door. "Teacher?" she called. A groan answered her.

Teacher was curled in a ball on the living room floor, gasping with pain.

"Oh my God," she said. "Oh my God. Grady, Mama's putting you in your room while I take care of Daddy, okay?"

Grady protested, shrieking, but Madonna detached him from her neck and put him in his crib, shutting the door behind her to muffle his high-decibel yells.

Back in the living room, she threw herself on her knees by Teacher. He knew she was there. He reached toward her.

"What's wrong?" Madonna asked, crouching on the floor by her husband. "Teach, what's wrong?"

"Pain," he whispered. "Pain."

"I'm calling 911," Madonna said. "Get you an ambulance."

He shook his head. "Noooo," he whispered.

"Why not?" she demanded.

"Payback," he said, after gathering himself.

"What you mean?"

He whimpered. He grabbed her hand and squeezed it until she winced.

"You mean *Fiji* is doing this to you?"

He managed to nod.

"I'm gonna kill that bitch," Madonna said, reaching for her purse, where she always carried a gun.

Again, he shook his head vehemently. And he drew a long, shuddering breath. He was able to take Madonna's hand.

"Why not?"

Teacher's body eased. "She caught me, and she's warning me," he said. "Fair and square." He took another deep breath, relaxed a bit more. "It's going away. It's over."

When Teacher could stand, Madonna helped him into bed. He told her three times that he'd be fine after a full night's sleep. "This has to stop now," he warned her, before he closed his eyes. "No dosing her food or giving her the stink-eye."

"But—"

"But nothing. She's not our target. I took a stupid risk and I got caught. I showed her my hand and got nothing in return."

Madonna looked down at him. "What kind of thing did you think you might find?"

"Some kind of clue why all the suicides are happening," Teacher said. "Some kind of reason. You can't tell me that isn't some kind of mystical shit. And Fiji is the witch, so I figured the two things must be tied together."

"She can't be causing them," Madonna said. "That's just not her."

"Well, I would have said the same thing right up until an hour ago," Teacher said, wincing as he eased into a more comfortable position.

Madonna cocked her head. From the silence, Grady had cried himself to sleep. She would skip his bath and his toothbrush tonight in favor of letting him stay that way. She raised a finger to her husband and slipped into the toddler's room to pull a blanket over him. She tiptoed out without waking him, to her relief.

Though Teacher was almost asleep, he roused enough to say, "She didn't call the cops. She didn't go running to her neighbors and ask them to come question me about it. She solved her problem herself."

And with that, Madonna made a sound of disgust, turned off the light, and left him to sleep. She was not content with Teacher's verdict, but for now she'd go along.

Madonna was not one to forgive and forget. She was more of the "get even" school.

She stopped herself from making plans for vengeance by reminding herself that Fiji was *not* the object of her paycheck these past two years. Madonna had to keep her eyes on the prize.

And it was a rich prize, indeed.

18

Lemuel said, "Bobo, the shop has to be closed tonight."

Bobo was standing in the doorway of his apartment above the pawnshop. Lemuel had come silently up the stairs while Bobo had been waiting for a pizza to come out of the oven.

Bobo thought of asking why, but if Lemuel had wanted to explain, he would have done so. "Okay," he said. "The weather's so bad I don't think you'll disappoint a lot of clientele."

"Thank you," the vampire said stiffly. He almost spoke again, but he seemed to think the better of it, and he went down as silently as he'd come up.

A few minutes later, Bobo saw Lemuel and Olivia climb into Olivia's anonymous gray Honda Civic and drive off. He shrugged and sliced the pizza. He was reading a book by Tana French, and he propped it up on another book while he ate his dinner.

He would have been very surprised to know that Lemuel and Olivia were on their way to kidnap a vampire.

. . .

"Her name's Christine?" Lemuel asked Olivia.

"Yep. That's what the Vampire Directory said. And this is the latest edition. The purchase had to go on your credit card. You have to be a vampire listed in it to buy it."

"I didn't know such a thing existed," Lemuel marveled. "And you say I'm in it?"

"You did ask me to search the Internet."

"I did wonder if you might be able to find the descendants of Arria Auclina and Dr. Quigley," he said. Lemuel was quite proud that he'd even imagined Olivia could discover such a thing, and he was even more delighted that once Olivia had understood what he wanted, she'd purchased the software and found his answer while he slept.

Lemuel had not been this pleased since Bobo had given him the hidden books.

"Do you want to look at your entry?" Olivia asked.

"I'm interested in hers," he said. "Mine need only read, 'Stay away from him.'"

Olivia laughed. "One person in a million would say that, Lem. Okay, Christine's entry says that she's the linear descendant of Arria Auclina. Christine was turned by Dr. Quigley thirty years ago to provide a gift for his sire. She is fluent in Etruscan."

"Where is she?"

"This is the best part. She's in Dallas right now, living in Joseph's nest."

"Then let's go." Lemuel was up and walking by the time Olivia's astonished look vanished, replaced by concern.

"What are we going to do?" she asked. "Lem, you can't just steal her." But she was smiling as she said it.

"Of course I can," he said. "And I may yet do so. But I plan to bargain." Lemuel was running up the stairs and into the shop. By the time Olivia caught up with him, he was looking in the old ledger, one of the earliest recording the pawnshop transactions. Whatever its original color, the book was now a mottled yellowish color with a dark brown spine.

Olivia didn't ask what Lemuel was doing. She knew that very soon he'd tell her. Lemuel turned to the earliest section of the ledger (which was about the size of a 9-by-13 baking pan), and within a minute he'd found what he wanted.

"It's still here," Lemuel said. "That's the beauty of keeping records." Laying the ledger on the counter, he went to the corner of the pawnshop where the magical objects were kept. Olivia studied the locked cabinets some nights while Lemuel was on duty, and she would have sworn she knew the appearance of each item, though not its use—for Bobo and Lemuel did not know the properties of all of them. But Lemuel unlocked a cabinet with a tiny key from his key ring and withdrew a ball the color of aged ivory. It was about the size of a softball, and it was decorated with tiny blue paintings of butterflies.

"Tell me a lie," Lemuel said.

"I'm a virgin," Olivia said promptly.

And the ball glowed from inside.

It was startlingly lovely lit this way, but Lemuel was not at all interested in the aesthetics of the ball. "It still works," he said with some satisfaction. "This will be a good thing to trade for Christine."

Olivia opened her mouth to protest that a woman should not be traded for an object, even if she was a vampire, but she closed it again. There were arguments you could win with Lemuel, and there were arguments you couldn't. This was one of those.

Lemuel slapped his pockets until he found his phone, which Olivia had given him the previous Christmas. She had also instructed him in its use, and now, with a glance to make sure she noticed, he checked his list of contacts and pressed one of the icons. He held the phone to his ear, and Olivia could hear it ring.

"Yes," said a cold voice.

"This is Lemuel Bridger."

After a pause, the voice said, "A great surprise to hear from you."

"Please tell Joseph that I need to talk to him this night and that I am on my way from Midnight."

"I will see if he has time to talk to you, Mr. Bridger."

"I am coming, anyway," Lemuel said, and hung up.

"If we're going to Dallas, we better get on the road now," Olivia said. "Are we taking the Vette?" Lemuel had a red Corvette, and Olivia loved to ride in it.

"I wish we could, but we have to bring back another person, so we'd better take yours," he said. "And you're right, let's start." He ran up the stairs to Bobo's door, told Bobo he was leaving, and in the next five minutes they were on their way to Dallas.

Joseph's large house was in a neighborhood of similar homes. His predecessor, Stan, had refused to move after the famous massacre several years ago. Joseph, too, had insisted the nest remain where it had been. The house had been carefully repaired. There was no sign that blood and death had ever filled the night in this upscale neighborhood.

Olivia had read all about the massacre, and she scanned the mansion's façade with some curiosity. She was rewarded at discovering a bullet hole on one of the window frames. Though it had been filled in and painted, it was detectable to Olivia, who knew her bullets.

Lemuel rang the doorbell. He said, "Olivia, don't leave my side in this house. If you have to answer the call of nature, I'd rather you do it in your pants than go somewhere alone with one of these vampires."

"You might have said that before we got here," she said, not knowing whether to laugh or make a dash for the bushes. "I can hold it." Olivia wished he hadn't brought up her bladder, though, because come to think of it . . .

Then the door opened, and Joseph Velasquez himself greeted them. He was not a handsome man; short and squat and flat-faced. But he was powerful and intelligent, which was attractive in its own right. "Mr. Bridger," he said, with just a hint of an accent. "And perhaps your companion is Miss Charity?"

"I am," Olivia confirmed.

"Very formidable," Joseph said, in a voice that conveyed the exact opposite. "Please enter my home." He stepped aside. Lemuel entered in front of Olivia, to take the first blow if there was an ambush. But none fell, and Olivia stepped inside behind him, trying not to feel shaken by the vibration of power as she moved past Joseph.

There were other vampires in the hall, and still more in the room to which Joseph led them. When the house had been built (by humans), this had been the family room, and it still served that purpose, though for a very different sort of family.

Olivia had never met any other vampire besides Lemuel, and she was surprised by how different they felt. She knew that Lemuel was unusual, but now she understood what a gap it made between him and the blood drinkers.

"Would you like a glass?" Joseph asked. He gestured toward a thin black-haired female who was carrying a tray of wineglasses.

"Thank you," Lemuel said, taking a glass from the central part of the tray.

"Would your human like something to drink?"

"Olivia?" Lemuel turned to her. There was a warning in his face.

"No, thank you," she said politely. Now was not the time to inform Joseph she could speak for herself.

"Thank you, no," Lemuel relayed.

"We are so pleased to be able to extend hospitality to such a famous vampire," Joseph said, slowly and carefully. "But since you have banned all such as us from your territory, I am quite interested to find out why you wanted to visit my own territory."

"I have come to ask for one favor in exchange for another," Lemuel said, just as carefully.

Their voices, you could hang icicles from them, Olivia thought. She was careful not to meet the eyes of any of the vampires around them. She'd read enough to know that. The mesmerizing eyes were not a trait of Lemuel's, and she was glad of that, because it would have been mighty inconvenient to dodge his gaze all the time.

"A favor?" Joseph was able to inject a lot of incredulity into two words. "From us? You astonish me."

"I was astonished to hear that daytime servants of yours had come to my town while I slept," Lemuel said.

"Ah. I will tell you why." Joseph inclined his head graciously. "I had heard that a human who did us great harm was hiding in Midnight," he said. "Rather than offend you by sending one of us at night, I thought humans in our service would be less intrusive."

"But of course, I heard of it," Lemuel said, and though calm, his voice was truly terrifying. "And it did seem to me that such an action might be considered a violation of our agreement of so many years ago."

"An agreement you made with Stan when he was young," Joseph murmured.

"An agreement with the head of a nest is an agreement forever, unless it is renegotiated," Lemuel said in return. No one in the room moved by so much as a whisker. Vampires could do that.

In the silence that followed, Olivia kept her eyes on Lemuel's feet. She would know if the time had come to fight by the way he planted his feet.

"Perhaps you could explain the favor?" Joseph asked.

"Certainly. I need the services of a young vampire in your nest. Her name is Christine."

The thin black-haired female with the tray moved an inch.

Busted, thought Olivia. It was the equivalent of jumping up and down screaming, "That's me!"

"This is Christine," Joseph said, and the censure was heavy in his voice. "She is a weak vampire, but a fair fighter."

He really doesn't like Christine. Olivia began to feel optimistic about their chances. Perhaps Lemuel would not have to give up the truth ball if Joseph was anxious to be rid of Christine.

"On the other hand," said a male with a blond crew cut, who had already caught Olivia's attention because he looked very retro-1950s, "Christine has proven her worth to us. May we ask why you need Christine, in particular?"

Does she have something we don't know about that we could use or exploit? Olivia translated.

"She is a weak vampire," Lemuel said, with the air of one being sadly blunt. "She has only one recommendation to me, and that is her lineage. Her maker, who calls himself Dr. Quigley, gave me less than fair value in something I bought from him."

Olivia found it draining to be so hyperalert to tiny movements. But at least no one was getting closer, and she could sense the vampires' interest. Olivia was finding the atmosphere in the house stagnant and cool, and she realized that the vampires had not turned on the heat yet, though the night temperatures were dipping into the low fifties. She was glad she'd pulled on a sweater for the drive.

The silence had lasted way too long, at least for a human conversation, and Olivia realized her thoughts were drifting when they should be most focused.

She'd heard that vampires could communicate with each other silently if they were connected by blood, and she figured that was what was happening.

"We are willing to give up Christine, for a price," Joseph said.

Good-bye, truth ball, Olivia thought.

"As it happens, I have something that may interest you," Lemuel said smoothly.

Forty minutes later they were driving back to Midnight with a very sullen vampire in the backseat.

Olivia realized that her sex life was on hold for the foreseeable future. Lemuel was so private he didn't admit in public that he and Olivia actually had sex, he had banned the F word from casual conversation, and he would never be induced into her bed with a vampire in the next room. Sure, there were more important things to face at the moment. But.

Well, shit, she thought.

19

Manfred woke up the next morning thinking about Mamie. Since he was a great believer in taking a hint from his own brain, after he'd had his granola-bar breakfast he called Safe Harbor. He was connected to the room she shared with Suzie, and it was Suzie who answered the telephone.

"Hello?"

"It's Manfred. How is Mamie?"

"Better," Suzie said immediately. "She's better! Your friend Fiji came, and she held Mamie's hand and prayed over her or something. By that point, we wouldn't have minded if she'd gotten out a feather headdress and danced around the bed with a rattle. But she closed her eyes and her lips moved, Fiji's I mean, and Mamie's sleep got better, more natural. Her legs quit moving, and she didn't toss and turn any more. This morning she woke up and asked for breakfast!"

"I'm so glad. Has she walked any?"

"Just to the bathroom and back, but that was more than she's done in days."

"That's great! That's just . . . *great*." Manfred couldn't think of eloquent words.

"We're so relieved. Maybe she'll gain her ground back, now."

"I hope so. I'll be over to visit in a day or two."

"Bring me a Hershey bar! With almonds!"

He smiled. Suzie had a sweet tooth, especially for chocolate. "I will," he said. "Let me know if anything changes, okay?"

"Sure, kid. Thanks for getting that Fiji to come. It's the weirdest thing, neither Tommy nor me can remember her leaving."

"What?" Abruptly, Manfred was less happy.

"Yeah. I guess we were so tired watching over Mamie that we fell asleep. She must think we're a couple of old farts. But that's okay with me. She pulled the iron out of the fire."

"I'm glad she could help." Manfred hung up. He didn't know what to make of Tommy and Suzie's falling asleep. But he felt much better, on the whole, so he was inclined to dismiss it.

Manfred knew—in the grand scheme of things, as Xylda used to say—that Mamie couldn't live many more years, or perhaps many more months or weeks, even. But if she could live and *enjoy* that time, he would be happy. She was such a sweetie. He couldn't remember her ever saying a bad word about anyone.

Except Shorty Horowitz, one of the other seniors who had been at the Midnight Hotel. Mamie hadn't been fond of Shorty.

And she'd said something less than flattering about Fiji, when they'd been eating at Home Cookin. In fact, she'd referred to Fiji as "lard butt," and he'd had to remind Mamie that Fiji was his friend.

Manfred had forgotten that until now. He considered the irony, that it was Fiji who had saved Mamie from mental torment. And he was sure that Fiji would have done so even if she'd known of Mamie's disparaging comment. Manfred postponed work to cross Witch Light Road and thank her.

He found Fiji sitting on her back porch, Mr. Snuggly at her side.

She looked stern, an expression he'd never seen on Fiji's face before—aside from the time she'd gotten so exasperated at a private detective named Shoshanna that she'd frozen her in her in place. While Shoshanna had stood there, immobile, in Fiji's driveway, Fiji had driven away. And her face had borne this same expression.

"Good morning," Manfred said, approaching cautiously.

Her face lightened. "Oh, hi," she said. "I hope your friend is better."

"That's what I came to tell you," he said. "She is. She seems at peace, and she got up and walked a little today. And not in our direction."

"Good to hear," Fiji said. "Want a cup of tea? Got the time?"

Manfred glanced at his watch. "Sure, I have a few minutes."

In no time at all, he was ensconced in the chair beside hers, with a cup of tea. He'd declined an English muffin.

"Does it bother you, what Chuy and Joe said?" he said, after a period of comfortable silence, broken only by the licking sounds of Mr. Snuggly cleaning his paws.

Fiji gave him a blank look.

"That they see ghosts. Did you know that?"

"No, it doesn't exactly bother me," Fiji said, though she looked uncomfortable. "I guess you mean, does it bother me that they see my great-aunt."

Manfred nodded.

"Maybe it should," Fiji said. "That might indicate her spirit isn't at rest. But I don't know that's actually what it means." Her shoulders rose, fell. "Maybe she made such an impression on her surroundings that a simulacrum repeats her actions. Maybe it means she's serving time in purgatory. I can't determine why they see her. So it would be kind of silly to get all worked up over it. I think I'm more—maybe 'concerned' is the word?—that they've been seeing ghosts all this time and this is the first I've known about it. Did they not trust me with the information?"

"I thought the same thing," Manfred said.

"It would be interesting to know exactly what these ghosts are doing. Are they creating new actions and actually living some kind of life? Are they simply repeating patterns they established when they were alive? Are these the same kind of ghosts that show up at your séances?"

"I wondered all that, too," Manfred said, relieved. "If they are the same, you'd think I could see them, right? After all, I'm kind of in the ghost business. Spirit business. Whatever. I guess I'm feeling some professional jealousy."

"Would you want to see ghosts like they do? All the time?" Fiji was very serious, and he gave the idea some thought.

"I don't think I'd want to every day," Manfred said finally. "But maybe if I could switch it on and off, it would be . . . interesting."

"I would *not* want to see Price Eggleston stab himself every day," Fiji said.

"God, no!"

"Or Aubrey." She'd been Bobo's girlfriend. "I didn't like her when she was alive. And she looked pretty awful dead. That's another question I want to ask Chuy and Joe. Do the ghosts look like their living selves?"

"Maybe we can just ask them."

"Maybe. We'd sure have to pick the right moment."

"Fiji? What are they?" This was the first time Manfred had dared to ask.

"I think you know what they are," she said.

"Are they . . . really angels?"

She raised an eyebrow.

"Yeah, what do I think?" Manfred translated her expression. "I think they are. But they're not the kind of angel that was in Jesus's tomb."

"No," Fiji said. "They're not. I'm sure they're fallen."

"What did they do wrong, you think?"

Fiji drank some tea while she thought about her answer. She said, "You know how when Jesus came, he brought a new philosophy. Before that, the word of God was always along the lines of, 'I'm going to smite your enemies if you're faithful to me, and you can take an eye for an eye.' Well, under the new policy, you were supposed to turn the other cheek every time you were struck. Here's my theory, and it's based on tiny bits of conversations I've had with them over the years. Chuy and Joe just couldn't make that change. They couldn't agree to turn their other cheeks. So here they are."

Manfred digested that, once he'd gotten over his surprise that she'd actually answered him. He said, "Their punishment was being banished to Midnight?" That was faintly amusing.

She laughed. "Yeah, doesn't seem right, does it? Let me remind you, this is just my theory. I only know they were humans hundreds of years ago, then angels, and now they're sort of in between."

"But they have families! I remember when Chuy's family came to visit."

"They reconnected with their descendants," Fiji said. "And somehow got them to believe they remember them. That's a lot of pronouns, but you understand. The descendants believe Joe and Chuy are current relatives. It's a comfort to Joe and Chuy, and they can do some good for their families that way."

Manfred nodded. "I can see that they don't believe in waiting for after-death justice," he said. "When I think about the Lovells."

Fiji nodded back at him. "Big clue," she said. She sat forward in her chair, and he realized it was time for him to go.

"Good-bye, Fiji, and thanks again for helping Mamie," he said. "You're a good neighbor to have, and I know she would tell you how much she appreciates it if she were a little more together."

"De nada," Fiji said. "I better open up the shop."

"Me, too," Manfred said. "Time to start answering phones." He reached down and scratched Mr. Snuggly's head, which the cat accepted regally. "Have a good day, Snug. Hey, how does it feel to know that Rasta's owners are angels?" The cat strolled away with his tail held high, as if he had barely noticed Manfred.

Fiji laughed as she stretched. "Are you trying to put him in a bad mood for the rest of the day?" She was only partially kidding. "Mr. Snuggly feels it very deeply that I'm just a witch, and Joe and Chuy aren't human anymore. On the other hand, Snug can talk. Rasta's just a bunch of fur and bone, Snug always says."

"I'll try to be more tactful," Manfred told her. He worried a little about Fiji as he was crossing the road. She'd given him much more information than he'd expected, almost as if she weren't thinking about what she was saying. Abstracted. She'd seemed abstracted. As if she were thinking about something else entirely.

He shrugged. She hadn't complained or asked for his help. As he went back into his own house, Manfred was thinking, *I know a pair of angels. I talk to angels. I live on the same street as angels. And across from a talking cat and a witch.* And yet, he admitted to himself, this didn't feel strange at all. It felt quite normal.

20

Fiji was not a happy witch. She remembered over and over that she'd deliberately caused pain to Teacher.

But she'd felt it was necessary, and nothing had happened to change her conviction. Necessary steps (maybe necessary evils) didn't always make you feel good afterward.

Plus, she'd called Bobo when she'd promised herself she would not do so again.

Plus, the creature was talking to her.

Its voice was not coming as frequently, which she figured was due to the fact that no one had died at the crossroad in five days, but she still felt it *thinking* at her.

Fiji was glad she had several customers that morning, and that not a single one of them was suicidal. Fiji would have enjoyed closing the shop for lunch and walking down to Home Cookin, but she wasn't ready to face Madonna.

Fiji had a strong feeling that Teacher would know why he had been stricken, and she was pretty sure he'd share that with his wife. If he did, Madonna was not the kind of woman to take an attack on her husband lying down. Madonna would find some way to retaliate, if she got the chance. Better, and safer, to eat canned soup and grilled cheese in her own kitchen . . . if only she'd had some soup. Her Piggly Wiggly trip had not been as comprehensive as she would have liked.

Feeling irritated with herself, and therefore the world, Fiji pulled on her jacket and walked over to Gas N Go. She had completely forgotten about the new manager until he looked up from his card game. Not tarot, she saw. Solitaire.

"Oh, hi, new guy," she said. "I'm Fiji Cavanaugh, I live in the house with the Inquiring Mind sign in the front." He was good-looking in a very stern and dark way, but she found she wasn't afraid of him as she often was of overtly lovely people.

"Fiji," he said, tilting his head courteously. "I'm Sylvester Ravenwing. Can I help you today?"

"I need soup," she said.

"Second aisle, second shelf on the left," he said, and went back to his game.

It was kind of pleasant to be left in peace. Teacher, in his interim stint as manager, had always been so glad to see someone that it had sometimes been hard to get out of the store, and Shawn Lovell had always been so eaten up by his worries that shopping had been something of an ordeal.

"So, you think you'll be here for a while, Sylvester?" Fiji asked. She put the can of Campbell's Bean and Ham on the counter.

"I do think so," he answered. "This all you want?"

"Yep. See you."

He nodded as graciously as Queen Elizabeth II and went back to his card game as soon as he'd handed over her change.

On her way home, Fiji realized that Midnight had its own little rainbow. Madonna and Teacher and Grady were African American, Sylvester was Native American, and though Suzie hadn't lived at the hotel for long, she had been born in Hong Kong. *Midnight, crossroads of the world,* she thought, and smiled to herself.

Back in her own warm kitchen, Fiji added some leftover vegetables to the soup as it was heating and got out her frying pan for the grilled cheese sandwich. She was so hungry she considered making two and sliced extra cheese.

Fiji was surprised to hear a knock at her back door while the first sandwich was sizzling in the pan. She sighed heavily, to show the fates how reluctant she was, before she answered the door. "Olivia," she said, trying to sound welcoming. "What can I do for you?"

"You can make me a grilled cheese sandwich," Olivia said. "That smells great, Fiji. And while we eat, I have something to talk to you about."

"Okay." Fiji was mildly interested. She and Olivia were not bosom buddies, but Olivia was never boring. Fiji popped another sandwich into the skillet. In a very few minutes, Olivia having declined any soup, they were sitting at the kitchen table together eating and talking.

"Lemuel has a new vampire buddy," Olivia said, apropos of nothing.

It was easy for Fiji to see this was not a good thing to Olivia. "I'm guessing you're not crazy about this development?" she said.

"It's a woman," Olivia answered.

"Oh. Gotcha." But after she thought about it longer, Fiji wasn't sure she really did. "Surely you don't think Lemuel is two-timing you?"

"No." Olivia's face was grim. "But she's got something he needs, and he bought her from Joseph Velasquez."

"What's she got that Lemuel needs?"

"She can read Etruscan."

"Well, shit. No way to compete with that." Fiji was bewildered but also amused.

Olivia laughed, a harsh sound. "Nope. Since I don't think anyone left in the world except a few vampires can speak or read fluent Etruscan."

"So why does Lemuel need an Etruscan speaker? Oh, wait. The travelogue, the one he's been trying to translate . . . and it was taking him so long, right? That's in Etruscan."

Olivia nodded. "So until the book is translated, we've got little Miss Subservient living with us."

"What's her name?"

"Christine something. She's from Dallas; she lived in a vampire nest there. Lemuel has nothing to do with them, especially Joseph, the leader."

"How did he know Lemuel needed an Etruscan speaker?" Fiji was confused.

"He didn't until we showed up asking for one. We found Christine in the Vampire Directory. So we gave Joseph, the sheriff, a present, and he gave us Christine. Whose maker was Dr. Parker Quigley."

"Am I supposed to recognize that name?" Fiji was embarrassed. "I don't."

"I didn't, either," Olivia said. "Don't feel bad. As I've since found out, Dr. Quigley was a kind of shady and scary guy in his day—surprise, surprise. Because of his research into ancient Egyptians and ancient Roman burial customs and rituals. Anyway, while he was doing more research, he eventually ran across an Etruscan vampire named Arria Auclina." Olivia pronounced the name carefully: Ar-REE-ah Aw-CLEE-nah.

"And this Arria Auclina made him a vampire."

"You got it. She was pretty excited that someone was interested in her people. And she taught Dr. Quigley Etruscan, to keep the language alive. And then he taught Christine. In another huge enormous totally unbelievable coincidence, Dr. Quigley was the vampire Lemuel ran across in New Orleans. He gave him a dictionary, to help in translation. But the dictionary was pretty crappy, as it turns out, so that's one reason Lemuel's had such slow going getting the book translated."

"This is kind of convoluted," Fiji said.

"No shit. Joseph, who evidently is Christine's boss, decided she was expendable. Turns out the vampires of Dallas have been feeling 'bad emanations' from Midnight."

"That's a lot of vampires thinking about us. I've always been glad Lemuel kept them away from here," Fiji said. "When the daytime people were here looking for Barry, it made my skin crawl."

Olivia looked at Fiji doubtfully. "You're not saying Lemuel makes your skin crawl," she said, in the tone of someone who is just making certain of a fact.

"No, I'm used to Lemuel and I talk to him the same way I talk to anyone else." *Though I almost always think before I speak with Lemuel,* Fiji added silently.

"He's one of a kind," Olivia said proudly. "Almost literally. At least, he's really rare."

Fiji carried the plates and her bowl over to the sink. "So I guess you have a goal in coming to visit? Not that I'm not glad to see you and share lunch and a good story with you," she said over her shoulder.

"I do have a purpose," Olivia admitted promptly. "Lemuel happened to be outside Teacher and Madonna's trailer last night, and he heard them talking about you. Teacher said he'd been in your house, and you'd caught him, and then evidently you paid him back?"

"I did both those things." Fiji sat down opposite Olivia. She didn't exactly feel defensive, but she definitely felt wary. "So?"

"Hey, I'm not critical! Because it turns out that the Reeds seem to have come here to spy on me."

This was unexpected news. "Sure you're not being paranoid?" Fiji asked gently. "Because he searched my house."

Olivia gaped at her. "Really? But I have to tell you, I'm pretty sure he's here because of my family."

"You have a—an unpleasant family background?"

"Yeah. I've got family issues. No big surprise there, huh?" Olivia's smile was bitter.

"Don't we all? You met my sister." Fiji waited for further revelations. This was sure a day for them.

"She was a piece of work, sure enough. But my father . . . well, he's rich and he's powerful. So it's most probable the Reeds are working for my dad."

"It might not be your dad?" Fiji was dazzled. The mysterious Olivia was finally unburdening herself.

"My father has a right-hand man, Ellery McGuire. My father would never believe it, but Ellery has been trying for years to position himself to take over the company. My dad is old, and he never has been great at inspiring love and loyalty; I'll just put it that way. My brother is dead, killed a few years ago in a ski accident."

"I never knew you had a brother," Fiji said, spellbound by the sudden spate of revelation. "Your family's really rich?" She thought that explained a lot about Olivia's confidence level. And maybe her ruthlessness.

"Yeah. Really, really rich." Olivia nodded.

"And you don't hang with them because?"

"Because when I was really young, my stepmother and her boyfriends molested me. And she made me call her 'Mother' while she did it."

"That sucks more than I can imagine. What happened to your real mother?"

"She and Dad got divorced and she remarried. She had some issues with alcohol—surprise, surprise. That's why my dad got custody of me. My real mom survived a few years, but then alcohol killed her."

"Did your dad know? What your stepmother had done?"

"He said he didn't when I confronted him," Olivia said, letting her shoulders rise and fall. "Some days, I believe him. Mostly I just hope not."

Compared to Olivia's family, Kiki was a walk in the park, Fiji realized. "Is your stepmother still alive?" she asked.

"No." And Olivia smiled.

Message received, Fiji thought. "So you figure not only your father is looking for you but also this right-hand-of-darkness guy? Ellery McGuire?"

"Yeah. I figure so."

"How do you hide from someone that rich?"

"It isn't easy. And, as you can tell, someone has found out where I am because—to get back to the original conversation—that's why the Reeds are here."

"To watch you."

"To watch me."

"And why are you here in my house, again? Specifically today? Just because I'm mad at Teacher, too?"

"Here's the deal. I'm sure Manfred told you Teacher hitched a ride with him to Killeen?"

Fiji nodded.

"And he told you that Teacher pumped him for information on the way?"

"I don't think he mentioned that, no."

"Well, he did. Asked him a lot of questions. Anyway, Teacher wanted to be let off at this hardware store, because he said he knew the owner really well and the owner was able to get Teacher some really great tools that Teacher needed. That sounds totally made up to me. Why couldn't the guy mail them to Teacher? Why couldn't Teacher order them online?"

"So?"

"So, you and I should go to Killeen and find out what we can about this man and about his business."

"And that will help us how?"

"That will help us know more. And knowing more is always good."

Hard to argue with that, Fiji thought. "Okay, do we have the name of the store?"

"It's on San Jacinto Street," Olivia said. "And the name of the store is Handyman Hardware. It's been under the management of this man for three years, about the same length of time that the Reeds have been at Home Cookin."

"Seems like they could have placed someone closer if this store guy's goal is to support the Reeds," Fiji said.

"Yeah, well. This is what we've got to work with," Olivia said. "When can we go?"

Fiji looked at her calendar. "I don't want to work tomorrow, anyway," she said recklessly. "Let's go then. What are you planning on doing to this man?"

"We'll wing it," Olivia said, smiling a very unpleasant smile.

They left early on Saturday morning in Olivia's anonymous gray car. Fiji figured Olivia would experience a backlash after telling her so much about her life, so she was prepared for Olivia to be extra snarly during the ride. To her surprise and pleasure, Olivia seemed more relaxed than she'd ever been in Fiji's company.

Fiji thought, *It's almost like being with a real friend.* The idea startled her; she'd considered Olivia more a companion in a shared experience, as though they'd gone through sorority hazing or a store robbery side by side.

"Have you heard from your sister since she left so abruptly?" Olivia asked.

"My mother called to ask me what I'd done to her," Fiji said. "She was crying. My mom, that is."

"Ouch."

"Yeah. One of the things Kiki told me was that my dad has Alzheimer's, and my mom is taking care of him full-time. Kiki wanted to find some excuse not to help her, I think; she separated from her husband before she knew what going back home would mean. Or maybe he threw her out. He's humping her boss, who fired her for stealing. And he's gambling. A complicated situation."

"Some people would be glad to have the chance to take care of their father," Olivia said, neutrally.

"That wouldn't be Kiki, and she's right there and was the favorite daughter," Fiji said. "If my mom asks me directly, I'll give her a break for a week." She felt anything but pleased at the prospect. "My dad isn't a bad man, but he's proud, and that's always made him hard to deal with. Maybe he's not anymore. I've heard the disease makes you the opposite of what you were. It would be really pleasant if Dad was the opposite of the way he was when I was growing up."

"You could ask this young woman Manfred's so hot for," Olivia said. "Estella. She's a part-time caregiver at the place where our old people are staying."

"I looked for her when I was there to see Mamie," Fiji said. "But I didn't cast eyes on her."

"If you were there in the afternoon, you wouldn't. She works at night and goes to classes during the day," Olivia told her. "She's a nursing student, I think. I checked up on her." Olivia said this very casually, as if that were normal procedure.

"I'm glad he's found someone. Since Creek left the picture."

"Me, too. Now we need to work on you," Olivia said.

"Oh, no! No, I'm . . ."

"Crazy about Bobo, I know. And he's been so broody lately I think he's screwing himself up to saying something. Did you two have a fight or something? That maybe opened his eyes?"

"We had a falling-out," Fiji admitted.

"But you're overlooking another possibility," Olivia said. She was smiling, too, but she was definitely serious in intent. "The tigers are nuts about you. If you can say tigers are nuts!"

"The *Rev*?" Fiji was incredulous.

Olivia laughed out loud, which was a sound Fiji had never heard before.

"No, not him. The Quinns, father and son."

Fiji gaped at Olivia.

"I'm serious," Olivia said, half-smiling. "You haven't noticed that John Quinn stays longer and longer when he stops in to visit Diederik?"

"Well, Diederik needs him," Fiji protested. "That's why he comes." But now that she was seeing things through a different lens, she was wondering.

"Riiiiight," Olivia said, and then wisely held her tongue.

Fiji stared straight forward for a good five minutes, thinking things over, reinterpreting encounters. She shook her head silently a couple of times.

"Of course, Diederik's too young," she said.

"Wait around a couple of weeks, he won't be," Olivia said, and Fiji laughed involuntarily.

"But I don't think that's true, actually," Fiji said. "Now that he looks in his late teens, it should slow down, Quinn said."

"Good, because he was going to wrinkle and lose his teeth in a year at that rate of aging."

"My sister teased me about Diederik, too," Fiji said. "And she was serious. That is, she was really considering him. But I remember buying him Superman underpants just a few months ago. He's definitely out of the eligible park. It's almost like thinking of Grady as a potential future partner."

"You sure? That Marina at the hotel seems mighty happy. I'm sure she and Diederik are doing the deed, especially after going in there the other night while he was doing janitor work and she was working the desk. I don't think either of them were exactly *working*."

"Why'd you go in?"

"I was being a good neighbor," Olivia said virtuously. "I noticed one of her tires was low."

"Did you tell her?"

"Oh, yeah. But I'm not sure if she registered what I was saying or not. They both looked pretty self-conscious."

"Half of me is saying, 'Oh gosh no, he's just a baby,' and the other half is going, 'Wowsers.'" Fiji shook her head. "I knew they were, ah, seeing each other, but I guess getting a specific instance makes it more real."

"Well, Quinn should be conflict-free, because he's definitely mature."

"No kidding," Fiji said, looking self-conscious herself.

"Yeah, I thought so," Olivia said with some satisfaction. "You can't be immune to his charm. Forget Bobo!"

"Does everyone in town know I've always had a crush on Bobo?"

Olivia nodded. "Maybe the Rev hasn't picked up on it, but he's not one to care about the feelings of the heart."

This had been a remarkable talk for both of them, and just as Fiji was thinking, *Wow, have I spilled my guts*, Olivia seemed to become aware of the same thing. They both fell silent. Fiji had no regrets. It had been fun to talk woman-to-woman. She felt empowered, though the word made her wince a little.

"I'm just gonna tell him," she said out loud.

"Sure. Long past due," Olivia said. "You know, I'm the only regular human in Midnight, aside from the people at the hotel. Oh, and Bobo."

Where did that come from? Fiji wondered. She fumbled with what to say.

"I'm just human," Olivia said before Fiji could come up with something. "I'm a drastically bad one. But human."

"So?"

"No, look. You're a witch, and I don't think we know the half of what you can do. The Rev, Diederik, Quinn—weretigers. Chuy and Joe—angels. Lemuel—vampire. Manfred is a psychic. The new guy at the gas station, he seems pretty . . . something, I don't know."

Fiji couldn't figure out why Olivia was making such a point of her own ordinariness. Fiji didn't think Olivia was ordinary at all. She thought Olivia was a sociopath, but one she could get along with. And she felt a little sorry for Olivia sometimes, while in the same moment she understood that Olivia had lethal skills and no qualms about using them.

"Olivia, you're complex," Fiji said. "It's what you are."

Olivia laughed again. It was already a red-letter day.

When they reached Killeen, they stopped briefly at a gas station to top off the tank and hit the ladies' room. With the aid of Olivia's phone, it wasn't hard to find San Jacinto Street, which was in the older part of downtown, the part with sidewalks and storefronts and angled parking. Olivia found a space a few doors down from Handyman Hardware. The front door of the store had a cartoon of a very muscular man with his arms crossed over his chest, a hammer in one hand and a drill in the other.

"Cute," Olivia said. But she wasn't laughing now.

Fiji pushed open the door. The store was old, too, and the tile floor rose and fell a bit. It was dim in the store's interior past the plate-glass windows, and no one was in sight, even though the bell over the door had issued an electronic *bing-bong*.

"Be right there!" called a male voice.

Olivia walked over to a display of mailboxes and open and shut several in an experimental way. Fiji was distracted by an array of planters; she wanted to put one on the cement balustrade on her porch. Geraniums or petunias, she thought, and wished she'd brought a tape measure to determine if the longest planter would fit the space. She was actually surprised when the man appeared.

"Hi, can I help you ladies?" he said. He directed his attention to Fiji, who was closest, but naturally, he glanced at Olivia.

Olivia turned around, and Fiji saw him literally twitch, though his face stayed pleasantly expectant. There was no doubt in Fiji's mind that this man had recognized Olivia. However, Olivia ignored the twitch and followed the cue of the bland expression. Fiji followed her lead.

"My friend brought me over," Fiji said, designating herself the main shopper.

"So what are you shopping for today?" he asked. The fingers of his right hand flexed and clenched in a fist.

Fiji glanced around, hoping she was making the scan casual. "Two things," Fiji said. "I need a hammer that's not too heavy for me to swing. Also, I'm interested in measuring this sort of window box to see if it'll fit on my porch." Behind the man, she could see Olivia nodding vehemently. Yes, she knew him, too. She was just better at hiding it.

"Let's take care of the hammer first," he said.

Good. She wanted to get Olivia close to some usable weapons. "By the way, I'm Fiji Cavanaugh," she said, as she followed him down the aisle to the left.

"Oh. Lucas Evans," he said.

"Have you lived here long, Lucas?" She strove to sound just interested, not flirtatious. In her own opinion, she hit the sweet spot.

"A few years," he said casually. "You ladies from around here?"

"Oh, no, we live in Midnight. Little bitty town, you've probably never heard of it."

"And this is the closest hardware store to Midnight?"

"No, there's one in Davy, and there are two or three in Marthasville," she said, managing to sound surprised. "But we're in town to visit a friend, and rather than get there too early, we thought we'd explore greater downtown Killeen before we went to her house."

"Who are you visiting?"

"Agnes Orta," Olivia said, not missing a beat. "We know her daughter."

They stopped in front of a display of hammers that would have delighted Thor himself. Fiji genuinely needed a hammer, and she took her time hefting a few. One of them pleased her, and Lucas Evans assured her it was top-of-the-line. After a glance at the price, Fiji believed him.

When they returned to the front of the store to measure the window box, she handed the hammer to Olivia very naturally before she lifted a trough to feel its weight. Now Olivia was armed; Fiji relaxed.

The hardware store owner was about forty-five, and he had a little gut and a soft brown mustache. He blended in perfectly; he was wearing a western shirt, plaid with snap buttons, and a rodeo belt and Levi's. Even cowboy boots. He was relaxing, too. Fiji could tell he was sure that Olivia was ignorant of his true identity.

Evans handed Fiji a metal tape measure that he had worn clipped to his belt. She had to admit to herself that he was good. If it hadn't been for that initial flinch, she would never have guessed that he was agitated inside. Now that she was tuned to it, she could feel it under his skin.

"I own a small business, too," she said chattily. "This is a great location. How many customers do you think you get a day?"

"Oh, depends on the season," Evans said. "Lots in the spring, fewer in the summer. Then in the fall it starts back up, and there's a boom around Christmas with people putting up lights and decorations and so on, repainting for the holidays. Course, most of them nowadays go to Walmart or Lowe's or Home Depot."

"Good to see a small business owner prospering," Fiji murmured. She double-checked the planter's measurements and turned to Olivia. "What do you think?" she asked. "Will it fit?"

"On your porch, I think it will," Olivia said. "But I'm wondering if it'll fit in my car."

"I'll buy it," Fiji said with decision. "If it doesn't fit in the car, I'll ask a friend if I can borrow his pickup." She paid for her purchases, trying not to wince as she handed over her debit card. She'd need to sell quite a few decks of tarot cards to make up for this shopping excursion.

Fiji and Olivia were about to each take one end of the planter when Lucas volunteered to carry it out to the car. Olivia said brightly, "That would be so great!" She ran ahead to fold the backseat down to accommodate the length of the window box, and Lucas, with a little help from Fiji, managed to slide it in at an angle. It just fit.

"See, it was meant to be," Olivia said.

"I think you're right, miss," Lucas said.

"Oh, I'm a Mrs.!" Olivia told him, with what Fiji could only describe to herself as a coy smile.

Lucas was clearly stunned—and so was Fiji, but she hid it better—for a long moment. Recovering, he said, "Sorry, but I didn't see a ring."

Observant, Fiji thought.

"Nope," Olivia agreed. "I don't wear one. Neither does he."

"Ah, welllll," Evans said, after a long and pregnant pause, "enjoyed meeting you ladies. Have a safe drive back to Midnight."

While he went back inside, Fiji climbed into the car in silence.

Olivia was quick to back out and drive away. "I don't want him to look out and see us talking," she said. "Looks too much like we were talking over him and our little visit."

"True," Fiji said faintly. "So he recognized you. Even," she added with an edge to her voice, "though you're a married woman."

"Yeah." Olivia gave her a delighted smile. "That was great, huh? I recognized him, too, but I don't think he could be sure of that. He worked for my dad's right-hand, Ellery McGuire. This Lucas Evans was pretty low down the corporate ladder, but I saw him at a company retreat."

"It's good you didn't have to kill him," Fiji said tartly.

"Thanks for getting me close to the hammers. But in a hardware store, you really can't go wrong. It's what they call a weapons-rich environment."

Fiji nodded. "I did want a window box," she said.

And they both sniggered.

"Are you really married?" Fiji said.

"Yeah," Olivia said. "I really am."

"To Lemuel?"

Olivia nodded. "The Rev married us."

"Why?" Then Fiji flushed. "I'm sorry, that was just rude."

"No, I know it seems unlikely. But if my father dies and I inherit, I wanted to be sure someone he would just hate would eventually get the money. Lemuel will outlive me by centuries."

"And Lemuel agreed to this," Fiji said, marveling.

"Sure. He loves me." Olivia's voice was rough.

"I'd say it was mutual."

"It is," Olivia said. "He knows I love him, and he understands the reasons I wanted to marry him. And he approved."

"I'm surprised you haven't been outed yet."

Olivia shrugged. "We didn't change anything. Didn't see the need. We got married at midnight in Midnight! Our witnesses were two customers who happened to be in the pawnshop. The Rev registered it with the state, as he's required to do, but the Davy paper doesn't print marriage notices. We checked first."

"I'm . . . flabbergasted. I hope you're happy."

This sounded so prim that they started laughing again.

"When did this happen?" Fiji asked.

"About six weeks ago," Olivia said. "Before Lemuel started looking for sources of information about the damn books. And definitely before Christine made her appearance."

"I guess that would put a cramp on any marriage," Fiji said. "Having another vampire with super hearing and super smell right next door."

Olivia nodded grimly. "Not that we were doing anything different since we went through the ceremony," she said, with the air of one determined to be fair. "But now we're not doing *anything*. Lemuel is weirdly straightlaced. Nudity doesn't bother him one way or another, but any action between him and me is strictly private."

"Then I hope she leaves soon, for both your sakes. If my guest bedroom were light-tight she could sleep in my house, but it isn't." She tried not to sound relieved about that, and she left a little silence to make it clear she was switching conversational gears. "We've strayed away from what we're going to do about your buddy at the hardware store."

"Now I'm certain that Teacher is being paid by my dad or his right hand to watch me. Teacher's really been hands-off, so I guess his orders are to keep track of me in general. He doesn't follow me when I leave town. I couldn't miss that. The man I killed in Dallas, the one waiting to snatch me at Rachel Goldthorpe's house? He was definitely working for Ellery McGuire. So I'm thinking Teacher is on my dad's payroll."

"But why would this Lucas Evans be situated so far away from Teacher? Seems like he'd be closer for convenience."

"But then I'd be much more likely to see him," Olivia said. "It's only the chance of Teacher's truck breaking down and him begging a ride from Manfred that tipped me off."

That made sense. "So are you going to do anything about it?"

"Eventually. Now that I've spilled the news that I'm married, I suspect something will shake loose." Olivia seemed pleased at the prospect.

They rode in silence for a while, each thinking her own thoughts. Fiji was worried, for her part. Olivia might "shake loose" something she couldn't handle. If Olivia's father was as powerful as she had said, even someone as capable as Olivia might not be able to stay on her feet if blow came to blow. Of course, Olivia's father's motives might be benign.

Then Fiji decided she would leave that worry to Lemuel and the future. She should be more worried about whether the planter would fit.

Luckily, it did.

21

That night, the visiting vampire, Christine, told Lemuel that in two days she would be finished translating the text of the travelogue about Texas supernatural sites.

"It is hard work translating this," she said. She had not grown on Lemuel. Her thin face and lank black hair did not impress him, she had no charm of conversation or character to soften his opinion, and her presence prevented him from mating with his woman.

"Who do you think wrote it?" Lemuel asked.

"Arria Auclina, obviously," Christine said, sounding positively snarky. Then she seemed to remember she was the underdog in the relationship. "She is the only Etruscan vampire I've heard of. She seems to have enjoyed writing this travel journal very much, and she wanted only other vampires to read it. Writing in Etruscan achieved that neatly." Christine sounded proud of her maker's maker.

"What point is there in writing a magical site guide for vampires in a language only three vampires can read?"

"I don't think Arria Auclina cared," Christine said, hardly listening. She looked exhausted.

"How can I find her? Is your maker in contact with his maker?"

"I have no idea. Dr. Quigley doesn't share his life with me any longer. I know Arria Auclina hasn't died the final death. I would have felt it. But that's all I do know. Can I go out tonight? I must drink. I can't subsist on the artificial stuff."

Lemuel, who hardly looked at Christine in the normal way of things, realized she did look peaked.

"Tomorrow night, if you've finished translating the next chapter. Here are the rules," he told her. "No one from this town. No one from Davy. Marthasville is the closest you can hunt. You can't kill anyone or leave them in an 'animal attack' state."

The visiting vampire looked rebellious. "Do you follow these rules yourself?" she asked angrily.

"When I take blood, I do," Lemuel said. "And I know you have to be discreet in Dallas, since the massacre." The Dallas massacre had impressed on all vampires the need to be discreet.

"I will follow your rules," she said, with poor grace.

"If I didn't need to work, I would take you to a good place myself," said Lemuel. "Do you drive? You can borrow my car, if you like."

"I'm not a good driver," Christine admitted. "Maybe you or your friend could take me. Since you work at night."

"We'll make a plan," Lemuel said.

"So after I translate this book, I'll be free to go back to the nest?"

"Do you want to? I don't think Joseph will pursue you if you decide to leave."

Christine looked startled. "You would let me go?"

"After you've finished the translation, you are free to go wherever you want," Lemuel said, making a sudden decision. In his opinion, he had paid more for Christine than she was worth, considering the intrusion onto his territory by the daytime servants. It would serve Joseph right if she chose to run, and Lemuel was sure it would not make Joseph really angry, since he clearly disliked Christine and had no respect for her.

Later that night, while Christine worked down in Lemuel's apartment, Olivia came up to visit with Lemuel. She had a lot to tell him. First of all, she reassured him that she missed him, and she made sure he missed her. When they stepped apart, Lemuel's eyes were not cold anymore. Olivia seemed to be very satisfied with that.

Lemuel said, "The girl needs to hunt. I didn't think about her hunger. She doesn't look good."

"What's her progress?"

"She is close to finishing, but I haven't read the newest stuff. However, I think I must let her go hunting tomorrow night. Since it has to be blood, one of us will have to take her to a bar." Lemuel's mouth pressed down tight with his distaste.

"I think it would be better if I watched the shop while you drove her," Olivia said.

"I was going to suggest the same thing. I would not have been so sure, if she had not suggested you driving her. That made me suspicious."

"I don't know if she means me harm or not. Probably, she does. I'm on the edge of wishing *her* some serious harm, myself," Olivia said. "So if you and your little buddy want to scamper off and get some grub, I'll mind the store tomorrow night."

Lemuel felt relieved and grateful. "You are the best woman I've ever met," he said. "All the way around."

Olivia gave him a slight smile. "Glad you think so, husband of mine," she said.

"I like hearing you call me that more than I ever imagined I would, wife," Lemuel said.

"Same here. Now I'm going to have a nap, down there with Miss Dark and Crazy. If you need me, ring the alarm." She winked at him; she knew he wouldn't. Bobo had had to use the alarm bell a couple of times, so far. Lemuel never had. He considered himself the trouble.

Lemuel watched Olivia leave with regret. She was good company, and he liked having her sit with him during the night shift. But he recognized that she needed to get some sleep. He hoped that soon their situation would get back to normal. Normal these days? Impossible to come by. Lemuel was glad he himself could not see dead people, as Joe and Chuy could. There were more new dead citizens of Midnight than there were live ones, even with the new convenience store manager. Lemuel had not yet had a chance to go to Gas N Go to meet Sylvester Ravenwing, but he'd had a full account from Olivia.

Lemuel usually enjoyed his night shift at Midnight Pawn. But now that people had started killing themselves, he caught himself checking the landscape at least ten times a night. He'd think, *Is someone out there?* He'd rise, go to the door, stand on the steps, look into the darkness. And every time, he saw no one: no human committing suicide.

But that night, the rats and mice began dying. Lemuel caught a tiny flicker of movement in the darkness, one so small only a vampire could have detected it. He went out into the parking lot. When he realized he was seeing a tiny mouse run toward the middle of the intersection, he took a step back out of sheer astonishment. The next moment, he was aware that he could detect many small movements, some larger than the first.

As a vampire, Lemuel had lost what little squeamishness he'd ever possessed, but he did not like vermin. Nonetheless, he stepped out into the street. He saw a few dozen creatures hurrying to the center of the road, and there, right under the stoplight, they died. After ten minutes, there was a noticeable pile of little furry bodies. A skunk arrived. Two raccoons.

How many of these will it take to equal one human death? Lemuel wondered. *The creature must feed to break out.* Though Lemuel did not yet know the name of what was buried under the crossroads, he knew it was dark and hungry.

Across the street, Fiji's front door opened, and she staggered out of her house. Afraid that she was headed to the crossroads, Lemuel threw himself across the road and ran to her, seizing her by the shoulders to stop her forward progress.

Then he understood that she was grieved for all these creatures, and she was weeping. "I had to shut Mr. Snuggly in his cage," she said. "He started to go out the cat flap, and he said he was going to die." There were scratches all over her arms.

"He put up a fight," Lemuel said.

"LET ME OUT!" screamed Mr. Snuggly from inside the house.

"That's it," Fiji said, and he understood she was crying not from sorrow, but from anger.

Lemuel got her back into her house a few minutes later, and he made her take two sleeping aids. For once, he was sorry he didn't have the power of glamour.

Lemuel came out of Fiji's house, shutting the door quietly behind him, and went to borrow the Rev's wheelbarrow and shovel from the little shed in the pet cemetery behind the chapel. It was not a surprise that the Rev was waiting for him under the traffic light, and he was praying. The mound of furry bodies was up to Lemuel's knees, but the herd of sacrifices had stopped scurrying to die.

"I don't think it's any secret what's here, Lemuel," the Rev said after his prayer was finished.

"We just have to find out how to stop it," Lemuel said. "The book is almost translated."

He and the Rev began their grim cleanup job.

"Did you feel the pull?" Lemuel asked. "Your animal nature?"

The Rev nodded to indicate that was a legitimate question. "I felt a tug," he said. "The boy, a strong one. His father held him down."

It was a long, long night. Finally, all the animals were buried and the road was cleaned up. The Rev trudged away to his house. Lemuel, grateful they had not been spotted at their corpse disposal, went back in the pawnshop to write Bobo a note, telling him that Olivia would be in charge of the shop the next night. Lemuel went downstairs feeling more tired than he could remember being, but he showered before he crawled into Olivia's bed before dawn. He smelled of small deaths.

When Lemuel's eyes opened at the next dark, he felt better. Apparently, he'd taken some energy from Olivia as he slept beside her. Soon they would not have to sleep together all night. He would have his own bed back. Lemuel loved being next to her, but he feared that he would drain Olivia by his proximity if that became a nightly situation. She was not in the room, or even downstairs, his senses told him. He dressed and made himself ready in a very short time.

He found himself a little excited at the prospect of escaping Midnight, even if the odious Christine would be with him when he left. The brooding atmosphere of *something bad's about to happen* was getting to him, the same way it was to the humans.

Lemuel swarmed up the stairs to find Olivia already on duty. She'd been chatting with Bobo. Bobo shook Lemuel's hand to give him a big sip of energy. Olivia leaned over to give Lemuel a long kiss on the cheek, and that, too, felt wonderful in more than one way.

"I'll be thinking about you," she said. "Don't let that bitch get you down."

Lemuel said, "That will be the day."

Christine stuck her head in the pawnshop. "I'm ready, Lemuel," she called. Since he was in charge of her, however temporarily, she should have addressed him as Sir or Master, but he had not insisted. Lemuel thought, *That was a mistake.* He walked out the side door and back to the residents' parking area slightly ahead of Christine, whose black hair was smoothly brushed. Christine had used the washing machine and dryer the night before, and her short dress fluttered around her legs as she made a beeline to Olivia's car. Olivia's Civic was way more anonymous than Lemuel's Vette, and vampires simply could not stand out if eating was on the agenda.

"I regret that I didn't ask you earlier about your hunger," he said as he buckled the seat belt.

"I thought it was your way of providing me with incentive to finish," she said, in such a matter-of-fact way that Lemuel was glad all over again that he didn't live in Joseph's nest in Dallas. "And I suppose it worked. I've finished translating the book."

A jolt of relief went through Lemuel, and he said, "At last! I can find out what to do, and we'll be safe, maybe."

"Yes," she said. "Maybe." Lemuel glanced over at Christine. She seemed faintly amused. He started to ask her what she'd read about Midnight, but his dignity stopped him. He would read it for himself, by himself, and determine his own course of action.

"Where are we going?" Christine asked him. "How long till we get there?"

Lemuel said, "I think we'll go to the parking lot of the Cartoon Saloon. By the time we get there, plenty of drunks will be coming out, and they're easy to sip from."

Drunks never questioned their recuperation time, either, another plus.

"After I've fed, if you will give me some money and take me to the nearest hotel, I'll work out where I'll go next," Christine said.

She was a strange piece of work, Lemuel thought. She didn't sound as excited—or, frankly, as grateful—as he would have expected, considering Joseph disliked her enough to send her to work for Lemuel, who had killed every vampire in his territory for over a century.

"What do you want your life to be, Christine?" he said.

"You haven't been interested before. Why are you interested now?" She was sullen. He could only see the back of her head as she peered out the window into the dark night. It was not as dark to a vampire as it would be to a human with regular vision, but she was certainly not sightseeing.

"I have been a bad host," he said. "I was so preoccupied by the threat to my community that I ignored your unhappiness and your hunger."

She didn't turn to face him. "You're like all men," she said. "It's easy for you to sound generous when you've gotten what you want."

Lemuel had to admit to himself that this was true. "I'm sorry that's so," he said. "Olivia tells me I live in another time, and there must be more truth to that than I thought."

"Oh, it's not your being a vampire," Christine muttered. "Men are the same, vampire or human or demon or . . . whatever they may be."

"I can't apologize for all of mankind," Lemuel said stiffly. "I can only tell you that I am sorry and hope you will excuse me. I'm afeared that in this case I was thoughtless."

She nodded, which might mean anything, and the rest of the distance to Marthasville was accomplished in silence.

When Lemuel turned into the Cartoon Saloon parking lot, enlivened by larger-than-life versions of familiar cartoon characters, Christine assessed the hunting. She watched a drunken couple staggering to the Ford F-150 two slots away, and she smiled. There was no one else in the vampire's line of sight or hearing. Quick as a wink, Christine opened the car door and was stationed by the truck door when the two humans reached it. Lemuel got out of the Civic but stayed a discreet distance away in a shadow.

"What . . . ?" the man said. He'd been reaching for the door to open it for his female friend, and instead he'd touched Christine.

"Sorry," said the woman much more sharply. She was not as drunk as her companion. "This is a private party, gal."

"Please," Christine said with a smile. "Pretty please."

She struck like lightning, drinking from the woman first, holding the man at arm's length. Lemuel watched, a little enviously. He came over once a month as the bar was closing to get a sip or two, but never more often than that. There were several other bars in Marthasville, which was a college town, and when the mood for blood took him, he visited each of them in turn.

Lemuel watched Christine, trying not to worry about her self-control. He was just about to go over and tap Christine on the shoulder to remind her that she couldn't drain anyone when she switched from the woman to the man. So far, so good, he thought, turning his back to the scene. He settled against the car. Soon, Christine would be through feeding, he'd take her to a hotel, and the next night she'd be on her way to somewhere else. . . anywhere, as far as he was concerned.

He need never see her again.

Then Christine was walking across the crunchy gravel to the Honda, and the couple was in the truck. They both appeared asleep. But the truck was running, and that seemed odd.

"What have you done?" he asked.

The vampire looked sulky. "They were hard to handle. If you had helped me, I would have found it easy."

"All you had to do was call," Lemuel said. "Have you killed them, Christine, after I gave you such specific directions?" His anger began to rise.

"I think the woman is dead," Christine said sullenly.

Lemuel threw open the car door and went over to the truck, which was shut up tight with the engine running. Christine was hoping the humans would blame the deaths on carbon monoxide, but Lemuel knew there would not be any air in the lungs of someone no longer breathing. The man was alive, but sure enough the woman was dead. At least Christine had used a dab of her blood to close the puncture marks on both necks.

Lemuel lost his temper. "You worthless bitch," he whispered. He'd taken Christine out to feed, given her guidelines, afforded her an opportunity to get away from Joseph forever . . . and she had repaid him with this trespass. His fangs ran out with the outrage. He was going to damage her for this. The only question was how severely.

Then Lemuel heard a sound that snapped him out of his anger . . . a revving engine.

Lemuel whirled to see the Honda coming right at him, Christine at the wheel.

He leaped straight up in the air, his feet barely clearing the car roof. Christine dented the truck at the spot where Lemuel had been standing. He managed to land on top of the car, knees bent, but his balance was off, and he tumbled to the ground. Just as Christine put the car in reverse, he rolled under the dented truck, and she missed him. He had his cell phone in his pocket, and he pulled it out and hit a button.

"Hello, sweetie," said Olivia. "On your way back?"

"Report your car stolen," he said, and hung up.

Lemuel scrambled to his feet on the other side of the truck. His first impulse was to let Christine go for now. He could hightail it into the cover of town, laying low until she'd given up and driven the car away. But then he thought of the blow his name would take, even if he tracked down Christine afterward.

The rare and feared vampire Lemuel Bridger had been bested by a weak bloodsucker younger than himself, other vampires would say, and they would challenge his territory . . . unless he solved this problem on the spot.

For a second, Lemuel regretted calling Olivia. She should have contacted the police by now. They'd be watching for her car. If the police stopped Olivia's car while the vampire was driving it, Christine would do her best to kill them. On the other hand, it was vital that Olivia be kept out of the trouble her vehicle had already caused.

It flashed across Lemuel's mind to call Joseph, who would be obliged to track Christine down and kill her for her rebellion since she was one of his nest.

But Lemuel discarded that idea immediately. Joseph would never let

Lemuel forget it. Lemuel was left with the appealing prospect of hunting Christine down and killing her himself, which he much preferred to do.

It was worth buying Olivia a new car.

Christine was cruising through the parking lot now, looking for him. While he'd been thinking, Lemuel had managed to keep out of Christine's sight by adroit ducks and dodges. He had to stop her from leaving, and quickly. He was surprised that the collision hadn't already alarmed the patrons of the bar. The noise level inside the Cartoon Saloon must be incredible.

Lemuel flitted from one row of cars to the next, trying to be seen. Christine spotted him and roared around the end, accelerating with every foot. Another leap put Lemuel on top of a Mustang, and then a Dodge Ram.

He and Christine played tag for a few more seconds. Even with his great strength, Lemuel was beginning to tire. Christine had gotten used to his leaping by now and was trying to time lunging the car at him to hit him where he would be.

Time to shake things up and end this.

Lemuel waited, waited, and then instead of jumping to the top of one of the next row of cars, he jumped on the hood of Olivia's car, plunging his hand through the windshield and grabbing Christine by the throat while she was still gaping at him through the glass. In her struggle, her foot left the accelerator. She thrashed and fought and scratched wildly.

Lemuel was not unscathed in this fracas. But he managed to gouge out a handful of her throat so she could not speak if she wanted to. He had to make sure she died before she could heal. He had to hurry. She was freshly fed, while he was getting weaker.

At least the car was no longer moving, but was lodged (again) against the still-running truck with its two silent passengers.

Lemuel, both arms through the windshield now that he didn't have to hold on to the car, was tearing at Christine with his fingers hooked. His head, mashed against the edge of the windshield, forced his eyes to turn to the huge cutout of Yosemite Sam with lettering in his talk-bubble that read, "Park here, podnuh!" Lemuel made an effort to reach even farther through the broken glass, even deeper. He snapped Christine's spine.

Even a vampire had to stop fighting with a broken spine. She went limp, but he didn't trust her and drove a finger through her eye to her brain.

"Lights out," he whispered, and came very close to losing consciousness. He thought he was dreaming when he saw Olivia appear beside the car with a stake in one hand, a gun in the other. He was so weak and addled that he opened his mouth to tell her he loved her, to beg her not to kill him. Instead, Olivia pulled open the car door and drove the stake into Christine's chest.

"You ruined my fucking car," she snarled. She pulled the stake out and sank it in again. "Asshole!"

"She's very dead," Lemuel said, feeling much more optimistic. "Olivia, can you give me a hand? And not one of Christine's, please."

Olivia turned to look at him for the first time. "Oh my God," she said. "Lemuel!" She eased him off the hood of the car and held him up while he wrapped his right arm around her neck. They staggered over to Lemuel's sports car.

"Go back," he said. "Open the doors of the truck and turn it off. Cover your fingers. No prints."

She ran back to the truck, which was still running, and did those things. "The woman is dead," she said. "The man is still breathing."

"Time for us to skedaddle," he said, and they climbed into Lemuel's sports car and eased carefully out of the back of the Cartoon Saloon parking lot, onto a side street where all the businesses were closed.

Olivia drove like a dream, never exceeding the speed limit and braking with such gentleness that it seemed surprising when the car actually stopped. She was trying to prevent jolting Lemuel.

"You followed me," he said, and closed his eyes to concentrate on his healing.

"Not quickly enough. But aren't you glad I did? I was almost to Marthasville when you called." He could hear the muscles in her neck as her head turned. He had never been so attuned to someone before.

"Why?"

"Why'd I follow you? I sat behind the counter for five minutes, and every minute I sat I grew more worried. I didn't trust that bitch. She looked at you with snake eyes. She was too resentful and too hungry."

"You should have . . ." But Lemuel couldn't finish the sentence. Sharp stabs of pain accompanied the healing, and his body jerked in response.

He felt her worry like a cloud filling the car. "I should have what?" she said tartly. "Should have killed her earlier? Should have remarked on how hungry she was? I figured you, as a vampire, should already know. Should have told you what a treacherous bitch she was?"

Lemuel managed to nod.

"Like you would have listened." Olivia said nothing else, which was a blessing.

"You left the shop closed," Lemuel scolded weakly, when she parked his car behind the store.

"Sue me." She ran around to his side of the car to help him out.

"I can walk," he said, and began moving carefully in a straight course for the side door. He walked slowly, but steadily.

Olivia ran ahead of him to unlock the door, and they paused for a moment on the landing while she relocked it. Then they went down the steps as quietly as they could, hoping they wouldn't wake Bobo on the top floor. Lemuel's apartment was open, as he'd left it, and he felt his way inside without turning on a light. He knew Olivia was hovering in the doorway of the bedroom.

"Come in here, if you please," Lemuel said. He'd taken off his clothes, which were probably ruined, and now he lay down on his bed. The worst of his wounds were healed, but he was exhausted. He wanted her closeness.

"Let me feed you," Olivia whispered.

Lemuel felt her hand patting to determine where he was. Then she was on the bed beside him, her warm neck pressed to his cold mouth.

Lemuel bit and felt her shiver, and then his mouth was filled with the most divine taste. Her flavor was bold and brave and bright, like Olivia. He was always mindful of the need for self-control with her, and he stopped just before he would have had to chide himself. He healed the ragged marks in her neck, and she shuddered again.

"Olivia," he whispered. Everywhere his body touched hers, he could feel the heat of her. "I admire you just as you are. But if you are ever weary of this life, I would gladly make you like me."

"I thought you'd never ask," she whispered back. "Let me think on it, Lemuel. Would we be able to stay together?"

"I am not like most vampires, as you know. We'd be able to, as long as it suited us. I know there are disadvantages to being both energy and blood fueled. But there are some good things about it, too."

"Disadvantages?"

Olivia already sounded sleepy. He put his arm around her. Possibly he could get her closer. "I can't hide what I am," he said. "Everyone who looks at me knows I am not human. And I'm not beautiful like so many of the blood vampires."

"You were changed by someone who loved you," she murmured. "That has to make a difference."

Lemuel had never thought of that. He did now, lying with Olivia in his arms, both of them on the verge of sleep.

"What happened to your wife?" Olivia said, suddenly sounding a bit more alert. It was not only Lemuel who was thinking of something for the first time.

"The man who'd changed her. He came to woo her a few years

later, and by that time we were strapped. Two energy suckers in an area with a thin population and very little transient traffic . . . it just wouldn't work in those days. I was trying to live as I had when I was alive, plowing the fields at night, moving the cattle around then, too. That wasn't working, either. I had never been anything but poor and a cowboy. I had always planted just enough for my wife and me. We'd never had any but stillborn children, thank God, because after our days and nights reversed, what would have happened to them?"

"So this man came back? And he took your wife away with him?"

"He did. By that time, we were broke with each other. She'd changed me to save my life, but the life we had together wasn't worth it. Yet we didn't have much of any idea of how to change it."

"Tell me the rest later?"

"Surely."

"Night-night."

He smiled over her head in the darkness, and then they were both asleep.

No customers came to Midnight Pawn in the hours before the sun was up, but three skunks, a fox, and seven opossums died under the traffic light that night.

The creature underneath raised a finger. It had not moved in almost two hundred fifty years.

22

Bobo rose early in the morning and went to the front window to check for dead people. The Rev was heading away from the intersection with a wheelbarrow full of limp animals. Diederik was trailing after the old minister, so Bobo didn't run down to offer his own help. He turned away, shaking his head. It was obvious this wasn't going to be an ordinary day, and Bobo wondered if there would ever be an ordinary day again.

Bobo dressed with some haste, and he took his bowl of oatmeal down to the shop with him. There was a new note beside the cash register, which he read with some bewilderment.

Arthur Smith walked through the door within the hour. Since he was the sheriff, he didn't have to wear a uniform, though he usually preferred to. Today, Smith was very well turned out in a navy blazer, sharply pressed khakis, and a starched white shirt. His tie was a cheerfully subdued plaid of blue and green and a hint of red.

"Looking good," Bobo said by way of greeting.

"Thanks," Arthur said uncomfortably. "Ah, I have a thing later."

"Okay. What can I do for you before you have your thing?" Bobo added together Arthur's discomfort, the fact that he'd been seeing Magdalena Orta Powell very steadily, and Arthur's romantic history. Bobo suspected that Arthur was about to get married again.

"I can't rouse your tenants."

Of course, Bobo had heard Arthur try the side door, so this was no news to him. He had wondered if he should intervene, but he'd correctly figured Arthur would come into the shop through the front door. "The side door stays locked until one of us goes out that way, Arthur. Of course you can't see Lemuel, it's daytime. I can't believe you tried. Olivia worked the counter in here last night, too. Is this about her car?" (The note had said, "Bobo, my car was stolen last night, so people may show up asking for me. Olivia.")

"Yes, mostly," Arthur said. He still looked grim. "Lemuel is all right?"

"As far as I know. I can go check, if you want."

"That would be a relief to me."

Bobo went out the side door to the landing and downstairs. He heard a little stirring in Olivia's apartment, so he knocked softly. She opened the door so swiftly he was startled and stepped back.

"What's up?" she said. She'd just showered and was wrapped in a towel. Her auburn hair trickled drops of water on her shoulders.

"Is Lem okay? The sheriff is upstairs asking. What happened?" Bobo whispered.

"Lemuel's fine. Tell Arthur I'll be up in just a minute," she said. "I can explain then." Her voice was at a normal level. "You could shout and Lem wouldn't wake up, you know."

"Right," Bobo said, a little embarrassed. Up the stairs he went to relay Olivia's message. He and Arthur had a calm exchange of pleasantries until she came in. She looked pale to Bobo, but he noticed she had put on makeup and an outfit that was nicer than her usual Midnight wear.

"Arthur, thanks for coming in person about my car. Did you find it?" Olivia was all hopefulness.

"We did find your car, but I'm afraid I have bad news," Arthur said. "There was a small amount of ash that was a different color in the front seat. We think it was a dead vampire. And the car was wrecked. It had evidently bounced around like a pinball between the cars in the parking lot at the Cartoon Saloon in Marthasville."

"A dead vampire?" Olivia seemed genuinely startled. "I didn't think there was enough left of them after they died. I mean, to tell a vampire was there."

"There was a pile of flaky stuff left," Arthur said. "I'd never seen anything like it, but I've read about it in law enforcement journals. It matched the pictures I've seen of vampire remains." He paused. "Were you were out last night?"

"Briefly," she said. "But most of the night, I was helping Lemuel. He had the night shift here in the pawnshop, as usual."

"And by 'helping,' you mean . . . ?"

"Keeping him company," she said promptly. "He's my sweetie."

The idea of Lemuel as a "sweetie" made Bobo turn away with a grin.

"And when you say you were out?" Arthur was persistent. It was his job.

Olivia turned to Bobo. "Don't get mad, but Lem and I took a walk. It was such a pretty night we couldn't resist. And we were only gone thirty minutes. But during that time, my car went missing! Or at least that was when I noticed it was gone."

"I don't suppose you left your key fob in it?"

"No," she said. It had actually been in Lemuel's pocket.

"Can you narrow down how long it might have been missing?"

"I used the Civic yesterday afternoon," she said, looking thoughtful. "I drove to Davy and back. After that, I didn't take it out. I can't remember looking behind the store for any reason. So I guess it was stolen between five p.m. and one a.m. I hardly see how it could have been taken in the daytime, so I'd imagine it was taken after dark."

Arthur didn't respond to that. "Could I see your key fob?"

She pulled a key ring out of her pocket and showed it to him. "Here it is," she said. "Plus side door key and apartment key."

"These haven't left your possession?"

"No," she said.

"What about your extra key fob?"

"I checked last night, and it's in a drawer in my apartment."

"That was some talented vampire," Bobo said. "Knew how to boost a car without keys. Hey, how is that possible?"

"Usually, your fob has to be within a couple of feet to open your car," Arthur said. "But there's a device called a power amplifier. If the fob is within a certain radius, it can open the car and a thief can start it."

"Damn," Bobo said, truly amazed. "I had no idea. And you say Olivia's car is totaled?"

"Looks totaled to me," Arthur said. "And not only did a vampire die and the car get totaled, along with a lot of damage to others, but the Civic hit a pickup truck so hard that the woman inside snapped her neck, and the man who was with her is in intensive care. At least that is what we're assuming happened to them."

"That's awful," Bobo said. "Do you think he'll make it?"

"Maybe," Arthur said.

"But surely Olivia can't be held liable for the woman's death and the man's injuries?" Bobo was indignant. "I mean, after all! Her car got stolen!"

"I'm really sorry for all of this," Olivia said. "But at least the dead vampire isn't Lemuel, and the man in the hospital may recover. I'll try to focus on that." She looked determined and brave. "Oh, by the way, and far down on the list, I called my insurance agent first thing this morning. Matt Wrigley. To alert him about the theft. Did he contact you?"

Arthur nodded. "One of my deputies talked to him. When he described the situation, Matt said he'd call you later today, after he'd seen your car."

"I've only had the Civic for three years, and I got a great deal on it secondhand. Now I'll have to go through the process again." Olivia's expression was sour.

She's genuinely chagrined about that, at least, Bobo thought. Abruptly, he longed to simply walk out of the pawnshop and across the road to Fiji's place. He wanted to sit on her back porch and drink any beverage she cared to offer him. He wanted to have an ordinary conversation with her. Maybe he could hold her hand while they talked. That would be so nice. He missed her so much. She'd called him when Teacher had searched her house, but since then she'd reverted to keeping her distance.

"Bobo!" From her tone, Bobo understood Olivia had said his name several times.

"Sorry, I was daydreaming," he said.

"If the insurance guy comes in here, can you call me to come up?" she said. "I'm going to be doing some research on another vehicle, on my laptop."

"Sure." That unnecessary instruction had been worth interrupting his thoughts?

"Olivia, at least you know what happened to your car," Arthur said. He, too, did not sound pleased. "I guess it's just an amazing coincidence that you happen to date the only vampire in a large radius, and then a vampire stole your car out of all the cars within that radius, and then that vampire died in that car after wrecking it for no reason."

"An amazing coincidence," Olivia agreed seriously.

And with that, Arthur left.

Olivia said, "He was looking good." She sounded very calm and innocent.

"My guess is that he's getting married again. He was sure dressed up." Bobo walked to the front window and looked across the road at Fiji's cottage.

Sylvester Ravenwing walked by.

"That's the new guy at the gas station," Bobo said. "What's he doing out of the store?"

"Speaking of looking good," Olivia said. "That guy is completely hot. And my second question would be, why's he going to Manfred's?"

They moved in unison to watch the new guy cross the lawn to the house next door.

"Huh," said Bobo. He was curious, too.

"Interesting," said Olivia.

And then an ancient pickup pulled up out front of Midnight Pawn, and an equally ancient man unloaded a large tin statue of a horse from the back.

"I'll leave you to all the excitement," Olivia said. "You better get the door for him."

"Thanks," muttered Bobo when she'd gone. After one more longing look across the street at Fiji's place, he hurried to open the door.

As the old man struggled into Midnight Pawn, Bobo noticed that Ravenwing was knocking at Manfred's door.

23

Hello?" Manfred said. His brows drew together at seeing a stranger, which did odd things to Manfred's piercings.

"You haven't been in the store yet to greet me," the stranger said.

"Ah, sorry? Who are you?"

"Sylvester Ravenwing."

"Okay, pleased to meet you. I'm Manfred Bernardo." He shook Ravenwing's hand and turned away to return to his desk. But Ravenwing didn't budge. "Ahhhh . . . did you want to come in?"

"I do. We need to talk."

Mystified, Manfred took a step back. "Come to the kitchen," he said. "I have some Coca-Cola. Or tea. Or I can make coffee."

"Tea is fine."

Manfred led the way back, and he just knew Sylvester's eyes were taking in the shabby, comfortable house.

Soon Manfred and his unexpected (and unwanted) guest were ensconced at the kitchen table. Manfred was vaguely aware that if he had been Fiji, he could have offered cookies or something, but that was very much not the case. He did brew the tea, and during this process his unexpected visitor did not say a word.

"You were brought up by your grandmother," Sylvester said, as soon as Manfred had put the tea on the table and pulled out a chair.

No other conversational opener could have startled Manfred more. "Why do you want to know?" he asked, then slapped himself mentally. By the sound of it, Sylvester wasn't asking a question but stating a familiar fact.

"I knew her," Sylvester said, and that was another earth-shaker.

"Then you probably know that after a certain point my mom couldn't put up with me so she handed me over to my grandmother," Manfred said. "And Xylda and I got along like a house afire. While my mother lived with the regret she had about that, and still does. Though she's happier now she's married." His eyes narrowed, he waited for Sylvester's next move.

"I knew Xylda when she was very young," Sylvester said.

"How?" Manfred was tired of all this pussy-footing.

"We were together for a while."

Manfred had three instant and equally violent reactions. He was struck dumb. He also had a hundred things to say. And he wanted to punch Sylvester. These did not blend well, and he began coughing. He inhaled sharply, held the breath. Then he slowly exhaled. The biggest secrets in his family had been the identity of his mother's father and the identity of his own. Sometimes Xylda had claimed the man she'd married had been Rain's father. Sometimes she had just smiled when he'd asked her.

"You don't look old enough," Manfred said, and congratulated himself on his even voice.

Sylvester said, "She aged, but I stayed this way."

"Are you human?" Manfred asked.

"Not completely." Sylvester's face was impassive, which Manfred simply could not understand. He had to be having an emotion about this—regret, or . . . something? Anything?

"Are you—my grandfather?" Manfred said, almost holding his breath at the enormity of this question. He wasn't sure he wanted to know the answer.

"I am," Sylvester said.

Manfred's breath whooshed out. He didn't know if he was relieved or disappointed. Mostly, he was terrified. After all these years . . . an answer. At least one. "Okay, a few questions," he began cautiously. "How come we don't look anything alike? I mean, at *all*."

"I don't always look like this," Sylvester said.

Again, not what Manfred had expected. "*Aaaaargh*," he said. "I'll come back to that later. Did you ever see my grandmother after your, um, fling?"

"I think two years is more than a fling. Yes, I saw Xylda from time to time. But not in her last ten years."

"So you know she died?" Manfred said slowly.

"Yes. Her light blinked out in my heart."

"Flowery. But you didn't come to her deathbed. You didn't attend her funeral."

"I was very fond of her, nonetheless."

"So just to be absolutely clear, my mother is your daughter."

"She is."

"But she's not anything like you. Or me. And she sure as hell can't change her appearance."

"No. Everything skipped a generation. That happens sometimes. Xylda told me that her grandfather was the one who'd had the power before her."

Manfred dimly recalled Xylda telling him the same thing. "Do we have to do this question by question? Can't you just tell me the story?" Manfred forced himself to take a sip of tea. His hands were shaking.

"I am not so good at telling histories. But I'll do my best. I was born to Chickasaws in the area now known as Tennessee. My mother, Squirrel Hands, was a wise woman. Her husband had just died, and she was childless. She wanted a son more than anything. She knew she had the sickness in her belly, the same one that had killed her own mother. When she met up with a demon named Colconnar—and she was never clear about how that happened, whether he had sought her out or she had summoned him—she struck a bargain with him. Her bargain was this: that in return for becoming free of the sickness, she would bear the child of Colconnar. Demons rarely breed to make their own babies, which perhaps you knew."

Manfred shook his head faintly.

"No? Huh." Sylvester seemed a little disappointed. "My mother got Colconnar to agree that she would have her child with her as long as she lived."

Manfred nodded. *This story is not going to end well,* he thought.

Sylvester nodded gravely back. He continued, "Colconnar—my father—had said he would take the cancer away. He did. But he did not guarantee Squirrel Hands that she would be healthy, and she didn't think of asking for that. Whether Colconnar caused it or not, my mother got an inflamed appendix, or maybe some womb infection—at least, those are my best guesses. I was about ten, maybe twelve, when my mother died, after considerable suffering. The moment she was dead, Colconnar came to get me."

Manfred had heard stranger stories and believed them. "There were other people there?" he asked. "Members of your tribe?"

Sylvester nodded.

"Did they see him?"

"How would I know? He took me. I didn't get to do any post-abduction interviews." Sylvester looked at Manfred as though he were wondering if his grandson was deficient.

Manfred reminded himself to be patient. "All right. So you went with your father. Did you know who he was?"

"Oh, he told me who he was right away. I believed him. If you had seen him, you would have believed him, too." And Sylvester shivered.

Manfred tried not to think about how frightening that must have been for a preteen boy. "So were things a lot different? With your dad? I know that's a stupid question, but I guess I want to know how you managed . . . in demon-land. I guess it's not actually below us."

"Different realm," Sylvester said. "A different dimension, I think. Different creatures. Different laws." All the lines of his face were drawn and grim as he told Manfred this.

"Why'd he want you?"

"Good question," said Sylvester, for the first time showing some approval. "He was preparing me to be useful, so he could offer me to his ruler as a servant. Colconnar was proud of having a son. I would have been a rare gift."

"But that didn't happen?"

"Colconnar sent me out into the earth. Time had passed differently. Everything had changed. There were white people everywhere." Sylvester Ravenwing looked sad. "He'd sent me here, though there was no town then, no Midnight. He ordered me to verify the report that a powerful witch was living in this area. Demons enjoy having sex with witches, especially virgin witches, though the witches don't always survive it."

Manfred winced. "So you found the witch."

"I did, and I liked her. I was so impressed with her that I confessed why I had come. My father would be coming for her. She had had a forewarning, and she was gathering people to help her, other people with magical abilities."

By now, Manfred could see where this story was going. "She planned to trap him?"

"Yes, grandson. She called together everyone of power she could find, because Colconnar was strong. If he gave me to his lord, the sacrifice of his son would gain him power. If he had sex with the witch, he would gain even more power. His ambition was to establish a kingdom on earth, a place all his own."

"What about the rest of the demons? Why didn't they want to do the same thing?"

"Do all humans want to conquer Russia? Or Australia?"

Manfred had no answer for that. "So did the witch and her crew bind the demon?"

"Yes, they did."

"How?"

"I don't know."

"But you were here!"

"No, I was not. My presence would amplify Colconnar's power, the witch said. And she sent me away to Tennessee."

"So you don't know what happened."

"I do know that Colconnar is still trapped."

"But not how." Manfred slumped his face in his hands. "And there's a demon under the crossroad. Okay, how'd you meet Xylda?"

"I traveled for years in what had become America. Sometimes I looked like my Indian self, and sometimes I looked like a white man. I kept going back to Tennessee, because it was my birthplace, and very beautiful. To my surprise, there came a sort of fashion for Indians, as we were called, and the remnants of my tribe held exhibitions there, of tribal dances and crafts and so on. Though I was a half-demon, and my Indian people knew that on some level, they still claimed me. They allowed me to use my magic nature to train as a shaman. It was very strange to be valued rather than killed off. At one of these 'Native American' events, I met your grandmother Xylda. She was lonely, and she was wild and beautiful, too." Sylvester smiled broadly. "Her gifts had made it hard for her to have friends. She was shunned in the community."

I know what that feels like, Manfred thought.

"She was delighted when we met. It was her birthday, and she had no one to celebrate it with. We came together by way of celebration, and we stayed together for two years. We were the first for each other, and I know she wore my necklace until the day she died. I could feel it."

"The necklace." Manfred searched his memory. "The freshwater pearls?"

Sylvester nodded.

"She did wear it always. But you *left*."

"She didn't think I would make a good father for the child, when she did a reading of your mother as baby. She married a human man to teach your mother how to be human. Since I couldn't."

"So why are you here, now?" *It can't be a coincidence*, Manfred thought. "You're not just here to do your grandparental duty by me."

"That's the important part." Sylvester looked even sterner than before. "I will tell you."

Sylvester's narrative style left a lot to be desired. Manfred was heartsick and had too much to think about to know where to begin. "Get to the point," he said.

"However the witch imprisoned my father, the spell has lasted two hundred fifty years, and it's about to wear out." Sylvester was pleased to have finally gotten to what he considered the main point.

"You're going to have to do some more talking," Manfred said. "Everyone needs to hear this."

24

That evening at Home Cookin, Quinn and Diederik were eating at the big round table the locals used, while the Rev was settled at his normal table for one. The Rev was not much for conversation during meals, or at any time.

Soon after the two weretigers sat down, they were joined by Olivia, and then Chuy and Joe. The two men looked incomplete without Rasta.

"We can check on him with our phones," Joe said. "We can see him in his kennel at the vet's. We miss the little fella, but until the situation here is settled, that's where he should stay."

"He's just too small a creature to handle all this," Chuy said sadly. "The suicides, the tension, and now the smell."

"Smell?" Diederik took a long drink of chocolate milk.

"Hasn't the air seemed different to you?" his father asked. Quinn tried to speak gently, but there was an unmistakable chiding note in his words. Weretigers should be alert to smells and sights around them.

"It seems a little bitter," Diederik said. "Like grapefruit, burned."

"Not a bad description," Quinn said, feeling relieved. "I'm wondering if you should be taken somewhere away from this. This is not a healthy place."

"Father," Diederik said sharply. "I'm not Rasta. I'm a man now, and I have to take my place in the world."

Bobo, who had just entered, paused in the act of pulling out a chair. He looked at Diederik askance.

"If we knew what that place was." Quinn didn't think of himself as a worrier, but this evening he was troubled. The only son he was ever likely to have was in a dangerous location, where the supernatural world and the natural world felt like they were coming closer to each other every night.

"My place is here, with the people who raised me," his son told him, with a definite overtone of "Duhhh."

"Diederik," said a rusty voice from the table by the window, finally breaking the silence. The boy flinched, glancing over at the Rev and then back to Quinn. What he saw in Quinn's face made him feel even worse.

"Excuse me, Father," Diederik said, his words tumbling over each other. "I know you've done your best to protect me, even if it meant your absence. I know I need to learn your business, so I can carry it on. But I love it here."

"Then you'll be glad to know we've bought a house in Midnight," Quinn said, trying to salvage the moment he'd thought would be so happy.

There was a moment of blank silence. Then Diederik started laughing, and Chuy and Joe smiled, and even the Rev looked a little less grim.

"You all are moving to town to stay?" Madonna had come to the table to take their orders. "Welcome to the neighborhood."

Everyone at the table was disconcerted, not by the purchase of a house by John Quinn, but because none of them had thought of the

Reeds as permanent residents. Before Madonna could take offense at that moment of silence, Diederik picked up little Grady, who had staggered over to the table on unsteady legs, and swung him high. Grady threw up his hands and laughed, and they all laughed with him. Diederik leaned over to kiss Quinn's cheek.

It was a very happy moment for Quinn.

Lenore Whitefield, who managed the hotel, came in then, and though the Midnighters continued to talk, they were all surprised. Lenore and her husband, Harvey (a jerk no one liked, except presumably Lenore), had kept aloof from the little Midnight community. It was natural they would not interact that often. The hotel bought its groceries in Davy. It only employed a handful of people: a cook from Davy at breakfast time, another one who came in for lunch and dinner, a maid, evening clerk Marina, and Diederik. Lenore did a large share of the maid work while Harvey sat at the desk.

Now, however, Lenore needed something. That was evident in her stance. "Mrs. Reed, do you have a moment?" she asked, perching on one of the seldom-used stools at the counter.

"I will in ten, fifteen minutes," Madonna said, glancing at the clock by the door to the kitchen. "If you can wait that long?"

"I can," said Lenore. She swiveled on the stool to look at the table where the others were sitting. "Hi, Diederik! Who's your buddy?"

"This is Grady, Mrs. Whitefield," Diederik said. He waved baby Grady's hand at the woman. "How are you?"

"I'm just fine." She seemed a bit bemused at Diederik's careful manners. "Hi, Mr. Quinn. I hope you're enjoying your stay at the hotel. We sure like to have repeat guests like you."

"Yes, it's very comfortable," Quinn said. "And thanks for employing my son."

"Not many people want to mop and clean anymore," Lenore said, shaking her head. Her short brown hair, heavily shot with gray, was thick and wiry, giving it somewhat the appearance of a dog's coat. The accepted opinion in Midnight was that Lenore was a nice enough person, not extremely bright, clinging to her job with desperate tenacity since it had rescued her and Harvey from dire straits. She seemed to be direct and honest.

It was a good food night at Home Cookin, but then every night was at least pretty good, ranging up to sublime. Madonna Reed might not have won any personality contests, but she could (dammit) cook. Even Chuy, who was quite the chef himself, took his hat off to Madonna, at least metaphorically.

"What are you eating tonight, Bobo?" Lenore asked.

"Catfish and hush puppies and slaw," Bobo said. "There aren't any bad choices, though."

When Madonna brought in the food, Lenore looked at their plates with keen interest. As soon as all the customers had been served, Madonna came to lean on the counter to talk to her.

"What's on your mind, Lenore?" Madonna had never wasted time on casual conversation.

"You probably know I have a cook coming from Davy to help with breakfasts for everyone, and then someone else comes to cook lunch and dinner for the residents. The nonresidents have to fend for themselves."

Madonna nodded, and everyone at the table scrambled to say something to each other so it would appear they weren't listening.

"Well, my morning cook is still fine. But my lunch and dinner cook is about to quit. Since we only have four residents at the moment, I think I can do lunch. Soup and sandwiches, that kind of thing. I was hoping you'd agree to do the dinners."

"For the residents, only."

"If that works out, maybe we could talk about supplying something for the transient guests? A few stay for weeks since they're doing contract work at Magic Portal." Magic Portal, the large company east of Midnight that manufactured games, was a major employer in the area and also responsible for the great Internet connections available in Midnight. Plus most of the hotel's clientele.

"But I'm just starting off with the residents. How would we convey the food? Four extra meals won't make much difference to my workload, I figure."

"I have a cart that Harvey can wheel over. Do you have plate covers? Cloches?"

"I have some in back, yes. Previous owner left 'em. They're very old, but usable."

"So I propose that Harvey would come to get the dinners for the residents at five thirty. We would have given them their choices earlier in the day."

"Harvey will also return the dishes?"

"Yes, he'll return them the next day by lunchtime."

"I'll give you an answer tomorrow. I'll have to figure out what to charge for this."

"Let me know. I'm really, really hoping you'll say yes."

Madonna nodded. When Lenore had gone back to the hotel, Chuy said, "You gonna do it, Madonna?"

"Hell, yeah," she said. "That's gonna add up. I might have to work an hour longer, but the money should be worth it. I'll have to do some figuring."

Nothing else exciting happened during the meal, though Madonna did ask all of them where Fiji was. "She hasn't come in here in days, and that's not like her," Madonna said, with a smile that struck Quinn as off. He also noticed that Olivia looked down, guarding her expression.

When they'd all eaten, Quinn told his son he'd see him later, and the boy left for his job, a smile on his face at the prospect of seeing Marina, Quinn figured. Quinn paid at the same time as Olivia, and when she left, he followed her to the pawnshop. As she was about to go inside, he hailed her.

"You following me, tiger?"

She didn't seem alarmed, but mildly irritated.

"It's not hard to walk in the same direction as someone in Midnight," Quinn said. "But I have to say that I'm really curious. What is the big secret between you and Fiji, the one about Madonna?"

He hadn't hit the mark exactly, Quinn told himself, judging Olivia's reaction.

"Big secret?" She smiled. "I don't know any big secret. I've always been curious about the Reeds. Haven't you?"

"You mean how they manage to keep the restaurant open? Of course, but there's something else about them. Something that seems significant to you."

"I don't know what that would be," she said. She went inside.

Quinn watched her go and then spun to face the shop across the road. Before he could convince himself it was none of his business, he ran across. His feet made almost no sound when they touched the pavement.

Fiji had just finished her supper and was washing up when Quinn knocked at her back door. "Quinn," she said. "Hi. Come on in." She took the chain off the door. Mr. Snuggly, who adored Quinn, appeared instantly and began basting himself against Quinn's ankles.

"Snug, stop it," Fiji said.

"I don't mind. Hi, little brother." Mr. Snuggly did not reply, but he did purr.

"Please have a seat." Fiji sat down in her accustomed place at the kitchen table and gestured at the chair opposite. Quinn worked himself into the small space and looked at her with frank appreciation. "Looking lovely," he said, and she made a little derisive sound. He ignored it. "I'm going to ask you some questions," he said, "and I hope you answer them. If you don't . . . okay."

"Let's have the questions."

"Is there a reason you haven't been to Home Cookin in a few days?"

"Yes," she said, without hesitation.

"Is Madonna angry with you?"

"Yes."

"Goddamn it, Fiji, this is like playing hot or cold with a kid."

"Yes," she said, and laughed out loud at his indignant face. "Okay, I'll tell you about it, like I told Bobo. But I'm not telling you the whole story, because the whole thing is not mine to tell."

"Fair enough," Quinn said.

Fiji told him about catching Teacher coming out of her house, about what Mr. Snuggly had told her, and about her subsequent reprisal. She also told him about Teacher's connection in Killeen, without going into any specifics.

"I get that you're leaving out parts of the story, and I feel like those parts have to do with Olivia," Quinn said. "What I don't get is why Teacher would search your house if he's here to watch Olivia. And that changes my ideas about Olivia and her background, because setting up a whole business and a whole family to watch one person requires deep pockets."

"Yes, it does," she agreed. "If you ask me, that's why the hotel got renovated."

"What does that have to do with anything?"

"Because—oh, shit, I'm getting into Olivia's business again!" Fiji was angry with herself. "I believe Teacher's been searching all our homes all along, whenever he had a moment, just to see if the rest of us were who we said we were."

"What's so important about Olivia?"

And Fiji stared at him, her lips pressed together. Quinn felt like shaking her to knock loose the secrets. Instead, he leaned across the table and kissed her.

It was a really satisfying kiss. She was warm and soft, and she smelled great, and she had that magic running internally that made every kiss zing through his blood. For the tenth time, Quinn wondered if witches were born or made. He was pretty sure that either you had magic in your blood, or you didn't. Fiji definitely did.

He was bent across the table in a strange position, so before he was really ready to stop, he had to break off. He sat back in his chair.

For a minute, Fiji looked dazed. After she recovered herself (and he couldn't help but be pleased that it took a moment), she said, "Okay, that was sensational. But I'm still not going to tell you." She smiled as she said it, just a little, so Quinn would know she didn't really believe he'd been trying to bribe her to spill all with a kiss.

"I like you," Quinn said directly. "And I have a suspicion that in private, you work magic that we can't even imagine."

Fiji smiled. "You're right. I do. No double entendre."

"You're not going to give me a hint about Olivia? About your problems?"

"Nope. Not mine to tell."

"So I'll have to approach Olivia herself." He shook his head.

"Yeah, good luck with that," she said. She stood, which was a pretty clear signal for him to leave.

He loped back to the hotel, not quite suppressing a smile. The kiss had been rewarding. *It's been too long since I had a good companion,* Quinn thought.

Diederik was on the brink of going out on his own.

In view of that realization, his kiss with Fiji took on a much more interesting cast.

25

Olivia said, "Telling him I'm married is sure to flush them out."

"And that's what you want?" Lemuel was reading the translation Christine had worked so hard on. He knew what Olivia was telling him was important to her (and therefore to him) personally, but he was pretty sure the text was even more important. At least in the Midnight universe, and just at this moment.

"I'm tired of this underhand game. I want to know who the players are and who's backing them." Olivia was exercising as she talked, and the flexing of her limber body was doing nothing to aid Lemuel's concentration. Since she'd slept extra during the day, she had cleared a space for stretching in the herd of chairs occupying the pawnshop's center. Lemuel watched from the high stool behind the counter, the handwritten translation before him.

He tore his gaze from the papers to look at Olivia. "If your father has tracked you down to watch you, he's done nothing to make you think he will harm you. The Reeds are acting on his behalf? They haven't raised a finger against you. In the past three years, there's been many a time they could have acted against you."

Olivia paused in her squats. "Okay, I concede that."

"The more serious threat, if I'm understanding you correctly, is that your father's right-hand man is watching you separately and unknown to your father."

She nodded vigorously as she began doing lunges. "He was responsible for the man who tried to grab me when I was breaking into the Goldthorpe house."

"Yes, you heard him say the name over his . . . walkie-talkie?"

"Cell phone. Yes, I did."

"So he seems bent on capturing you. However, we haven't seen his agents here."

"One of them is responsible for the hotel."

"But which one?"

"My dad owns the company that renovated the hotel. Manfred traced it back, and back, until he got to the source. Of course, he didn't know that the president of the company was my dad, whose name is Nicholas Wicklow."

This was the first time that Lemuel had heard her father's name. "Thanks for trusting me with it," he said. "I wondered if you would."

"My real name," she said, with air of someone doing a very necessary but distasteful task, "is Melanie Horton Wicklow."

"No, that's your birth name," Lemuel said. "Your real name is Olivia Charity."

She smiled at him, and his heart felt at ease. "Though she always made me call her Mother, my stepmother's name was Tiffany, and I hope she never rests in peace."

"What about your real mother—your biological mother, as they say now?"

"I didn't know her very well. Her name was Cara," Olivia said.

"From the pictures, I look like her. Maybe another reason for Mo—*Tiffany* to do what she did."

"But you're uncertain about your father's knowledge of her abuse."

"I waver back and forth," Olivia said, almost reluctantly. "Now I feel he didn't know. But I also think you don't know something like that if you *aren't paying attention*."

"Yes," Lemuel agreed.

Olivia sat on the floor cross-legged, bent forward, and stood on her hands, her legs still crossed. Lemuel eyed her with admiration and a touch of exasperation. "Woman," he said, "we have to talk."

"I thought we were."

"We have to talk about another topic, as interesting as I find this rare conversation about your family."

Olivia rolled back into a sitting stance and looked up at him, her eyebrows raised in query. "What is it, Lemuel?"

"We must call the town together," he said. "I think we are about to be killed."

Her phone rang.

"Olivia," said Manfred. "We have to have a town meeting. Sylvester's forty-eight hours are up."

26

The ground floor of Midnight Pawn was far larger than it appeared from the outside. The bare boards of the old floor creaked as the people of Midnight assembled and chose seats. Part of the fun of gathering in the pawnshop was trying out the eccentric assembly of chairs that had accumulated over the years.

But those coming into the pawnshop were somber, in no mood for fun. Bobo descended from his apartment as rumpled as if he'd already gone to bed, though it was only nine o'clock. When Fiji arrived, she looked exasperated. She'd been in the middle of practicing something, Lemuel deduced, from the stained bib apron still covering her T-shirt and jeans. Also, she smelled like sage.

Manfred entered and took a seat, but he didn't greet anyone. He sat staring down at his hands as if he had something very much on his mind. Diederik left work to run over to the meeting. He smelled of Marina Desoto. Quinn came with him. No one objected to his presence. It seemed right.

Chuy and Joe sat side by side, holding hands, Lemuel noticed. It was unusual for them to display affection in public.

Olivia had told Lemuel more than once that she didn't understand how he could be so tolerant of other people's sex lives and reticent about his own with her. Lemuel thought, *I have always liked privacy for myself.* And his strongest emotions were personal emotions, saved to be savored between himself and one other person.

With no fanfare or tentativeness, Sylvester Ravenwing slid silently through the door and took his seat among them. He sat by Manfred. Ravenwing nodded to Lemuel. They had met once, both out on a stormy night. Lemuel didn't challenge the newcomer's right to be at the meeting. He was definitely a Midnighter. Chuy and Joe, however, stared at Sylvester Ravenwing with some suspicion.

"What's up?" Bobo asked, once they were all assembled. He was doing his best not to stare at Fiji, Lemuel noticed. And Fiji resolutely kept her face turned from him. It was sad to see trouble between them.

"I was kind of in the middle of something," Fiji said. A couple of faces turned to her. Fiji had never sounded this snappish before.

Lemuel waited until they all were paying attention. It didn't take long. "I just finished reading the translation of the text I hoped would explain what is happening here," Lemuel said. "And I will tell you. Manfred has told me that Sylvester Ravenwing also has things to tell us."

"What did you find, Lemuel?" Olivia asked. She was sitting on the edge of a wooden chair at least fifty years old.

"The creature buried under the crossroad is a demon, and he's about to rise," Lemuel said.

There was a long moment of silence.

"The demon's been talking to me," Fiji said.

Everyone else was frozen in place by this revelation. Finally, Quinn said, "Okay. Let's hear about this. Maybe starting with Lemuel."

"Crossroads have a lot of magical connotations," Lemuel said. "Places to put magical sites, like cairns. Places to worship, places to bury suicides, places to execute criminals and to leave the bodies as warnings."

"I think we're all aware of the magic of crossroads," Chuy said, and Joe placed a warning hand on Chuy's shoulder.

"Not me," Diederik said cheerfully.

Manfred cleared his throat. "Maybe I can shortcut this process. I think you've all met Sylvester, who's taken over the Gas N Go. Sylvester has told me he's my grandfather. It's his father who's buried out there." Manfred jerked his head in the stoplight direction. "The demon. My great-grandfather."

After another long, significant pause, Fiji got up and went over to the two. She looked down at Sylvester, whose dark eyes met hers with a sort of recognition, a kinship.

"You didn't say anything when I came in the store?" she asked, because of that look. "You've had magical training."

"I had to talk to Manfred first," Sylvester said. "Yes, I studied shamanism with my people. I'll need the skill. The time is close at hand. You say you've been hearing his voice?"

"Yes."

"Demons love witches, for their power. They like to consume it," Sylvester said, in a disturbing, matter-of-fact way. "But no mistake, you have the power to imprison him again. So he wants you on his side."

"So this demon's tried to pull people who don't like me to the circle, and get them to kill themselves, to make me believe he's on my side. A *demon* has been talking to me," she said slowly, as if this were the worst thing that had ever happened to her. Maybe it was.

Sylvester nodded.

"Your father is a full demon?" said an echoing voice.

Everyone jumped, and they all looked around for the source of the voice.

"It's Joe," Diederik whispered. "His wings are back."

Chuy's were, too. The two men were standing in a haze of light, and they had drawn swords, and their wings reached almost to the ceiling.

"Yes," Sylvester said. "I helped to imprison him. His name is Colconnar."

"Don't speak his name," Chuy said, his voice echoing like Joe's. "It's an abomination."

The Rev stood, too. The scrawny old man looked terrifying. "Brothers," he said. "We all stand together this night."

Olivia ducked her head. She whispered, "*Wow.*"

"Joe and Chuy, your presence is glorious," said Lemuel. "But Col— the demon's return to earth is a crisis we can forestall with Sylvester's help."

The swords gradually vanished, but the outline of the wings remained. Sylvester went down on one knee before the angels to show respect and then sat. He nodded at Lemuel as if to give the vampire the floor.

"Before Christine so justly passed away, she completed the translation. I'm glad I obtained her services, since we have only a few days to spare." Now Lemuel was satisfied he had everyone's complete attention.

"The witch who sent Sylvester away gave a full account of the ritual, and Arria Auclina recorded her words. We all have a part to play," Lemuel began. "And I will ask each of you to do a few things. But if we don't do this together, we will die. And we will just be the beginning of the death."

Olivia took in a deep breath through her nose. "That's an incentive," she muttered.

Lemuel continued, "The witch then was a powerful virgin. I know that seems unlikely, but it was the case. She accepted the role of bait in luring the demon to the circle. The circle was drawn in salt and ash, and it was very large."

"We're going to be busy," Diederik whispered to Quinn.

"All the people the witch assembled had a part to play," Lemuel said. "And I don't think it's any coincidence that this crowd echoes that one. There were angels, psychics, vampires, shapeshifters. Men and women who were brave enough to face a demon. They all focused their beliefs and what magic they had on the witch, who was powerful in and of herself. This girl was stuffed with magic in every orifice by the time the shaman started the summoning. Colconnar manifested with a roar, determined to have sex with the witch and then eat her. He never wasted part of a human."

Everyone in the room looked as though they had something to say, but Lemuel motioned them all to be silent so he could finish his story.

"Colconnar emerged from his realm in the circle where the witch was waiting, but instead of permitting him to have sex with her, the group threw a magic net over him, imprisoning him in our world. He was sealed in the circle. Then a shaman had sex with the virgin witch on top of his prison, sealing Colconnar in the earth with virgin blood. That magic was strong enough to keep the demon buried for two hundred fifty years. But now he stirs. And we have to reenact the ritual to rebind him."

There was a long silence.

"Is there a virgin in Midnight?" the Rev said. "I am not one." His gaze went to Diederik. The boy turned red and shook his head.

"Me, neither," he said.

They all exchanged glances, but it was so evident that Lemuel, Olivia, Quinn, Bobo, Joe, and Chuy did not qualify that everyone looked hopefully at Manfred. Manfred said, "Sorry, not in the club."

"Um," said Fiji.

All eyes went to the witch.

"I appreciate your assumption that I couldn't possibly be, ah, untapped. But actually, technically, I am. A virgin." She couldn't have been more embarrassed if she'd said she was a shoplifter or an embezzler.

Sylvester nodded happily, but everyone else was clearly flabbergasted.

"Unbreached," Lemuel said, as if he could not quite believe she understood what "virgin" meant.

Fiji nodded, her lips pressed in a grim line and her eyes fixed on the floor.

"Well, damn," said Quinn as if he were having a very pleasant fantasy.

Bobo stared at her, but she did not see him.

"Sooooo . . . what does this mean she has to do?" Manfred asked.

Lemuel said, "The moon is waning, and it is also very close to Halloween, Samhain. A very powerful day. But since Fiji has her annual party, we have to think of a way to seal off the town so no bystanders will become involved. Also, we have to draw a magic circle of large dimension that includes the crossroad, and that circle must be reinforced with . . ." He bent to look at the translation again.

"Salt and ash. Hawthorn, probably. We can find it here," Fiji said. She still avoided looking at anyone else. "I've got bulk salt from Sam's Club."

"Thank you, Fiji."

"Yay, a modern twist," Olivia muttered.

"Once the magic circle is drawn, one of us—not you, Olivia—must enter it with Fiji before it's activated. The rest of us must focus our own power and magic and will on the circle. The one inside it with Fiji must join with her just as the demon emerges, so Fiji's virgin blood will reinforce the spell."

"The suicides will stop," Chuy said with some relief.

"Yes," said Lemuel. "Maybe some of you didn't know this, but the Rev and I have been disposing of animal bodies every morning. Since the humans haven't been coming, the animals have. They simply die on top of him. He's getting their essence, and it's strengthening him."

"As much as people?" Bobo asked.

"I think Fiji has been turning all her will to keeping people away," Lemuel said. "Is it not so?"

Fiji nodded. A tear ran down her face. "When I realized that most of the people he was pulling in were people who hadn't thought good thoughts about me, or who'd actively tried to do me harm, in Price's case, I cleansed myself of bad intent over and over. Especially after I punished Teacher for searching my house. I was scared he'd be next. Then the animals started. But that was better than the people."

Lemuel had a hard time looking compassionate, but he did his best. "The demon fears you and he hates you, but he must not have you. If he does, it's the end of Midnight."

"We would all be honored," Sylvester said abruptly. Fiji looked directly at him, surprised. "To be chosen to enter the circle with you," he explained.

Fiji appeared to be completely flustered by all this attention and Sylvester's obviously sincere compliment. "How will you pick?" she asked in a choked voice. "I mean, is it a magic thing, or can I . . . ?"

And then they all fell self-consciously silent as every man in the room wondered if he would be the one in the circle with Fiji.

"You can, my dear," Lemuel said. "But I am out of the running, as wonderful as I'm sure the experience would be. The Rev and Fiji already know that Olivia and I are hitched."

This was another stunning piece of news.

"And the hits just keep on coming," Quinn muttered.

Joe said, "Blessings on your union."

"This is turning out to be a completely *amazing* evening," Manfred said, and no one contradicted him.

"So, how will you pick?" Diederik asked Fiji. The boy was wide-eyed and smiling, delighted to be a man in the running for Fiji's big evening.

Quinn said, "Son, tone it down. This is not a date to the prom."

Suddenly, Fiji turned her back on all of them, and from the way her shoulders were shaking, Lemuel was sure she was crying.

"We'll talk about that later," Joe said. "And for the record, either Chuy or I can perform this act for you, Fiji, and it would be an honor and a privilege—though one that would be appreciated more by another man."

"Thanks," Fiji said, her voice muffled. "Can we talk about this later? I've had as much as I can stand. I know there isn't much time. But a little later."

Everyone trailed out, except for Lemuel. Olivia went downstairs to her apartment, Bobo went upstairs to his after a long hesitation, and Fiji finally uncovered her face and turned to face Lemuel.

She was *laughing.* "Lemuel, my heart is broken," she said, trying to sound serious. "You alone will not have sex with me? Even the gay guys would do the deed. But not you."

Lemuel said, "Well, darn, Fiji, if you really want me . . ." But he was smiling, too.

"You know, friend, I really don't," she said, and laughed even harder. She sat on the nearest chair and fanned her face with the apron. "And I thought the most exciting thing that might happen this evening was finally getting the truth-and-candor spell to work. I certainly didn't need it tonight." She wheezed for a second more, and then sobered up.

"I am sure the prospect is daunting," Lemuel said, feeling his way. He was not sure what to say to a woman who'd just gotten the news that the first sex she was to have would be public. And if the ritual didn't work (for any reason), a demon would rape her and eat her. A woman who still had dried tear tracks on her face, and yet had laughed until she bent over with it. Lemuel was proud to know her.

"No shit," she said. "'Daunting' is the word. And you know what my first thought was? I wondered if I could lose twenty pounds by Saturday."

"You look very nice," Lemuel said, puzzled. "You are a fine figure of a woman, Fiji." He was quite sincere, and he was at a loss when he saw that she raised a skeptical eyebrow.

"Of course I am, that's why so many men are knocking at my door," she said.

Lemuel had no trouble understanding her this time. That voice was bitter.

"What do you expect in a town the size of Midnight? There is only one man you want at your door, Fiji, and I think he realizes that he should have been there months ago."

"So where is he now, Lemuel?" she said, getting up.

"I think he is upstairs as you told him to be. I think he is berating himself for not having rid you of your virginity very privately and long ago."

"Oh," she said blankly. "Well, that would be something he should tell me. No one else. But I thank you for trying to make me feel better."

"You are welcome," Lemuel said. "You are a strong woman, Miss Fiji, and I respect you."

"Ahhhhh . . . thanks," the witch said, a little doubtfully, and with no more ado she left for her house. She was neither crying nor laughing, but she was deep in thought. Lemuel thought that might be worse.

27

Back in her own kitchen, blessedly alone, Fiji slumped at her kitchen table, the spell she'd been working on abandoned before her. Her spell bowl was full of odd ingredients, and she'd been rapt in her work until she'd gotten the phone call to go over to the pawnshop . . . and the absurdity of being a virgin in this place and at this moment had come back to bite her in the butt. Maybe literally.

Now that she'd had a little laugh at the absurdity of her situation, she was bleakly aware this was one of the worst days of her life.

After she did a quick riffle through bad-day memories, she revised her evaluation.

This was *the* worst day.

Not only to have her virginity common knowledge—but to be required to have public sex to stop the end of the world as she knew it.

"All right," she said out loud. "Let's pretend I don't feel this is all about me."

"Something you want to talk about?" Mr. Snuggly said from somewhere under the table.

"Yes," she said simply. The cat emerged from his hiding place and jumped up onto the other kitchen chair, then to the table. He looked at her expectantly. "Get on with it," Mr. Snuggly said. "I can't read your mind, even if I wanted to."

Fiji explained.

She had to go over some points a couple of times, because Mr. Snuggly did not understand why it was embarrassing for a human to have sex in front of other humans. He also did not understand why she cared who saw her body. "It's only a vehicle," he said, clearly puzzled. "You just ride around in it."

"Well, true enough," she said, "but I sure need to take my vehicle in to the shop and get some dings hammered out."

"There's nothing wrong with you," the cat said. He seemed to be digging around for something nice to say. "You're soft and warm," he said. "You smell pretty good. You would look nice carrying cubs."

"Oh my goddess," she said, letting her head fall to the table with a dramatic *thunk*. "What if I get pregnant?"

"You would have to spend a lot of time with a baby," Mr. Snuggly said, looking much less pleased. "You might forget to feed me."

"How could I forget?" she said, raising her head to cast a baleful eye at the cat. "You remind me often enough."

Mr. Snuggly looked off into the distance regally. After a moment, he abandoned the pose and asked, "Will you need me for the ceremony?"

"I'd think, as my familiar, you'd definitely better be there. You boost my power."

Mr. Snuggly looked as pleased as a cat can look. "I can't transform into a big man," the cat said. "So I'm afraid I can't help with the sex thing."

Fiji thought she'd thrown up in her mouth a little bit at the idea of Mr. Snuggly becoming a man to have sex with her. "Thanks, anyway," she said in a strained voice. "I have some candidates."

"Splendid," Mr. Snuggly said. "Will they draw straws for the honor?"

Fiji glared at him. "You're being a jerk, Snug."

The cat looked bored.

After a second, her anger collapsed under the weight of her worry. "What would Aunt Mildred have done?" she asked Mr. Snuggly.

He looked somewhat more interested. "Mildred would have used a spell to determine the right sperm donor," he said, after some thought.

"What about her personal preference?" Fiji looked away as she asked.

"That would have been interesting to know. I think, though, that the spell would have been her choice. Mildred was not a hot-blooded woman. She did not think highly of humans who let their lust get the better of their judgment."

"Not helpful," Fiji muttered.

"Oh? Did you want me to tell you to follow your heart? In that case, just call the blond hunk across the road and tell him he's the one."

"He's a nice guy," Fiji said defensively, knowing that the words were inadequate.

"That's what you should go for, then. A nice guy." Mr. Snuggly's words dripped with sarcasm. He lifted a leg and bent to clean his butt.

"There's nothing wrong with a nice guy," Fiji said, in a voice that was almost a snarl.

"Oh, gosh, no. Let's skip three powerful weretigers, both the mature one and the younger one and the really young one. And the angels. And the psychic. And the half-demon hunk with the long black hair. And the vampire. Let's go for the plain-vanilla human with the tragic life." He turned away pointedly.

"If you weren't a small animal, I'd take you down," Fiji said. She was so angry it took her a moment to realize how ridiculous that was. Her mouth twitched.

"You could try," Mr. Snuggly said coldly, and turned around to give her a glare. "Oh, you think that's humorous!"

Fiji couldn't manage to laugh, but she smiled. "You'll definitely have to be there," she said. "All hands on deck. It'll be dangerous."

Mr. Snuggly said, "The upside of this whole situation is that Rasta has been gone. I suppose they'll bring him back afterward."

"Sure. If there is an 'after.' Joe and Chuy miss Rasta."

The cat made a sound just like hacking up a hairball. Fiji realized he was laughing. "Manfred should have let him get run over that day," Mr. Snuggly said. "Brainless ball of fur."

There were many things Fiji could have said in return, but she kept her mouth shut. She decided that the next day would be dedicated to looking up a spell to help her choose her deflowerer. "And that sucks," she said, as she brushed her teeth.

28

What happens if this doesn't work?" Diederik asked his father.

"Nothing good," Quinn said, after a moment. He and Diederik were taking turns spray-painting a white circle. It encompassed the entire crossroad, and to be sure it was large enough they were including corners of sidewalk, edges of buildings, and one fire hydrant by the Midnight Hotel. Quinn cast an eye along the curve of the line and decided it was good. He continued, "I guess the town will disappear, or the demon will kill all the people living here and then begin to rampage, to make up for lost centuries. Diederik . . . I think it would be better if you leave town. I'd like to send you to stay with a friend of mine in Louisiana."

"Run?" Diederik was outraged. "No, Dad, I'll fight with you and the Rev. We are tigers!"

"I don't think even weretigers can beat a demon, Diederik. It's not like ordinary prey."

"I've never seen a demon." Diederik took the spray can from his father, taking his turn drawing a section of circle. As the traffic went through the stoplight, they had to wait until it was cleared either way to continue.

"I have. I fought a half-demon in the pits. Like Sylvester. And it tore me up."

"But you won." Diederik glanced at the center of the circle, under the stoplight. He estimated they were making the circle fairly even. Quinn had stood under the light for a moment, holding the string, and Diederik had run with it, stopping every few yards to put down a reference mark. They'd had to do it quickly, but it had worked.

"Yeah, I won. But only, I think, because she had already had a bout that day, and I was fresh."

"Tell me about the pits."

They'd stopped painting the circle while they talked, and Quinn glanced up at the evening sky. He was tired. It had been a busy day. "I'll tell you if you'll keep walking while we get this done," he said.

"Was it like *Gladiator*?" Diederik asked. He'd just watched the movie on the hotel television.

"Yes, except real. My own blood. My own pain. My own fear. Every time I went in, I was not sure I would come out. Every fight might be my last. I didn't like the person I became while I fought. But I had to fight."

"To save your mom and your sister."

Quinn nodded. "To save them."

"Were they grateful?"

"I think they were, way down deep," Quinn said. "But my mother, because of her ordeal at the hands of hunters, was crazy. And there are some obligations that are too painful to acknowledge. Some debts too big to be paid."

"I hope I never owe anyone a debt like that," Diederik said.

"I hope not, too, son."

The circle was almost complete. Quinn thought it would have been better to allocate the painting to Lemuel, who could have done it at night. There were interested spectators in the windows of the hotel, but no one asked any questions or tried to stop them, which was one of the benefits of living in Midnight. Quinn looked up at the man on the upper floor, the one who rented the room with a great view of the pawnshop. Their eyes met. The man's face stayed blank.

"How are we going to keep people out of the circle that night?" Diederik said, after they'd worked for a while in silence. "Regular people?"

"Considering only five cars have gone through the light while we've been trying to get the circle sprayed, and it's evening now, I'm not too worried about that. I'm more concerned that some of the hotel people might look out their windows and get alarmed at seeing a couple having ritual sex in the middle of the road. If they call the police, the consequences will be really bad. But I expect defense of the circle will be up to Joe and Chuy. And maybe Sylvester can conceal us. I don't know how good a shaman he is. I think it was a late calling of his."

"Joe and Chuy aren't anything like I thought they were when I met them," Diederik said. "There's something cold and scary about them, when you go below the surface."

"They're way more than they seem. And it's a deep difference. They're very good at acting like regular guys." Quinn looked down at the section he'd just painted. The circle was now complete.

"I think of Joe and Chuy like they were my uncles. But they kind of scared me at the meeting." It cost Diederik something to confess this, Quinn could see.

"That's a reasonable reaction, Son," Quinn said. "You don't mess with angels, even fallen ones."

"The demon . . . was he a fallen angel, too?"

"Good question. And they don't always tell you the whole story. This is . . . God stuff. But my understanding is that demons, and devils, used to be angels, too, yes. But God, whatever name he or she wears, can read hearts and minds, and know the degree of evil and rebellion in each. The lust for power can corrupt even the best. So some got banished utterly and early to a different realm, and some were thrown to earth after the New Coming, like Joe and Chuy. But . . . maybe that's all bullshit. I know some half-demons who are really good people."

Diederik made a face. "Doesn't that make you feel weird?"

"Talking about gods and demons? Yes, it does. I should spend more time thinking about it than I do."

"I don't like to think about a god looking at me and judging me."

"I don't think anyone *enjoys* that idea. The love part, yes, but the being-found-wanting part . . . we're all worried about that."

Diederik gave Quinn a startled look, as if he'd supposed his father wouldn't venture into such deep waters. "Not you," he said. "Not you, Dad."

Quinn laughed and put his arm around Diederik's shoulders. They'd been standing outside the hotel, and now they went in. Marina, behind the desk, smiled at Diederik in a very womanly way, and Quinn tried not to sigh. He'd had "The Talk" with Diederik when Diederik was a little tyke, because he'd known all too soon Diederik would need to know the facts. Diederik was good-natured and charming, and also outstandingly handsome, but there was a touch of feral about him that made the boy truly magnetic.

Quinn didn't think he himself had ever been as attractive as his son, so he was really proud of Diederik's lack of conceit. That was where the Rev had proved to be a good guardian. Vanity didn't stand a chance with the Rev around.

Quinn ran up the stairs to his room, as Diederik and Marina exchanged a few words before Diederik went back to his job of dusting, vacuuming, and mopping the lobby and the bathroom off of it.

The apocalypse might be coming, but work had to go on. Quinn called up the diagram of the venue of the next wedding he was hired to produce, in this case a true production—almost a three-ring circus, he thought. Velda and Ramon, both true shapeshifters, would be tying the knot in two weeks.

He paused for a moment when he pictured the bride and groom. He wondered if he'd ever get to have his own conventional marriage. His mate, Tijgerin, hadn't survived, and his mother, too, was dead; they'd been the only two full-blooded female weretigers he'd ever known. But he had a son, which was all he could ask for. Quinn decided he'd be glad to find a woman of any heritage.

I'm a little old to be making such a resolution, he thought. But he was smiling. It was doable.

29

Nothing the next day went as planned. Nothing.

While the inhabitants of Midnight were preparing themselves for one crisis, which would fall in one more day, another presented itself without any of them seeing it coming—even Manfred, the psychic.

Just at eight o'clock in the morning, a big vehicle rumbled into town from the east. Joe and Chuy were running the water (the shower and the sink respectively), and they didn't hear the sound as anything special. It roused Teacher, though, because he'd driven a vehicle that sounded like that at one point in his life. He pulled on his shoes and hurried out of his trailer.

No one in the hotel, except the man who lived in the front room overlooking the pawnshop, gave it a second's thought. And he only thought how out of place it seemed.

The rumble gradually subsided into silence in front of Midnight Pawn. Lemuel's shift was over and Bobo hadn't come down yet, so no one came out of the shop to see what was happening.

"This vehicle is an abomination," the Rev whispered, when he heard the noise of the motor. He was kneeling in prayer before the bare altar in his church.

The Rev liked to start the day with prayer. Diederik lived with the Rev, so his attendance was obligatory, and that morning Quinn had joined them, too. The Rev had spent the previous day reducing a chunk of hawthorn tree to ash, and Quinn had to put the ash in a bucket. But all that was on hold as the Rev cut short his prayer and the three men came out of the church to look at the abomination.

"That's a stretch Hummer," Quinn told Diederik, who had never seen one before. Since Quinn was an event planner, he was well versed in ostentatious vehicles.

Diederik was impressed, but Quinn saw that the Rev was having a bad reaction to the Hummer. The older man's eyes went golden. He was sensing a threat, so his tiger was getting close to the surface. At his age, the Rev could change any time he wanted, as could Quinn. But Diederik still had to have the moon's help, so if it came to fighting . . . Quinn laid his hand on his son's shoulder. "You have a key, I think. Run. Wake Olivia. Tell Bobo to get out of the shop. *Hurry.*"

Diederik streaked across the road to unlock the side door of the pawnshop. He disappeared inside. Standing on that landing, he could yell upstairs for Bobo and downstairs for Olivia.

There were men getting out of the Hummer, now, men as unlike the Rev and himself as it was possible to get. They wore suits but with gun belts underneath. They had rifles in their hands. They looked in all directions. They might as well have had "HIGH-CLASS HOODS" tattooed on their foreheads. There were five of them, plus the driver, who got out but remained by the vehicle.

This looked a lot like a small invasion.

Quinn didn't want to transform in public in broad daylight, but he didn't have a weapon, and he was certain he was going to need one. He wished he hadn't sent Diederik into the pawnshop, a wish that was confirmed when he saw all the armed men turning toward it.

The pawnshop was the target.

The newcomers began to move in the direction of the front door. They walked spread out, not in a clump; they knew what they were doing, Quinn thought. The men were watchful, glancing from side to side, but they seemed not to fear the Rev or Quinn, maybe because the two stayed still.

Quinn couldn't risk making a move, though, not until Diederik reappeared. Every second made him tenser. Just as he was about to run across the street to put himself between the invaders and the pawnshop, the Rev took an unexpected step.

"Fiji!" the Rev bellowed in his deep voice, and out of her front door the witch popped. Fiji looked like a fluffy puppet in her nightgown and rose-colored bathrobe. Her eyes widened as she took in the armed men and their approach to the pawnshop. Then she came off her porch and down the path to the sidewalk, her hands held ready as if she were about to perform surgery. Her zebra-striped slippers thwacked against the concrete in the eerie silence.

Not too surprisingly, the invaders did not recognize Fiji as a threat until she got halfway across the road. And then she froze them.

"I feel like a one-trick pony," Fiji said. The Rev ran to stand by her. Quinn was right on his heels. Quinn stopped to examine the closest gunman, as still as a department store dummy. He was so overwhelmed with relief that he couldn't find the voice to tell Fiji how grateful he was.

"No shame in that, if the trick works," the Rev said practically. He began going from man to man, divesting each one of weapons and telephones. The telephones were Quinn's suggestion, and Quinn helped.

Bobo unlocked the front door of the pawnshop as if he were opening for business on an ordinary day. But he stepped out with a shotgun in his hands.

Fiji, who had set the spell firmly, was going from man to man in the Rev's wake, looking into each face to make sure the man was good and frozen.

"They all seem good for ten more minutes," she pronounced. "Enough time for Olivia to come check 'em out."

"You sure she needs to be here?" Bobo said. "She might want to start getting in some licks. Olivia's not going to turn down an advantage. Why can't we just call Arthur Smith? Any reason why we wouldn't?" He looked hopeful.

"I think this is about Olivia," Fiji said with conviction.

Quinn thought so, too. Then he expelled a lungful of relief, because Diederik exploded through the front door with Olivia at his heels.

Olivia strode down to the loose cluster of men, gun in her hand and an incredulous look on her face. "You did this?" she asked Fiji.

"I did," Fiji replied, her hands held ready at her sides. Olivia spared a second look for Fiji's bathrobe and slippers.

"Good work," Olivia said, with a straight face.

"Looks like the word of your marriage really did *stir something up*," Fiji said to Olivia in tones of the deepest sarcasm.

Quinn saw Teacher Reed running across the road. Teacher was carrying a shotgun, too.

"You coming to help these men out?" the Rev called, and his voice hung over them like the reverberation of a bell. All the Midnighters turned to look at Teacher.

"No! I'm coming to protect Olivia!" Teacher yelled back.

"Protect. Huh!" Olivia said. "I wish Lem were awake. He'd love this." She walked over to the front door of the limo. "Let's see who rented this baby." The driver was one of the men with guns. She glanced inside the driver's seat, but evidently she saw no paperwork, so she went to the back. Fiji had reached the fourth gunman, but she caught Olivia's movement from the corner of her eye.

"Olivia! I didn't check inside!" Fiji yelled at the same moment the

Rev bellowed, “Wait!” But Olivia flung open the limo door, and there was a loud crack of noise. Olivia seemed to be pushed back a step, and then she folded to her knees.

Olivia fell over sideways, still trying to raise her own gun.

And Fiji, with a wide-eyed intensity, dropped to her knees by Olivia, but she did not look down at her friend. Instead, she looked inside the Hummer. Her face was like nothing Quinn had ever seen. It shone with power and determination and a complete lack of pity. Fiji extended her hand, and she *concentrated*.

The man inside began screaming. And he didn’t stop until he was dead.

After it was over, Fiji sagged to one side, exhausted. She couldn’t say a word or stand. But by then the ambulances were there, because the Midnight luck had run out. A passerby who’d stopped for gas at the convenience store had seen the shooting. He’d run inside Gas N Go to get away from the bullets, and he’d called the police.

Within seven minutes of the call, the approaching sirens split the morning air. But in that seven minutes, the Midnighters worked hard. Teacher was positioned with his (perfectly legal, he assured them) shotgun pointing at the invaders, who were sort of walked into a close formation by Quinn. He found it was like moving department store dummies, too, but they were quite a bit heavier.

The Rev put the guns and telephones in a heap in the pawnshop parking area. Bobo and Teacher stood guard. Diederik was sent into Fiji’s house to keep out of sight, since he had no official existence. Sylvester simply stayed in Gas N Go, Madonna and Grady stayed in their trailer, and Chuy and Joe in their shop. Manfred, who’d poked his head out just in time to see Fiji take action, closed his front curtains and laid low. The hotel people were all out on the sidewalk, craning and marveling.

Fiji released the imported gunmen from her spell just at the right moment as the police arrived. They all swung around belligerently, confused and angry at having been disarmed and corralled, which they didn't remember at all. The police asked Teacher and Bobo to put down their weapons, which they did instantly and with every sign of being glad the police were there to take over the bad guys . . . one of whom was unwise enough to take a swing at Deputy Garcia. She cuffed him in the blink of an eye.

As the police got the situation sorted out, and EMTs began to work on Olivia and Fiji, who was unconscious, Lemuel slept the sleep of the dead. Diederik sat in the Inquiring Mind looking out the window as his dad had ordered him to do. The boy was distraught at the sight of Fiji and Olivia being strapped onto gurneys and lifted into the ambulances. But he could see Quinn was not in handcuffs and the police were listening to him, so Diederik knew at least that part of it would be all right.

"If Olivia'd gotten shot at night," Quinn said to Bobo very quietly, "we could have just carried her downstairs to Lemuel."

Bobo looked a little shocked. "Do you think that's what she'd have wanted?"

Quinn nodded. "I think so. If she gets through this, we'd better ask her."

"She just has to recover," Bobo said. "And Feej has to be okay. She just has to."

"I've seen this before. I think she's exhausted from using such big magic," Quinn said, trying to sound reassuring. "And she's never killed anyone before, I'm sure. That'll take it out of you."

But Bobo, after he'd been accepted as one of the good guys, sat on the front steps of the pawnshop and stared into a future too bleak to endure.

He tried three times to get into his truck and go to Davy to be with the Midnight wounded, but the police wouldn't let him. They had too many questions to ask.

30

Fiji woke up in the hospital, shivering and bewildered.

I killed someone. That was the first thing she remembered.

He'd been gray-haired and mean-looking, the pleasure and triumph of shooting Olivia still stretching his lips into a smile.

That had sent Fiji off the deep end. It almost didn't matter that he was about to shoot Fiji, too. She'd unleashed death on him. It hadn't been a real spell, but sheer will. As she lay in the pale green hospital room all by herself, she wondered where the power had come from. As best as Fiji could remember, she'd simply had a clear, consuming conviction that this man must die for what he had done to Olivia.

And he had died, but not quickly. His face had turned blue and his mouth had foamed, and he'd screamed with a dreadful catch, as though finding the air for screaming was a struggle. Then he'd kind of rattled deep in his throat. That had been that.

A girl in scrubs came in and bent over to look at Fiji. "How do you feel, Miss Cavanaugh?" she said.

"Cold," Fiji said through trembling lips.

"I'll get you another blanket."

Fiji nodded and soon felt deft hands spreading another blanket over her. She was so grateful she could have cried.

"Is that better?" the girl asked.

"Yes, thanks. How is my friend?"

"Your friend?"

"The woman brought in same time as me. Been shot."

"She's in surgery, but don't worry about her. She's got a good doctor working on her. She's in good hands."

This was not real information. She was being soothed. Fiji expected that next the nurse would offer to pray with her. "I need something a little more specific than that," she said, but her voice was too weak to have authority.

"Now that you're awake, a doctor's going to come talk with you," the nurse said. "She'll be here in just a minute."

It was more than a minute. In fact, Fiji went back to sleep. She woke when an older woman in a white lab coat came in.

"Ms. Cavanaugh, I'm Dr. Sheridan," the woman said. Her gray hair was in a smooth pageboy, and her glasses, hanging from a chain, had flirty red frames. "Can you tell me what happened to you?"

Fiji decided to tell the truth with some omissions. "I saw my friend Olivia get shot and I went to pull her to safety," she said slowly, editing as she spoke. She was finally feeling warm, and her voice came out stronger. She'd stopped shivering. "When I saw the man in the car who had shot Olivia, he pointed the gun at me. I was really scared he was going to shoot me, and I couldn't protect Olivia or myself. Then his hand kind of fell on the car seat, and he had a fit, I guess? I was just . . . I couldn't breathe, and I thought he was going to kill me, and maybe I fainted."

"I don't think you fainted, which is a momentary thing," Dr. Sheridan said gently. "I'm not sure if you hyperventilated, or had a severe panic attack, or both, but you were unconscious for a good ten minutes. We have to rule out some kind of heart event."

"So that's a long time to be out?" Fiji said.

"That's a long time to be out." Dr. Sheridan was obviously trying to make Fiji understand that she'd suffered a serious event, while trying to avoid setting off another "panic attack." "When you came into the emergency room, we ran an EKG, and the results were fine, so that's good news. Your blood work isn't all back, of course, but nothing popped out at a first look."

"I kind of remember that," Fiji said, trying out a smile. She'd been woozy but awake by that time. "Aside from feeling really tired, I feel much better now." Fiji knew exactly what was wrong with her. She'd strained her "magic muscles" when she'd channeled too much energy into killing the old man. She suspected she'd probably expended way more energy than she'd actually needed to use, and in consequence her body had shut down to protect its depleted resources.

She'd know better next time.

For a few minutes, the doctor took Fiji over her medical history, which was very simple and blameless, and then over her family's medical history, which was quite typical of any fairly healthy family.

By the time that was done, Fiji had decided she liked Dr. Sheridan.

"I'm glad to hear you're feeling better. But you need to consider having some tests run. We sure don't want to see you back here again." The doctor smiled at Fiji benevolently. Fiji had been enjoying the conversation, because it was free of the man she'd killed and the demon under the road and who she was going to have sex with. But now she felt tired, and reality crept up on her again.

"Let's talk about any more tests later," Fiji said. "I'm really feeling better."

"Of course. Right now, the sheriff wants to talk to you. Do you think you're well enough to do that?"

"Yes," Fiji said. "Thanks for everything."

Arthur Smith himself came in. Fiji was both glad and sorry to see him. Arthur was in uniform, and he looked tired, but he also seemed curiously content. After a second, Fiji decided that Arthur looked relaxed. So apparently he hadn't been, the whole time she'd known him.

"Hey, Fiji, how are you feeling?" He reached to take her hand, and then withdrew his own so quickly Fiji almost thought she had imagined the gesture. Perhaps he had rethought it after remembering she had some explaining to do.

"Better," she said. Now that her core was warm, she felt drowsy. She wished passionately that she were home in her own bed with Mr. Snuggly purring beside her. After all, she was still in her own nightgown, though her bathrobe was hanging on a hook on the wall, her slippers on the floor underneath it.

"Did anyone check on Mr. Snuggly?" she asked, suddenly afraid something had happened to the cat.

"I saw him," Arthur said. "The kid in your shop coaxed him out from under the Hummer."

Fiji stared at Arthur. "He was under the car," she said, almost asking a question. "Oh, poor Snug," she added hastily. "He must have been terrified."

"The boy carried him off, and I didn't see them again," Arthur said.

Fiji relaxed. Diederik would feed and take care of Mr. Snuggly, or the cat would nag him relentlessly. Now if only Arthur wouldn't start asking questions about Diederik. His lack of paperwork would be awkward.

"If you feel you're up to it, I do have some questions to ask you," Arthur said. He was standing by the bed rail, gripping it lightly.

"Sure," she said, trying to make her own hands relax. "About the shooting."

"Sure. Had you ever seen that man, the one in the stretch Hummer?"

"Never."

"Any of those men familiar to you?" Arthur's wide blue eyes were fixed on her face.

"No." It was a pleasure to tell the plain truth.

"What happened? Just take your time. We're trying to figure this out. Every detail helps."

Fiji was glad he'd told her to take her time. She did. "I heard all the commotion across the street, and I came running out," Fiji said. (Best to omit that the Rev had called her. That was not explainable.) "The Rev and Quinn were standing in my front yard. Diederik was just going in the side door of the pawnshop, or maybe Quinn told me he'd gone in. I don't remember which."

Arthur nodded, to show her he was listening.

"I saw all the men had guns. They were moving toward the pawnshop. Slowly."

"Did you realize there was someone left in the Hummer?" Arthur asked quietly.

"I never thought about it at all. The windows were tinted dark. The doors on the pawnshop side were open."

"What happened next?"

"I thought all the men were going to go into the pawnshop. I was scared for Bobo. And Olivia and Lemuel." Fiji took a deep, shuddering breath, remembering the fear. If she had really been uncertain how she felt about Bobo, she now knew. "Then Diederik and Olivia came out. And Bobo."

"Do you have any idea, however out there, about why these armed men would be going into the pawnshop?" Arthur's voice was gentle, but his eyes were intent.

"No," she said. "I was stunned."

"*Someone* has to know why those men showed up," Arthur said. "They're not talking, except to ask for a lawyer."

"Maybe Olivia can tell us? How is she?" Fiji asked cleverly. Information!

"Still in surgery, and it'll be a while before she can talk," Arthur said.

"Can you tell me about her?" *Dammit, someone's got to tell me.*

"About her wound? Not in any detail. One of my deputies talked to the doctor who's operating, and he seemed fairly certain she'd pull through."

"Good." "Fairly certain" was something.

"Just a few more questions? I can tell you're tired." Arthur looked concerned, and he might be, but he was also a cop.

Fiji nodded.

"What happened to Ellery McGuire?" Arthur said.

"Who . . . ? That's the name of the man in the limo? The one who shot Olivia?"

"Yes. The guy who was filling up his car at Gas N Go said you stretched out your hand to him. What was that about?"

"I begged him not to shoot again," Fiji said. "He was pointing the gun at me, and Olivia was bleeding." She shook her head. "It was horrible." And it had been. She could feel again that burning intensity that had seized her when she'd realized what she must do.

"He didn't think you spoke. The witness."

"I'm not saying I made a speech. But I said at least, 'No, no!'"

"Okay. Then what happened?"

Then I killed him. "He sort of crumpled and his hand dropped," Fiji said, as she'd told the doctor. "And he turned really white, and stuff came out of his mouth. I guess he's dead?" She'd known he was dead, but she had to play this out.

"Yes. He's dead. But you had no weapon, right? So you couldn't have harmed him physically."

"I had no gun or Taser or anything," she said truthfully. "I just wanted him to *stop*. I was so scared that Olivia was dead." And she shuddered, remembering Olivia's blank eyes and the blood coming out of her abdomen. And knowing Lemuel was asleep and could not wake to save her. And knowing this meant the hospital, and the chance Olivia would really die. *And being very, very angry*.

Fiji began to cry, and that pushed Arthur to finish up in a hurry.

"She's not dead, Fiji," he said, in as comforting a voice as he could manage. "And we have all the attackers under arrest. I don't know how Bobo and Teacher rounded them up, but they had those assholes under control."

"But those assholes are not talking?" She was really curious how they were going to explain their presence.

"Not a squeak." Arthur's mouth pulled down at one corner. "Not until their lawyers get here."

"Smart," Fiji said. "And professional. I want to go home."

"You've got some insurance," he said, smiling. "Why not stay a while? The doctor wants you to spend the night, make sure you're okay."

"She seems like a nice woman," Fiji said. "But there's nothing wrong with me that time and rest won't cure. I was just overstressed and really scared, and I blacked out."

"That's between you and the doctor," Arthur said. "You feel like having some company?"

"I guess," she said, cautiously. Depended on who the company was.

To her mild surprise, Chuy Villegas came in. Chuy was wearing his usual casual clothes: khakis, a polo shirt, loafers. He looked as unlike an angel with wings as she could imagine.

He put his hands on hers. After glancing over his shoulder to make sure Arthur was out of hearing, Chuy said, "Thanks to you we are all alive."

"I don't understand," Fiji said.

"If you hadn't cut off the head of the snake, I think they would have gone through Midnight killing everyone they encountered to cover up the fact that Olivia was the target."

"Surely . . . you can't be killed?" She felt almost embarrassed, pointing that out.

"But they didn't know that," he said. "And getting shot always hurts."

Fiji didn't want to take any credit that wasn't her due. "I killed a man, Chuy. On purpose. I only thought of saving Olivia from getting shot again."

"You did what was necessary. Don't fear judgment from Joe and me. We live under the old code," Chuy reminded her. His voice was cool and stern.

"I wonder if I can go home soon," she said. She couldn't think of right and wrong any longer.

"I think the correct thing to do is to call a nurse," Chuy said gravely. "She is supposed to remove the needle. What is going into you?"

"Just fluid, I think, so if they had to give me medicine, they could administer it through the tube." She had to dredge hard to come up with the word "administer."

"You weren't hurt?" Chuy said, as if he were pretty sure that was the case but had to check.

"I used all my magic," she explained wearily.

"I understand. You need bed rest and soup and to keep warm." Again, he sounded like he was reading from a manual on the care and feeding of witches. But Fiji didn't mind.

"That sounds so good," she said.

Chuy said, "I'll do what I can to make that happen." He turned to leave her room.

"Chuy," she said. "When I killed the man, the demon laughed."

His shoulders slumped. "I was afraid of that," he said, and went to secure her release.

Evidently, Chuy was very good at greasing the hospital skids. Faster than she would have believed, she got her release papers and was in a wheelchair, riding out the door to the curb. With some hesitation and faltering, she maneuvered herself into Chuy's car. She would have liked to see Olivia before she left the hospital, but apparently Olivia was still in surgery.

"Three days until Saturday," Chuy said on the drive back to Midnight, and suddenly Fiji understood why he was so anxious to have her back in town. She had to be in Midnight to make her own personal sacrifice.

"I'm sorry you brought that up," Fiji said. She'd been feeling fairly warm and cozy with Chuy, but not any longer. She rested her head against the cold glass of the window. She was far beyond caring if her hair got lopsided.

"I *am* sorry," Chuy said, sounding awkward. "I know you are thinking about what you have to do. But I am thinking about the next century, and longer."

"I think it's more like I'm thinking *me* and you're thinking *you*," she murmured. He didn't respond; either he thought she was saying something stupid or he completely agreed. "Have you felt him moving?" she asked.

Chuy sighed. "I have," he said.

Soon I will rise, the demon had told her.

She had not heard his voice in a day or two. She'd felt him, looming in the back of her mind, always present, but he'd been silent.

She hadn't missed his voice a bit.

Her homecoming was oddly anticlimactic. Fiji had left in the middle of a tumult. She came back in the middle of nothing. There was no one on the street. The limo was gone, the body was gone, all the people who'd been in the street were gone. She didn't even see Olivia's blood in the pawnshop parking lot. Chuy pulled behind her house and ran around to open her door, helping her out of the car as solicitously as if she'd been an aged *abuela*. Her back door was unlocked, as she'd left it. Chuy offered his arm to help her manage the step up to the porch and the back-door sill. She was so weak; she hadn't felt this way since she'd had mono as a teenager.

Chuy was seldom inside Fiji's house, so she was ridiculously glad she'd made her bed first thing this morning. In fact, she'd been just about to take off her nightclothes and get in the shower when she'd heard the Rev shouting. Chuy folded back the covers neatly so Fiji could climb into bed. "Anything else I can get you?" he asked.

"Just some water, please," she said, feeling almost shy about having him move around her house. Chuy returned from the kitchen with a glass of water and a bowl of soup with crackers on a bed tray. Fiji had never seen the bed tray before, but the soup was Progresso minestrone. She sat propped up and consumed it all. She felt much better.

When Fiji was done, Chuy silently removed the tray. Fiji scooted down in the bed and turned on her side. Her comfort was complete when Mr. Snuggly padded into the room, jumped up beside her, and curled up by her hand, nudging it and even giving it a raspy lick. Fiji scratched his head and he purred, the most soothing sound in the world. She heard the back door opening and closing; Chuy had left.

Glad you're home, the demon murmured.

"Fuck you," she said. And she fell asleep.

When she woke up, it was dark outside.

Fiji felt almost normal. She started to get up, but then she realized someone else was in the room. "Lemuel?" she said, almost certain she could smell him.

"Fiji," Lemuel said from the shadows. "I'm here to thank you."

"I was glad to be able to do something," she said. She wasn't quite sure what to say next. "Thanks for being here," she tried.

"And yet I wasn't able to be there early today when you saved Olivia, my wife."

"We wished you were awake," Fiji said. "We were afraid we would lose her."

"You protected her with your body, and you killed the man responsible."

"Yes," Fiji said bleakly. "I killed him."

"You're not sorry you saved Olivia?"

"No, of course not. He was about to shoot again—me or her. I had to do it. But it doesn't sit real well."

"I can remember once I felt that way," Lemuel said after a moment.

He came closer, perched on the edge of the bed. He took her hand. His was very cold.

"Fiji, you are a young woman. You haven't seen a lot of life. I don't want this for you, to have to kill. And I wish I could say this is the only time you'll have to step up to defend this town and its people. But how can I know that?"

"How did Aunt Mildred handle it?"

"She was a pip," Lemuel said unexpectedly. Fiji choked back a laugh.

"What does that mean?" she asked.

"Mildred was one of a kind," he said. "She was sarcastic and downright, and she said what she thought. People were a little afraid of her, and they respected her."

"I liked her a lot," she said. "Aunt Mildred had a sense of humor."

"She kept it well hidden," Lemuel said dryly. "And she looked forward to seeing you every year, when your family would visit."

"I don't remember meeting you, those summers."

"I wasn't supposed to exist, when you were a child. When you were a teenager, Mildred was afeared meeting a vampire would be so exciting that you'd tell your parents. They wouldn't have let you return."

"You think I'll get arrested?" she said. It didn't seem likely to her, but she wanted another opinion.

"No. The medical examiner will say the old man had a heart attack or stroke or something. The coroner would never say, 'I think a witch killed him with magic.' Am I right?"

She nodded, smiling just a little.

"I am more worried about what will happen to Olivia. Surely her true name will be known now, and her father will try to make amends to her. She never wanted to see him again."

Fiji thought of Teacher charging down the sidewalk with the shotgun. "At least now we know the Reeds weren't on the side of the gunmen," she said. "But when I feel a little better, I'm going to have to understand Olivia's past."

"We'll tell you," Lemuel said. "Sleep now, friend. I'm going to Olivia."

And before too long, Fiji did fall asleep again.

31

After a long internal debate, Manfred drove to a little bakery in Davy and bought two croissants and two muffins for Fiji. He did not try to pretend he'd made baked goods for her. He took the box to Fiji's. The front door still had the CLOSED sign up, so he went around back and knocked quietly, as befitted the house of an invalid.

"Come in," Fiji called, and he opened the door to see her sitting at her kitchen table. There were big circles under her eyes and her skin looked as if someone had erased all her color.

"Feej, you look like something the cat dragged in," Manfred said, and then cursed himself, especially when he heard a raspy laugh coming from under the table where Mr. Snuggly was sitting.

"I know," she said. "I got all drained, Manfred. But I feel better today, and I know I'll be up to the ceremony on Saturday. I hope I'll be able to help prepare."

"Tomorrow, Quinn and Diederik will go over the circle with salt and hawthorn ash. The Rev got the ash done."

"Sounds good."

They both looked away, embarrassed. Neither of them wanted to talk about the public sex. What was there to say?

"Here," said Manfred, putting the box down in front of her as though that would erase all awkwardness. "You're always cooking for us. So I went and got you something." He shrugged. "I thought about making them myself. You're lucky there's a bakery!"

"Please, have a seat," she said. "Get a cup of coffee, if you want. Or I have tea." Fiji had recently invested in a Keurig and was happy with its versatility.

"Thanks," he said, and happily made himself a cup of tea and Fiji some coffee. He also accepted a croissant after Fiji had said firmly that she absolutely could not eat two croissants and two muffins. Somehow the butter dish appeared between them, with a knife, and two little plates, though Manfred did not notice how that had happened. After a moment, he realized Fiji had set the table, though he'd come over determined she would not have to stir a finger.

Guiltily, Manfred asked her if he could feed Mr. Snuggly for her. He was relieved when she nodded. He also went out to check her mailbox and to bring in her newspaper, and he put the dishes in the sink. He felt better about himself after that.

By the time Manfred left, he thought Fiji was looking a little healthier. She told him she was going to shower and dress and open the shop. He remembered to ask her if there was anything else he could help her with before he left, and she thanked him again for the breakfast.

Manfred left feeling pretty good about himself for helping Fiji, though he didn't realize he'd left the pastry box in the middle of the table, the dishes undone, and the butter out of the refrigerator.

Fiji found it made her feel more like normal to do some cleaning up, though she was moving slowly. She still felt a bit weak, though not as much as the day before. Moving at a snail's pace, but steadily, she pulled off her nightgown and got into the shower, which truly felt like heaven. It was crisply chill outdoors, and she turned the hot water on hotter. When she was very clean she turned it off and toweled herself with as much vigor as she could summon.

Fiji decided not to make any decisions this morning. She pulled on the first pair of jeans her hands encountered in the closet, the first sweater in the drawer. The first pair of sneakers she saw in her closet. The first pair of socks her hand lit on. Fiji was not terribly clothes-conscious, but selecting things at random according to convenience was a new level of carelessness. It was liberating.

To complete the pattern, she put on the first pair of earrings she touched (eyes shut) in her jewelry box.

As Fiji turned the sign to read OPEN, she was feeling pretty darn good about herself.

It would have lasted, too, if her first customer hadn't been one of the few people Fiji truly disliked, one of the women who sometimes came to her Thursday night class of witch wannabes.

When she wasn't behind the counter at the Walgreens in Davy, Willeen Elliott dressed in ensembles she imagined made her look authentically Wiccan and therefore interesting. Today, Willeen was wearing a peasant blouse, a voluminous skirt, and a dramatic shawl that encircled her and was tossed over one shoulder. Since Fiji had cancelled that night's meeting, Willeen had come to tell Fiji her theory about the suicides.

"We got to get our little group together," she said, as if no other conclusion was possible. "We got to stop them by working magic at the crossroad." It was amazing to Fiji how close to the truth Willeen had gotten for entirely the wrong reasons. Willeen explained her plan at length and scolded Fiji for not stopping the suicides on the spot.

Amazingly, Willeen hadn't heard of the shooting the day before, which was an unexpected ray of sunshine. Fiji certainly wasn't going to bring it up.

"You just don't have any get-up-and-go," Willeen said, snorting. "Fiji, you live right here on the spot where all this hellish activity is going on, and you have yet to cast a spell or say an incantation."

Fiji didn't think she had to defend herself. Willeen was hardly entitled to know the whole story of what was happening in Midnight. But at the accusation that she had done nothing, Fiji had to respond.

"I live here, and I think I do know what's going on," she said with some heat. In fact, she stood up behind the counter, her chair almost bouncing with the suddenness of her shift. Willeen took a step back.

The woman actually bridled. Now Fiji knew exactly what writers meant when they said that. "When are you going to do something about it?" Willeen demanded.

"You don't know what I've done," Fiji said, exasperated. "For all you know, I could have a cauldron of wizard lips and bunny tails simmering on the stove."

Willeen looked very startled and actually made a move toward the hall door, but Fiji said, "That's private, Willeen."

"Are you really doing something?"

Fiji nodded.

"Are you facing the powers of evil?"

Willeen was incurably dramatic. She had rescripted her life to resemble a daytime drama.

"Yes," Fiji said on impulse. "I am."

Willeen gaped. "Really? Do you . . . need my help, at all?"

It was brave of Willeen to ask, really, but Fiji didn't want to torment the woman. "It's being taken care of," she whispered with great significance.

Willeen was delighted and frightened, all at the same time. "Goddess be praised," she breathed, though if Fiji was any judge Willeen didn't have any conception of what goddess she meant.

Fiji rang up the tarot deck and the mystical greeting cards Willeen had picked out. At least Willeen always purchased something. *But she just buys things so she can carry around her purchases in an Inquiring Mind gift bag, so someone will ask her what kind of shop it is,* Fiji thought. She gave Willeen a courteous nod as she handed over the bag with the charge slip inside.

Willeen nodded back very seriously, as if they shared some great and portentous secret. She departed in a flutter of skirt and after a complete redraping of the shawl.

Fiji collapsed back into the rolling chair behind the counter. She wondered if it would be so very bad if she had *two* grilled cheese sandwiches with her soup at lunch. *If I'm thinking about food, I must be getting over being a killer,* she thought.

Mr. Snuggly gathered himself and jumped up onto the low work area below the counter. "I have been over to see the Rev," the cat said. "He has prayed for that man's soul. So don't worry any more about him."

It was just weird how the cat often divined her moods and the subject of her thoughts. Of course, he was supposed to be her familiar, but Mr. Snuggly seemed more familiar with his own wants than with how to help her do witchcraft.

"How did my aunt get you to actually do some work?" Fiji asked.

"That is a . . . tactless way to put it," the cat said stiffly.

"I was just wondering. I know you were her familiar, but how did that relationship work? That's a more accurate question, right? Now you're mine, but I haven't seen you do anything that was familiar-like."

"Mildred picked me out as a kitten," he said. "I was adorable, of course, and she knew I was special."

"Did she?" Fiji was far more interested than she would have been under other circumstances. "Were there any other kittens in your litter that could have been, ah, special cats like you?"

"I had an excellent mother and five siblings," Mr. Snuggly said rather stiffly. "They were very striking, of course."

"Of course."

"So when Mildred came to see us—we were born under the church, you know—"

"I did *not* know that."

"We were! The Rev was most kind. He put food and water out for my mother so she wouldn't have to leave us for long periods of time, and he found us homes."

"Ahhhhhh . . . I don't suppose any of your siblings could talk?"

The cat glared at Fiji. "Of course not. Though they were all *delightful*."

"I'm sure they were. Could you always talk? From birth?"

"No," Mr. Snuggly said, in a tone best described as "frosty." "I only discovered this ability when I was several months old and living here."

"I wonder if you would have talked if you'd lived with someone other than Aunt Mildred?"

"I don't know," he said. He jumped down and walked away. She could hear his voice trailing away as he went down the hall, and she stood to look after him. "Come to give a little comfort, and she asks about my family. My family! As if they could help being good, honest, plain cats . . ."

Impulsively, Fiji called, "How come you were under the car?"

The cat looked at her over his shoulder. "I was there because you needed a focus point. You needed to give him the biggest dose of bad you could, and my proximity helped. And that is what a familiar does."

"So how did he die?"

"You took his air," Mr. Snuggly said. "You pulled it all out of him. Felt like a tiny storm in there."

"I took his air," she said, trying to really understand it. "I held out my hand at him, and I took his air."

The cat nodded. "You did. And more power to you. He was a bad old bugger."

32

The day following the death of Ellery McGuire, the Reeds were afraid to come out of their trailer. "We're in the open now," Teacher said. "I went down there with a shotgun when McGuire showed up. They know Melanie's dad hired me."

"Olivia," Madonna corrected him. "We've called her Olivia for two years; we might as well keep on going."

"Mama play?" Grady asked, bringing her one of his puzzles.

"Sure, honey," Madonna said, sitting on the floor with him. Since this was not her usual answer, Grady was delighted. His broad smile was so happy that Madonna had to smile back. "We may have a lot of time to play, little man," she told Grady. She dumped the puzzle pieces out between them and said, "You put one in first."

The puzzle was big and wooden, and Grady's little hands fumbled a bit, but he put the boat in the boat-shaped cutout, and Teacher clapped. "You're smart, Grady," he said, and bent to kiss the child on the head.

"We may need Grady to get us out of this mess," Madonna said.

"It's good that one of us is smart. We got to make a living, and since we weren't open yesterday . . ."

There was a knock on the trailer door, which was such a rare occurrence that both the Reeds started. Madonna held out her hand to Teacher, who pulled her up off the floor easily. They faced the door.

"I have to answer it," Teacher said finally.

"All right," Madonna whispered. She opened a cabinet that was above Grady's height and pulled out a Sig Sauer P220. "I'm ready."

Teacher grabbed up Grady and went to the door. He took a deep breath and opened it from the side, awkwardly. He didn't want to block Madonna's line of fire.

Joe stood on the steps. His face was calm, and his hands were clasped in front of him. Madonna's gun hand fell to her side without her willing it to do so.

"We're cool," Joe said. He nodded, to show that was his entire message. Then he left.

"This *town*," Madonna said when Joe was out of hearing. "This damn town!"

"At least we know," Teacher said, more philosophically. "Couldn't ask for more straightforward than that."

"You're sure he means it?" Madonna returned the Sig Sauer to its hiding place.

"Yes," Teacher said, not even taking a moment to think it over. "That was Joe, and he speaks the truth."

"I've never lived in a place like this," Madonna said, shaking her head. She took Grady from Teacher and nuzzled his neck. "Mama loves you, little man."

"Mama," Grady said, and patted her on the cheek. "Play."

Mama did play with Grady for twenty minutes, and then she decided to open the diner for dinner, at least. Teacher said he'd help, since she'd told the local boy who bussed for her to take the day off. Madonna was glad she hadn't given Lenore Whitefield an answer about making the nightly meals for the resident old folks in the hotel, because she would have had to scramble to get anything prepared in time.

The little Reed family walked over to Home Cookin, and Madonna felt much better when she began food preparations. She was a woman of many talents, but this was the one that made her happy.

Teacher's cell phone rang as he was setting the tables. He pulled it out of his pocket and looked at the caller. "It's the man," he called to his wife, and answered the phone in a completely different voice.

"Yessir." He listened. Then he spoke. "She's going to be fine. I bribed an orderly to listen and look. Two more days in the hospital, maybe. Then home." He listened some more.

"No, I don't think you ought to come, Mr. Wicklow," he said, trying not to sound horrified by the idea. "Her next of kin now is her husband. He might not want you to see her. You're the boss; you'll do what you want, of course. But if you wait until she gets out of the hospital . . . all right, then, good-bye."

"How's Wicklow handling the situation?" Madonna said, popping her head out of the kitchen. Her husband was putting his phone away, and he looked relieved.

"He's plenty worried about her. But now that McGuire is dead and Olivia's out of danger, I think he's scared of actually facing her again. And maybe the old man doesn't really want to know what Olivia does to make her money."

Madonna shrugged. "Girl's got to keep alive."

"I think everybody in Midnight knows Olivia's business. Everybody but us," her husband said bitterly. "And that would be a good thing to know. He'd be sure we were on the job. We just can't get anyone in this town to *talk* to us."

Madonna said, "You better take that from Grady."

Teacher swooped down on his son and took the pepper shaker away. "You'll sneeze and wheeze if you eat that stuff, Grady," he chided.

"Neeze," Grady said, and Teacher laughed.

For the first time since the break-in, Fiji came to eat in the café that evening. She gave Teacher a very direct look, and he looked back, and after that she behaved as though the incident had never happened, or at least as far as Teacher could tell.

Fiji seemed wobbly to Teacher, and he noticed that the other Midnighters all took a moment to hug her or pat her or just say a quiet word. And when she'd eaten, the Rev himself walked her home, though Bobo wanted to, Teacher could tell.

Madonna and Teacher cleaned up the kitchen and were out the door by eight thirty. The night was dark and cool, with a promise of rain. Teacher stood looking up for a moment at the heavy clouds skidding across the sky, driven by the wind.

It was less than seven yards to the door of the trailer, but in that short space Teacher went from thinking of playing a game on his laptop to fearing for his life. Lemuel stood between Teacher's family and home.

In the only light available, a weak security light over the rear door of the diner, Lemuel's white skin seemed to glow like mother-of-pearl. Teacher bit back a scream, Madonna made a gulping noise, and Grady stirred sleepily on her shoulder.

"If Olivia had died, you would have died at this moment," Lemuel said. "You were coming to her aid, they tell me. So you are saved." And then he was gone.

"Oh my God," Madonna said, after a moment of shuddering silence. "Oh my God." Teacher felt even more unsettled by the whole incident when he realized that Madonna had tears running down her cheeks.

He had never seen his wife cry before.

33

Later that same night, in the hospital in Davy, Olivia woke when a cold hand took hers. "Lemuel," she said weakly.

"I was here last night, but you slept the whole time," Lemuel said. "I understand you will recover. I talked to the doctor myself."

Her room was dim but not dark, and she could see his outline against the light coming in the partially open door. "Lem," she said. "I almost left you for good. If he'd gotten an inch to the left or an inch to the right . . ."

"And me sound asleep," Lem said bitterly. "No use to you at all."

"He shot me," she said. "Fucking asshole."

"He's a dead asshole now," Lemuel said.

"I thought I heard one of the EMTs say that," Olivia murmured. "I expected to see Fiji or Bobo today, but they said I couldn't have any visitors. Was that your doing?"

"Yes, that was my doing. I'm sorry if you wanted company, but I was scared someone bad would come in, and I would not be here to protect you. Now that we are married, I had the right to prevent it."

She nodded. "Okay with me. I didn't feel like talking. Did I see Teacher with a shotgun? Guess we know for sure why he's in Midnight."

"I've had a talk with him and Madonna," Lemuel said. "Now that I know your father hired them to protect you, not to kill you, we've come to an understanding."

"Did you scare 'em to death?" Olivia said. She smiled at him.

"Pretty near. I'm going to stay here until I have to go, close to dawn," he said, smiling back.

"They're gonna come in here to check my blood pressure," she said, protesting, already half asleep.

"Yes, I know. But they won't turn me out," he said. "I'm your husband."

"You know what's silly?" she breathed. "For a little while yesterday, I forgot!"

"You've been shot and you're weak," Lemuel said practically. "I'll do the remembering until you're better."

"That's good," she said, and a little smile crossed her lips before she was out again.

Vampires like Lemuel did not have the gift of glamour, so he couldn't hide himself from the nurse who came in an hour later, even if he'd wanted to.

"How'd you get in here?" she demanded. "No one's supposed to be here!"

She wouldn't have been so abrupt if he hadn't scared her, he figured. That was why he kept his voice calm when he replied.

"I came to sit with my wife as soon as it was dark and I could rise," he said in a very reasonable voice.

Olivia opened her eyes at the sound of voices.

"Ma'am, do you want this man here?" the nurse asked Olivia directly.

Olivia said, "Yes, very much." And that was that.

The nurse took a half step back because she couldn't help herself, and she said, "Don't upset the patient, sir." Then she wheeled around and marched down the hall, her rubber-soled shoes squeaking as she hurried.

"It feels weird to have someone looking out for me," Olivia said, a bit to Lemuel's surprise.

"I feel the same," he admitted. "It's strange. But strange-good, as Fiji says."

"Fiji!" As if the word triggered a flood of memories, Olivia gasped and tried to sit up. In an instant, Lemuel was on his feet and pushing her down with a hand that was like a weight of iron on her chest. Olivia lay back. Her eyes were wide and she was panting with remembered panic. "Lem, he was going to shoot me again and she saved me! What happened to her?"

"She's fine," he said. "Now, hush, Olivia. Hush. Calm."

"Tell me!"

"It was Fiji who killed McGuire."

Tears began oozing from Olivia's eyes. They trickled down to her hair. Lemuel took a corner of the sheet and patted her face.

"Poor Fiji," Olivia said. "She had to kill someone because of me."

"She was willing," Lemuel said cautiously.

"I always hoped that Fiji could stay . . . herself."

This didn't make a lot of sense to Lemuel. Fiji was still herself; she'd just added another experience to her repertoire. But he could tell it was an important thought to his Olivia, so he simply waited for her to elaborate.

"She won't be the same," Olivia said.

When it seemed clear that she wasn't going to say anything else, Lemuel said, "She's always been stronger than anyone seemed to think."

"I know, you're thinking, 'Olivia never liked Fiji that much, anyway, so why is she so upset?'" Olivia said.

Lemuel hadn't been thinking any such thing, but he felt it was wiser to nod.

"The thing is . . ." Olivia stopped, and turned her head a little.

Lemuel realized that was his cue to wipe her face again, and he did so with tenderness. "The thing is, I do like her. I was just envious. Everyone likes Fiji. She's sunny and cheerful. She bakes bread. I wanted her to stay that way . . . while I kind of hated her for having all that."

"So now that she's killed someone, and she has to complete a ritual in front of an audience, you are distressed." Lemuel understood. "Sooner or later she was bound to do something that would serve to keep herself safe, and sooner or later she was bound to have sex, Olivia."

"That is not the point," Olivia said. "And you know it."

Lemuel felt completely at sea. "I'm sorry," he said, because that seemed a safe thing to say.

"Me, too," Olivia said, in a voice so low he had to bend forward to understand her, even with his sharp hearing.

"I have to be there for her," Olivia said, in a stronger voice. "I have to get out of the hospital in time to be there."

"If they won't let you go, I'll give you some blood," Lemuel promised. "Would you like some now?"

Olivia said, "We've only done that during sex before."

"It's wonderful to exchange blood when we are being man and woman. But you would heal faster now if you had some of my blood."

"I would love to heal faster. Bring it."

Lemuel had wondered, at first, if Olivia was seeking a relationship with him because his blood would heal wounds much faster. In her line of business, quick healing was an undeniable plus and might mean the difference between life and death. Lemuel hadn't volunteered blood-giving or -taking when their connection had become sexual; he had been waiting for Olivia's cue. If she had brought up blood first, he would have been even more cautious in letting their relationship develop. But Lemuel had become assured that whatever Olivia wanted from him, quick healing was not on her agenda.

Without hesitation, Lemuel opened his own wrist and offered it to her. He was amused to see that she made a little face. A little bite in the heat of passion was very different from this exchange.

But his Olivia was nothing if not determined. She managed several good gulps before she fell back on the pillow. "Thanks," she said, in a somewhat stronger voice. "Not fun, but functional, huh?"

"When you come home, dearest dear, we will spend good times together," Lemuel promised.

"Sounds like a plan," Olivia said. "Sounds great." She smiled at him and fell asleep.

Lemuel stayed by her bedside until nearly dawn. Olivia slept while the nurses came in and out, checking her vital signs. They mostly pretended he wasn't there, or gave a little nod in his direction without meeting his eyes. He was used to this, and it didn't bother him. The price he paid for being able to take energy rather than blood from people was that he stood out sharply from the herd, was unmistakably not human. Even when he did take blood, he did not look lifelike.

Now Lemuel wondered if he, along with the other citizens of Midnight, would live to see many more days.

It all hinged on Fiji.

To Lemuel, who had never been modest about his body, Fiji's sacrifice seemed—maybe not trivial, since to Lemuel sex was a very private thing—but a low priority in the grand scheme of things. A woman Fiji's age should not balk at such a sacrifice. Lemuel himself would not.

If she had been a dewy teenager, he might have held another opinion. And Lemuel understood the procedure would not be pleasant, but then, having a demon loose on the town would not be pleasant, either, and that would affect many more people.

Though Lemuel had told Fiji that he must be off her list of potential partners as a married man, during the long hours of night he wondered if some chance occurrence would force him to take the role. In that remote case, Lemuel hoped that Olivia would forgive him. Olivia's forgiveness was not an easy process. Lemuel sighed, the air stirring in his dead lungs. He watched her sleeping profile. He would do anything for her. *You're caught, good and proper,* he admitted to himself.

When the vampire could feel the very first tinge of dawn approaching, he slipped out of the hospital and got in his car. He siphoned energy along the way: from a sleeping orderly slumped on a chair, a visitor in the waiting room who was dead to the world, a middle-aged woman recovering from minor surgery. A sip of life force here, a sip there.

Lemuel was in his room below the pawnshop thirty minutes before the sun rose. He slept the sleep of the dead.

34

Fiji had trouble focusing the next day, though there was plenty to keep her busy. The past few years, children from Davy came to see her decorated Halloween house and take a cookie from her heaped tray. Her yard was deliciously scary, and most of the Midnighters helped her out in one way or another. She had celebrated Samhain by herself, and that was a pleasure, too.

But this year Halloween and Samhain were on the same Saturday night as the waning moon. Midnight was going to be scary for real. Fiji had to get the word out, so trick-or-treaters wouldn't flock to the Witch's House, as her Halloween extravaganza was called. She set about spreading the news in as many ways as she could.

Manfred made a list of local online sites, like the area Swap N Shop page; Fiji wrote a notice for Manfred to post on every single site. Fiji called the Davy and Marthasville papers to ask if they were doing a Halloween activities story. Both were. "In view of the recent deaths in Midnight, I thought it would be in bad taste to have a big celebration here," she explained. "I'm sure everyone will understand. To cut down on the disappointment, it would be so helpful if you could include that in your story."

"I didn't want to add, 'And you may get eaten by a demon,'" Fiji told Manfred, who'd dropped by because he thought he really ought to. In truth, he was feeling more than a little self-conscious around her, Fiji could tell.

Fiji was horribly aware that her virginity and its impending loss was on everyone's mind. It would be harder to be in a more humiliating situation. She considered several plans to extricate herself from this predicament, but every step she pondered seemed to end in making things worse, not better. In her most hidden heart, Fiji wondered what would happen if *nobody* volunteered to . . . partner her. "Oh, my God! How scarifying would *that* be?" she muttered.

Fiji was not often stupid or silly. She realized that a public ritual was not a love tryst. But she harbored a hope that the man who completed his part of the deed at least showed some—well, some *enthusiasm*. If one of the angels had to sacrifice himself to do that, she would not be able to show her face for the rest of her life. The idea of poor Joe or poor Chuy on top of her, pumping away without lust or love . . . well, it just made her wince with mortification.

"You have company coming," Manfred said, and she pulled herself out of her black thoughts. Fiji's back was to the door, and she turned to face it. She was regretting opening the shop. Her customer was probably the odious Willeen or some other dabbler.

Fiji was surprised to see Lenore Whitefield from the hotel. She seldom saw Lenore and had only spoken to her once or twice. Lenore was bursting with things to say, there was no mistaking the look, but she stopped in her tracks when she saw Manfred.

"Hi," Fiji said. "Was there something I could help you with, Lenore?"

"Uh, yeah," Lenore said hesitantly. "Your name is Fiji, right?"

"Right. And this is Manfred Bernardo from across the street."

"Sure. Hi, Mr. Bernardo. I hope Tommy and Suzie and Mamie are well? I miss having them at the hotel."

"They like Safe Harbor, but they do miss Midnight," Manfred said, trying to be tactful. "Please, call me Manfred."

Still, Lenore hesitated.

"Something's on your mind, Lenore?" Fiji tried to be gentle, but she was conscious of the clock ticking.

Lenore took a big step into the store, committing herself to a conversation. "When the hotel opened, the project manager kept telling me that market research had proven that the hotel was in a good spot for its purpose. A place for old people to stay while they waited for an opening in assisted living. And if we had the divided use, with part of it being for regular hotel customers and part of it being for more extended stays, the hotel would be able to make a profit."

She paused, and to give her some kind of confirmation that they were on track, Fiji said, "Right."

Lenore said, "Me and Harvey, we needed jobs, bad, and we were really glad to be picked out of the other couples who applied for the job. That Eva Culhane, she ran the interviews."

It took Fiji a few seconds to remember that Eva Culhane had been the project manager who'd been on site while the hotel was being renovated. She had not, by Joe's account, been warm or fuzzy or anything but brisk and efficient.

"I noticed that the couples who got asked to come back for a second round, they were like us," Lenore was saying. "They didn't have any other family with them. Well, even that made sense. Not too many people with little kids would want to settle in Midnight."

Manfred and Fiji nodded in unison, like bobblehead dolls, Fiji thought.

"Naturally, I talked to the other women while we were waiting," Lenore said. "As you do."

"Sure," Fiji said. Manfred looked blank.

"And it seemed to me that we were the saddest of the lot."

Fiji opened her mouth to say something to refute that, automatically, and then she realized she had better wait and see what the bottom line on this conversation was going to be.

"What do you mean?" Manfred asked, practically.

"I mean that we didn't have any kids at all, not even grown kids who would come to visit, or anything. Or living parents. Or brothers or sisters. Well, Harvey's got a brother in Alaska, but they haven't talked in five years, I guess."

"No close connections," Manfred summarized briskly.

Lenore nodded. "This didn't make any difference to my husband, but it worried me a little. Some of the other couples, the man was a good plumber, or carpenter, or had some executive experience, like running a couple of Holiday Inns or the like."

"But not Harvey," Fiji said.

"Not Harvey. He worked on the line at a factory that made salsa. For twenty years. When he got laid off, he couldn't find another job to save his soul. He tries to help, but he just hasn't got the skills. So we hire Teacher to come do repairs. I kind of lied to Ms. Culhane about that."

"I understand," Fiji said. "I suppose I would have, too." Eventually, Lenore would get to the point.

"Culhane didn't check up on us that much," Lenore went on. "And that seemed pretty strange to me, considering how finicky she was about everything else. It was like she was looking for the least qualified, rather than the best qualified. See what I mean?"

Fiji, nodding again, said, "I do see."

"But I was so glad to get the job, which included a place to live," Lenore said doggedly, "that I ignored all the signals."

If Fiji nodded one more time, she thought her head would fall off. "I understand," she said. It was impossible to read Manfred's expression. He was watching Lenore with apparent fascination.

"It come to me too late, after we'd already gotten here, that we'd been sucked into something that might kill us," Lenore said.

"Okay, why do you think . . . ?" Manfred didn't have to finish the question.

"Me and Harvey, we're expendable," Lenore said with some dignity. "To them, anyway. I've tried my best to make the hotel nice, to run it so it makes money. I knew the first batch of old people we got, them from Nevada, they weren't really waiting for assisted-living places. They were window dressing, to make it look like the hotel was really what Culhane said it was."

"You're absolutely right about that," Manfred said. "Someone has paid to put them in an expensive place, but you know that. I want to know who's actually footing the bills, and why."

"It's something to do with Olivia," Lenore said.

Fiji could have danced with relief. The point was in sight. "What about Olivia?" she said.

"I don't know," Lenore said. "But it's to do with her. I'll tell you something. Some of the guests really do go over to Magic Portal every day to consult there, whatever that means. But whoever's in the top front room on the corner stays in almost all the time, watching."

"I think that you were brave to come tell us this," Fiji said to Lenore. "I really appreciate it. And while you're here, I have a thing or two to tell you. I was going to come by later today."

"Really?" Lenore seemed a little excited that Fiji had planned on visiting her, which made Fiji feel like a scumbag.

"Here's the thing," Fiji said. "This year, Halloween is going to be quiet in Midnight."

"Oh?" Lenore looked doubtful. "I know that last year lots of people came to town to enjoy your house and yard."

"Yes, and that was fun." Fiji smiled at Lenore. "But this year, we've heard that with the weird suicides, and the shooting, something really serious might happen."

"That sounds pretty bad." Lenore sighed deeply, her eyes fixed on the wall as she thought. "Okay, I'll arrange for a party for the residents in the dining room, and I'll talk to the transient guests. I really do appreciate the warning."

"No problem. I should have come by earlier," Fiji said. She felt both awkward and unworthy.

"Harvey especially should stay in," Manfred said abruptly.

"What?" Lenore turned to face him, looking puzzled.

"You know I'm a psychic," Manfred said, trying to smile and failing. "I think Harvey will be in extra danger."

It was clear to Fiji that Lenore was conflicted. The hotel manager didn't know whether to be pleased that Manfred had thought enough of Harvey to warn him, or if she found the whole idea so ridiculous that she didn't give it any credence at all. "Thanks," Lenore said. "I'll remember that." After she left, Manfred and Fiji were left to look at each other in a resigned way.

"It was a real vision," Manfred said finally.

"I know," Fiji replied. "And you've told her. If she doesn't believe, she doesn't believe, and frankly, I think we have enough on our plates to worry about."

"Are you still hearing the voice?"

"Not today. But I feel him move, more and more. He's flexing. And I saw the Rev carting off more dead animals this morning. He's building up his strength."

Abruptly, Manfred said, "If it's me, Fiji, I'll man up. I promise you." He smiled at her in what he meant to be a reassuring way. But Fiji had a suspicion he was thinking of Estella.

"Thanks, Manfred," she said, trying to hide her own lack of enthusiasm under a steady voice.

When she was alone, Fiji felt dismal again. Even the guys were worried about having sex by appointment. (Well, at least one guy.) Though she realized that had little or nothing to do with her as a woman and she understood the sacrifice required of her, she was unhappy and anxious to get it over with.

Which is not the way you should feel about the first time you have sex.

At least, that had always been her impression.

If she survived to see November 1, her life would be her own again.

35

The next day was Halloween. And Samhain. And Saturday. And the waning moon. And the longest day in the history of the world, if you were Fiji.

To everyone's astonishment, a warm front came in from the west. The skies poured rain in the morning and early afternoon. The roads and sidewalks were washed clean. The front window of Midnight Pawn was streaked with drops that blew under the awning. Fiji's garden, in its last hurrah before winter, looked fresh and vivid; inside the Inquiring Mind, Mr. Snuggly tucked himself under Fiji's counter to be safe from the thunder.

The Rev went to the chapel under a giant and ancient umbrella. He'd asked Diederik to dust and vacuum his house, which Diederik was glad to do. It didn't seem like a good morning to be kneeling in the little chapel.

In his room at the Midnight Hotel, Quinn worked on the details of a sort of quinceañera within the half-demon clan in New Orleans. When he couldn't distract himself with that any longer, Quinn again read over the translated account of the ritual as Arria Auclina, Etruscan vampire, had written it down scores of years before. Auclina had heard this account firsthand from the witch involved, but she hadn't been present. Lemuel had sent them all copies so they would understand what had to be done.

Quinn had to hope that nothing essential had been lost in translation.

Fiji was studying the ritual, too.

Olivia came back to Midnight, fetched by Bobo. Over her protests, he'd carried her in, wrapped in a raincoat. He helped her down the stairs and turned down the cover so she could climb into bed in her own apartment in her own pajamas. Though Olivia was doing so well her doctor was dumbfounded, the transition exhausted her. After Bobo left, she promptly fell asleep. She woke to lightning, which she could glimpse out of her windows peeking just above the ground level. Lemuel still slept, of course, but she knew he was in the next room. She was the only person in Midnight who was deeply happy.

Diederik worried about his part in the evening's preparations as he cleaned. The salt, now mixed with the ash of the hawthorn tree, was in a tub in the chapel. He and his father were charged with sprinkling the mixture on the circle they'd drawn around the crossroad. But if it kept raining, he didn't know what they'd do. Underlying his worry about the weather and the excitement of the potential demon rampage, Diederik was hoping Fiji might choose him to participate in the final part of the ritual. Diederik was more than ready.

Manfred was busy with his usual workload. He paused, though, to think about Estella Hardin. He'd gone out with her a couple of times now, and those evenings had been very good. He hoped like hell he would have more evenings with Stell. But that week he'd been avoiding the intimacy that would lead to sex, because he simply couldn't face having sex with Fiji (if that was his lot), and then going back to Stell, while keeping this evening's events a secret.

Joe and Chuy missed their dog and clung to each other. They put the CLOSED sign on the shop's door. No one shopped for antiques or manicures in the rain in Midnight. And they alone had faced a demon, so they knew what could happen to them this night.

Lenore and the cook at the hotel collaborated on doing all the prep work for a Halloween dinner for the residents and those of the transient group who wanted to participate. Lenore had talked to Madonna about making a pumpkin pie and a devil's-food cake, and Madonna was in the kitchen at Home Cookin working on those as she and Teacher did the normal lunchtime preparations.

The night before, Lenore had given Marina the task of preparing Halloween goodie bags containing hand lotion, tissues, candy corn, peanuts, an orange, and other odds and ends. Lenore had pointed out that Marina seldom had anything else to do, a point that Marina had felt was quite unnecessary to emphasize.

In truth, Marina was having a little trouble keeping up with the apparently unflagging sex drive that kept Diederik ever at her side. Marina actually thought it would be nice to have an evening off. To the girl's surprise, after she'd prepared the goodie bags, Lenore had sent her home with instructions to come back in two nights. "Take Halloween off," Lenore had said, with a weak smile. Marina thought of calling Diederik, then decided she'd go party with her friends from school instead.

Bobo had gotten all the accounts of Midnight Pawn in order. *Just in case,* he told himself. *Just in case.* All the online forms were filled out, he'd gone over the inventory, and he'd made sure his will was in his bedside drawer. Bobo was determined to step forward for Fiji, but he wondered if he would survive the process. He wanted to be ready.

He thought of Fiji every other minute and was sorry this day would be so fraught for her. She was so kind and good.

Despite Manfred's warning, Lenore did not keep tabs on her husband, which was a pity.

Harvey Whitefield hadn't had a binge in a long time, but that day something about the pounding rain made his resolution collapse utterly, and he drove to Davy to a liquor store and bought a bottle of bourbon, saying nothing to his wife, who was very busy in the kitchen and in the hotel, putting out decorations for the party. That suited Harvey fine. He got a liter of Coca-Cola and a glass from the pantry, put some ice in a bucket, and retired to an empty room in the hotel to have his own private party. He watched the game show channel on the flat-screen. Though he wasn't good at remembering the answers, the questions made him feel smart. And he was gleeful at having successfully dodged his wife.

The three senior citizens who were in the Midnight Hotel suites, waiting for an opening at the assisted-living center in Davy or the one in Marthasville, played cards and read or listened to audiobooks, according to their eyesight acuity. They liked the break in the monotony provided by the rain and thunder, and they had a pleasant, cozy day. It got dark even earlier than usual in October. They were all glad to switch on the nearest lamp.

The four people who were "transient guests" at the Midnight Hotel went about their business. The three genuine tech support people actually drove to Magic Portal, even on a Saturday. They had a productive day at the gaming company. Their Magic Portal colleagues invited the three to a party that would start immediately after work that day, and they all accepted gladly. Working with the Magic Portal people was more fun than anything they'd ever done.

The fourth person was the man renting the second-floor front room, which overlooked the pawnshop. Lenore understood he was a writer, and that was why he stayed in his room almost all the time. There was certainly a laptop in his room, and he always seemed to be working when Lenore cleaned his room. The past two days, he'd seemed very jittery, and he was never without his phone in his hand. He'd told Lenore he might check out at any time. He seemed surprised and pleased to get a special Halloween treat brought up on a tray by the boy who usually worked in the evening.

"Why are you on duty during the day?" the man asked.

"The girl quit," Diederik answered. "Enjoy."

Left alone with the tray, the man had to admit it looked interesting. There was a small pitcher of sangria with lots of fruit in it (carefully covered with a paper frill) and a cheese and cracker plate with a bit of honeycomb. The note on the tray said, "Have a happy Halloween!" He took the tray to his chair and table arranged by the window to keep his vigil. He drank the pitcher of sangria and picked at the cheese and crackers and honeycomb. He didn't wake until three a.m. the next morning, courtesy of Joe and Chuy, who'd entrusted Diederik with the delivery.

Underneath the rock, dirt, and asphalt the demon Colconnar stirred. He was not *quite* strong enough yet. He needed more blood. He would rise. He would have the witch in every way it was possible to have her. He began summoning anyone weak enough to listen. Ah! He found someone very weak, and very close.

Harvey Whitefield had dozed off from the liquor and the drumming of the rain in the empty hotel room. He woke, thinking he'd heard someone call his name. He felt a surge of guilt, because he was sure his wife was looking for him. But to Harvey's astonishment, the voice was one he'd never heard before. Harvey lurched to his feet, looking from side to side to find the source of the summons.

He went to the door and listened. Nothing on the landing. But he could still hear his name. He opened the door just a bit and looked around. There was no one there. He could hear, very faintly, the sound of the old geezers in the common room on the ground floor. They were talking about how to play Texas Hold 'em and debating how many books Nora Roberts had written.

Harvey wasn't interested in either subject, so it was easier for him to listen to the voice. In fact, he found it impossible to ignore. After a second, he stepped out of the room and went down the stairs, unsteady on his feet. It was unlucky for Harvey that the stairs were carpeted, or he would have made quite a lot of noise and maybe someone would have stopped him.

But that didn't happen.

Harvey was supposed to be on duty at the desk, of course, but who'd even noticed that he wasn't there? No one! Marina would be on duty in a few minutes. (Harvey did not know that Lenore had given Marina the night off.) There was a bell on the desk, anyway, to summon help if a traveler should stop in. Like anyone ever did! This damn place!

Harvey hardly realized he was crossing the lobby floor to the doors. No one saw him leave, and the tinkle of the chime on the door didn't even register to the little group in the common room. They could only hear the rain beating down.

Harvey was soaked to the skin within seconds of stepping outside. He dimly understood what he had to do, now that he could hear the voice more clearly. He didn't have a gun or a knife or anything sharp-edged with him, which he realized was his fault. The two queers across the road could sell him a blade, but their knives were all antique. The pawnshop had knives, but they were under lock and key. The bitch who ran that witch shop had knives, but she always looked at him like he was a problem she had to solve.

Then the demon supplied him with a good idea. Harvey lay down on the road just a little out of the direct radius of the stoplight. In the heavy rain, the next truck that came along passed through the green light without even noticing the bumps.

The demon was delighted at this rich meal, and he felt more blood a bit farther afield. He began pulling the really ripe one, the really tasty one, the one the witch despised.

And Kiki, who'd been staying at a motel in Marthasville with a cowboy she'd met at the Cartoon Saloon the day she'd left Midnight, accelerated in her drive to the crossroads. Where she had to be. NOW.

36

The rain stopped at four thirty though the clouds did not clear, and Quinn and his son went out immediately to sprinkle the salt and ash on the outline of the circle. In the gloom, the two didn't spot the body until they were halfway around. More than one truck had passed through by then, so it wasn't a recognizable shape.

Though Diederik had the strong stomach of a tiger, he vomited after he realized he was looking at Harvey Whitefield.

"We can't call the police," Quinn said. "They'll be here forever, and we have to do this tonight."

"But Mrs. Whitefield," Diederik protested. "She should know." He liked Lenore, who had always been nice to him, unlike Harvey. Diederik wasn't grieving for the man, but for his wife.

"She should, yes, but we can't risk a demon rising while the cops are here," Quinn said reasonably.

"What do we do with him?"

"Let's move him to the side, so no one will worry about him until the ritual is over. And if the ritual doesn't work, his body will be the least of our worries."

They did move the body, which was very unpleasant, and they covered it with an old sheet of plastic the Rev used when he was digging graves in the animal cemetery. Then the two weretigers resumed their task. The salt-and-ash mixture stuck to the painted line very well because of the damp air and wet pavement.

"Do you think Fiji is scared?" Diederik asked quietly. He was carrying the bucket, and Quinn was using a large scoop to distribute the mixture.

"Sure she is," Quinn said. "For a human, this must feel degrading. They're very modest about no clothes in public."

"Let's switch," Diederik suggested, and when they had swapped scoop and bucket, he said, "They don't like to talk about sex even when they've had it, either. Even when they've had it with *you*."

"You have to go with their feelings," Quinn said philosophically.

"If she picks one of us and she gets pregnant, will the child be one of us?"

"We talked about this when you began to want Marina. The baby would grow up to be a very healthy person its whole life. And the chances are also good that the child would be athletic and strong. But no, it wouldn't be able to change."

Diederik clearly pitied such a child. "I hope someday I can find a tigress, Dad," he said.

"I found your mother," Quinn said. "And I'd given up hope."

"If there's one tigress, there can be more."

"Absolutely." Quinn looked over at the chapel to see the Rev standing on the steps.

"Diederik, run tell the Rev about Harvey and ask him to say a word over the body," Quinn said, and Diederik hurried over to the old cleric. Quinn saw the Rev nod and walk unhurriedly to the deformed corpse to kneel beside it.

The moment he did, a half-familiar car swerved up and almost hit the Rev, who proved he still had excellent reflexes. The old man threw himself to the left. Diederik and Quinn were only a few feet away, and they both leaped farther, startled and furious.

A woman got out, a woman who smelled familiar, too.

"It's Fiji's sister!" Diederik said, but Quinn was already moving to intercept Kiki, who was staggering toward the intersection. Luckily, no vehicles were coming, but Kiki lay down to wait for her death. She screamed when Quinn yanked her up by her arm. Fiji's door opened and she ran out, afraid the demon was breaking free early. She dashed toward the struggling group.

The demon screamed, too, in outrage and desire. And he moved so powerfully that the ground began to tremble.

As doors flew open and the people of Midnight poured out of their houses, Kiki struggled with the weretigers. She was intent on dying. The Rev sent Fiji to fetch a rope from the toolshed to bind her, and the three men managed to get her into the chapel.

Fiji said, "I need to be with her!"

Quinn said, "No, we can deal with her. He called her to hurt you. You have to be mentally ready for tonight. He's trying to distract you."

Fiji began to protest, but then she thought, *He was drawing people who didn't like me. He was able to draw my sister.* And she trudged back into her house. The chapel was cold and damp, but at least Kiki couldn't commit suicide if she was secured inside.

Kiki was tied up hand and foot, as a matter of fact.

As the three weretigers left the chapel, the Rev (for the first time ever) locking the door behind him, Bobo held open the front door of the pawnshop while Lemuel carried Olivia out. Bobo reached in to grab a stadium seat with an awning, and after he'd expanded it, Lemuel lowered Olivia into it with great care. Olivia looked pale under the pawnshop light; she was dressed in flannel pajamas with a padded vest over them and socks with moccasins on her feet. Lemuel covered her with a blanket. He was taking no chances.

Joe and Chuy, hand in hand, walked down from their store to stand at the corner opposite the pawnshop. Manfred emerged from his house to stand with Bobo.

And to everyone's surprise, the Reeds walked over from their trailer to take a post on the sidewalk in front of the hotel. Grady was bundled up in a pram-type stroller. Madonna looked resentful but resigned, and she glared around as if daring anyone to make something of her presence. Teacher looked almost pleased. They were both carrying guns.

They nodded at Sylvester, who was wearing jeans and nothing else. He was ready at the Gas N Go corner.

Midnight seemed to fall silent.

37

Inside her front door, Fiji was praying, and praying hard. She thought of all the lives that had been lost at the crossroad in the past few weeks, both human and animal, and she knew she had to stop this from going any further. But this was a bitter pill to swallow, and she almost choked.

She shook her head angrily, exasperated with the weak side of herself, and told herself to be more like her aunt. She flung open the door and stepped onto the porch, Mr. Snuggly at her side.

Fiji's hour had come. She felt weirdly like the bride arriving at the entrance to the church, except instead of wedding regalia, Fiji wore a green silk robe. She'd saved it for a big night that had never happened.

Tonight she got to appear naked in front of everyone she knew, have sex, and save the world. If that didn't constitute a big night, she didn't understand the meaning of the phrase. She'd also dropped five pounds since she had learned she'd have to "drop her drawers," as Aunt Mildred had put it. But that had been from sheer anxiety.

Standing alone under her front porch light, knowing everyone was waiting for her, Fiji struggled to suppress her squeamishness and her bit of vanity and her performance anxiety. For a split second, she was tempted to scream and run back inside. Though it was night, the clouds seemed to be skittering away and the moon was out. Fiji remembered her sister, so anxious to meet her own death.

And Fiji could feel the demon below, moving and murmuring, yearning for her. She felt Mr. Snuggly's soft fur rub against her leg.

Her lesser concerns about her body, about the feelings of the men around her, fell away. These were small issues. She had big work to do.

The relief of this realization was sublime.

Fiji began to cast the spell she'd found in Aunt Mildred's spell book. Its purpose was to close the town to outside notice. She didn't know how often Mildred had had reason to use the spell, but she also had no reason to doubt its efficacy. Sylvester, whom she saw standing under the awning at Gas N Go, was using a similar spell.

And as she repeated the words over and over, her hands moving in a disseminating circle, she began to feel the cone tightening over the crossroad, enclosing all of them inside. She had a fleeting impulse to giggle, thinking of the "cone of silence," but it vanished as she could discern more clearly exactly what it was she was sealing them in with.

The rest of the world drifted away, leaving only the people of Midnight and the demon. Lemuel stood up and walked forward as Fiji stepped down from her porch and walked to the intersection to stand under the stoplight. Abruptly, the stoplight froze on yellow. They were caught in its eerie glow.

Lemuel read from a page. "Fiji Cavanaugh, witch of this town, do you agree to protect this place with your body and soul?"

Fiji nodded. She had hoped it would be a graceful gesture, but she felt her head jerk. She took a deep breath, trying to relax. Then she gave that up as impossible. "I will," she said. Her voice was level.

Lemuel said, "Do you agree to sacrifice your virgin blood to appease what lies below?"

"To seal the demon below us for another two hundred fifty years, I agree," Fiji said. She turned east. "I call on the air for wisdom." She turned south. "I call on the fire for courage." Her voice faltered. After a moment's recovery, she rotated another quarter turn to face west. "I call on water for cleansing." Another quarter turn. "And I call on the earth for strength, most of all." She paused. "Help me defend this town and these people against the demon who threatens them. Bind him into the earth so he can't harm the earth's children."

"Men?" Lemuel said, without raising his voice. But they all heard him.

All the males in the town except Teacher came to stand beside Lemuel, who was glancing down at the pages of script. Fiji could not meet anyone's eyes. Mr. Snuggly glided smoothly past her and sat looking up at the men.

And then she realized that one of them had moved.

Bobo had fallen to his knees. Silently, he held out his hand to Fiji. And there was no way even an insecure woman like Fiji could misinterpret the invitation.

"Really?" she said, embarrassed that her voice was shaking.

"It would be an honor," he said, and even Fiji could not doubt his sincerity. There was love in his voice. "I failed you before. I won't fail you now."

She tried hard not to cry, but a tear ran down her cheek. The other men stood silent, waiting, all of them with emotions she could just detect. To her astonishment, some of them were disappointed when she took Bobo's hand to lead him to the center of the circle. And she held her head a little higher.

Chuy and Joe revealed their true selves as they moved apart to opposite sides of the circle. Their swords glowed. Their wings spread. Manfred took a place a few feet away from Chuy, and Lemuel an equal distance from Joe. Sylvester stepped into place, and he was chanting in a language none of them could understand. Teacher moved into a vacant spot with his shotgun, and Madonna, too, joined the circle. The three weretigers joined in, and finally, as if she could not help herself, Olivia rose and made her way, painfully, slowly, to join them.

Fiji raised Bobo up, and he bent to kiss her. It was everything she had ever hoped for. Even under the public circumstances, she began to feel heat moving through her, and there was no mistaking the fact that Bobo was feeling the same way.

This was not a time to speak. Wordlessly, she loosened the tie of her robe and let it slip down, and stood back. Her eyes straight ahead, she held herself rigid as Bobo looked at her, until he said, "Look at me." She did and read only delight there. Bobo stripped off his sweatshirt, and she stepped in to unbuckle his belt and unzip his pants. He dropped them in a heap, and Mr. Snuggly sat on the discarded clothes, his golden eyes glowing.

Though it was nipping cold, Fiji, full of magic, willed them to be warm, and they were. She had power she had never imagined, and it dazed her.

Fiji knew the moment when Colconnar realized the ritual was taking place above him. He began to move with increasing violence and purpose, clawing his way to the surface, slowly and sluggishly.

She should have been terrified. Instead, Fiji was possessed by a sure confidence: in her power, in her womanhood. She and Bobo kissed again, longer, and this time they lay down on the road. Bobo tried to interpose himself between Fiji and the cold, muddy asphalt, but she said, "I have to touch the ground." He nodded, and she lay on her back. She looked up at him, knowing he could see that she loved him. She was not afraid, now, of his knowing that. She forgot other people were there.

"Are you ready?" Bobo asked, his blue eyes intent on her face. They could both hear the demon now, and they knew they could not spend any more time on preliminaries.

"Oh, yes," she said, surprised to find it was true. She lusted for him with a pure brightness. He pushed into her. It stung. She knew she had bled a few drops and was thankful. She thought, *Not a virgin anymore.* They could stop right now, and the ritual would be satisfied.

But she would not be. Her body had a mind of its own, and that mind said, *Hell no.* She realized in a far part of her brain that she need not have had performance anxiety. She *certainly* knew how to do this. She and Bobo moved together as if they had done it a dozen times. Despite everything that should have prevented her pleasure—the spectators, the weather, the discomfort of lying on cold pavement—Fiji found herself getting close to a climax, which she had never expected.

The magic was gathering around her and Bobo like a thick cloud. But Colconnar was very close to the surface. He was still moving upward. So it wasn't just the virginity or the virgin blood that counted, she realized dimly.

A taloned hand burst through the asphalt. The demon was dark red, or at least it looked that way in the glimpse Fiji had before her body demanded all her attention. The other hand appeared, and Colconnar began to heave himself out of the ground, but still Fiji and Bobo kept up their movement.

Colconnar's talons were almost at Bobo's leg.

Fiji saw the shadow of a lion, small but unmistakable. She knew it was there to protect her. She forgot it, let the magic build and build, her body moving with Bobo's, her hands on his back stroking, digging in, urging him on even when a dark talon pierced his leg and his blood spurted, blending with hers. He screamed, but with her hands on him he did not stop moving in and out of her. With his second scream, he exploded inside her, and at that moment her power flared outward.

Colconnar bellowed.

The sound was so loud Fiji's ears rang. The demon's emerging arm, as big around as a man's thigh, flailed to try to reach Fiji. But

Bobo stayed on top of her to protect her, though his injury was terrible.

The shadow lion stood over them, and it had grown to giant size. Its shadowy form snarled and bit the demon's arm. Bright purple blood spattered the ground, already stained with Fiji's and Bobo's blood. Fiji's brilliant power lit up the scene like a floodlight, and that light made the demon's skin bubble and hiss.

With the terrible sounds of a building collapsing, Colconnar slid back underneath the Texas soil.

In the sudden silence, Fiji heard someone begin clapping. Then everyone joined in, many hands.

As she and Bobo looked into each other's eyes and he kissed her yet again, she figured the clapping was the only way the residents of Midnight could think of to express their profound relief that they were not going to be eaten, and to thank her for her protection and sacrifice.

"Not so much," she said. "Not such a sacrifice."

"Maybe we can get in a warm bed and sacrifice again, real soon?" Bobo seemed reluctant to get off her and get up, and she could understand that. She would like to revel in the moment, too. But the world intruded, and she knew her magic would not be able to hold the scene for long, even with Sylvester's chant.

"That sounds very good to me."

She could tell the moment Bobo felt the full impact of the injury. He hissed and rolled off to her side. "Plus, we need to look at that leg of yours," she said prosaically.

"It hurts a hell of lot. Damn. This is literally anticlimactic," Bobo said, and she began to giggle. He sat up, and she scrambled to her feet. She looked around for her silk robe and found it lying in a dirt-streaked heap a few feet away. Bobo's own clothes were not in much better shape, and his jeans were decorated lavishly with cat hair, though Mr. Snuggly was nowhere in sight. Perhaps he was enjoying being a lion.

Lemuel and Quinn helped Bobo to his feet and half carried him to Fiji's house, after a moment of hesitation.

"You have some cleaning up to do," the Rev said, in his creaky voice. "You're still . . . beaming."

After a moment, Fiji realized he meant magical cleaning up. She was the source of the light around the crossroad. Okay, she would figure this out.

She ratcheted down her magic, unfocusing her will to dissolve the bubble that had kept the world out. As she did so, she saw that all the ghosts of the town were clustered around the ash-and-salt circle, interspersed with live people. Aunt Mildred was standing next to Chuy, and a Mexican cowboy in clothes of a hundred years before was looking at Olivia, who'd resumed her seat on the steps of the pawnshop.

Though she was fascinated and would have liked to spend moments looking at every face, the next instant a car's headlights were coming from the west, from Marthasville, and the cold pinched her skin, and she realized she had to get inside or risk getting arrested. She felt her weariness in her bones . . . plus a very pleasant sense of relaxation and a slight achiness.

Fiji caught a glimpse of the body of Harvey Whitefield, but someone else would have to take care of that particular problem.

Fiji gathered up their clothes hurriedly and started for her house. She sensed someone in front of her and looked up to discover her sister, who had somehow wriggled out of her bonds.

"What did I just see?" Kiki said. "Were you humping in the middle of the road? Did I just see something coming out of the asphalt?"

"What do you think you saw?" Fiji said, and took a step around Kiki. "Go home, Kiki, and don't come back."

She walked over to her house, finally locating Mr. Snuggly. He was sitting on the little wall around the porch next to a planter, and he looked proud—which meant he looked like all cats. But he nodded to her in a congratulatory way, and then set about cleaning his paws.

For a moment, Fiji hesitated at the door, looking back. She could see a shadow surrounding the cat, a shadow that didn't match the domestic shorthair feline outline at all.

But Fiji had opened the door an inch, and she could hear the water of the shower running. She could imagine the warmth of the water and the clean smell of her soap, and she knew Bobo was waiting for her to join him. She hoped Lemuel had healed his leg. If not, there was bandaging to do. She even looked forward to that. Fiji stepped inside and shut the door behind her.

38

The next morning, Fiji woke feeling like a new woman. The crisis was over. The demon was imprisoned. Bobo was asleep beside her. She had saved the world! She had had sex! Bobo loved her!

She tried to track down the essential difference she felt in herself. She was still Fiji, still the least important person in a contentious family, still a witch in a society that did not like witches, still round as a honeydew in a nation that revered stiltlike women.

But now, she thought, *I am powerful.* It was a fact. Her feeling that she was transforming had begun before last night—in fact, when she had frozen the gunmen the day of the assault on Olivia. The day she had killed McGuire. Arthur Smith would never stop asking questions about that day, and she would never be held responsible for any of it. She knew that. And despite the fact that everyone was always talking about how nice she was, she didn't feel guilty for having killed Ellery McGuire. It had been the only way to prevent the deaths of people she knew—people who were in her care.

She wondered if Sylvester Ravenwing would stay, and she rather hoped he would. She wondered if Olivia would decide to become a vampire. She wondered if Joe and Chuy would ever be able to re-attain heaven. And what would Teacher and Madonna do, now that Olivia's father might come talk to Olivia directly? There was no need to protect her from Ellery McGuire any longer, Fiji figured.

It felt good to have a future in which to contemplate all these things.

She felt a little movement beside her and knew Bobo was awake.

"Hey, beautiful," he said. Another thing she knew was that he meant it.

Joe and Chuy had gotten up at their usual time, but instead of Joe going for his run and Chuy preparing breakfast, they'd jumped in their car and driven to the kennel where Rasta had been boarded. The Peke was bathed and groomed and ecstatic to see his people. Everyone who worked at the kennel agreed that if all gay people were as nice and modest and normal as Chuy Villegas and Joe Strong, they wouldn't mind having them around.

Joe and Chuy drove back to Midnight. "If we can't ever go back home," Joe said, "at least we have a dog."

"'God' spelled backward," Chuy said. It was an old joke, but they always enjoyed it.

Joe gave a silent sigh. Sensing the near-emergence of the demon had activated a hunger in him, a deep need he had suppressed for decades. He had wanted to fly, to defend heaven.

But they had promised each other not to fly, and he was shackled to Midnight.

"So you got to see Fiji buck naked," Madonna said, apropos of nothing, to her husband.

"Me and everyone else in town," Teacher said cautiously.

"How'd that make you feel?"

He'd been folding laundry, and he kept on folding, though he also felt her eyes on him. "Sorry for her," he said promptly. "She didn't want to do that, and she's no kind of exhibitionist."

"You didn't think you'd like to get a piece?"

"Madonna!" He was genuinely shocked. "You know I haven't touched another woman since we've been married."

"Uh-huh. But I also know you like women with curves, and that Fiji has got 'em. And they're not as jiggly as mine."

Teacher said, "Fiji has got nothing that you haven't got, and I love you."

Which was absolutely the right answer, if it wasn't exactly accurate on all counts.

Later, Madonna said, "You think Mr. Wicklow will keep us here? Let us stay?"

"Now that McGuire is dead? Well, I hope so. I like it here, to tell the truth. You?"

"I'd like to try to make the restaurant a real concern," Madonna said. "I've been kind of playing at it, because I knew he'd keep us solvent, no matter what. But if we really work, advertise, and get us a hook—maybe we'll have the best pie in Texas, or something—maybe we can really make some money. Grady can have a car in high school." Madonna had always envied the teens in her area who could afford that luxury. That was her idea of the best you could hope for.

"He could learn the value of work that way," Teacher said. He tried not to sound excited.

"We wouldn't be beholden to anyone," Madonna said. "Of course, we also wouldn't have a pension plan or health insurance."

"Let's see what the man says." Teacher said. "Might be he has a plan we'd love."

"Might be," Madonna said. She was already thinking of new things she'd like to put on the menu.

Buying the house next to Fiji's had been the quickest real estate transaction in the history of home sales. The sole heir had been delighted to get thirty thousand for a property he hadn't thought about in ten years. Today, Quinn and Diederik started work on their new home. Quinn had some carpentry knowledge, and he enjoyed teaching his son what he knew.

"Marina broke up with me," Diederik said suddenly, just as he'd finished prying up the old tile in the bathroom. "By text."

"How do you feel about that?" Quinn continued on his way to the front door, where he tossed an old kitchen cabinet into a rented Dumpster.

"I liked Marina," Diederik said. "But I liked having sex with her more than I liked her, I think."

"Let me give you some advice. You may think that, but never, ever, say it out loud to a woman."

"Why not?"

"That's what every woman fears. Every woman wants to be liked because of who she is, her personality, not because she makes her sex organs available."

"So I should pretend?"

That was a puzzler. Quinn thought about it. Finally he said, "The perfect answer? Never to have sex with someone you don't genuinely like enough to hang around with."

"How'm I going to do that?"

"We're going to have a lot of conversations about this," Quinn predicted, and he was right.

Though he didn't share his disappointment with Diederik, Quinn had hoped that Fiji would choose him the night before, that it would be him curled up beside her in her bed next door on this chilly morning.

But Quinn looked at his son, and he realized that if he'd had so much luck already, maybe he would have some more.

The Rev knelt in his chapel and prayed. There was always something to pray about, and the God of animals and humans was ready to listen. At least this time, the Rev could thank God for a long list of things. He was especially grateful that Kiki Cavanaugh had recovered from her spasm of madness enough to drive away all by herself late the night before. He would be even more grateful, he confessed to God, if he never saw the woman again.

Lenore Whitefield had woken at four a.m. She could not have said exactly what had happened the evening before. She and the people in the hotel had stayed in all evening, not even approaching the windows, and had had a pleasant Halloween celebration playing games and eating candy.

But Lenore had been mighty irritated with Harvey because he hadn't shown up. She figured he'd gone to a bar to binge-drink, something he did from time to time. He'd always come home before, but now the other half of the double bed was cold. Lenore rose and wrapped a fuzzy bathrobe around herself, made some coffee in the large kitchen. While it was perking, she looked out at the little parking area for the staff, and she saw that Harvey's truck was still there. Lenore found that somewhat reassuring. After she'd had her coffee and gotten dressed, she began searching the hotel. Harvey was nowhere to be found, though she discovered a rumpled bed in one of the unoccupied rooms. There was an empty bottle and the television was on to the game show channel, all signs that Harvey had hidden in there to drink. Her worry congealed into a lump in her throat.

Next, Lenore called Harvey's cell phone and listened to it ring. She tracked the sound back to the room he'd used, where she found it under the edge of the bedspread.

This had never happened before. If his truck was here, Harvey was here. If Harvey was gone, the truck was gone. But he always answered his phone, and he always came home.

By the time the sheriff knocked on the back door, Lenore had admitted to herself that she was pretty sure Harvey was dead. She was sad. And she felt free.

Olivia woke suddenly, aware that she was still in bed with Lemuel, that he was cold and dead for the day. The previous evening had exhausted her, though she spared a smile and a moment to wonder how exhausted Fiji might be after spending the night with Bobo. They'd gotten off to a good start, if Olivia knew anything about sex at all, and she believed she did.

Her phone rang, and her hand shot out to pick it up before the sound could disturb Lemuel. It was a silly reflex. Ringing would not disturb Lemuel in the slightest. "Hello?" she said, in a normal voice.

"Melanie," said a man's voice.

"No, this is Olivia," she said calmly. "You have the wrong number."

"Don't hang up, it's your father," he said.

She froze. It had been years since she'd heard his voice. And she hadn't recognized it because it had changed so much.

"All right," she said, unable to settle on one feeling.

"I'm so sorry, Melanie," he said. "I'm so sorry."

"For what, specifically?"

"For leaving your care to your stepmother."

"You finally admit I told you the truth?"

"I do."

"Hmph." Olivia pulled the covers up until only her hand holding the telephone and her head remained uncovered. She wriggled closer to Lemuel, which was only a comfort emotionally.

"I just didn't want to see it or believe it," Nicholas Wicklow went on, when she didn't speak. "I told myself that she needed the company of her younger friends and that it was nice she was paying so much attention to you. It never occurred to me that she was abusing you in such a terrible, terrible way."

"Even when I told you so. Even when my brother told you so."

"Even then. Melanie, did you . . . was her death really an accident?"

"You're not famous for actually wanting to hear the truth, Dad." And Olivia hung up.

She wasn't sure what she would do the next time he called. But there would be a next time.

Maybe she wouldn't hang up then.

Manfred Bernardo was taking Stell to lunch. She did not have to go into work tonight, she'd aced her last test, and she was in a good mood. They drove over to Marthasville with comfortable moments of silence and pleasant conversation when they thought of something to say. Despite the fact that he'd been up late the night before, or maybe for that very reason, he was delighted with the bright cold day and the smooth, clean lines of Stell's face. He admired her red sweater and jeans and boots. He was learning more about her on every date. More importantly, all he was learning was good.

Manfred liked women who could, and expected to, make their own way in the world. Both his grandmother and his mother had proved themselves capable of that. Manfred also liked women who didn't judge, and Stell didn't seem to have an issue with Manfred's occupation. She asked questions as she would about any unfamiliar job.

He'd offered a choice of an upscale Mexican restaurant or the best Italian place in the area, and Stell had picked the Italian place. Manfred had only been there once, but the service and food had been good, so he was hoping that would prove to be the case that day. A large party went in right before them, but for once Manfred wasn't irritated about that. It would give him longer to talk to Stell.

Their conversation covered the agonies of high school, the thrill of graduating and heading out into the world, Manfred's one year of ju-co while he tried to figure out how to make his psychic talent pay for him, Stell's ongoing education and how many years she had left. He asked her what kind of work she wanted to do when she got her degree.

"I would be glad to work in a hospital for a few years," she said, and Manfred could tell she'd thought about it. "But eventually, I think I'd like to work in a doctor's office. Less pay, but regular hours, and closed on weekends."

"You've got a plan."

"Yeah, you bet I do. My dad is on a yard crew for a landscaper, and my mom cleans houses. They're great people, but I don't want that for me. I have some ambition."

"I like that," Manfred said. He looked at her sitting across the table, and realized he knew so much about her. Her head and soul were telling him things about Stell that her mouth would not speak on such short acquaintance. "I like that a lot," he added, with emphasis.

And she smiled back.

Sylvester Ravenwing stood just outside the door of the convenience store and surveyed Midnight. The traces of the previous night were erased. He'd followed Kiki to a hotel in Davy and watched her check in. She would awake there sometime today and do whatever struck her fancy. He'd helped Quinn and Diederik to hose the salt and ash off the white circle, and when he'd called 911 to report the death of Harvey Whitefield before dawn the next morning, he'd felt a deep content.

Sylvester liked this little town and his new job and his grandson. He thought he'd stick around for a while.

Arthur Smith didn't spend much time thinking about the death of Harvey Whitefield. Harvey's record contained a dismaying number of DUIs. It was kind of ironic that he hadn't killed anyone else by driving, but he himself had died by being driven on. And there were a few questions about Harvey's actions.

Yes, it was weird that he'd gone out without a coat on a cold and raining night. Even drunks didn't get out much in that weather. And it was odd that he'd left his cell phone in the hotel room in his own hotel.

But the results of the autopsy were pretty cut-and-dried. Harvey had been stinking drunk. Either he'd been hit by a truck while bending over, or he'd passed out on the road. Being run over had killed him. "That's all there is; there ain't no more," as the doctor said when he called Arthur after the autopsy. The doctor spared a moment to marvel that Harvey had been able to walk to the street, as drunk as he'd been.

Arthur Smith listened with half of his attention. After all, it wasn't like Harvey had been murdered.

The next night, Mr. Snuggly sat on the back porch of his house and listened, with some disgust, to the noises coming from within. It had been a long, quiet day. "The pawnshop isn't open," he muttered. "Neither is Fiji's shop. This is wrong and bad. How can she buy my food if she doesn't make any money today?"

Fiji had explained that on slow days she still made a little money. But if the shop was closed (reasoned Mr. Snuggly), she would not make any, and therefore he might go hungry. He padded into the little pantry and counted the cans of cat food. He would be good for a week, and in that time she would get tired of staying in bed with Bobo Winthrop and she would open the shop to sell things.

Mr. Snuggly very generously decided to let Fiji have her way today and tonight. Tomorrow, though, he would be sure she went to work.

After all, a cat had to eat.